Harold Heath has wo[illegible] nol-
ogy teacher, occasion[illegible] and
freelance music writer [illegible] an a
house music productio[illegible] and
remixes alongside sev[illegible] pe.
Harold has recorded fo[illegible]'s Oblong Records, remixed art-
ists like J.T. Donaldson and Terry Lee Brown Jr. and released two full-length artist albums. Having retrained as a music technology teacher, Harold now works full-time as a music writer for the likes of DJ Mag, Beatport, Attack Mag, Roland, iDJ Mag, 5 Mag etc. Aside from DJing and making music, he also enjoys listening to, reading about and thinking about music too. Harold lives in Brighton with his wife and teenage son.

LONG RELATIONSHIPS

MY INCREDIBLE JOURNEY FROM UNKNOWN DJ TO SMALL-TIME DJ

Harold Heath

VELOCITY PRESS

First published by Velocity Press, 2021

velocitypress.uk

Cover photo
Cleveland Aaron
f5point6.co.uk

Cover design
Ronaldo Alves

Typesetting
Paul Baillie-Lane
pblpublishing.co.uk

ISBN: 9781913231088

CONTENTS

The air in the community centre is musty, tinged with a hint of disinfectant. A circle of middle-aged men and women sit on scuffed plastic chairs nursing bad coffee in styrofoam cups. Their chairs tiredly squeak on the tattered lino. There are faded posters on the wall about addiction and recovery. I clear my throat:

"My name is Harold, and I am a DJ."

ACKNOWLEDGEMENTS

Many thanks to:

Annie Heath for everything.

Colin Steven at Velocity Press for publishing my first book.

Sally Rodgers, Colin Dale and Carl Loben for helping out.

Danny 'Fannah' Pont for being pushy, needy and most excellent.

Matt 'Wolfie' Rowley and Chris 'Frostie' Frost for being ace for all these years.

Fannah, Wolfie, Frostie, Leigh Morgan and Matt Sayers for reading various drafts of the book and telling me what was right and what wasn't.

Cleveland Aaron for doing a great job with the photos.

'Design' Dave Hampton for the HH logo.

Some names have been changed in this book.

If you ever bought one of my records, downloaded one of my tunes or came and danced to me DJing, then this book is absolutely dedicated to you, with much love.

INTRODUCTION

RICH IN PARADISE

An event marquee, 2 pm on a drizzly Sunday afternoon in a park on the outskirts of Brighton, 2017. Everywhere I look there are parents with small children, many of the parents already looking harassed, many of the kids already overexcited, teetering between euphoria and frenzy. There is face painting, a bar with a ludicrous ticket system that makes everyone annoyed, fizzy pop, lots of noise, and me. I'm behind the decks on a small sound system. I've been booked to play at Big Fish Little Fish, a kids and parents rave and I'm cueing up 'Let Me Love You For Tonight' by Kariya, a record I first bought around 30 years ago and which has since become a classic in the house music canon. Weirdly, although the crowd is exclusively parents and their toddlers, Carl the editor of DJ Mag is here with his young son too as he's a local.

I'm playing on Pioneer CDJs, the industry-standard music player, all my tunes now existing as digital files rather than the vinyl records I bought and played all those years ago. I haven't played some of these tunes since I was young, bursting with energy and hungry for adventure. When nights out were brand new expeditions into the territory of unknown thrills. In the marquee this afternoon, the bleeps and sub-bass of LFO's UK house classic 'LFO' take on a surreal air, as toddlers and children are encouraged to dance by eager parents, whilst some of the other Mums and Dads look on with a mixture of emotions ranging from bemusement through to teary-eyed nostalgia.

I'm playing what feels like my final DJ gig. I've played two or three gigs this year, and the amount of clubbers who would be willing to pay to hear me is now probably under a hundred worldwide. I've pretty much stopped releasing house music and only put out a couple of remixes over the last twelve months. This final revisiting of 30-year-old records feels like it would be an appropriate gig to draw the line under my career.

It isn't my last gig, of course, there's no such thing as a last gig for a DJ, there's never a final gig. A true DJ is always ready for the call, should it come. DJs may pack away their decks, put their records into storage and deactivate their Soundcloud account, but they never really stop being a DJ. The DJ instincts are always there in the back of their mind, subconsciously noting the BPM of the tune on the radio in the background. It's like the mafia: you never really escape being a DJ.

You won't have heard of me because I was never a famous DJ. Whether I was a successful DJ would entirely depend on how you defined the word success. House music was my thing, although I love all sorts of other music too. I've been buying records and mixing them together in public since the late 1980s. I've DJed in good clubs and bad, at raves and restaurants. I've released loads of tunes on credible underground labels, which used to get reviewed in the pages of dance music magazines like DJ Mag and Mixmag. I have a few club night flyers where I'm the headliner.

Decent DJs used to play my music, BBC Radio 1 played my tunes a few times, and Channel 4 used one of my tracks on a campaign once. I was a briefly popular DJ in Eastern Europe. I managed to stretch this all out into a half-decent credible dance music career for a few years whilst never really reaching the heights, or playing the best clubs. There were a couple of brief periods where all my earnings came from DJing and music-related work, but for most of this tale, I was also working part-time, temporary, seasonal, occasional jobs too.

There's a pyramid of DJs, with a small amount of phenomenally successful DJs at the top, a slightly larger quantity of very successful DJs below them, then a bigger third tier and so on. At my DJ career height I was perhaps tier five, maybe briefly tier four. I've not achieved the success of a Derrick Carter, a Gilles Peterson or a Dangerous Dave Pearce. I reached a low-middle tier and then plateaued. It's a question of scale; there are lots of DJs I've heard over the years who are excellent, they have great music collections, they know their chosen musical backwater very well, they're brilliant selectors, excellent technicians and utterly committed to their craft. And they equally are in no way 'famous' either; there are just too many of us for everyone to be globally successful.

The level in the DJ pyramid I reached was still good fun though, at times unforgettable. My various releases and remixes gave me enough of a profile that I was able to register with a couple of DJ agencies, and for a few years in the 2000s I got some lovely gigs in the UK and (mostly Eastern) Europe. I had a couple of DJ residencies, and I also got to play at parties that I had been going to for years.

I loved nearly every economy, budget-class second of it. In some ways, I achieved everything I could ever have wanted. My moment in the DJing sun lasted a few years then slowly and gently petered out, as though the dance music industry didn't so much chew me up and spit me out, as smell me and give me a brief derisory lick before simply turning away out of lack of interest.

Despite never reaching the upper levels of the DJ pyramid, me and countless low-level DJs like me, kept going long after it was sensible, because nothing else was ever really going to measure up to what it was like to be at the helm of a brilliant party where the entire room is locked in.

What other job can compare to when your hands are shaking with sublime anticipation because you know that the next tune you're about to drop, the one you spent three months tracking down, is going to make an entire room of people throw their hands in the air with a collective shriek of joy? Where else are you going to get that sense of community, transcendence and sheer freedom that you get when a good party truly goes off? It's irresistible. It's not like drug addiction, because DJs can manage for years without a decent gig and still describe themselves or think of themselves as DJs. It's something else, like a scar on your memories, a fold in your recollections that will always be there. Deep down, a DJ never truly retires.

House music and its many offshoots have been well chronicled, from the roots in disco and the Black and Latino gay clubs of America to the world-dominating force it is today. The tale is usually told as a story of individual trailblazing producers and DJs, who created this culture out of an urge to transcend the everyday and the mundane with weekends of hedonistic escape. Which is true.

But there is another part of the story, that of all the other DJs who weren't influential, at least not globally. All the local heroes, the nearly-made-its, all those amazing DJs who never quite got that big break, or couldn't turn their small success into anything bigger. I always wanted to write a book to celebrate these DJs and to try to understand and explain how and why we continued with our love of dance music and DJing, long after any chance of making a decent living from it had passed. I wanted to tell the tale of how DJing and dance music changed all our lives, and how for many of us, club culture created moments of such utter unadulterated joy and freedom that we brought some of that positivity back to our everyday lives. This is a story for all the DJs who didn't 'make it', at least perhaps not in the traditional sense but who were changed for the better, and whose lives were shaped and enriched by DJing and by club culture.

This is my tale, the story of just one of the countless DJs who fell in love with the potential contained in nothing more than some fantastic music, a dark room and a bunch of mates. It's my love story.

1

PASSION

'HORIZONT', VARNA, BULGARIA, 2008

It's nearly 3 am. I am purposefully taking a mental Polaroid of everything around me, as I want to remember this moment always. I am DJing, the main guest for the evening. I am having a moment of pure indulgence, playing one of my own productions, on a beautiful high-end hand-carved artisan sound system which was forged in the embers of a dying sun. We are at an open-air bar in Varna, Bulgaria, on a hill overlooking the Black Sea, on a magical summer evening. The ocean seems completely still from up here, and looks almost entirely black, apart from the silent reflection of the silver moon. Someone comes up to me and begins a conversation, but as I drop in the next song, she exclaims "Oh I fucking love this tune" and is gone, back to the dance floor.

Every tune I play seems to be the perfect piece of music, out of all the available pieces of music in my CD wallet, for that particular moment. Each tweak of the EQ and cross-fader adjustment seems to increase the energy and magic in the air. About 45 minutes ago, I began to realise that this might just be one of those nights that lives up to or even surpasses the early evening anticipation. Where we will actually feel, as we dance to our favourite music, with our loved ones under the stars, something special: synergy, connection. This venue is pretty isolated; no one is going anywhere else, we're a closed group, here for the duration. This has become more than a bunch of people drinking and dancing together; the whole is greater than the sum of its parts; we are all part of a single mass now.

Something semi-sacred happens at a really good party. It's not caused by the DJ or the venue, or the sound system; it's not any one single thing, it's a new thing created out of all the individual elements. It's a shared experience, a group emotion that can be a genuine power for good. Some people return to the 'real' world and their normal lives tired but happy, improved; and the intense weekend experience can positively affect how they see the world and how they interact with those around them. Of course, some others return to the real world tired and a bit depressed, have a bath and lie on the sofa for two days eating Pringles and main-lining skunk; not everyone receives a transcendent experience every time they go out.

The sound system here is superb. It's owned by a local DJ who spent a long time obsessively setting up and tweaking it. At one point, he firmly tells me not to play any Mp3s on it and to only play vinyl or wav. files, as though a largely indiscernible difference in audio quality might somehow infect his amp and speakers. The rig is loud, clear and full, with not a hint of distortion. There are no rattling monitors; nothing's going into the red, there's just the irresistible pulse of the best in house music, drawing all to the dance floor.

For a lower-mid-tier working club DJ like me, this might be as good as it gets. I am completely confident that what I will play here will go down well. Everyone here is a seasoned clubber, the scene here is really healthy: they love to party, and they love their house music. No one will make requests; they know that they're going to get exactly what they want and there's no air of hoping this will get better or wondering if this is just somewhere to be before going on elsewhere.

It may sound obvious, but if you're getting your flight and hotel paid for and you're getting a nice fee too, and all you are expected to do is turn up to a party and play some music for a few hours, then you had better make a good job of it. You have to have some very good music on you, really, it had better be the very best in your genre. And you better be connected enough to have a few secret weapons, a few unreleased bits that no one else has got. And you need to be strong in the mix, you need to be able to handle the decks and the mixer like a pro, and put it all together cohesively, excitingly. No mistakes, no fuck-ups, no inappropriate selections, no fear, no weakness, just be the best.

They'll expect you to present brilliant music seamlessly, perfectly. They'll expect you to ride the EQ and effects but not to overdo it; they want to know that they can completely relax into the groove, knowing that you won't suddenly haul them out of their trance by making a gauche programming decision. Most of all, you need to somehow work out what they want, even if they don't know themselves, then serve it up to them until the lights come up at the end of the night.

I had got this gig because I made house records that were briefly popular with a tiny demographic across Europe. When I DJed, I usually played house music: tech house, deep house, underground house, techno and disco if you want to get into genre definitions.

This next section is important as it details the emergence of tech house, a genre that I worked in for most of my DJ career. Genre distinctions are the absolute heart and soul of DJing and dance music, so forgive me whilst I painstakingly explain exactly which brand of 4/4 doof-doof music I DJed and made.

Tech house has been going since the early 90s in some form or another, and that's a long time in dance music, though it has changed so much during that period that to many of its former adherents it's now unrecognisable. It's important to our tale because I was really into it in the mid and late 90s, enough to build a home studio and start making it. It was these productions that allowed me access to the next couple of tiers of the DJ hierarchy, so tech house came to dominate my life for the next few years.

It was originally a DJing style, not a strict genre. As the name implies, tech house is a techno and house hybrid. But it began with

DJs like 'Evil' Eddie Richards, Terry Francis and Nathan Coles from the Wiggle parties in London, Mr C, Layo & Bushwacka! at The End and some others too wanting to recreate the acid house vibe from a few years previously.[1] Tech house was a reaction against commercial 'handbag' house along with the descent of UK rave into hardcore. At the beginning, it was very much defined by what it wasn't as much as what it was: it wasn't hardcore, it wasn't trance, it wasn't hard techno, it wasn't uplifting house. It emerged from the gaps between the genres. DJs picked music which contained the abstract musicality or raw intensity of techno but also the shuffle and swing of Chicago house. So techno records might get pitched down, and US garage dubs sped up, certain electro and progressive house tunes – if they contained the right amount of funk – might also get worked in. Tracks were given a new identity simply by their placement with other pieces of music in the context of a DJ set. It was irresistible: a genre comprised of some of the best elements of other genres, wide open to interpretation, interesting, exciting, and absolutely killer on late night dance floors.

Tech house was also brilliant as its birth coincided with the appearance of internet newsletters, groups and chat rooms, thus providing virtual spaces in which to argue about tech house. You could join a group that would CC you all day long on email conversations from DJs and producers all over the world, all arguing about what tech house was or wasn't. In fact, apart from its subtle melding of some of the best elements of house and techno, tech house was defined by constant arguing about what tech house was.

Still, the music was superb. The whole nuanced mood that a lot of

1 There were plenty of other folk – DJs, producers, record shops, promoters, journos etc. – who were also involved or who influenced what went on too, so if you feel that I've missed out an important name in this section, you can rest easy that I'm probably aware of that person, I just haven't included them in this very brief history of tech house, mainly because I'm keeping it short in an attempt to avoid alienating my readers, not all of whom are tech house purists :o)

late 90s tech house records had, teetering between seedy, scary and sublime, really appealed to something in me and set me off on my DJ and production career in a direction that would eventually win me the respect of my peers with very little financial reward. I knew this and entered the pact happily. This was underground music that was specifically made to work on certain dance floors, in certain types of venues for certain types of clubbers and there was something in it that I found irresistible.

Artists and labels began to make music that sat somewhere between house and techno, specifically 'for' the tech house scene and I became one of those artists. My productions were released on some labels in the scene, some of the DJs played and charted my stuff, and I was certainly very influenced by this particular genre, so I became a minor member of the UK tech house scene.

Tech house has since grown into something of a clubland monster, becoming phenomenally successful worldwide but for lots of DJs at my level gigs outside of the UK were often in Eastern Europe. A friend running a DJ agency brought me up to speed. For her (bigger, more successful) DJs, the higher fees they could command for playing closer to home meant they often didn't take the Central or Eastern European gigs. However, me and my tech house compatriots were more than happy to fly out to Bulgaria or the Czech Republic because the crowds were made up of genuine party soldiers who truly loved what we did.

I'd been DJing since the late 80s – in pub back rooms, student unions, in nightclub second or third rooms, in restaurant basements and at house parties – when, in a short serendipitous period in 2001 I lost a marketing job I detested, negotiated myself a good pay-off, updated my home studio and began to make house music for release. Within a few months, I had signed a few tracks to a well-respected label from Canada, Stickman Records and was pushed up a couple of tiers in the DJ pyramid.

Producing dance music is often seen as a logical next step for a DJ, as the two disciplines, although fundamentally different, do share certain elements. For me, DJing and producing are two entirely different skill sets. It could be strongly argued for example, that auditioning snares on your Mac in your bedroom will not equip you with the necessary social skills, composure and confidence to provide several hours of audio entertainment for a dark room full of a thousand people in various stages of intoxication. Certainly, a decent DJ should have some idea of what will work on the dance floor and therefore have some idea of what might work in a dance tune. But being a good producer is no guarantee that you'll also be a great DJ and too often the opposite is true. I was lucky in that by the time better gigs started for me as a result of my heightened profile, I had been DJing in some form for years and was at least competent.

However, my music industry success was never mainstream. I had underground kudos, lots of it. But I didn't end up playing at the Ministry of Sound, or Space in Ibiza. I never played in Berlin, Chicago, Detroit or New York. I once DJed in Dartford in a disused carpet warehouse which smelt like old ham. I rocked flat-roofed pubs called things like The Dockers Fist. I played at some decent clubs and parties, and for a memorable mid to late 2000s purple patch, a few clubs abroad too.

There was always a hierarchy of DJs, and although I was successful in comparison to the local amateur DJ I had been previously, I wasn't very successful. I wasn't residency-at-Cream, or guest-at-fabric successful. That was where an awful lot of other semi-pro/semi-amateur DJs and I were aiming, but that was not where I ended up. As the role of DJ became easier and more popular, larger DJing success inevitably became about luck, contacts, networking and timing in addition to talent. No matter; the underground house scene promised and delivered countless nights of unmissable fun.

I select another tune, change my mind and select something different. A gig like this is a joy for many reasons. The people, the setting, the equipment, and obviously the pay, but perhaps the very best thing is that my particular specialism, the type of music that I play, is loved by this crew. That's why they're here: to hear the very best of my music collection, put together as perfectly as possible. They know that I'll play some of their favourite tracks and that they'll fall in love with some new music as well. I'm excited in the way a parent is before Christmas morning when they know their kid is going to be beside themselves with joy when they open up their presents.

Any DJs who worked before digital music became the norm will know that there were dry spells when there weren't many good new releases about. When you might listen to a stack of vinyl as high as a pint of lager and only find one B2 dub that you thought you might be able to use. When you go to every record shop in Soho and leave with nothing except a US double pack and an acapella compilation, both of which you're starting to have doubts about. And so you head out to the suburbs.

I lived in different parts of east and south-east London for years so got to know where outside of the West End you might get a few decent records being sold. Cruisin' Records in Welling, the back of that weird furniture shop in Plumstead, Sounds Right in Stratford. Or it might be a dedicated dance music record shop like Bluebird in Bromley, Paul for Music in Whitechapel, Music Power in Ilford. There was a shop on Lee High Road in Lewisham that specialised in jungle and hip hop, where they played everything at nightclub volume making anything more than the simplest conversation virtually impossible. I always found it a little intimidating in there, even when they were selling my Harold Heath 12" productions in their tiny house section.

And then there are times when it seems that every week there's a bunch of brilliant new tunes to play, and then the following week, the next batch just blows away last week's stuff, as though the producers are all collectively going through some kind of accelerated-creativity phase. This gig is one of those times, and I'm in full-on DJ Santa mode, itching to deliver the new profane medicine to the acolytes, my bag packed full of musical spells to beguile and weapons to slay the dance floor.

I realise now that often in my clubbing and partying years, we thought that we were just going out, just having a laugh, but in fact we were actually having experiences and creating friendships that would live with us for the rest of our lives, and which would shape, at least to some extent, the kind of people we were. House music and partying might seem, from the outside, to be superficial activities, low-level mindless hobbies and blind hedonism, and obviously, at some level they are. But for us it meant more. We were dedicated and committed to the scene, I think because we all knew how good it could be. If you needed a cure for your working week blues, then this was where it's at. Looking for a sense of community in an atmosphere of outrageous enjoyment? Step right up. People have been gathering at night to dance together for longer than there has been house music, we just were lucky enough to be doing it in an age where the music and sound system technology had caught up enough to seriously increase the intensity of the enjoyment and pleasure.

I was booked for this particular Varna gig by a much-loved disco sprite and force of nature who is no longer with us. Ivan Boiadjiev was always smaller in real life than I remembered, his personality looming large in my memory. Even as we sat eating seafood and drinking vodka together that afternoon before the gig, whenever he got up from the table, I was always surprised at how small he was; his character always seemed much bigger. Gently mocking my cheap sunglasses, telling his long stories, smoking endless cigarettes; if you suggested a caper, he'd be up for it but would probably already have done it and have a superb story to tell involving schemes, predicaments, a third entirely bizarre and random element and much hilarity.

I work the EQ; I hear the chink of glasses near me, the sound of people shouting to each other in Bulgarian (and, occasionally the incongruous sound of someone Bulgarian speaking English with a very distinct home counties twang. Later I found out that he had been to school in Surrey in the 90s). The dance floor is now packed and has achieved its own momentum, becoming a single, churning organism. Like starlings performing a murmuration, different parts split off and re-join, but the main space in front of me will now remain packed until we finish. The bass drops in, and everyone shifts up a gear. We share the moment, just one of many over a time-stretched dream of an evening. The beats and low-end wash over the crowd, the steady 4/4 pulse the only constant, anchoring the dance floor into a sublime state of now, time stretching out behind us and in front of us as we all lock into the present moment.

A young man comes up to me; he's simultaneously rubbing his belly and shifting his weight from one foot to the other. He nods vigorously, and grinning, says something in Bulgarian, nods again, grabs my hand and enthusiastically shakes it for what seems like a minute, then jogs the five steps back to the dance floor as the next tune drops. I completed the mix – EQ and volume tweaks and all – all one-handed whilst shaking his hand, no one noticed, and I'm secretly pleased.

The tune I've just dropped is going down way better than I expected, always a nice bonus when it happens. Moments like this are the only times DJing when my hands shake. Because the floor is already heaving and whooping and I know that if they like this, then they're going to love the tune I'm about to drop. Just when everyone thought we'd peaked, everything is going to become bigger, badder, more intense. A delightfully sweet sense of anticipation takes over me, and the adrenalin manifests as a clenching in the gut and a slight tremor in my hands. It's nerves too, no doubt born from the vinyl days when one tiny slip or error could completely ruin a moment like this, and you'd have to start building the atmosphere up again almost from scratch. No more, though. The tune is cued up on the ever-reliable Pioneer CDJs, the DJs-digital-dream-deck. The faders are correctly positioned, the crowd is supremely primed, they're like an arrow in a pulled bow, just waiting for me to let go. Now, I wait. I have perhaps two minutes before I'm going to start to mix the next track in.

By the time I played this gig, CDs had pretty much replaced vinyl as the standard DJ format, and would soon be superseded by USB drives. There was still vinyl about and most venues still had Technics 1200s or 1210s record players, but many of them functioned purely as stands for CD decks and laptops. Previously, DJs had never discussed formats because there weren't really formats, plural, there was just vinyl and cassette, and no one DJed off cassette. Format was utterly irrelevant, never mattered. Still doesn't really, it's the music that possesses the magic, not the delivery system. Hasn't stopped DJs arguing about formats ALL THE TIME FOREVER INTO AN ENDLESS ETERNITY though.

For the DJ, playing a set with CDs is remarkably straightforward compared to vinyl. You still need a sense of rhythm and timing and to understand the concept of bars and beats, and you still need the ability to listen to separate pieces of music at the same time and make judgements about their relative pitch and so on. But the actual physical act of getting those two pieces of music to play in sync is much easier using CDs than vinyl.

You don't have to physically move the needle back to the start of the record; there's a button for that. You don't have to interact with the platter as though it were made of fragile glass crystal because you can't jog a CD the way you can the needle on a record. There won't be a build-up of fluff on the needle that causes the stylus to slide across the record to its paper centre where the sound of the needle scraping the label will be amplified through the pristine 12K club sound system to the abject terror of everyone in the place.

The introduction of digital technology removed much of the stress of DJing, as messing up a mix in front of a crowd can be a humbling experience, and it pretty much eliminated the possibility of losing it the way you could with vinyl. People could use digital technology and still DJ very badly indeed, but, in terms of the tunes going out of time in the mix, that kind of mistake at least was pretty much eliminated. If your tunes still went out of sync when you were DJing on a pair of CDJs then you might need to go home and have a bit of a practice before attempting to DJ in public.

By reducing the amount of time needed to beatmatch, the introduction of CD decks slowed the pace of DJing down and opened up more creative potential. DJs now had more time to loop a section of a track, drop in an acapella or work the FX. Some of the things that had always been tricky to pull off on vinyl – particularly looping, but also anything involving cueing up different parts of a track – suddenly became much easier too, opening up all sorts of possibilities for live remixing. And in a final strange irony, despite the role becoming demonstrably easier with the advent of CDs and laptop DJing, many DJs chose this point in dance music history to start teaming up in twos and threes, at the exact point when the technology made such a thing entirely un-needed.

On this night, I spend the extra couple of minutes afforded me by the digital revolution watching and waiting, savouring the anticipation, basking in the moment. I catch a couple of eyes on the dance floor, take a sip or two of my drink, and needlessly adjust my headphone volume. Finally, it's time. I hit the play button and gently nudge the jog wheel to get the next track playing in time with the current. I can hear them both in my ears, while the crowd can still only hear one song. This is the secret world of the DJ: we always hear that bit at the start of the record that punters never get to hear.

The beat is locked in, so it's time to blend it in with the current tune. I'm tense with excitement, trying not to frown as my wife has told me I can look a bit angry when I'm really concentrating. I've EQed out the low end and mid-range, and I'm just dropping the hi-hat in and out. Then I leave it in and drop in the mids. Just this tweak causes a ripple of excitement, and an already active crowd becomes more – more everything – they move, whoop, shout, laugh, and dance more. I've not yet dropped the bass in; I'm stretching the moment to rinse every last drop of anticipatory emotion out of it. I'm adjusting the volume levels, easing out the low end on the other track; I switch the filter in, slam the crossfade across and back again whilst giving the filter a tweak – essentially creating a funky, squelchy on the spot percussion-fill – then in an instant, I slam the crossfader back across whilst simultaneously snapping the bass EQ up.

The tune drops in perfect time, its impact on the dance floor is instant and intense, and it's as though everyone has had exactly the same thought at exactly the same time, as though they are no longer individuals, and the entire crowd suddenly go at it with even more urgency, cheers and shouts than before. It's exhilarating and even now, the memory of the shivery rapture of a group moment on the dance floor can cause goose-bumps on my arms and a leap in my gut.

This is where you can really see the power of DJing. Get it right and you become a cog in a magnificent human machine, your musical choices and programming decisions seeming to create pace and energy. You can almost ride on some kind of unseen wave from the room, controlling its torque with the EQ, the FX, feeling that sonic power as you drop a kick drum in and out and it makes the room shudder, keeping that essential pulse going, supplying audio-electricity to the mass consciousness that is emerging in front of you.

Each tweak has a target, the bodies on the dance floor and each sonic adjustment aims to further connect the audio to the physical. To not only make them dance but to constantly involve them in the current moment, the now of the mix, so that they forget about last week and next week: to create an immersive, ever-mutating luminescent cloud of sound in which dancers can truly lose themselves.

Get it wrong however, and you may quickly become the subject of a room full of high, twisted and drunk people's ire. That ever-mutating luminescent cloud of nonsense I just mentioned can dissipate in the blink of an eye.

It's just past 3 am and I am having a near-perfect DJ gig. I am relishing the moment, treasuring it, locking it away for future reference, to prove to myself that I was here, that this happened, and it was worth remembering. I glance at the moon's reflection on the Black Sea and then back to my happy dance floor, then breathe in deeply, metaphorically rubbing my hands.

2

VALLEY OF THE SHADOWS

LOS LOCOS, COVENT GARDEN, LONDON, 2003

Anton is on the Los Locos dance floor, dancing by himself, very badly. He's enthusiastic and spirited and what he lacks in self awareness he seems to make up for in elbows. A strange and ungainly young man, he would strut and smoke his way around the club as though he were a modern-day James Dean, sometimes offering me a no-look fist bump as he passed the DJ booth on his way to the toilets. Imagining himself detached, cool, edgy, a silent king of the dance floor, he in fact was an awkward, wiry bean of late-adolescent tension. Always first on the dance floor, he would dispatch his suite of weird angular movements, looking like a collection of arms and legs disagreeing with each other. A wisp of a moustache graced his upper lip, a cardigan draped louchely over both shoulders, his perfectly shined penny loafers glinting in the strobe light.

It's 10:40, Tuesday night, in a small basement club called Los Locos, just off Covent Garden in central London, a tourist plughole surrounded by similar bars and clubs where tourists accidently ended up if they weren't swept away to the West End proper. There were three universities and countless language colleges within walking distance meaning that usually at least half my audience were students, and sometimes it was essentially a student night. The other half were a broad mix of disparate groups: tourist, local, mistake, office-party, don't-get-out-much, Megan's birthday etc. Much like a wedding reception, from a DJing point of view, my audience was a near-impossible demographic.

This evening, I have the Anton issue to attend to. When Anton was on the floor by himself, no one else would come and dance, as though sharing the space with him would incur some kind of guilt by association. As the DJ for the night, this was a genuine problem for me. The only way to avoid a difficult evening where the punters become disgruntled was to get the room moving. I don't need Anton performing the role of a dance-floor-clearer, I've got a huge deep house collection thanks. When the floor is full he's welcome back and he can come and do his weird kung fu/jazz hands as much as he likes. And on their night bus or cab ride home, non-regulars will talk about 'crazy moustache guy'; but no one will get on the floor when the only other occupant could qualify as entertainment. He has to go.

Anton's a regular here and I've developed a straightforward technique to get him off the floor. A deliberately jarring change of musical mood would usually do the job and he would grimace as I purposely car crashed Ja Rule into Girls Aloud, upping the tempo by 20 or 30 beats per minute in a couple of seconds and completely ruining his flow. He would ruefully shake his head, just slightly, as though he wasn't so much annoyed, as disappointed. Then he would sashay off to smoke another cigarette, one eye on the mirrors around the wall, cardigan perfectly in place over his shoulders.

This is DJing but it's not the DJing that I wanted to do – this isn't about rare grooves, taking the listener on a journey, working the EQ and playing upfront promos. This is musical crowd control; it's audio fodder for the masses, the sonic equivalent of Harry Ramsden's fish and chips or Saturday evening ITV: solid, reliable, dependable light-entertainment, unchallenging, simple and undemanding. This is DJing but not how I wanted it.

A punter, about five pints into his evening, props himself up against the DJ booth and surveys the gradually filling room. His breath smells of stale lager, cigarettes and some kind of fast food grease. He's down with his mates tonight: "Firm-handed bro, we're kind of running things here yeah?" he says, only half-joking. He suggests I play the three biggest tunes of the last 12 months, tunes that I play every week here without exception, sometimes twice in a night if pressed: 'In Da Club', 'Crazy in Love', and 'Toxic' by 50 Cent, Beyonce and Britney Spears respectively.

By far the best tactic for dealing with this kind of input is to agree and get on with looking for the next tune, although whilst doing this, there is still a tiny part of me that bristles with resentment. The 'true' DJ inside me who thinks of DJing as, if not an art form then at least a craft, where the gigs involve technical skills, encyclopaedic knowledge of obscure, underground music, communion with the audience, integrity, and commitment... that DJ is secretly resentful that drunk man-in-bad-shirt thinks he's given me some quality advice. And worse, later on when I drop Beyonce's 'Crazy in Love' to rapturous reaction, with perfect timing, having spent two and a half hours artfully building the atmosphere and tension, drunk-shirt will catch my eye and give me the gun-fingers as though to say "See mate, see, I told you if you played this they'd love it. You're welcome".

To point out to kebab-breath that his suggestions are akin to telling a footballer that they might want to attempt kicking the ball into the opposing teams net should they wish the match to go well would be unwise. Anything other than "Sweet bruv" or some similar shouted exhortation would break the spell – because this period, from 11ish to 12ish in a commercial UK nightclub – is the magic time. It's the time when the number one rule is, don't break the spell.

It's the time when the club fills up, pre-peak time which here wavers between about half 12 and 2. It's before the post 2 am thinning, before the nights' winners and losers can be starkly differentiated from each other. Young people, high on sugary alcoholic confections and raging hormones can look across the dance floor through the smoke and ultraviolet lights and for a time, it's almost as though we're all on MTV, in one of those videos where everyone isn't at the club, they're 'in da club', and they're all beautiful, attractive, popping corks, dancing and flirting as the DJ plays their favourite songs.

For a moment they ignore that their feet stick to the carpet, or that the smell of disinfectant and stale beer is still discernible behind the fog of Lynx body spray and cigarettes. The Tex-Mex paraphernalia on the walls showing the venue's daytime role as a theme restaurant fades into the background. The punters are transported somewhere they imagine to be better. This is the best time of the evening, whilst the alcohol is still bringing people up, creating excitement, when a DJ can build anticipation, even a DJ bound by unbreakable laws to always play 'In Da Club', 'Crazy in Love', and 'Toxic', every night, without exception. Even a DJ so restricted gets to know what tunes work best to build a room up, how to programme them, to tease the crowd, to seduce them before letting them have it. That skill is still relevant here, away from Ku and Amnesia, fabric or the Sub Club, no matter how far removed from authentic club culture I may have drifted.

And for a while, I can create a con, a mass deception in which everyone in the room takes part. Even I buy into it sometimes; the atmosphere is somehow light and giddy, potential hangs in the air, mingling with the smoke and perfume. There's something about loud music in a dark room with coloured lights which triggers some kind of synaptic activity in my brain, reviving old memories of raves and nightclubs, and perhaps earlier memories of parties and discos as a kid, triggering a rush of adrenalin. And there it is, that exquisite sense of anticipation you get at the beginning of a night out: anything could happen this evening.

US mainstream r'n'b and hip hop: Jay Z, Justin Timberlake, Destiny's Child, J-Lo etc. was a large part of the music 'policy' at Locos. I had tried to introduce a more challenging/interesting music policy to no avail and following a constructive conversation with the management ("Stop dicking around with that doof-doof shit and play them what they fucking want") had accepted that a diet of hip hoplite and pop/indie/dance that would work equally well at weddings and student nights up and down the country was what was required. The money was good, the drinks were free, there are worse ways to earn, so I acquiesced. I figured the money would help me support my "actual DJ career". It wasn't like I was getting regular gigs playing the music I loved every weekend anyway. If I was lucky, at this point, I was probably playing somewhere decent maybe once or twice a month, but some months went by when Los Locos was the only place where I wore headphones professionally.

"My actual DJ career." It's funny looking back, how I had a regular paying DJ gig, two nights a week which I didn't regard as my DJ career, and then I had intermittent bookings over the year playing underground house in cool clubs which I somehow instead regarded as my actual DJ career.

Outside of Los Locos, I had a truly tiny but dedicated following. But no one at Locos knew or cared about who I was. No more than if the bartender were a decent photographer, or the doorman a well-respected journalist, it would be irrelevant to the role we play in the club. On Mondays and Tuesday evenings at Los Locos, you won't hear any underground house or rare disco re-edits. No obscure one-sided white-labels, no acetates, no promos, and there's no mixing really. I rarely touched the EQ or the effects on the mixer, although I occasionally beatmatched to relieve the boredom.

When I DJed outside of Locos – 'proper gigs' – I generally played house, or funk and disco. I was a fully paid-up member of the underground club scene, and so I always viewed the music at Locos as a necessary evil, one that I would interact with as little as possible. I kept it at arm's length, rarely properly listening before downloading, never hearing in the club as I wore insomnia earplugs, as though too much contact with it might corrupt my underground sensibility. There was always a slight scent of bad faith about working at Locos, as though I was betraying 'true' DJing. To use my skills for the good of the dark side, to bring the programming excellence, sense of flow and fastidious attention to detail that had contributed to me becoming a competent club DJ to the masses, whilst playing the worst kind of commercial, sell-out music. However, it turned out that I had my price, and I went into it fully aware of what was involved.

I originally got the job following one of the most misleading job interviews ever carried out in the history of recruitment. My old friend Snake Eyes was managing Locos at the time. Snake eventually moved on to manage various venues south of the river, but had been very clear about what music I should play when offering me the Mondays and Tuesdays DJing slot at Locos, and it's one of those conversations that has stuck in my mind through the years:

Snake: "It's a student night, they'll love your tunes – bit of funk and soul, all that, they love it."

Me: "Really, that sounds brilliant – what about contemporary stuff?

S: "Oh yeah, they love all that, house, hip hop, you can play anything really."

Me: *thinks: this almost sounds too good to be true* "OK, I'm in. Six hours, 9 to 3, Mondays and Tuesdays – funk, rare groove, soul, hip hop, house, breaks, disco, and jazz, right?"

S: "Yeah brilliant. Totally. Umm."

Me: "What?"

S: "What?"

Me: "You said 'Umm'."

S: "No. No, brilliant. All good. You might need to play you know, a Blondie track or something like that occasionally but you know what you're doing right?

Me: *thinks: Oooh I can do that mix I do with Grandmaster Flash's 'Adventures on the Wheels of Steel' and Blondie's 'Rapture...* "Sure no problem mate, of course."

S: "Excellent. Drink?"

Snake and I had hung out together for years, united by a love of clubbing and music. He was one of the few people I've ever met in my life who seemed genuinely happy pretty much all the time. A red-haired Liverpudlian bursting with the joys and possibilities of life, who steadfastly refused to ever dwell on anything bad that happened, or indeed to ever consider the consequences of his actions.

Consequently, he was terribly good fun, and you could either stand at the sidelines tutting or join in. I remember he borrowed my new red coat once when we went to a Spiral Tribe warehouse rave. The next day, he told me that he had carefully left my coat in the corner of the warehouse for eight hours and couldn't understand where it had gone at the end of the night. He was once seeing a friend of mine whilst simultaneously having an affair with a member of his bar staff. Whilst I was admonishing him about his conduct, Snake looked me in the eye and said with complete seriousness: "It's alright Harold, I've got a plan. I'm going to carry on until I get found out, and then I'm going to apologise."

Bearing all this in mind, I perhaps should not have been surprised when I played my first Monday night the following week and found that the music policy we had carefully worked out was complete and utter nonsense. They wanted hip hop and r'n'b but not the kind of hip hop I liked, no Mike Ladd, no De La Soul or Jurassic 5. I wrote down everything they asked for as I realised that this gig was not the dream gig I thought it was going to be. I went home and thought about not doing it. Then I thought about the money and got some music piracy tips from my flatmate Long Tall Jim. Next week, I arrived tooled up.

Aside from J-Lo, Jay-Z, J-Kwon and such, the Locos crowd also loved a bit of pop trance. For many in the underground house/techno DJing fraternity, slightly bizarro Dutch 90s pop trance act Alice DJ were the epitome of everything that was wrong with cross-over commercial dance music, a pale, mocking shadow of acid house culture, a beige bastardisation of something pure and raw. I completely agreed with this analysis, but I went ahead anyway: I did it. I wore the earplugs and I played Alice DJ. And at what I also considered a particularly low point in my DJing career, I used to play Bon Jovi's 'Livin' On A Prayer' every Monday and Tuesday night for two years (perhaps not so much a low point as a low period). Usually, around 2 am, and to my shame, when it got to the chorus, I would pull down the volume at the second 'Woah', ensuring the entire, drunken, shameless room would holler together "Woah, Living on a pray-er". Indeed. My prayer was usually: please God, make them all leave soon so we can knock off half an hour early.

Tonight the pop requests mount up quickly, so I move into Britney territory, unselfconscious pop music, at which point a girl comes up to the booth and asks for hip hop and r'n'b. "I've been playing hip hop and r'n'b for the last hour," I say. "I was sitting down then," she says. I tell her I'll play some in a bit and before she can say anything else a group of very drunk young men on a stag night, dressed as World War One flying aces, start shouting at me to play "something from World War One".

I write down the requests on a growing list, which I will curse later as I can only read the first two or three that I wrote down. The legibility of my writing quickly deteriorates as the list progresses until I appear to have taken a request to play 'shitcunny Hitler' which I'm pretty sure I don't have with me.

Many of the tourists here have made a terrible mistake. They wanted to be at fabric or another of London's 'proper' nightclubs but had somehow ended up in front of my booth, scowling at how their holiday in one of the world's clubbing capitals had gone so wrong. Sometimes they would pull themselves out of their funk just enough to ask if I had any M.A.N.D.Y., or was I going to play anything from John Tejada, referring to the early 2000s club trend for restrained, sophisticated and stripped back 'minimal' techno tracks, knowing full well that even if I did have any of this kind of music with me, a dance floor heaving to the strains of Usher, the Black Eyed Peas and Liberty X really aren't going to be interested.

There's something particularly saddening for a DJ to see a very good record clear a floor, and I could guarantee that a slice of classy European minimal-tech house would clear this particular dance floor in the time it took for the hi-hat to come in. Or worse, they'd stay on the dance floor but refuse to dance, eyeballing me until I played something 'everybody knows' or something 'everybody can dance to'. You pick your battles. You wouldn't try to force the main room at Ministry to dance to S Club 7 any more than you'd get Los Locos to move to Ricardo Villalobos.

Every week, me and thousands of other resident DJs went off to work, in clubs, pubs and bars, comedy venues, village halls and bingo halls. Others played weddings, birthdays, anniversaries. This wasn't about underground music, fashion or genres; this was what DJing was like before DJing was cool. This is DJing with no pretensions to art or technique, although it definitely involves the same processes of empathy and communication as any other DJing. Because it turns out, and here's a little DJ secret for you, that even people who like music you don't, really love to dance together. It's not just us clubbers with our dub mixes, rare acetates and exclusive remixes, it's everyone.[2] We all work hard every week and everyone deserves a few hours in the dark getting down with their mates.

Every night is different, yet somehow the same: you go to work. You stand in a greasy wooden and perspex booth, tucked at the back of the club, the bar on the right, toilets on the left, dance floor directly in front, in a building with poor ventilation and the lingering odours of stale beer, bleach and, back then, cigarette smoke.

2 A dub mix is an alternative version of a song, a practise taken straight from Jamaican sound system culture. In house music terms, you can think of a dub mix like a remix, but one where they've taken a lot of the music and vocals out and replaced them with weird noises and far-out studio effects, or, sometimes, with just lots of beats. When it comes to DJing, there are certain types of DJs, myself included, who always head straight to the dub mix if there is one.

You play music for the drunk, the happy and the lonely, and for those who couldn't care less what you play, using a mixer that has seen better days and a pair of off-brand CD players that are embarrassingly low spec. There's a pair of Technics 1210s, the industry standard for playing vinyl records, plugged into the mixer too, but they function purely as plinths for the CD players.

Sometimes the CD players stick, disks refuse to play or to eject, and you make sure you bring cleaning disks and that you clean the decks every night before you start. You'd better have an Mp3 player plugged into the mixer for when things go wrong too because any DJ will tell you a complete sound failure to a full room is a humbling experience. Momentarily, the only sound is the hum of the air con and the whirr of the spotlights, the clink of glasses and bottles behind the bar and the tramp of feet on the dance floor, but after a second the calm turns to a full-on crowd verbal assault. Better gigs, in better clubs, you might have a sound engineer to help you out or just to frown at as though it were their fault to divert attention – but then again, in a better club, in a better gig, the CD decks wouldn't be Sainsbury's own brand and prone to sticking.

The sound equipment is well past its best and beset with problems, from crackling connections to unexplainable volume variations. You learn quickly to bring basic tools and gaffer tape for all eventualities. There's also a laptop in the booth, but it has no sound card or internet connection and is good only for semi-controlling the lights and for playing solitaire between 9 and 10. Occasionally a particular nerdy punter will attempt a conversation about what operating system is running. (I wear headphones and earplugs all the time, smile and shout "Great, bottle of Becks please!").

You keep up to date with new releases, burning a CD or two a week. You bring two or three CD wallets packed full of disks, in an attempt to have most things that most people might ask for. There will always be occasions when someone requests something like 'Old Shep', and you have to admit to not having that particular tune in the bag this evening but essentially, you get to know your punters, what they want, what they need, and what they didn't realise they wanted ('Long Train Running' by The Doobie Brothers: never requested, always killed when I played it). You prepare all your music, gather your headphones, cleaning equipment, torch, gaffer tape, earplugs, pen and paper, spare cables, kiss your loved ones goodnight and head off into the evening.

You go to work and attempt to successfully soundtrack the peaks and troughs of a couple of hundred mostly-drunk people in a tiny, disorientating space on a night out. If you've done your research properly and if you play it correctly, if you observe the room and react to it, if all the stars align, you might have an OK night, a night where you get pleasantly low-level drunk, have a few shouted conversations with half-cut strangers, play some music, make some people happy, keep the place rammed so that the bar makes a decent take, and get out of there by ten past three with your soul intact.

3

GOOD LIFE

Growing up, I loved discos. Discos were a big part of the 1970s British childhood. Discos at birthdays, Christmas, Halloween, school discos, community centre discos. My favourite was the thrillingly named Gary's Disco at our youth club. I have a bizarre early memory of attending Gary's Disco in what must have been the very early 80s. A crowd of girls singing along to Toni Basil's 80s pop classic 'Mickey' but changing the keyword in the chorus so that they sang "Oh Gary, you're so fine, you're so fine you blow my mind, hey Gary." I instantly understood, at a basic level, what was going on here. Gary wasn't a particularly attractive man as I remember, and anyway, you could barely see him as it was pretty dark in the crypt and he had his traffic-light disco show on full blast. Equally, the girls weren't particularly attracted to Gary, and his fineness or ability to blow anyone's mind wasn't the issue.

I realised he'd woven some kind of night time magic, a brief spell that was broken the moment the music ended and the main lights came on. Then, the artifice instantly dropped away, you saw behind the curtain, and Gary was just a records nerd with wooden boxes of 45s, arranged chronologically (50s, 60s, 70s and 80s) across the table behind him. But the combined effect of loud music, night time, disorientating lights, dressing up and dancing: I could see straight away that it was a potent concoction.

From my older brother Si, I inherited a love of audio equipment. In the 1970s, kids built up hi-fi systems from 'separates': a Marantz amp, Pioneer tape deck etc. I got into speakers, high-quality cables, gold connectors. Si had specialist accoutrements to clean his vinyl, little brushes and bottles of liquids, purpose-built shelves for his records, the whole peripheral world of the home listener. All this I thought was very good indeed.

Mum worked at a massive music publisher's warehouse, where I spent many happy school holidays. It was dusty, noisy, with rat traps in the corners and a vending machine that dealt the illicit delights of various Cadbury's products that seemed unobtainable anywhere else. The warehouse stored sheet music and books about music, piled in boxes on pallets on huge shelves the height of a house, the top only accessible by forklift. But a nimble 10-year-old could climb up, if you had the balls and were careful not to get caught, crack open a box and curl up in a dusty cardboard den, reading about David Bowie, Peter Tosh, The Sex Pistols, Donna Summer, Fleetwood Mac, The Who, Adam Ant, Velvet Underground; some I knew and some I had never heard of, I didn't care.

Lying in my dusty book-nest, reading about the music industry, about live gigs, touring, session musicians, recording studios, guitars, mixing desks and cars in swimming pools, I ate it all up – the facts, the commentary and the myths. Looking back, I can see now how getting to hang out in a massive warehouse full of music books might have had something of an influence on my future career development, and it was certainly a key to a door behind which was a world of excitement, glamour and debauchery – the music industry – where magic was created. I wanted in.

However, I still had to decide what my allegiances were going to be. Records were a big deal in the 70s and 80s. The music you bought and the tribe you belonged to defined you, much more than they do now. In the 1970s and 80s, kids picked a side. You were either a mod, punk, new romantic, soul boy, rude boy. And it was important. Your identity is made during the teenage years, and we literally wore our identity through our clothes. Si's solid attachment to heavy metal and his insistence on playing it really loudly in our shared bedroom may well have contributed to my becoming a dance music devotee. Timing played a role too: 'Planet Rock' by Africa Bambaataa and the Soul Sonic Force and Malcolm McClaren's 'Duck Rock' were both released in 1982 when I was 11, at exactly the right moment for me.

Hip hop was the first sect I joined, aged around 11 or 12, rapidly abandoning my Stray Cats posters, Shakin' Stevens records and Elvis Presley belt buckle which had previously seemed so cool. Hip hop was an all-involving, exciting scene which aside from not being in any way rockist was a complete package with its own codes, language, ethos, art, dancing, music and clothes. Most importantly, for my future career, hip hop was a DJ based culture.

Me and my mate Frostie learnt some moves and would breakdance in the school playground. We met at school when we were 11, and we've luckily stayed friends ever since, but it was touch and go at the beginning: soon after we first started hanging out, he revealed his favourite records were Natasha's 'The Boom Boom Room' and 'Living On The Ceiling' by Blancmange, both records I strongly disliked, which could have led to serious disagreement between us. However, a sudden rush of culture was about to make any such concerns irrelevant: Desmond Corrigan was over in the corner of Sister Carmel's classroom doing something weird. He'd woven his fingers together and was undulating his arms as though there was an electric current going through them. He'd seen body-popping and breakdancing on John Craven's BBC Newsround the night before. It looked really cool and Frostie and I rapidly embraced a young life of popping, locking, breaking and battling.

Hip hop was new, and even though we stole it wholeheartedly from America, it became ours. Hip hop gave me a gang I could join. We wore the same clothes and could identify each other in the street. It gave me a code to live by, a set of cool things to be into – breakdancing, electro and rap music, DJing and scratching, clothes and graffiti art. Hip hop, and the allegiance I made at that tender age to dance music/Black music and club culture as opposed to the forces of rock, affected many decisions for years to come: clubs, not gigs, record decks not guitars, dancing not fighting, trainers not shoes, hoodies not shirts.

We bought knock-off Nike wind-cheaters and, briefly confused by the clothes in the Breakdance movie, black leather driving gloves. One day, Frostie brought his new Nike trainers into school to show our 'crew' and we were all equally envious and impressed. That's right, we were a crew. We had a name, we were called the Street Crew. Then we were called Sidewalk. And then we were called StreetFunk. There was definitely a theme. We stopped changing names though because I was drawing custom made T-shirts for the entire crew and had to re-do them every time we came up with a new crew name.

I spent hours practising breaking in preparation for Saturday afternoon 'battles' in Bury St. Edmunds town centre for which the ever-reliable Frostie would bring a role of lino bigger than him on the bus from Sudbury, bless him. I developed a reputation for having 'The Fastest Backspin In Bury', something I'm still proud of. Looking back, it's funny that we called them battles when clearly they were dancing competitions. 'Dancing Competition' just doesn't have the same kudos as 'battle'.

The music was all electro and early rap. I bought early electro classic 'Renegades of Funk' on 12" from Andy's Records in Bury after having first mistakenly bought 'Renegades' by Brass Construction, and took it into school to show my mates and also so that I could carry it to and from home.

Electro was brand new machine-music; it was unearthly, it was what robots would listen to on the moon, and yet here it was right now. I had heard synths and drum machines on pop records by Depeche Mode or Gary Numan, but they were still pop records. Electro sounded like it had been made by aliens, it was the music that should have been playing in the cantina scene in Star Wars. On 'Street

Sounds Crucial Electro Vol. 1', DJ Herbie the Mastermind seamlessly mixed the entire album together so you couldn't tell where one track started and the next one ended, a process I thought was just amazing but which was also at this stage beyond my comprehension.

One day, at the Howard Estate youth club, one of the bleached, musty halls we used to gather to breakdance, a kid called Spicer (never found out his first name, that's not how things worked), turned up and busted out a backspin that utilised my particular technique (I wonder if he too now suffers from a lower back compressed disk and a nagging problem with his sacral ligament?). Up to this point, I had been very proud that I was generally acknowledged as the owner and practitioner of the best backspin in Bury. Spicer was a direct threat, but I wasn't fazed; I'd seen Breakdance, Wildstyle and Beatstreet many times and I knew that the day would eventually come when I'd have to defend my crown. I had prepared not one, but two tricks with which to destroy any potential backspin usurper.

Spicer busts out of his backspin into a perfect freeze, a cool pose you pull at the end of your routine. I let him leave then sauntered on. Breaking was ALL about sauntering. If you couldn't saunter, then you'd lost before you'd even begun. The accepted route when battling was to warm up with some footwork – fancy jumping around but still remaining on two feet, then launching into a couple of cool moves – before you let loose your show stopper.

However, due to what was clearly a challenge to my backspin mastery, I decided to forgo all that, and launched myself into my signature backspin before slamming my arms on the ground, stopping dead, and then performing my unique never-before-seen-in-public reverse backspin (this I think may be partially responsible for the twisted vertebrae in my middle back that started making itself known in my 30s). Then, having already delivered the killer blow to a rapturous reception, I served up a final coup de grace and performed my 'bouncing back spin' a move described perfectly by its name. I won the battle. And poor old Spicer will likely also endure a lifetime of low-level back trouble but still came second.

All too quickly breakdancing became passé. Much to my dismay, my mates began spending their Saturdays going to the football in London instead of spinning on lino and unsuccessfully chatting up girls. This was an alarming development. Not only did I have minimal interest in sport generally, but as far as I could make out, there were no girls at football. When we were breaking in the park, there were girls, music, fun, and excellent showing off opportunities. Going to the football supplied none of these things. In fact, London's football grounds in the early 80s were often far from a pleasant fun day out. I remember a lot of racist chanting, loads of punch-ups, coin throwing, and a generally intense macho culture that I found intimidating.

Spending Saturdays standing in the freezing rain on a terrace, hemmed in on all sides by seemingly huge, drunk men in shirtsleeves who pass the time sieg-heiling the other fans and singing songs about gas chambers just didn't appeal to me. One particularly grim afternoon, I spent an hour or so standing two streets away from Upton Park tube station in the mid-to-light icy drizzle, as the police attempted to keep us away from opposing fans and to control the sporadic alcohol-fuelled fighting. Then a police horse bit me on the shoulder leaving its thick bubbly spittle on my new Ellesse ski jacket, and the policeman riding the horse told me to "Fuck off cunt". I decided that even though the football casuals dressed really cool, this wasn't for me. You picked your sides in the 80s, and I didn't want to be on this one.

Looking back, I would happily compare myself to Crazy Legs from the Rock Steady Crew, who in the late 70s travelled the five boroughs of New York, keeping the breaking flame alive until hip hop was ready to go global. Except that in Bury St. Edmunds there was literally no one to battle anymore.

Instead, I retreated into my record collection. In the mid-1980s, in sleepy Suffolk, compilation albums were my escape and the resting place of my dreams. Like countless other kids across Britain, Street

Sounds and Kent were the record labels that initiated me into the wider world of Black and club music. Aside from their hugely influential Electro compilations, Street Sounds also released collections of the latest street soul, jazz-funk and dance tracks while the Kent label released a steady stream of brilliant compilations of old rare music covering sixties soul, r'n'b and northern soul.

The mixtapes I made from them were my initial DJ training, learning about juxtaposition, context and timing. Music rushed in to fill the vacuum left when everyone stopped breakdancing and when carrying lino around the town centre on a Saturday became uncool. It broke my heart; culture had let me down, the vagaries of fashion and whim had killed off my thing, the thing I was brilliant at (did mention I had the fastest backspin in Bury?), where I had met loads of new friends. I guess in larger cities an underground hip hop scene continued, but there was no underground scene in Bury St. Edmunds, or if there was, 14-year-old me couldn't find it. But hip hop culture had left its mark on me, even as my mates abandoned trying to learn how to do the Windmill.[3]

Hip hop culture instilled in me a love of vinyl and collecting records, which naturally led to a fascination with nightclubs and DJing, way before I could actually attend nightclubs or go and hear a DJ in a club. This was before DJing was cool. Record collecting had no hipster kudos; it was just something people did. I used to buy records whenever I was happy and also whenever I was depressed. And as a self-indulgent teenager with no real angst to deal with, I still found plenty to be 'depressed' about and consequently bought plenty of records.

3 The windmill was a particularly impressive breakdance move that looked a little like if an actual windmill came to life and then rolled around on the floor. It required a fair bit of practice to nail. It's since been superseded by a new generation of extreme and acrobatic breakdance moves that make the humble windmill look a little old fashioned, but when we were kids, it was the mark of a true breaker. Anyone could do the worm, most people could bust out some passable footwork, but the windmill was a breakers right of passage.

You could also borrow albums from your local library and record it onto your own cassettes, like a very labour intensive version of torrenting. Buy the cassettes, get the record from the library, clean it, get the recording levels right, play and record both sides, write the song titles on the cassette cases. I thought it was the most brilliant thing.

I made mixtapes for me, but as part of the teenage mating ritual, I made them for girls too. Making a mixtape for a girl is one of the more bittersweet memories of my teens. Putting together a list of tunes that somehow say something about the person receiving the tape and the person giving it; and maybe if I make her the perfect mixtape, she'll go out with me. In fact, girls tended to really like the mixtapes and not go out with me, but this never deterred me in my mixtape-based romance endeavours. Just like the jobbing DJ ever hopeful for their big break, hope springs eternal for the lovelorn teenage boy.

My friends and I would regularly get turned away from the door of Bury nightclubs 'Taps' and 'The Reflex'. I managed to sneak in a couple of times by clinging to a group of older boys who'd I'd known when we were breakdancers and one night watched absolutely entranced as the DJ mixed Cameo's 'She's Strange' into the Fatback Band's 'I Found Lovin''. It was brilliant. Then he started chanting 'You wot, you wot, you wot you wot you wot' over the record, and everyone responded in kind. 80s clubbing was weird. I was so impressed with the whole thing that I drank way too much Pernod and black and threw up purple vomit in the toilets. As the doorman escorted me out I threw up some more and got some on his suede shoes.

The Caister Soul Weekenders were a short drive away from my home in Suffolk, and some of my friends' older siblings used to go. The realisation that whilst I sat watching TV with Mum and Dad there was an underground dance music scene taking place this very evening, just a few miles up the motorway, where DJs were playing amazing music you never heard on the radio, felt like an unavoidable cerebral itch that would, at some point, have to be scratched.

DJs in the 80s were archivists and collectors. Music-loving nerds with dirty fingernails from flicking through endless dusty boxes of second-hand vinyl. They were grafters, technicians, blue-collar workers. Superstars they were not. Their work routines involved the transportation, setting up and maintenance of equipment. There wasn't a flight to be caught; there was a transit van that needed diesel. Their skillset was to play popular music and create a fun atmosphere, they supplied the sound, flashing lights and personality to make your party.

They were called things like Sight and Sound, Rainbow Roadshow, and, of course, Gary's Disco. They didn't post their mixes to Soundcloud, play their own productions, weren't consummate media professionals and didn't provide constantly updated relatable content via a suite of social channels to their ever-growing international fan base. They advertised their services via an advert in the back of the Bury Free Press and a couple of cards in newsagents' windows.

A mobile DJ had a section in their record crates for the 'slow dance', a tradition completely forgotten now in clubland. Also known colloquially as the 'erection section', the DJ would play a slow ballad or two and encouraged the audience to briefly pair up for a slow, awkward stumble around the dance floor. It seems almost bizarre now, a lost tradition from another time. Mobile DJs had to play the hits and the classics. Never a B-side, never an album track, just what people knew. They got on the mic to make announcements, if someone's car was blocked in, or to wish Natalie a happy birthday. They played 'Oops Upside Your Head' by The Gap Band and got everyone to sit down and row an imaginary disco boat.

In the 1980s, a DJ became a DJ because they wanted to work with music and because they had amassed a record collection. They didn't do it for the fame or fortune, for the chance to 'appear' at a festival or to release a record. DJs DJed because they loved music. This is why I wanted to DJ. Because I knew that I owned some music that other people hadn't yet heard, and I felt sure that they would want to experience the feeling I had when I first heard certain records. DJing is an odd hybrid of community service and consumption.

The urge to share was driven also by the reality of musical scarcity when it was genuinely difficult to obtain all the music that you wanted. I used to have 'want lists' of records that I had heard rumour of but had never seen; taxonomies of exotic song titles, archaic artists, defunct labels and obscure or emerging genres: like Chicago house music.

Anyone who's been into house music for a while will know that one of the many ongoing unresolved controversies in the scene is the "Who played house music first in the UK?" argument. It's a somewhat futile discussion, as every day that passes, the memory of every single person involved degrades just a little more. Still, I'm happy to throw my hat into the ring.

The first time I knowingly played a house tune was Marshall Jefferson's 'Move Your Body (The House Music Anthem)', which was on a compilation album called 'Upfront 3' ('Over 90 minutes of the latest club hits!') in spring 1986, at St. Benedict's Upper School in Bury St. Edmunds. I had taped it off my mate Mackie's uncle Jackie and we all went to listen to it in the school music room on their massive cassette player. Amid the mid-80s street soul and clunky hip hop beats of the latest club hits there was this mysterious self-titled anthem.

I remember me and my mates being really into it but we didn't see it as a huge, life-changing moment. It would be a couple of years from when I first heard house music to having a full-on, road-to-Damascus, evangelical conversion. All the pieces weren't quite in place yet. Aside from anything else, we were in the music room at lunchtime in a Catholic upper school in provincial England and not in a Chicago warehouse.

We thought this new music was cool, it was kind of like fast electro, but we had no idea what it would become, it was just the latest thing from the US. With much head-shaking and a palpable pity for us, my older bro Si and his mates Nigel and Haggerty informed us that it clearly wasn't music, not proper music, we were idiots. They grinned knowingly to each other, feeling sorry for us because when they were young, music was so much better. They sounded exactly the same as most DJs my age when they listen to grime.

In June 1987, I was 16-years-old. Thatcher scored a third victory in the summer. In August, Danny Rampling, Paul Oakenfold, Nicky Holloway and Johnny Walker went to Ibiza to visit Trevor Fung and, so the narrative tells us, accidentally invented Balearic beat and kicked off acid house. That summer I went to Great Yarmouth for a week with my mates Fat Man Joe, Elmo and Andy. While the 'Ibiza Four' were holding hands in a swimming pool and listening to 'Moments In Love', we were practising drinking and trying to chat up girls by the seaside. And while me and my mates had been listening to the slick US soul of Luther, Janet Jackson, Cameo and the Fatback Band, much of London's clubland had been rejecting the shiny drum machine uptown r'n'b mainstream and was going through a brief appreciation of older funk records with the rare groove scene.

Rare groove was a club scene that began in the London warehouse parties of the early 80s, based around an obsession with obscure funk records from the late 60s and early 70s. It briefly went overground with a flurry of influential compilations before being completely overshadowed by acid house in '88. To me it was a gateway to the underground, and I became beguiled and then obsessed with rare groove, even as its brief club dominance faded and acid house exploded.

For the provincial town-dwelling kid, amassing a collection of original funk 45s was not really possible, so compilation albums were vital to people like me who were falling heavily in love with the lost soul sounds of the early 70s. Luckily, in 1987 the best compilation album ever released came out. The Urban Classics albums (for there were three, the first two were brilliant, no one likes the third one) were an attempt by the Polydor record label to capitalise on the rare groove scene, as a number of their tracks had been selling in their thousands on illegal bootlegs.

Your career in music is punctuated by pivotal moments that perhaps don't become clear until after the event. Just like discovering electro a few years before, this one single compilation album opened up a musical wonderland to me that I never knew existed. It almost seems a little twee, to look back over one's life and see that a single compilation album seems to have such a hold on you 30 years on and to ascribe so much influence to what was essentially a money-making exercise by a major record label; but it just proves that you should be mindful of what music you fall in love with at sixteen as it will live with you forever.

It was a Sunday evening, towards the end of the summer. I was in my Habitat bedroom, all red tubular furniture, listening to Busta Brooker on Saxon Radio, our local station. Busta Brooker did a soul show, playing 'upfront dance', a mix of early hip hop and prehouse dance music, what my family would have still called disco, along with some classic soul and funk. I had got back from our lads holiday in Yarmouth and was bored and lonely. Busta Brooker was one of the few conduits through which I dreamed of escaping from sleepy Suffolk because he played stuff that you didn't hear anywhere else. His show and Robbie Vincent's soul show on BBC Radio 1 were the musical highlights of my week. Busta hyped this new compilation album and said he was going to drop a killer tune after the adverts. I cued up my Alba tape deck and waited expectantly.

The ads finished and the pretty string figure that opens 'Hot Butterfly' by Gregg Diamond Bionic Boogie featuring Luther Vandross filled my room. The union of chords and melody, the very notes Luther chose above all the other notes he could have chosen, the whole thing was somehow imbued with twilight emotion and it perfectly matched what I was feeling. Those longing lyrics chimed with the frustration a 16-year-old boy feels on a lonely late summer Sunday evening. 'Hot Butterfly' is brilliant by the way, a richly produced slice of 70s dance floor soul, defined by Gregg Diamond's unique funky honky-tonk piano and, of course, Luther Vandross's effortless vocals floating on top. But it was more than a great track, to me at that moment it somehow summed up how I was feeling, frustrated, full of ideas and passion, feeling stifled in a tiny town where nobody understood me or my music, man.

'Hot Butterfly' was part of something bigger, there was a whole world of superb and undiscovered music being played in unknown clubs and warehouses, and it was all out there, just waiting for me: the underground. A world of unimaginable excitement and excess. As the song finished I decided that if a single piece of music could affect me so deeply and so instantly, and could somehow mean so much then I was going to be involved in music and DJing. I didn't know how, but I remember being very clear that a decision had been made.

I went and bought the album from Andy's Records the next day; the thrill of the record in its plastic bag knocking against my leg as I walked out of the shop, getting it out on the bus journey home, and just looking at the cover, turning it over, reading the song titles, the credits, the small print, smiling to myself. When I got it home I discovered that it was a treasure trove of rare funk featuring a set of tracks that have since been played to death and back to life again, and that have been sampled countless times too. Bits of these records and others from the rare groove scene would appear again and again over the following decades, sampled, cut up, morphed and re-worked, used as raw audio material for hip hop, house, hardcore, jungle, drum & bass and more.

That album pushed me over the edge, solidified my path; I was decided. Somehow I was going to work in music. I wasn't sure if I wanted to work in a record shop or deal rare vinyl, or design record sleeves, or DJ, or run a record label – it didn't matter at 16-years-old. I had a focus, that was enough.

1987 was also the year that all my football mates promptly left school on their sixteenth birthdays. Luckily for me, I was about to get a lifelong partner in crime in the shape of soon-to-be-best mate Wolfie. He was a new kid in school, from somewhere weird in the Midlands and he wore cool clothes. His garments and effortless charm was extremely effective with the girls of the sixth form of St. Benedict's Upper School, a fact I was simultaneously impressed with and envious of, as I was gauche and clumsy around any girl that I actually liked. Like, literally walking-into-lampposts-while-trying-to-talk-to-them clumsy.

Wolfie had an MA-1 Flight Jacket, wore Levis 501s and used Black & White brand hair wax. In life, he was an eternal optimist with the sunniest disposition and the broadest smile. Once on acid I watched fascinated as he slowly melted into a conglomerate of all the friendly loyal dogs I've ever known. Although he and I were very different from each other, we were completely and utterly united in one thing, the absolute primacy of music in our lives. Wolfie was as much a music obsessive as me, he bought tunes, made mixtapes, liked clubbing and read books and mags about music. And girls thought he was hot and he knew someone who could sell us hash – what more could you possibly need from a mate? Quite why he chose to hang around with me, the human personification of Eeyore the miserable donkey from Winnie the Pooh is beyond me. He was best man at my wedding a few years ago and he and Frostie and I met up with our respective partners just the other day. I'm a very lucky man.

It was inevitable then that my first DJ gig would be with Wolfie beside me and so it was that we played a church hall in Sudbury for Frostie's little sister's birthday party. I'm pretty sure that (a) the birthday attendees didn't think much of it and (b) we played 'I Believe In Miracles' by the Jackson Sisters, which was our jam that summer, more than once, along with Public Enemy, S-Express, Eric B & Rakim, the Jackson 5 and plenty of James Brown. Wolfie and I loved it, although we barely knew how to make the equipment work.

They had a Citronic DJ deck with the record players, mixing controls and all connections contained in the same great big slab of bakelite and wood, with an attached mic. Despite not really understanding just how DJ beatmatching and mixing actually worked, I quickly decided that perhaps I should move from record collector to DJ.

In my mind, I was already headed to the Funhouse in New York, the spiritual home of hip hop where John 'Jellybean' Benitez DJed. If this were a film of my life, this would be the perfect point for a montage, perhaps soundtracked by Ollie & Jerry's 'Breakin'... There's No Stopping Us', as I get in training for playing at the Funhouse, working two jobs to raise the airfare, practising my DJing skills, buying tunes etc. However, I didn't actually end up playing at the seminal New York club. Oddly, no one from the Funhouse had caught Wolfie and me playing our rare groove compilation albums in the church hall in Sudbury, so they never called me to arrange the gig. So I just carried on buying more records, in case the call ever came.

Wolfie and I drove around Suffolk with our mates, listening to hip hop and rare groove, getting high, wondering vaguely if we should start a funk band. I bought a wah-wah pedal for my Fender copy guitar and dabbled with a hip hop band who in the extremely short time we were together was called The Glass Bead Game, Howzit, Dub Connexshun, Jupiter X, Atlantic Ultimo before settling on Atlantico. Band names are super important when you're in a band. I played two gigs as rhythm guitarist in legendary short-lived art-school group Purple Kevin who clearly didn't get the importance-of-band-names memo. On the infrequent occasions I DJed I didn't have a record box or bag and would never have spent the money to buy one, not when there were records I could buy instead so I carried my tunes around in a ragged blue plastic crate. We knew another pair of local DJs who also rapped, they transported their records, microphones and mixer to gigs in a liberated Sainsbury's shopping trolley.

We paid weekend visits to London, eyes wide open from the white cross trucker-speed pills we used to take. We went to the Electric Ballroom, Wendy May's Locomotion at the Town and Country club, got turned away from The Wag for not being cool enough. You could go to Dance Wicked at the Electric Ballroom in Camden and Paul 'Trouble' Anderson, Trevor Madhatter, Judge Jules, Norman Jay and Gilles Peterson would be DJing across two floors, £4 to get in!

Hearing club DJs like these mix tunes together and seeing them work their dance floors in their own particular style was inspirational. I'd try to act cool whilst sneakily studying what they were actually doing with the mixer and decks, working out how they were making two records sound like one.

We would buy records, clothes and the Soul Underground fanzine. I braved the fear-filled trip to the intimidating record shops of Soho and Camden. Club DJs in London were also generally unapproachable too; I occasionally just wanted to know the name of the track they were playing (I always just wanted to know the name of the track they were playing) and got the brush off many times by super cool scowling DJs who would literally neither look at nor speak to you.

By the time rare groove reached Suffolk via compilation albums in 1986 and 7, the scene in London had already peaked and begun to dissipate. Still, it was really important to me; it demonstrated the plain truth that lies at the very heart of DJing: that the best stuff isn't the most popular or well known.

In the interest of balance, it's worth mentioning at this point that whilst all this talk of rare funk records and cool clubs might infer some kind of teenage cachet or kudos on me, I was in fact, a gauche, awkward teenager, prone to poor sartorial choices and with a terrible haircut that never, ever worked. When we paid our first ever visit to Gilles Peterson's legendary Sunday session at Dingwalls, people by immaculately dressed jazzers and rare groovers, I was literally the worst dressed person there.

Wolfie, Frostie and I went to the seminal James Brown gig at the Brixton Academy in 1987, I got roaringly pissed and apparently fell off Wolfie's shoulders although I don't remember getting up there, spraining my wrist in the process. I then wandered to the bar feeling a little rough and promptly passed out, banging my head on the sticky floor of Brixton Academy. Woke up in an extremely unglamorous first-aid room with a sore wrist and a slightly sticky head, feeling, as my mates delighted in telling me I told them later, somewhat "woozy". I think the JB's were going into 'Soul Power', James Brown may have been exhorting Maceo to blow, whilst I lay on a gurney with the room spinning, a matronly first aider looking down at me with a mixture of pity and very mild disgust. Say it Loud, I'm a Sex Machine.

HAROLD'S TOP 1987 RARE GROOVES

The Mighty Ryeders – Evil Vibrations
Maceo and the Macks – Cross The Tracks (We Better Go Back)
Reuben Wilson – Got To Get Your Own
The Jackson Sisters – I Believe In Miracles
Bobby Byrd – I Know You Got Soul
Larry Young's Fuel – Turn Off The Lights
Clarence Wheeler and the Enforcers – Right On
Bohannon – The Fat Man
The Soul Searchers – We The People
Patti Jo – Make Me Believe In You
Roy Ayers – Running Away
Coke Escovedo – Wouldn't Change A Thing, Runaway
The Jimmy Castor Bunch – It's Just Begun
Eliminators – Loving Explosion
Eddie Harris – It's Alright Now
The Notations – Superpeople
Eddie Bo – Check Your Bucket
Cymande – The Message, Bra, Brothers On
The Fatback Band – Keep On Steppin'
The JBs – Pass The Peas
Fred Wesley and the JBs – Damn Right I Am Somebody, Blow Your Head
Magic Disco Machine – Scratchin'
Sisters Love – Give Me Your Love

Foster Sylvers – Misdemeanour
Sweet Charles – Yes It's You
Lynn Collins – Think (About It)
James Brown – She's The One, It's A New Day, Give It Up, Turn It Loose, Funky President
Sir Joe Quartermain and Free Soul – (I Got) So Much Trouble In My Mind
Hodges, James & Smith – Turn The People On
Nature Zone – Porcupine
Kool & The Gang – Funky Stuff, Rated X, N.T.
Oliver Sain – Bus Stop
African Music Machine – Black Water Gold, Tropical
The El Dorados – Loose Booty
Chakachas – Stories
Rosetta Hightower – Rocking Chair

4

PROMISED LAND

Growing up in the UK in the 80s we were afraid of nuclear war, the Bermuda Triangle and 'Britain's most haunted house' Borley Rectory. The threat of nuclear war in Europe between Russia and the USA was quite real in the 80s. It was always on the news, people knew the names of different missiles, we had all seen maps and leaflets showing the estimated width of bomb damage to the surrounding area that would occur if local RAF bases in Suffolk were bombed by the Russians. We were also afraid of Thatcher who was battling striking miners, dismantling the unions, scapegoating single mothers and attacking gay people with Clause 28 and the Tory party eventually turned their attentions to the rave scene.

Acid house and its associated culture felt to us like it was the birth of a brave new world. Although many have pointed out that rave entrepreneurs were products of Thatcher's relentless drive towards individualism, it felt as though the whole rave endeavour was the complete opposite of Thatcherism. It was communal, egalitarian, open, tolerant and fun. Perhaps for many, it was just pure hedonism and nothing more, but there were overtly political elements like the Freedom To Party campaign and travelling sound systems like Spiral Tribe. And the very act of staying up all weekend long and being in no state to go to work on Monday morning was inherently oppositional to the status quo. Living for the weekend, finding value outside of the 9 to 5 and building organic communities that crossed class, race and gender boundaries: these were all political acts that bucked the system.

It sounds slightly ridiculous to say now, but for a while, acid house and raving seemed as though they were life-changing, even world-changing. Perhaps they were but maybe not in the way we felt at time; the dance music explosion certainly had a massive impact on popular culture and for me and countless others, our experiences in house music and clubs went on to at least partly define us for the rest of our lives.

I had my first acid house clubbing experience in an unremembered city centre club in Ipswich at the top of several flights of stairs. A big dark room with a DJ playing 4/4 909 beats and 303 acid house. This was still before rave had broken big and there was no mass euphoria yet, but you could tell something was happening, something new was developing. We arrived late and it was already rammed. Some were very clearly on drugs, others were pretending to be, and others stood back observing the churning mass of bodies, simply bemused by the whole affair. There was lots of 'acid dancing', the beginnings of the litany of raver dance moves.

The robotic beats and relentless drive of early acid house sounded really rather good on a big sound system in the dark. However, being Ipswich in the late 80s, the club shut at perhaps 2 or 3 am, and we had missed our last train home. Quick tip, don't imagine for a moment that the casualty department of a city hospital will be busy and disorganised enough for you and your circle-eyed mates to just hang out and use the vending machines till the trains start in the morning. It won't be, and they won't let you. Not for the last time I passed an entire jaw-clenched night wide awake hanging around the empty streets of a city waiting for the sunrise and the trains to start again.

Analysis of the late 80s dance music explosion has often focused on the 'Ibiza four' and the UK tabloid's version of the 'second summer of love'; this was the accepted acid house 'backstory' and obviously, all that stuff definitely happened. But history is always written after the event and inevitably by the major players; events are collated, edited and put back together to tell the cohesive story of acid house and rave in the UK. But there are many other stories to tell too. For plenty of people like me who were outside the main cities in the late 80s, we had a different experience. It wasn't so much an overnight thing, from listening to hip hop and funk to suddenly thousands of kids gathering in fields at weekends and all the smiley t-shirts, bandanas, and dungarees. Instead it was more of a slow burn over a longer period where for a while, hip hop, rare groove, Balearic, acid, Belgian new beat, garage and techno all existed together.

Living in a small rural town, far away from the metropolitan centres, underground culture always took its time to reach us and was often no longer underground by the time it did. Pre-internet, new youth movements and musical genres really did ripple out from metropolitan centres to the provinces gradually, and in the process they were filtered and dissipated, taking on some of the character of where they ended up.

For us, in Suffolk, this meant that the weekend parties courtesy of older local hippies in run-down houses out in the countryside benefitted from our introduction of good music. Instead of the Led Zeppelin and Pink Floyd that had previously soundtracked these leisurely rural bacchanals, rudimentary sound systems were created and the music changed to hip hop, funk and early house. I DJed at one of them, playing rare groove and US garage from my collection of compilation albums along with a few precious 12"s, learning the hard way that vinyl albums are often pressed way, way quieter than 12"s. I also learnt that some people felt strongly that Led Zeppelin were better than Adonis and would attempt to discuss this at length with you while you were DJing if you let them.

I had spent a year at art college in Ipswich before realising I wasn't going to be an artist and instead enrolled on a humanities degree at the University of East London. This got me within a tube journey of the clubs and record shops I had coveted for so long, and I squeezed my growing record collection and off-brand decks into a tiny room in West Ham.

Our mate Tones had moved to London a year before me, and he took me, Frostie & Wolfie to the Astoria on Charing Cross Road. White Lightnings were the brand of LSD we took that evening, along with wraps of speed resulting in a headlong assault into the very deepest recesses of my consciousness whilst simultaneously rushing to every single point in the universe, observing the electrical signals in my brain splitting down into their constituent atoms and then reassembling themselves in the shape of time itself; one of those types of night. It really was nearly too much, but dear old Wolfie was there to help me keep it together and then suddenly I popped out of the acid-bubble of doubt back into where I was: a room full of people, overflowing with joy, going completely fucking primal to some of the best music ever invented.

It was Orbital's 'Chime' and the huge roar that greeted it that pulled me out of my hole, as every single body in the place became connected, part of a churning, organic machine, driving the rave forward, the pressure building up, and the pleasure unfolding in unceasing waves, exponentially growing. Unforgettable; a slick of hot sweat covered my back, the acid gave everything a heightened sheen of ultra-mystery and hyper-reality; it seemed that every point in the room had someone dancing in it, no-one was sitting around, or chatting, or posing, or pulling; an entire generation it seemed, locked into the same brand new groove, all of our own.

And then there was Methylenedioxymethamphetamine, or as we knew it, White Doves, Blue Calis, Dennis The Menaces, Snowballs. We cunningly referred to it by its secret code name 'E'. The subject of much myth and conjecture at the time: it's all made in giant secret warehouses in Russia by a single crime family, this latest batch actually has strychnine in it, E was originally created by the CIA as a truth serum, those red and white capsules were created by a private lab on behalf of the Metropolitan Police and contain a tracking agent that latches onto your DNA...

Like the countless others who had this experience, I can clearly remember the very first ecstasy pills we took: a handful of white doves, quickly shared out and nervously dropped, ironically at the Fitness Centre in London Bridge. Ironically because the Fitness Centre had been home to the legendary Shoom parties a couple of years before, where Danny Rampling had preached his message of Balearica to his devotees, but by the time I showed up, they had moved on from a dingy gym-by-day in Southwark. I believe that it might have been a Promised Land party, but no one who was there with me is especially certain on dates or who might have been DJing.

Tones had arranged to meet me at the Fitness Centre; he was late, I was early, for some forgotten reason we didn't arrive en masse, so I spent about half a precious hour by myself inside as it warmed up at the height of the rave/acid house scene. It was precious because, although I didn't know it at the time, things were about to change, and I was enjoying my last few moments of pre-E naivety. I sat nearly opposite the stairs and watched in wonder as some scary-looking men came up to me, and were then simply lovely. Likewise, a few minutes later a stranger approached me, offered me some of her chewing gum and we chatted for a while. Meanwhile, the Fitness Centre was filling up. It was a tiny venue, windowless, at least as far as I could see, but then they rarely turned off the smoke machine. You entered by a staircase, the bar area (water or soft drinks only) on your left as you came in, and the smoke-filled dance floor to your right.

I remember being nervous but excited that I had ended up somewhere so illicit, so clearly debauched. And the atmosphere, the very clear joy from everyone who came bounding down the stairs, the welcoming bonhomie for newbies like me, the complete acceptance of anyone, that was all there, very clearly in place. I found myself part of a larger thing, chatting to the kind of blokes who would have been frightening me at the football a few years earlier, but now everyone seemed blissfully accepting of each other. Then my mates arrived and things sped up.

We all had it, that moment, that evangelical beginning, when you suddenly realise that you and the rest of the room are rushing, full of psychic joy, all in perfect sync with each other and the music. And you realise that you feel as light as a feather and you can actually feel the music, it plays through your body, causing goose-bumps on your skin and visceral excitement in your gut. Here comes the rush.

Whoever was DJing at the Fitness Centre that night played those spine-tingling, moment-defining anthems Joe Smooth's 'Promised Land', and Derrick May's 'Strings of Life'. You heard them everywhere you went during this period, lifting entire dance floors off the ground. I clearly remember the unique shade of UV blue covering everything, the continuous smoke machine, and the music, a perfect mix of acid, Italian piano house, techno and some US garage for good measure.

This was music from space, from another time-stream, built from exotic materials and engineered with unknown future techniques. Some of it was so fresh, so alien, it opened up new possibilities simply by existing. It shifted the concept of what music might be, and opened a corresponding metaphorical door within the listener's mind too, presenting a broadening of possibilities.

I had an experience that countless other kids across the country were having, an epiphany, some kind of magical moment of pure synergy where this new music, the people, the moment, the substances coursing around our young nervous systems, the shared, brand-new emotions of the entire room, all coalesced into a greater whole. Weightless, hovering above the floor, lost in the smoke, whoops and sweat of a grubby cellar south of London Bridge. From that moment forward, we were living for the weekend.

My first summertime visit back to Suffolk after moving to London: lilac hoodies, Kickers, lads with that curtains haircut or a ponytail, long summer nights, meeting at service stations for illicit nocturnal escapades. I have a clear memory of sticking my young dumb head out of the sunroof as we drove and clocking the line of cars behind us, each one filled with young people looking for the rave. That night around 50 cars ended up following the wrong car, driven by a civilian on his way home. He was completely freaked out, wondering why on earth a small mobile village of bright-eyed youths had followed him home to his little Suffolk cottage.

Memories of several hundred wired teenagers aching for excitement and adventure gathered together around their car stereos on a hot Friday evening, a perfect recipe for Big Fun. Like party-animals of the British Savannah, drawn to the oasis of the Esso Services, we would gather in the evening sunlight in a petrol station car park on the edge of town. As the tarmac slowly cooled and the shadows lengthened, every car arriving would be playing their mixtapes. We were waiting for a signal, for someone to receive a message on a pager or a big phone and then suddenly everyone would pile into their cars and set off in another convoy of adventure.

The police were a constant background presence. We would get stopped and searched on the way to raves and so became adept at hiding drugs about our persons. Late one night they turned up to Club Labyrinth, the home of hardcore raving in East London. They wandered slowly into the main room, the heat, moisture, smoke and volume obviously disorientating them. They were looking at us, all deep in it, with a mixture of apprehension, disgust and sheer bafflement, the whole situation a perfect embodiment of the generation gap.

Labyrinth was held at the Four Aces club in Dalston, East London and was mass physical abandon, bacchanalian and debauched. It was where the full power and intensity of our new thing was consolidated and intensified, distilled into its purest form, before rapidly over-ripening and turning sour. The Four Aces was a literal Labyrinth, an old sprawling Victorian Theatre that you'd barely notice from the street that had been converted into a live venue in 1969; Desmond Dekker and Bob Marley had played there. By the time we showed our membership cards, paid our tenners and walked in, Labyrinth had become a rave warren, seemingly constructed of corridors, backrooms, side rooms, lobbies, stairwells, steps to nowhere, basements, nooks, crannies, hideaways, all dark and soaked in UV. It was like raving in a day-glo Escher painting. Open till 6 am Friday and Saturday nights, packed with a real mixed London crowd, that brilliant mash-up of classes and cultures that the best London scenes are made up of. Labyrinth was fun, exciting and edgy as fuck.

We took a friend one night, his first rave. A small-town boy, football hard-nut, salt of the earth. He found the whole thing alien and to be fair, Club Labyrinth in early 1990 was pretty fucking full-on. He spent the first couple of hours convinced that people were 'eyeballing' him, worrying that a fight was about to kick off, his adrenals on full alert, before succumbing to the charms of the night people and all we had to offer, ending up with his hands-in-the-air at the breakdowns, hugging sweaty strangers, all that stuff. It just did it to you, the combination of music, people and drugs and the permission that was implicit in it all, the permission to be as wild and carefree as you wanted. It did the same thing to everyone willing to let their guard down: broke down a few barriers and allowed strangers to share magic moments with strangers.

It sounds like amyl-tinted nostalgia, and maybe that's part of it, but the early rave scene for me and my friends was characterised by meeting and mixing with people and classes who didn't usually socialise together. The kids who DJed on the pirate radio stations we all listened to clearly weren't from the same background as me and my mates, but it didn't matter. It was like what hip hop and breaking had been for me a few years earlier; social barriers briefly became unimportant. Hip hop and then acid house were, momentarily at least, more powerful than the English class system.

But even in the depths of the rave, you could still find some traditional English class snobbery. Hardcore rave music quickly became thought of by some as the music of the plebs. The clubbing underclass, uneducated – the 'acid teds' who didn't know any better. This eventually had a strong influence on how I approached DJing. I decided that I knew what was good, or what was cool, and no one else. I knew what worked on the dance floor because I had experienced it and nobody's opinion of what might be cool or fashionable would ever impinge on my own judgement. This became my approach to DJing. I put the hours in, listening to all those 12"s that the cool staff in the record shops of London were trying to sell me, looking for the rare jewels amongst the fodder, and I spent endless hours mixing them all together until I knew them all intimately. I've put in the hours, so I'm going to play exactly what I like, regardless of what anyone else thinks I should or shouldn't play.

In those early days, you'd see other ravers in the street during the week, catch their eye and share a moment: we were those that know, members of our secret club, our private community of pleasure and mayhem. Travel Fox trainers, whistle posse, Can You Feel it?, sharing water and chewing gum, Rizla, the ever travelling Clipper lighters passing from hand to hand, changing ownership countless times a night. We loved it. We loved the music, and the scene and the people we met, and staying up all weekend, then cocooning back home with curtains shut, coming down with the gentle pulse of Electribe 101 or Massive Attack soothing us back into reality.

Both albums were an integral part of our weekend ritual, which we felt wasn't just clubbing, it was a lifestyle choice. It was based primarily around the most exciting music I'd ever heard, but also including clothes, dance, MCs, pirate radio, and a bunch of new music-consumption rituals, as well as an unspoken acknowledgement of a mass shared experience. It felt like a cult. Those weekends at Labyrinth, Telepathy, Eclipse, Fantazia and the Tasco Warehouse, finding timeless periods of sublime ecstasy whilst simply dancing with your mates and a bunch of like-minded strangers, all together, hoping the DJ was going to play our favourite tune.

There is definitely a degree of remembering only the good parts, and no doubt there were unpleasant elements too. If there was a lot of amphetamine around that night, the atmosphere could turn a little paranoid, tense. Rumours used to travel around raves that the blue pills contained methadone, or the capsules were laced with rat poison. The Tasco Warehouse in Plumstead could be a little rough with people getting taxed or being sold fake pills. We went to a warehouse rave once where there were no toilets, just a near-lightless room where everyone pissed on the floor. At other raves there would be no lights anywhere except in the main room and you could find yourself lost in the corridors of some pitch-black warehouse. But the real dark side, the drug-related violence, the football firms, the gang warfare behind the scenes, we saw none of that while we were punters, and for a while at least, we revelled in our innocence.

We lost Frostie one night at a rave back in the Suffolk countryside and found him as the sun rose, in a hay-bale den of his own creation, gently singing to himself "You're in my hut now". Captain Simon used to sell a few wraps of speed down the Fitness Centre and one night asked us what we thought would happen if he just took them all instead. I remember us telling him that we weren't prepared to sit up with him for a week, but he did it anyway. He didn't sleep for a week. And then he slept for a week.

A guy we used to rave with called Goober, probably not his real name now I think about it, he used to get so into the rave, he'd start doing star jumps or drop to the floor to do some push-ups. In the middle of a packed, near pitch-black warehouse, the sounds of fledging hardcore enveloping us, the strobe playing tricks on your eyes anyway, and wait, is there a guy over there doing gymnastics? He'd catch himself and look sheepish, apologise to people who couldn't hear him and didn't care and then soon find himself star jumping again.

My thoughts of DJing had to take a back seat for a while, as I soon moved into a squat in a lovely Georgian house in Chelsea, an impractical set-up in which to store a burgeoning record collection, which I temporarily stored in my Dad's garage. The squat was full of art students; painters, sculptors and conceptualists who never, ever, did the washing up. I had lived away from home for a few months and ended up in a bohemian haven for groovy creatives all wearing big jumpers. Sometimes the water got cut off and often there was no electricity. We lived by candlelight by necessity, but it was a necessity that for me, always free to run home should we actually get thrown out, simply added an extra layer of beatnik glamour. I was holidaying in Bohemia.

My friends and I simultaneously wanted to tell the world about what we had experienced, whilst keeping it secret for fear of spoiling it. Afterwards, we spoke of nothing else; the melodies and riffs of unknown songs haunted us. For a while, I was obsessed with 'The Suitcase Song' after hearing it at Telepathy in Stratford. It was 'Break of Dawn' from Rhythm On The Loose, one of the finest rave tracks of the era, an absolute masterclass in melancholic bliss which samples soul and disco legend Loleatta Holloway singing "I'm surprised to see your suitcase at the door...". "It's about a suitcase" I would tell record shop assistants hopefully, "the suitcase song, you must have it."

The rave scene and acid house arrived in time for DJ and sound system equipment to be up to the job, following decades of various innovators and assorted nerds working out how best to amplify music to fill a space and how to enable a DJ to mix between a pair of tracks. Pioneering disco and hip hop DJs had given us a set of mixing techniques. The new music was created to be mixed by DJs, to facilitate a seamless, ever-evolving audio soundtrack that would keep dancers moving. DJs were able to add another layer of meaning and intent to the music through their selections and through careful use of context and juxtaposition; a DJ could programme disparate or related pieces of music to add drama, increase tension and sometimes to create something new from the source material.

I tried to take it all in, and would still sometimes haunt the DJ booth like one of the booth-spectres who would watch me DJ years later. I was looking for clues, about mixing and about tunes. Quick hint from the past for up-and-coming DJs; there is absolutely no point in asking for a track ID when you've double-dropped, haven't got any means to record or write down the answer and when you can't hear the answer anyway. Didn't stop me asking though.

I eventually left the squat, moved my records and my second-hand third-rate turntables back to East London and bought a new DJ mixer. I loved it; it had two sliders, two tiny screens with needles that indicated volume and a crossfader. I felt like I was at the helm of a sonic space ship.

The key to mixing records was something called pitch control, which not every record player had, but that my rickety old off-brand pair of decks did. The pitch control was crucial, as it allows the DJ to subtly speed up or slow down a record incrementally, allowing two tunes that are different tempos to be matched, and then, in theory, perfectly synchronised and blended together: beatmatching. This was the secret, the key to being able to mix and blend, the single most important thing you had to learn when you first bought your decks, and it was a challenge that required practice.

Many DJs will happily tell you that learning to beatmatch took them an afternoon and was no effort. Good for them. For most of us it was something of a challenge and for me and my friends, it was some kind of dark art, a branch of audio alchemy, which took much practice and gnashing of teeth to perfect. Your ability to hold down a vinyl mix for a minute or two became a badge of honour. The first time I got two records to play in time I left the two records on the decks and didn't dare move the pitch controls from their position for about a week afterwards.

First you put a record on, let's call it record A. Then you put record B on, but only in your headphones so only you can hear it. In your headphones, you move B to its exact starting point and hold it there, with the record platter still spinning beneath it. DJs use a circular felt mat (called a slip mat) to sit between the vinyl and the platter to allow the platter to freely move whilst the vinyl is held still. Then you have to wait for the exact moment, at the beginning of the next eight-bar section, and you simply let go of B in perfect time with A.

Then you simultaneously listen to A on the main speakers and B in your headphones and adjust the pitch of the one playing in your headphones to match the speed of the other. When you're content that they're the same speed, then you can begin to blend them together by gradually increasing the volume of one and decreasing the volume of the other to transition from one to the next and you might use the bass and treble for the same purpose too. Looking back, it all seems a little quaint and over-engineered, all that equipment, investment and time, just to synchronise two pieces of music. It's a dying skill now anyway as most DJ technology will take care of it for you with ease. But learning to beatmatch used to be a big thing for DJs.

Tones had got his Technics 1200s a couple of years before and had taught me the now accepted teaching method of learning to mix. I spent hours at the decks, staring at the mixer, the pitch control and the mesmerising tiny strobe effects of the onboard light by the platter. You had to tap your foot in time to the music, that was essential apparently. So you tap your foot to the beat, and you have to count, in fours, in eights and in 16s. You locate where in the sequence of bars you are in the song. Tap your foot, count one, two, three, four, then next time around when you get to four you're going to let the platter go with a gentle nudge and it will all fall into place: one, two, three, four, let it go. Gentle nudge, careful adjustment fuck fuck fuck why won't the stupid fucking thing fucking mix. These decks are broken, there's something wrong with this record, it's the pressing, it must be a weird pressing. The decks could definitely do with a service right? Fuck it. back to the start. Tap your foot in time, count one, two, three, four, cue up the other one, switch the headphones, one, two, three, four...

Pro DJs used the famous Technics 1200s or 1210s record players which came with a long smooth slider that allowed tempo control up to plus or minus 8%. Techno mavericks would occasionally open up their decks and fiddle with the machinery inside to give them larger pitch ranges. The off-brand record decks I was using had a small plastic wheel on the front which sped up or slowed the platter down to an indeterminate degree and which seemed to fluctuate with the vagaries of the British weather. Playing on Technics 1200s after learning to mix on them was like riding a bike with stabilisers having learnt to ride on a rubber unicycle with a puncture.

The reason that beatmatching is a big deal for DJs is that if you make a mistake at home and one record goes out of time with the other, there are no consequences, other than it sounding rubbish. However if you do it amplified on a huge nightclub sound system, in front of several hundred people, it is a quite different experience. The perfect blend you were executing quickly mutates into the sound of a hugely amplified one-man-band falling down the stairs and you will suddenly pull people out of their groove back into harsh reality, a harsh reality where they are all looking at you, and quite possibly booing. It's called train-wrecking, car-crashing, or dropping a mix and is the subject of one of the cardinal rules of DJing: Don't train-wreck your mixes. Get a bunch of people dancing at any social event, then suddenly mess up your mix and everyone instantly feels awkward and self-conscious, because the spell is broken and you, the DJ, will become the subject of their irritation.

I remember once furiously giving a record the finger mid-gig and saying to it in all seriousness, "Fuck you you fucking fucker" after it had drifted out of time whilst I was mixing in a club, something I was happy to hear a friend of mine report they had seen DJ Richie Hawtin do a few years later.

I emerged from a couple of years dedicated raving and clubbing with a poor degree from the University of East London and a first from Club Labyrinth college of hardcore-on-the-dance-floor.

I started making mixtapes again. Here's a nice story: Frostie's little sister Lou, the one whose birthday party me and Wolfie had ruined a few years before, moved to Bradford to go to university and took a couple of my mixtapes with her. She and her mates used to listen to my mixtapes as they got ready to go out raving. Ten years later I met one of Lou's friends and she remembered those mixtapes. Her name was Annie and I ended up marrying her.

I moved in with as many of my mates as we could squeeze into a rented house in Woolwich, South East London, and put my decks and Gemini Mk 2 Made2Fade mixer in the kitchen.[4] All the elements were now in place. I had been DJing at people's house parties for years (also often in the kitchen), but now I was about to start DJing for paying audiences (£3 to get into the Student Union at Greenwich University, £2 for nights at the Polytechnic of East London thank you very much). My friends and I did what any sensible young people would do; we decided to put on our own night.

HAROLD'S 1990 CAR CASSETTE 'GOOD GROOVES'

Izit – Stories
Snappiness featuring Dina Taylor – Sweet Inspiration
Fidelfatti Featuring Ronette – Just Wanna Touch Me
De La Soul – The Magic Number, Eye Know
Inner City – Watcha Gonna Do With My Lovin'

4 The wonderful Gemini Mk 2 Made2Fade was many DJs first mixer. It had a crossfader, individual track volume, master volume and headphone volume. You could switch between line or phono inputs and it also came with a nice chunky on/off switch; that was it, that was the extent of its functionality. We all learnt to mix on it and later on Fannah and I taught ourselves basic scratching on it. The sight of one in a second-hand shop or online instantly fills me with excitement for records I'm not going to buy and gigs I'm not going to play, a very strange sensation.

A Man Called Adam – Barefoot In The Head
Electribe 101 – Talking With Myself
Richie Havens – Going Back To My Roots
Young Disciples – Get Yourself Together
Young MC – Know How
Main Source – Looking At The Front Door
Soul II Soul – Back To Life, Keep On Movin'
Raze Presents Doug Lazy – Let It Roll
D-Rail - Bring It On Down
High Tide – Time Unlimited
Charles Wright And The Watts 103rd Street Rhythm Band – Express Yourself
Soft House Company – What You Need
Richie Rich – Salsa House
Last Rhythm – Last Rhythm

5

SOUND OF EDEN

January 1992, one of my first paid gigs: I'm DJing, for actual, real money. The gig is in the basement of a Chinese restaurant in Streatham, so I've not quite achieved my Ibiza residency yet (note: I never achieve my Ibiza residency). It's for a mate of a mate's sister's birthday party. I have brought my decks and mixer with me, which are now patched into a greasy amp which in turn drives the selection of various speakers available, some in pairs, some single, all of varying quality and each with its own particular technical problem. The carpet is sticking to my feet, a sensation I will forever associate with DJ booths. Everyone is shrieking-drunk-excited to be in the dank basement, lit by one single traffic-light disco light. There's a glitter ball too but it sits dusty and motionless on one of the speakers. Luckily for me, Sister Sledge and Stevie Wonder records exist, so I'm golden.

Little DJ tip for you here: there will be gigs that you take because you really need the money, where you know you're not being booked to play your latest underground one-sided white-labels, your job is to simply manage some over-excited people for a few hours. For these gigs, bring anything that Nile Rodgers produced: Sister Sledge, Diana Ross, Chic, etc. and some Stevie Wonder tunes. When all else fails, these records will save you.

I've had a steady stream of requests all night: "Sorry mate, I don't have Charles & Eddie, KWS, Right Said Fred, Jimmy Nail or Annie Lennox" (and weren't the charts shite in the early 90s?) "But I do have

SL2, Bizarre Inc, KLF, Prodigy, Crystal Waters, Candi Staton, Altern 8, K Klass, Xpansions and Kym Sims" (and weren't the charts brilliant in the early 90s?). I remember being slipped an envelope of cash halfway through the evening, which has since been my preferred method of payment for any kind of employment: brown envelope, delivered with a wink and a smile, halfway through the job, thank you very much.

By the time I was finishing university I had decided to "concentrate on my DJing yeah?" If anyone said that to me now it would instantly ring a tragic little alarm bell in my head but in the early 90s, this seemed like a perfectly reasonable thing to do with my twenties. So I did.

Club culture was splintering off into a variety of exciting subgenres, but there was still a blurring between the scenes, all the rigid genre barriers had yet to be put up. Djum Djum's 'Difference' in 1990 had been a very clear early signal of the way ahead. I bought it in the excellent Paul For Music record shop in Whitechapel because the bloke in the shop – may have been Paul, not sure – said I should, and he was right. I brought it home, listened to its spindly indie guitar line, dub b-line, sampled tribal chants and simply irresistible percussion-heavy drum track and wondered what the hell was going on, a feeling that would return again and again through my years of obsessing over new dance music records.

The thing about dance music is that it just won't sit still, it won't settle. Just when you think you've got a hold of it, it's already moved on and morphed into something different. It's always the same; a dark room with a strobe, a decent sound system and a DJ, but it's always different. Alternate qualities and flavours are emphasised or played down and over the years, the mood of dance music ebbs and flows from euphoria to detachment, from transcendence to introspection, back and forth, experimenting with slightly different emotional content each time.

In December 1992 DJ Mag gave away a cassette of Hacienda DJ Graeme Park mixing the back catalogue of Union City Recordings and we played that mix to death. It's a good representation of the kind of music my mates and I were into in the post-rave world. There was the continued commitment to generating euphoria but with a subtler approach, epitomised by Gat Decor's 'Passion' from 1992 on Effective records. It drew on the rave tradition by making music that was effectively enticing in the club/drug environment, but turned down the pace, aggression and the lunacy, replacing it with clear, functional production and a song that slowly built and then, gloriously, released the tension. It wasn't 'nutty' or 'bonkers', this was more considered, but it still sent a tingle up your spine every time it embarked on its journey towards its blissful zenith.

You can find the Graeme Park Union City mix on YouTube, along with the reams of misty-eyed comments. If you ever wanted tangible proof of the positive effect those days had on people, then have a quick read through the joy-filled nostalgia-fest that is the comments section on old school house mixes on YouTube and have your heart briefly warmed.

Having set my heart on being the world's greatest ever DJ, I was working part-time in the warehouse of Argos in Woolwich three mornings a week, unloading garden goods, ironing boards, Lego and consumer electronics. I played a few DJ gigs at my former student union in East London, playing flailing sets of all sorts of house music to students who generally preferred The Doors or Bob Marley. Apart from going clubbing, I tended to neglect my social life, family and friendships, obsessing over records and mixing, and staying in to practice on the decks. I was strangely driven, overly focused to the exclusion of everything else.

Lots of my mates were DJs; at least in the sense that we all owned records and decks. In that sense of the word, we were all definitely DJs. And we all loved clubbing, raving, house music, DJing and everything associated with it. Which was good, as it gave me an entirely skewed view of the world, one that allowed me to think that trying to be a DJ was a great career move. As part of my early 'concentrating on becoming a DJing' plan, I employed several strategies, including:

- Deciding what DJ name to have
- Talking about DJing a lot
- Thinking about DJing all the time
- Buying records
- Reading DJ Mag, Mixmag, etc.
- Recording mixtapes
- Sending mixtapes to DJ Mag, Mixmag, etc.
- Sending mixtapes to nightclubs

This last one may have been the most useless of all my strategies, even worse than talking about DJing all the time. Making mixtapes and then posting them, with a brief note, to nightclubs in the naive belief that this was how DJs got work. If nothing else you have to admire my tenacity, although I can now categorically state that this is not the preferred industry method of getting DJing work. Perhaps occasionally someone got a gig because of a mixtape sent to a venue but not often. Within a couple of years, I would be working in a nightclub myself and would see how utterly pointless sending a demo tape to a club was as Action Man Ron did the first pass on the mail, separating out the bills and official stuff from the various DJ and live act promo tapes, the vast majority of which he wordlessly flipped straight into the bin. If the guy who's in charge of keeping the local gangs from shooting anyone in your club is also the guy who sorts out the mail, then he's probably not going to be super-interested in your mixtape and earnest accompanying note.

I had moved on from the mixtapes of my teens, which tended to feature rare soul and funk tracks, carefully programmed and segued together, with handwritten track-lists and personally illustrated tape labels. Now they were a succession of deliberately chosen house tracks, beatmatched and mixed together, travelling slowly through varying tempos and moods. Making a mixtape was now a serious business for me, one that I tried to complete at least once a month so that I could proudly give copies to my mates of my latest monthly instalment.

Mixtapes were the 90s equivalent of social media promotion, an important DJ promotional tool, carefully curated audio gifts that you'd distribute to whoever would take them, and each tape had your phone number on it, just in case. You'd showcase all your new tunes, a few current big tracks, a few b-sides and more obscure things to show off your crate-digging credentials. Maybe use a film quote or sound effect at the start, search for tunes that were in the same key to mix together, drop in a couple of flash mixes with two copies of the same tune, but don't overdo it, less is always more…

You'd practice the running order, press record, listen back to the transitions, knowing that a good mixtape would get listened to until it snapped. Then when you were finally happy with it you copy, tape to tape from the master. Label them up, hand them out, post some. And then go and buy some more records and more blank cassettes for the next mixtape. If you were really splashing out, you might buy 'Metal' or 'Chrome' cassettes.

One place my mixtapes had succeeded was Greenwich University student union, a university I didn't attend, but where some of my friends from home including Wolfie had ended up, and I was soon playing my tunes on university campuses across South East London. You might get £30 or £40 for a couple of hours, maybe a couple of drinks. I thought I was big time.

I became mates with one of the other university DJs, Mel the Amphibian, who kindly gave me my first grown-up record box. We played a few local gigs and went record shopping together. We once got a gig in Liverpool, and I drove us up in my then girlfriend's raggedy old brown Mini, with the Amphibian who was a massive great muscle-man, in the front and our record boxes in the back.

We got stopped by the police for a missing tax disc, and for the first and I'm betting only time in my life, I was briefly mistaken for a 'squaddie'. I was secretly pleased that a copper would think me tough enough to be a member of Her Majesty's armed forces, although if I'm honest, it was probably the Amphib's massive shoulder muscles barely fitting inside the Mini that briefly fooled them.

I took every single gig I could, Greenwich University's various campus bars and clubs, parties back in Suffolk, more gigs in restaurants than you would perhaps imagine, warm-up gigs in many of South London's picturesque nightclubs, bars and pubs, 'guest spots' at mate's attempts at raves and house parties of course, honing my idiosyncratic mix of Italian piano house, UK progressive house and US garage. I nearly played at Club UK in Wandsworth. That single sentence, perhaps more than any other, sums up my DJ career: Harold Heath: nearly played at Club UK.

We were going clubbing to SW1 Club, the Gardening Club, Bar Rhumba, searching for something to match the intensity of our earlier rave experiences. After one evening out, all of us sat back at our shared gaff, tapping our feet to the beat from hours ago, someone, possibly lifelong house music soldier Panno, suggested that we put on our own night at the student union at Greenwich University. The university was packed with lots of kids with a bit of disposable income, all into having a good time, what could possibly go wrong? As it turned out, pretty much nothing, for a while anyway.

Every scene needs a facilitator. Every party needs a person who makes it happen. One of those people that gets described as 'larger than life'. One of those people who quite like being the centre of attention, but whose stories actually are good enough to deserve the limelight. A bit overbearing, a tendency to exaggerate, funny, loyal, irrepressible, irresponsible – in fact, they might be an absolute liability – but they make it happen. Every successful party needs one of these.

Ours was Fannah, a bragger, blagger, and a drama queen, full of life and drive, a uniting force, a born leader of men; trouble. A great big bonkers bear of a man, he once hugged me so tightly he put my back out. Rugby, lager and Saturday night punch-ups were his world until he found acid house. Fannah always had plans and was full of big talk. He acted all tough and as his later successful careers as a doorman and then psychiatric nurse showed, he clearly was, but underneath it all, he was as soft as the cotton wool he was secretly afraid of. He would hide his girlfriend's awful steaks under his mattress rather than either eat them or offend her. A great teller of tales, with stories which always had to be run through the 'truth-or-fan' filter, he was our facilitator and we loved him.

Among his many gifts, Fannah was superb at bestowing nicknames. His own name has no interesting story behind it; it's just what his family called him when he was young, in the same way my family called my sister Bo Bo and me Paulie. Which brings me neatly to mention that Harold isn't actually my real name, it was bestowed upon me by Fannah and stuck with me ever since, to the point where hardly anyone calls me Paul. The name Harold has served me very well indeed in the industry. Had I used my actual given name then whenever I phoned anyone in the industry up and said hi it's Paul, I'd then have to explain Paul who. But whenever I phone anyone up and say hi it's Harold, they know it's me because for a good few years there were no other Harold's in house music. Still aren't many. Fannah's nickname has stuck with me throughout my life.

Snake Eyes, or Snake for short, got his name because he was the only person we had ever met who, when surprised, would genuinely exclaim 'Snakes alive!' Wolfie was a keen lefty and trade union man, so was named after Wolfie Smith, hero of UK 1970s Marxist-revolutionary-from-Tooting sitcom 'Citizen Smith'. Panno was so called because he was from the Wirral, where apparently they sometimes eat something called a lovely pan o' scouse. The Amphibian, I'm not sure, I think he just looked a bit like an amphibian. Other nicknames that stuck and entirely replaced given names included Crofty, Pleasant Dave, Six Killer, The Cleaner, Alicetinian, Shameless and The Orc. Fannah christened me Harold after both Harold Larwood the cricketer (no, I've no idea either) and Harold Bishop from TV soap 'Neighbours', as he said living with me was what he imagined living with Harold Bishop would be like, a reaction to the trauma of sharing flats and houses with me for years.

We were the perfect odd couple. Him: loud, gregarious, funny, constantly making bad decisions leading to interesting adventures. Me: reserved, gloomy and darkly dedicated. Years later he revealed that if I was in a hurry to get out in the mornings, he liked to creep into the kitchen when I had put the kettle on and my bread into the toaster and was off looking for my shoes. He'd turn the kettle off and pop my untoasted toast up, sneak off and then quietly rejoice at my swearing from the safety of his bedroom.

It was Fannah who booked the aptly named Cellar Bar at the Student Union in Woolwich for me, Wolfie and our Yorkshire pal Hawkman (yep, that one's not a real name either) to play at 'Blow Your Own'. I definitely wasn't there when the name of our night was decided, and I'm not really sure why it was chosen, but it quickly became a compound noun 'Blowyerown' that simply signified 'our thing'.

Wolfie carefully hand-drew the charmingly amateur flyer then thought he'd better learn to mix before the gig. We had a Phonic MRT60 4 Channel mixer with 'Single Mixing System' (a crossfader) set up in the kitchen, with my crusty old off-brand adjustable pitch direct-drive decks. Panno and Wolfie went halves on a pair of Technics 1210s, funded by their student loans, and we moved to a house where the decks could have their own room. Wolfie says he remembers me giving him two copies of Robin S's 'Show Me Love' and, in a teaching style that I would now, as a qualified music-tech teacher heavily criticise on a number of levels, told him to "Just get those two playing at the same time", left him to it and went out record shopping.

All our record collections rapidly expanded, our tunes in different boxes, crates and shelves all over the room. Recording more mixtapes, so many mixtapes, listening to each other's mixtapes, being secretly envious when someone bought tunes that I liked. Wolfie,

Hawkman, Panno and I had this never stated yet cast-iron rule that if one of us bought a tune, it belonged to the discoverer and no one else could play it at BYO. They'd found it first, they had the right to play it. I don't remember us ever discussing this and neither do any of the others, it was a completely unspoken thing. Wolfie had very similar taste to me and occasionally sullied a decent tune by buying it before I'd heard it, thus disqualifying it from my DJ sets.

"I'm playing out this weekend," we used to say. "When you next playing out?" people would ask. When I was ten-years-old, playing out meant building dens, riding my bike or blowing up model armoured cars via the medium of crushed match heads. When I was 20, playing out meant a DJ booking.

I had more DJ experience than the others, having owned decks for years and also having actually played out before. I was also much more comfortable than my DJ peers to play a crowd-pleasing set rather than go off into some experimental glitch-step techno or play a set of entirely unknown new tracks. So as we put on more parties, Fannah often awarded me the prized last slot, when everyone was going hard, completely lost in their own little shared nirvana, and all the other DJs had done a very nice job of building it all up. All you had to do was play good records and you could tear the roof off.

This was my first experience of pre-mix hand-tremor, not from fear but from that delicious anticipation, knowing full well that the next tune was going to hit harder than the last. Looking back, I've always thought of those days of my DJing career as very innocent and I was utterly dedicated, obsessed with it. There was a genuine love of the music, coupled with a real urge, need almost, to share it. We were a relatively closed community; in many ways, a student union is the perfect audience for a party. Lots of them know each other already, and they've not got to get up for work on Monday. We knew our audience and they knew us, and in our isolation from outside influences, the whole thing rapidly grew into something good.

Blow Your Own put me at the helm of creating our own moments of rave paradise. It was furiously addictive. There really is no comparable feeling to DJing to a room full of friends and strangers and doing a good job of it, and them all being committed to having the very best time they could. Never had I been more ready to have something come in and take over my life. It seems so small now, a monthly house night at a university campus, but it became the most important thing in my life and the centre of my focus.

All record shopping was done with this gig in mind, and we all prepared in our own ways to make the night as good as we could. Sometimes we experimented getting extra sound or lights in. We gave out fruit and ice pops. Our flyers said things like '7 watt 4 colour laser', '20 K sound system', 'Stunning lights and decor, dance platforms, chill out area'. And we all 'practised' our DJing, getting to know our tunes, slowly working out how to build a mood through a succession of records.

For one Blow Your Own we got extra sound in from Kev who had worked on the sound at Labyrinth. He set up a huge wall of speakers across one of the walls in the cellar bar. Sounded amazing, but Kev thought it would be a good idea to get on the mic and MC over our progressive house, US garage dubs and occasional Italian piano screamer. It was good for a couple of minutes but the sign of a good is MC is knowing when to stop, the art of restraint. We soon had to have a hurried, awkward booth conversation in which we discussed the huge sound system (we liked it) and his MCing (we didn't like it). It turned out that diplomacy was quite an important part of the DJs role.

Adrenalin was a big feature of our nights and we all veered between cocky confidence and feelings of mild peril when we DJed. There were occasions when we misjudged the pitch control on the two records and found that they were falling out of time. One of the quickest ways to introduce self-consciousness into a room is to mess up a mix. Panno remembers the very first time he played out he had a list of the tunes he was going to play and what pitch he was going to play each of them at to ensure a smooth flow.

And of course, all it would take to sync them back in would be a well-timed careful little nudge to the platter or a push on the actual record label, just the merest little push. And nine times out of ten you'd perform this manoeuvre and it would be ok with just a brief wobble. But the tenth time, you'd adjust the wrong platter unintentionally speeding the record that needed to be slowed down. Because you're in the heat of the party, it's 2:30 am, you've had a few drinks, you're tingling with the rush, there's sweat pouring down your face, your headphones are crackling, Fannah is proper wigging out on the strobe control and smoke machine next to you, and the two records sound really similar. So you adjust the wrong one, the records now sound way worse than when you started fiddling with them. You try to counteract it and make an adjustment to the other one, but you're heavy-handed and overcompensate and in those three seconds, you've gone from a smooth transition to full on train-wreck.

So although we were super focused on buying way too many records, we were also hyper-focused on mixing well. This was when DJ Sasha was in the ascendant, and we all loved those long, drawn-out transitions he did, and we all aspired to be able to mix tracks together for minutes at a time. I loved it. It was terrifying because it would be so easy to break the spell, to pull the wrong track out of time by accident, to knock the needle, but that just made it even better when you managed to pull it off.

DJ Sasha. The name conjured up more than he could ever live up to really, but his mixtapes, passed around from friend to friend, from group to group, were precious rave gems. Sasha's sets were legendary; he played an Eclipse rave that we went to. At that time he was championing the Italian piano house sound, playing records that were full of innocent energy, intended to soundtrack hedonism, unselfconsciously jubilant. Sasha's DJ fame was based around the euphoric house he played, the musical sensibility he brought to his craft and his ability to stay in the mix for weeks on end, all of which I used as a template. It was in this spirit that I approached Blow Your Own. I was going to be Sasha for the students of South East London.

In 1993 Sasha remixed US vocal group Jomanda's 'Never', turning it into a ten and a half minute swirling prog-house epic. It had a huge intro with a subtle hint of 'I Feel Love' to it and it built up oh-so-slowly, full of the detailed production ticks and quirks that Sasha would become famous for, and then it had this dramatic, portentous vocal.

It's a killer track, right up my street and always worked when I played it. Then I discovered that I could mix it on top of Underworld's 'Dark and Long' (it's the song from the 'Trainspotting' soundtrack when Renton is coming off heroin, you're welcome) which came out a few months later and they complimented each other musically. If you got it right, the vocal from one would drop perfectly when the chords of the other came in and it just used to sound sublime. Not that either track needed to be meshed into another, they're both excellent records, but if you ever get the chance to travel back in time to the early 90s and to mix those two bad boys at a DJ gig for five or ten minutes, I firmly recommend you do so, it was exhilarating. When it worked, when those two tunes were sailing together, each one stroking the other and you were suddenly making something momentarily bigger and better out of two already-pretty-tasty building blocks – it was like standing on the edge of a cliff in a hurricane, it was like flying.

Fannah has a few precious photos from those parties. They're a stream of blurred young faces rushing through the night, smiling, laughing, cheering, dancing. Some of their faces we can put names to, remembering that peculiarly practical English university naming system: Brummie Matt, Spanish Jo, Big Sam, Little Mel. All those old friends, the ones you don't manage to hold onto, most of them are still walking the planet, going about their business. I can't help but wonder how Blow Your Own lives in their memories, if it does at all.

Giddy used to take a razor blade and make a small incision on his forehead. He would then neatly slot a single tab of acid in the cut,

White Lightnings were his preferred tipple but he wasn't overly fussy, and then seal it in with a tightly wrapped bandana around his head. "That's how Jimi used to do it" he informed us with a wink. Seb was completely bald, helluva build, top off from the kickoff, really high voice, never took any drugs, literally never stopped dancing all night.

The Ph Avenger started small. A slight, eager-faced party aficionado he came to the first party just dressed in red and pink and possibly some kind of eye mask. The following party he definitely had his cape and declared himself the Ph Avenger. The next one he'd got matching gloves and boots, proper superhero eye mask, cape, and a logo on his chest. And you knew you were at a Blow Your Own, because the Ph Avenger was giving it large on the stairs, and Carlos was on the bongos, and Seb's smiling across at you, and Lou was kung fu dancing, and the Hawkman was dropping Fly Baby's 'You Must Admit': we had somehow become a crew, a little rave family. A couple visiting from France came to a BYO and then travelled back to the UK once a month just to come to our party. After each event, we continued the sessions back at our huge shared house in Woolwich, high up a hill overlooking the rest of South London. That spring we all lost weight and photos from the time show these unfamiliar, pale-faced, skinny, but extraordinarily happy versions of ourselves.

BIG TUNES AT BLOW YOUR OWN IN THE CELLAR BAR

DSK – What Would We Do
Lil' Louis & The World – Club Lonely
The Good Men – Give It Up
Klatsch! - Oh Boy (Extended Mix), Dance (Fresh) (Extended Mix)
D.O.P. - Groovy Beat, Here I Go
Robert Owens – I'll Be Your Friend
Spooky – Land of Oz
X-Press 2 – Muzik X-Press, London X-Press

Fire Island – In Your Bones, Back To The Bones
Murk – Bugged Out
The Club Kids – During Peak Hours – (Mood II Swing Dub)
Degrees of Motion – Shine On (Farley and Heller Junior Style Dub)
Roy Davis Jr. – Mind Power
Gat Decor – Passion
Kathy Brown – Turn Me Out
Brothers Love Dubs - Ming's Incredible Disco Machine, The Mighty Ming
Hustlers Convention – Hustlers Dance EP
Coyote – Jekyll and Hyde (Magic Potion Mix)
Lost Tribe – Gimme a Smile – The Delorme V The Dharma Bums Mix
Kinky Riba – Check It Out
Ln's – Disco Inferno
Inner City – Back Together Again (East Village Dub)
Cool Jack – Try The Feelin' (Xen Mantra Remix)
Lionrock – Lion Rock
Bump – I'm Rushing
Smells Like Heaven – Londres Strutt (Gypsy Remix)
Gipsy – Skinnybumblebee
Flybaby – You Must Admit
Dee Patten – Who's The Bad Man
Reefa – You Can't Stop The Groove
Country & Western – Positive Energy
Jump – Funkatarium
Rejuvination – Work In Progress
Leftfield – Song Of Life
Djum Djum – Difference
Floorjam - Stoneage
Back II Front – Viewfinder (I Want You All Night)
TC 1992 - Funky Guitar
TC 1993 – Harmony

B.M.EX – Appolonia
Atlantic Ocean – Waterfall
The Aloof – On A Mission
Liberation – Liberation
Jomanda – Never (Sasha Remix)
Underworld – Dark And Long
Jaydee - Plastic Dreams
Hope A.D. – Tree Frog
House of Virginism – I'll Be There For You
Arizona featuring Zeitia – Slide On The Rhythm
Glam – Hell's Party
Direckt – Two Fatt Guitars
Disco Evangelists – De Niro
Desert Storm - Desert Storm, Scoraig 93
Zero The Hero – Direct To You
Bedrock Feat KYO – For What You Dream Of
Slam – Positive Education
Golden Girls – Kinetic (Cubic 22 Mix)
Jam & Spoon – Stella
Chubby Chunks – Testament 1, Testament 4
Funky Green Dogs From Outer Space – Reach For Me
Kamasutra – Running Away (Black Sky Version), Night Walk (Black Horses), New York Communications (PSG Mix)
Londonbeat - Come Back (Morales Deep Dub Mix)
Nightcrawlers – Push The Feeling On (The Dub Of Doom)
Hardrive – Deep Inside
MK featuring Alana - Burning, Always
Direct 2 Disc – Morning

6

SUCH A GOOD FEELING

We learnt a lot from our first parties; about how to put on a night, about music, punters, each other. And we learnt a lot about DJing. We discovered that if you play two copies of the same record back at exactly the same time and then gently touch the platter to put them slightly out of time, it created a lush whooshing effect called phasing which sounded as though the record were taking off. In a world where effects were largely absent from DJ setups, this was a little trick that could elicit a huge response.

And then there were rewinds. Although they weren't invented at acid house raves, they're another element of dance music that came straight from Jamaican sound system culture, it was at raves that I first heard a rewind. A rewind, also called a reload, is when a DJ plays a record so good that it makes the crowd go off, so the DJ stops the record and rapidly winds it back to its start, then plays it again. It's a brilliant, joyous, messy, ear-blowing technique, a proper bit of audio pantomime. And like all the best bits of DJing, rewinds should be used sparingly for their effectiveness to be appreciated in all their majesty. A good rewind can make a party explode.

My favourite rewind I ever performed was in the mid-90s, in a club in South East London, at Fannah's birthday party. We had the whole place to ourselves, a couple of hundred people inside, everyone's in for the duration. The management has gone home which means we can go as long as we want, or until Action Man Ron (no job title, worked at the club in a general sorting-things-out capacity) pulls himself up from his barstool and decides that enough of Sunday has elapsed for him to think about closing up.

I'm on the decks, we're in the bar area rather than the main club, making for a more intimate affair. Many of my friends are on the dance floor in front of me. I'm not sure how long I've been DJing; it might have been twenty minutes or four hours. It's approaching dawn I think, but no light comes in here anyway. My skin feels smooth, slightly glistening, taut. I'm simultaneously hot and cold, regularly getting goose-bumps from the tunes I'm playing, my eyelids fluttering in divine confusion as I attempt to hold down my mixes. I cue up the Prodigy's 'Your Love', a big tune from a couple of years previously, hit stop on whatever is playing and drop it.

It launches straight into a piano break, simultaneously euphoric but with a hint of melancholy, the type so beloved of the rave scene. It's a tune that triggers instant reactions from those who first heard it in their early days of ecstasy consumption. Something happened in those wild days and long nights, some kind of chemical/cerebral interaction that tied the music to the experience, and that meant when we heard that music again in the right environment, it gifted us a free mini-flashback of sublime exhilaration. Such was the case here.

Head doorman, champion cage fighter and local crime boss Tirpitz is in the booth with me. He takes hold of my weedy young shoulder with his huge slab of a hand, pulls me in close and in his unforgettably deep, south-east London accent, plaintively says in my ear "Rewind, bruv." I rewound, bruv, and it was beautiful.

The venue for our first year of Blow your Own parties was a little subterranean bar, no windows, split level, with a dance floor down a couple of steps, a bar in one corner, a DJ booth in the other. The split level aspect was one of the ingredients to its success. There was something about the whole rave experience that had led to the introductions of podiums and raised spaces for dancing. Being able to see other dancers, lock into their groove, to briefly make eye contact with someone across the room at those key moments when a big tune drops, all that stuff, was brilliant. But you really needed split levels for it to happen. And there was something about ravers wanting to take it all in too, to look out and see the entire churning groove, soaking up a free psychic high just from viewing the group as a whole. With its split-level hexagonal dance floor and tucked-away DJ booth, the Cellar Bar was a near-perfect mini-rave setting.

It had a maximum capacity of 170 and sometimes we would unofficially squeeze a few extra bodies in the place to get it rave-level packed. I loved the DJ booth in the Cellar Bar. The monitor speakers were on the right-hand side which I always preferred as I tended to wear my headphones on my left ear. The booth was completely enclosed, a separate little room with a glass front looking out into the bar, quite unusual for DJ booths. The glass inevitably created a barrier but actually also meant that people left us alone in the booth and everyone, as the cliché now goes, danced facing each other and not the DJ. All us DJs had to do was turn it on and the dancers made it happen. Panno remembers the first party we did there going off like no party before or since.

Playing in this booth was when I discovered just how many requests would turn out to be concerned with coat storage rather than tune selection. Throughout the evening the coat pile would grow exponentially into a little garment-based sovereign state. Once when looking for my coat, I uncovered an actual small human nestling in the dark embrace of the hoodies and puffa jackets (his name was Lee, and once told me that he could clearly see my then-girlfriend's glowing golden aura, right, nice one Lee, that's not at all weird). At least one visitor to the DJ booth always spilt their drinks on the coat pile, it must be the law or something.

Aside from coat island, there was just a pair of Technics 1200s, a mixer and the lighting console, strobe and smoke machine. Fannah always made a point of over-working the strobe and smoke machine to ridiculous levels. He loved John Boorman's King Arthur film Excalibur, where everything is always sheathed in mist and the breath of the dragon, and that's what our parties were like. We turned the house lights off, had as minimal bar lighting as we could get away with, made it as alien and disconcerting as possible, then – Fannah loved doing this – when the piano break came, switch the main spots on and off in time with the record.

Much like the first time you pick up an electric guitar plugged into a big amp, DJing with vinyl on a club sound system is both enthralling and very slightly nerve-wracking. The slightest nudge of the needle if you catch it with your sleeve by accident, or you lean over to shake someone's hand can cause the stylus to go careening across the vinyl.

There was a time pressure when DJing with vinyl too. Records are finite and they'll run out soon, so you'd better put another one on pretty quick, obviously making sure that it's a good one, one that compliments the last one and sets up the next one. You only have a limited amount of time to do the boring pitch adjustment stuff, and when you're as uptight as me, even the slightest pitch wobble is completely unacceptable so the process of spending a minute or two in the mix required deep concentration.

The process became way more intense in a club environment where the music was sometimes so loud that it drowned out what was in your headphones, especially if there were no monitor speakers. Sometimes the bass rumble would be so intense it would cause the needle to jump out of the groove and you'd have to play a gig with a penny stuck to the head shell with chewing gum to weigh it down.

DJing with vinyl always had an air of frisson, there was a fragility to the whole set-up and there were so many things that could go wrong, that you had to monitor, including your own dancing. There are a few occasions where I've knocked the decks whilst dancing to my own selection, caused the record to skip and in doing so briefly killed the mood of a room I've spent 90 minutes building up. Everything was fine as long as nothing entered an imaginary exclusion zone around the decks, but a single drop of a drink or hot-rock from a spliff dropping on the vinyl could mess the whole thing up in an instant.

Vinyl records are fragile, vulnerable, they deteriorate with repeated playing, and you had to hold them carefully, by the edges, as though there were fragile audio snowflakes. But in the heat of a gig they get chucked around and stuffed back in the record bag because you can't find the sleeve. Slowly over time, the vinyl picks up dust, which adheres to the greasy finger marks you left on them when you were in the middle of a hectic gig and had no time for the niceties of record handling and storage, contributing to the gradual sound degradation. Vinyl also gets tiny scratches, causing an audible pop or crackle when played. Some DJs say that this creates some kind of extra layer of voodoo magic, some additional atmosphere to the music which adds to the mystique and inherent superiority of vinyl over other formats. They're wrong of course. As if Aretha Franklin or Carl Craig somehow need some extra 'atmosphere' added to their recordings in the shape of the pops and crackles of ageing vinyl.

If you had a big DJing weekend you'd get Technics blisters from constantly laying your fingers lightly on the spinning platter to adjust the tempo. Your record box or bag also brought its own mysteries to the party: a good record bag could make a record completely disappear for an entire gig, only to mysteriously appear as soon as you get off the decks. Same thing with record sleeves: your bag or box would seemingly eat them up throughout the gig so that you end up just putting your tunes in the box sleeveless, or cannibalising other records' outer and inner sleeves. Come the next day, the record box would give up all the missing sleeves and records as though they'd been there all time. Also some of the inner sleeves were in on it, they would be fine until you took a record out, but then when you tried to put it back in five minutes later the sleeve would have magically shrunk by just enough to make it impossible to get the record back in.

And then there was the experience of hearing your records that you'd only ever played on a tiny home system, on a serious club sound system. Some of them sounded completely unrecognisable once they were away from the home listening environment. The bass response is huge in nightclubs and completely changes how records sound. Sometimes you had to check that you were playing what you thought you were, the difference was so big. Of course, the converse of this was that weird thing that often happened when you got back from the record shop after blowing £70 on a bunch of new imports to find that the one that sounded so amazing in the shop now sounded like some old pots and pans being rattled in a wheelie bin.

The atmosphere of our first year of parties, it was like being on a football terrace with England winning the World Cup in the last seconds of extra-time, on your birthday, which happens to be on Christmas Day. We had regulars, the same faces, a hardcore, who brought their mates, newbies who got pulled into our web, each time seemingly better than before. From inside the booth, you could hear the roar of the crowd. We caught some kind of wave of lucky synergy, all the elements were in place: a captive and ripe audience, a team of overly dedicated DJs, a frankly brilliant period in the history of dance music, a great little venue, that's all it takes and you can create magical memories that will stay with you for life.

We were nervous, over-prepared. Brought way too many records with us, and overthought the whole endeavour, but then I always thought that that was part of the reason I was a good DJ. I was entirely prepared for any eventuality, I knew all my tunes so well, that I couldn't fail, I had a musical option for every possible situation or occasion. Our first party went off, so we were invited back next month. We were such amateurs we left the date off the flyers, so had to stick labels on them.

The early 90s were a tumultuous period. Blair became Labour leader, Mandela got the presidency in South Africa, the IRA announced they were putting down their guns, there was Ace of Base: these were eventful times. And then there was the Criminal Justice Bill. In 1987 Thatcher had infamously said "There's no such thing as society" and then was proved utterly wrong the next year as acid house and rave swept across the country. A movement based around ideas of community and togetherness, made up of countless thousands of mostly working-class young people, organised via secret networks of mobiles phones, pagers, flyers and pirate radio. Why, it's almost as though there was such a thing as society after all. At the time, many saw the Tories Criminal Justice Bill of 1994 as a direct response to the rave movement and to house and techno in particular. We started putting references to the CJB on the flyers for our fully legal, licensed till 3 am parties at the student union. Let no one say we didn't fight the power.

The final party of the summer, according to Fannah: "We blew the doors off, full roster of BYO DJs playing, squeezed another hour or so in the running time, really good pills, I hammered the granny out of the strobe, Harold playing 'Gimme A Smile' at the end, was one of the greatest rave moments ever: period."

The piano/guitar-tastic song 'Gimme A Smile' from the Lost Tribe on Stress Records (Delorme V Dharma Bums mix if you're looking for the authentic version) had become an unofficial BYO anthem. 'Gimme A Smile' was nearly seven minutes long and started with a rigid sequenced bassline and a churning collection of bubbling synths. It's a reasonably innocuous intro and not instantly recognisable until the vocal sample sneaks in. I used to mix it in and just watch for the first person to realise what it was. Then one by one the energy would spread, little clusters of recognition rippling out across the room until they're all grinning at each other because they know what's coming. The first break features an unselfconscious funky guitar that would send any serious techno fan straight off to the bar in a flash but used to do the job very nicely on our dance floor. Then it potters off for a couple of minutes on a vaguely trancey UK progressive house-via-Italy journey, building a little tension, taking its time to work up to the main piano break. It was unashamedly jubilant, executed with glee, making no concessions to cool, just tapping into whatever magical bliss-source the piano-break draws its power from.

It had lyrics ("For the future!"), so everyone used to sing along, which added to its adoption en masse by BYOers. It had got such a good reception the first time I played it, I'd started to play it regularly, something that may have irritated the other BYO DJs. who were getting into a more sophisticated underground house sound. Not me, at the time I was a sucker for a massive crowd-pleaser, always have been.

The mood in our camp soured as Panno and I fell out over set times and came to blows a few simmering months later. Which just demonstrates how seriously we all took DJing: way, way too seriously. As Fannah would say to me when I would mention being nervous before a gig "It's just playing records Harold". He was right of course; this wasn't worth you and your mate punching each other in the head. And he was completely wrong too. It could never be just playing records.

Summer of that year we attempted to move our party to local nightclubs in South East London and found that the reality of such was quite different from the student union. Once I stepped outside the university DJing bubble, violence, drugs, dealers, fights, smashed glasses, ripped shirts, girls crying, vomit, minicabs, the late-night tension of the kebab shop, and the general tragic events of a UK Saturday night became much more a part of the job. We had some out-there folk at our university parties no doubt, but the more I DJed around south London's venues, the more wide-eyed young men I met who had the prefix 'Mad' before their name; it was like every bar and every club had at least one. So many of them, so very nearly handsome but with a fluctuating seething rage and crippling fear simmering just below the surface that would subtly pull their young features into a snarl, gently removing any beauty, quietly replacing it with the South East London screw-face; a very slight sneer and their eyes sizing you up as though you were prey; ready to pounce. Tough to DJ for.

This was a world where you might get knocked for your wages, or witness another DJ get thrown out of a club: actually flying through the air like in a cartoon, until he landed when it suddenly became very real indeed. The punters were different, less loved-up than the students, harder to please. And there were no bongo players in the clubs and bars of South East London, not ones I DJed in anyway. And whereas previously, perfectly pleasant relationships with a variety of mild-mannered student union Entertainment Managers had been maintained with ease, I was now often dealing with some very dubious characters.

Your fee was sometimes difficult to get. Promoters or bar managers who were supposed to pay you would disappear from the club. If you were lucky they were still there; you just had to find them. Search the bar, the dance floor, are they outside, make your way through security round to the back office, and yep, there it is, the mini-party-within-a-party, the promoters inner circle. They'd usually be taking cocaine; I think it's in the promoters rule book or something, you have to do a certain amount of nose if you're promoting.

One evening I was playing house music with another DJ I knew from a record shop in Welling, DJ Simon Green. Not Simon Green, but 'DJ Simon Green', that's how he introduced himself, "I'm DJ Simon Green". He had the biggest hands you'd ever seen and we always used to wonder how he managed to mix with such clunky great fingers. To be honest, DJ Simon Green didn't generally do a great job, favouring bland vocal house and the safe, unfussy eight-bar fade transition, never wavering from his commitment to the most predictable and dull mixing technique. But he knew a promoter who was paying us to play our records so I was warming up for DJ Simon Green, which was fine with me.

I knew that a group in the corner was made up of mates of local criminal, Simon 'Shooter' Michaels, who got his name from his career choice as an armed robber. I also saw that Shooter's younger brother, Hungry Johnny was there too. Shooter was no bother to me simply because he didn't know I existed; I was small fry, not on his radar. Hungry John though, he'd talk to anyone and start with them, just to see what might happen. He was tall, blonde and thin, his pale skin taut across the awkward contours of his still adolescent, angular face. He told me once that he was fine with his upcoming court case where he was certain to go down, as prison was actually great for him: he got to play pool, got three meals a day, all the drugs he wanted, and he could fight as much as he liked.

Johnny walked past me on his way to the toilet and said 'Alright mate!" in a friendly fashion. I responded similarly. A couple of minutes later he came out again and walked straight round the back of the decks and stood staring at me from the side. I turned to speak and he asked me sweetly "Did you just call me a shitcunt?" I said no. "Did he call me a shitcunt?" Johnny said to a non-existent audience. He tilted his head, holding his finger up to me in a gesture intended to politely ask me to hang on a second while he got his response from the invisible person he was addressing. They clearly agreed with him because he then said: "You did, you called me a shitcunt". Then nodding to the invisible crowd that was gathering he said: "He did, didn't he, he called me a shitcunt". No doubt, they all agreed.

I tried to tell Hungry Johnny that I hadn't called him a shitcunt and that I was just going to put another tune on, we're good though mate yeah? But I think that everything I said was drowned out by the roar of the baying invisible mob. He began to wind himself up, standing so close to me that I can see the blackheads on his nose, the flecks of pus-yellow in his empty blue eyes, and smell his classic English Saturday evening aroma of aftershave, cigarettes and lager. My impending doom was only curtailed when doorman Tirpitz suddenly arrived and expertly manhandled Johnny out of the booth. Tirpitz then lumbered back over and apologised to me for John's behaviour, careful to placate me to avoid any further trouble as though I were the kind of person who would later try to extract some kind of revenge, and who would need to be placated. When in fact, I really just wanted to leave, get some chips and go home.

There were very occasional punch-ups at student unions, and a bit of low-level drug dealing, but it was generally a pretty low-risk environment. This was different. One of the many things that ecstasy and acid house culture created was a dense smokescreen over the criminality often involved in nightclubs. It was a willing blindness to reality, based on drug-induced empathy which engendered a belief that pretty much everyone was cool man. But once house music moved back into the clubs from illegal raves in forests and warehouses, it returned from a shady illegal world to an equally shady legal/semi-legal world instead.

Bosh ran the door at the club in South East London where we promoted our first non-university night. He had been part of a punk group in his somewhat chequered past and was banned from the home counties for incitement to riot. About nine feet tall, his voice alone was enough to make you realise that if it came down to any kind of physical altercation, you were fucked. Eyes that looked you up and down, performed an instant physical assessment, then zeroed in on your psyche and tried to get in for a poke around. I once saw him walk across the club to throw someone out, pick them up by their throat, and carry them out across the crowded dance floor, all without once actually making eye contact with them.

We once found ourselves in the back room at the end of a night, surrounded by piles of cash and bags of drugs. All the security crew were crowded in this tiny office, and they're all fucking huge, all doing coke off big shiny knives that they all have just produced from inside the black leather jackets they're all wearing. At one point one of us, can't remember who, probably Wolfie, asked them if they'd seen that episode of US sitcom 'Friends' where Ross and Chandler get bullied at Central Perk. They hadn't.

At another booking, I went to the bar and was standing behind a man with a navy leather holdall casually open at his feet, showing its contents of, I reckon, maybe ten greasy-looking handguns. He was talking to himself extremely quickly. I remember he must have been very small because I could look down on his bald patch, and his long greasy comb-over Terry Nutkins-style hair. He got his drink and then with a nod of the head was taken through the 'Staff Only' door, leaving ten minutes later bagless.

If it was a Blow Your Own, then Fannah would have to deal with the big boys to get our wages, but if I was gigging on my own, then I had to go and find Bosh or his equivalent and get him away from his bag of nose for five minutes to pay me. One evening he didn't even look up, just told me that there was no money for me. I actually found myself kicking up a fuss. I'm not sure who was more surprised, me or Bosh, who had his partner-in-terror Keith with him.

The pair of them, craggy-faced hard bastards that they were, turned and listened to me for a moment, as though genuinely interested in what my plan might be. But the moment I stepped up the mood changed and the mask dropped. I remember immediately and instantly regretting ever entering their club, genuinely fearful that I was about to get a serious kicking. It's a unique experience, the expectation of violence, one that produces a very specific combination of chemicals in the brain, producing a particular flavour of fear that you really don't get in any other circumstances.

Bosh pulled himself up to impressive full height, jabbed my weedy chest and enquired as to exactly what I planned on doing about it. Strange how a show of strength can change how strongly you feel about something, but suddenly I wasn't so bothered about my fifty sheets anymore. Bosh's question was rhetorical: they marched me through the warren of corridors at the back of the club speedily, with a minimum of fuss and some low level 'cunting' and 'wankering'; I had time enough to wonder if I would be beaten inside or outside the club and to wonder if fighting back would make it better or worse, but they simply pushed me out the back door with complete disdain, as though I was of no consequence to them at all.

However, my records were still in the DJ booth as I hadn't fancied carrying my record box across a heaving dance floor and through the secret paths to the back office. Packed record boxes were super-heavy, surprisingly so. You could easily be mugged for your records as you could never run away whilst carrying something as heavy as a packed record box. But then of course you'd be able to catch the mugger instantly as they'd not be able to run away from you because of the weight of the records. But then they'd be able to catch you... if you're not careful you could get stuck in an eternal DJ space-time loop.

I figured Bosh and Keith would be returning to the office to do more nose, so I went straight back around to the front door, paid £10 to get back into the club I'd just been playing in, walked through the packed dance floor and up into the booth. Picked up my box of records and my hoodie and left. I paid a minicab driver £20 to drive me home. After drinks I was about £50 down on the night and I'd left my new mini Maglite torch in the booth too. Another great evening in South East London's clubland.

I once got a gig in room two (so many room two gigs, and a fair few room threes as well) at what turned out to be a serious fetish event, which then developed into a full-on sex-party. At the end of the night, the lights came on and the various rubber-clad and chain-ridden party-goers made their way to the cloakroom, apart from a single middle-aged couple who were still banging away furiously at the front of the stage. The poor security man waited patiently for a couple of minutes, then tapped them politely on the shoulder. "Hang on mate," says the gimp-mask and he suddenly breaks into fifth gear, puffing like an asthmatic hay-fever sufferer, presumably going red in the face although who knows what's going on under his gimp mask. Just when you think his heart's going to give out, he goes "Fuck it, I'm not going to come anyway" and withdraws from his grateful partner, with the air of a man who gave it his best, but is literally out of juice.

Once you start promoting your own nights you also come into contact with the poster campaigns of other local venues, the local rivalries spilling over into threats and violence if someone put their poster over another current event, or postered an area exclusively reserved for a certain club.

The poster team, the flyer team – there was a whole behind-the-curtains crew who made a nightclub work. Bar staff, sound engineer, DJs, club owner, promoter, cloakroom staff, the licensee, admin, accountant, cleaner, caretaker, a tiny little world of people doing things behind the scenes to keep it all functioning.

Out of everyone in the club, security generally knows what's going on, and they'll be the ones who you'll turn to if you get chased from the venue by an angry mob who didn't like your set of exclusively Mood II Swing dubs. Only the stupidest DJ gives security any grief. I once saw a very well known DJ attempt to get free entry for a huge entourage by pulling the whole "Don't you know who I am" thing. The security team literally didn't know who he was and simply ignored him. Some were nicer than others. One of the Friday night door crew at one of the clubs we put on a Blow Your Own was Mack, known as Mack the Murderer aka The Human Hand Grenade; piss him off and he'd nick your sweets off you for sure. Mixed martial arts expert, drug dealer, armed robber, career criminal, occasional doorman. Even the venue's resident 'Mad'-prefix-guy Mad Steve was afraid of him.

More than any other place apart from maybe bus stations, there are always people just hanging around nightclubs. People who are just often there. On the fringes. Slightly involved. Drifting in and out of legitimacy. Associates of the sound engineer, friend of a promoter, endless DJs, chancers and wannabes. The club owners' weird polyester husband, a silent 'caretaker' with dubious credentials. People who always seem to be at the end of the bar chatting to staff as though they worked there. And always drug people. Dealers, drivers, runners, enthusiasts, participants, customers. People who wished they were dealers, who pretended to be big-time, and people who pretended not to be who actually were.

G Man and Quick Nick used to hang around a venue I worked at for a while. "What do you actually do?" I asked them one day. "Oh, we're in antiques," they answered. "You sell 'em?" "Nah, we nick 'em". I was told a sad tale one night about the head of security at a venue I was working at. Apparently, he'd had to serve a few years inside because he'd got unlucky and someone he'd punched had tragically died. I later found out that this was true, but that the victim was tied to a chair at the time of the fatal punch. The same summer a friend of ours was taken hostage and pistol-whipped over a drug debt. Even I, with my high levels of nostalgia, can't say that it was all fun, it wasn't, nightclubs can be a dark world, one that in many ways we were all unprepared for.

But I was very happy to pick up any DJ gigs and despite the ups and downs, was still very single-mindedly focused on 'making it' as a DJ; bad gigs were just part of the process, you chalk 'em up and move on. I played in bars and clubs in Catford, Greenwich, New Cross, on the Old Kent Road, Peckham, Brixton, Deptford. I played my first gig in central London in a brightly lit bar on a tiny, tinny sound system and was comprehensively ignored by everyone there. The Amphib and I returned to Liverpool and put on a triumphant night of uplifting piano-bosh house for the lovely scousers in a sticky-carpeted pub, then had a most excellent after-party, hey la, before heading back to London in a wide-eyed round trip of exactly 24 hours.

If clubbing and DJing had an air of glamour, it didn't really come from the clubs themselves. The buildings were shabby, tattered, unremarkable spaces which smelt strongly of several odours, none of them good. The back rooms, corridors, storerooms, changing rooms and stairwells that were the preserve of staff and guest DJs were poorly maintained and equally seedy. Sometimes I'd be there early before anyone had arrived, other times I'd be there when all the punters had finally left for the night, and it was always unnerving to see the actual cold hard reality.

Each venue was the same, a collection of tricks, literally smoke and mirrors, to fool punters into thinking they were somewhere magical. Using the simplest deceits, venue after venue was somehow transformed into a dreamlike space at night: make it dark, coupled with flashing coloured lights and UV, maybe a strobe and a smoke machine, and very high volume music. Any glamour or excitement is generated by the people in there and the success of the night depends on just how much they're prepared to suspend reality and buy into the magic tricks. And here comes the DJ, party facilitator, vibe enhancer, low-rent shaman, nerd, with their bag of arcane audio and sublime sonic treats to encourage a brief session of wild abandon. Another gig: best get that tune cued up.

HAROLD'S FAVOURITE CLASSIC PIANO TUNES

Snappiness featuring Dina Taylor – Sweet Inspiration
Don Carlos – Alone (Paradise)
707 Boyz – Emotions
True Faith featuring Bridgette Grace with Final Cut – Take Me Away
Outrage - Tall 'N' Handsome
Double Dee featuring Dany – Found Love
Manix – Feel Real Good
X Ray Xperiments – Take No Chance
Bass Construction – Dance With Power
Liquid – Sweet Harmony
FPI Project – Everybody (All Over The World)
Jinny – Keep Warm
Bassheads – Is There Anybody Out There
Brothers In Rhythm – Such A Good Feeling
Liberation – Liberation
Alex Lee – Take It
Electric Choc – Shock The Beat
Dr Mouthquake – Love On Love (Mouthquake Master Mix)
Gat Decor – Passion
Jimi Polo – Better Days (Sasha Remix)
Shades Of Rhythm – Sound of Eden

7

INTOXICATION

SOUTH EAST LONDON, THE EARLY 1990S

I am gazing up at the stars on a cool clear night, the sound of the bypass a mile away audible above the low-level hum of Sidcup hospital. I'm dressed from head to foot in a white protective suit with a hood. The elastic around my face is too tight and I am sweating profusely. I look a little like a member of rave outfit Altern 8 but I am not at a rave. The air is filled with a vaguely unpleasant smell that I can't identify. The huge incinerator behind me churns on. I'm about to unload a lorry. Two days ago, I took a job from a temp agency in Lewisham to 'unload lorries'.

If you're going to be a DJ, then you're going to need to support yourself until your career takes off; hence this job. I had done this kind of work previously. I'd spent a week unloading Tate & Lyle bags that weighed as much as a small human, from metal container lorries that had been sitting in the August sun for a couple of days. 'Smile, it's Tate and Lyle' we had said to each other as we ripped open a bag, grabbed a handful of sugar for energy washed down with huge gulps of water, to be sweated out quickly and effectively by our young systems over the next half hour till the next sugar break. So I assumed this would be something similar, hard work, but good pay, and in no way interfering with my DJing.

I hadn't asked and hadn't been told what the lorries I would be unloading would actually contain, so I was dismayed when we opened up the back doors of the first lorry and a leg-shaped yellow bucket dropped out. It had a leg in it. I was unloading clinical waste: boxes of needles, amputations, bags of swabs, removed appendixes, etc. I worked the shift with Tattooed Pete who had worked there several years. I think he may have given himself the nickname. He said he was called Tattooed Pete because he had his own name tattooed inside his lower lip – "Pete" – and he would pull down his lip to show anyone he met. I used to think you work in a hospital incinerator mate, you should wash your hands before you do that.

Disposing of South East London and Kent's clinical waste was just one of many ways I contributed to society whilst supporting my early DJ career. I took a succession of temporary agency work as I studiously avoided any idea of a real job to pursue 'being a DJ'. I cleaned factories, sat for long hours at intersections taking traffic surveys, I filed things, packed things, unpacked other things, moved heavy things from one place to another and met a succession of people for whom this was their life, whilst I was just passing through until I 'made it'. I had Blow Your Own, and was playing regularly around other student union campuses. I was also starting to pick up other DJing gigs mainly through word-of-mouth and recommendations. Lots of them were opening, or 'warm-up' gigs.

There are two types of warm-ups. There are the warm-up DJ sets where there are some people to warm up. The idea behind DJing a warm-up is that there is some kind of progression to the night and that this should be reflected in the music. So early on, the DJ plays a 'warm-up' set, of more restrained, laid back, slower tempo music, nothing too intense, or full-on. The intention is to welcome everyone and create a mood, to build anticipation for the onslaught that is about to follow. So a DJ playing that sort of warm-up has a chance to play those gorgeous bits of music that they can't drop at peak time because they're not banging enough, an opportunity to experiment and to manipulate mood through selection.

A good warm-up set can be hugely rewarding for a DJ: there's a special kind of magic to enticing the first few people out onto the floor, because there always has to be a first person on the dance floor. How are you going to get them there? Warm-up sets are all about observing your audience and picking out those who clearly want to dance and getting inside their heads to work out what they want. There's a definite art to it, it needs insight, restraint, it requires some decent music knowledge and the ability to create rapport with music. Peak time is brilliant fun, no doubt, and generally gets you all the DJ glory, but bringing a room to the boil and then handing over to someone else is fantastically satisfying too.

Then, there are the other kinds of warm-ups, the ones that I started to get in the clubs and bars of South East London. The Amphibian got me a gig warming up for KISS FM DJ Graham Gold at a club in Deptford. For years, whenever Graham Gold's name came up in conversation, Fannah would always say 'He's bald and old is Graham Gold'. So obviously when I met him in this DJ booth for a hurried DJ handover, instead of saying Hi Graham, like a normal person, to my horror I said 'He's bald and old is Graham Gold'. Luckily we were in a nightclub with the sound system playing at near-full whack so he clearly didn't hear what I said and replied with something like 'Brilliant, nice one'. I have believed this ever since but now that I write this I wonder if perhaps he heard me perfectly well.

There was, literally, no one in the club when I got on the decks. Then I put on my final record at 10:55, at which point the club filled up and whereupon I promptly trainwrecked the mix. By 11:05 Graham Gold was mixing into his second track to a rammed dance floor.

I was once booked for a warm-up by the DJs who ran a South London record shop to play at their night in Beckenham. One of them bore a very passing resemblance to Ray Manzarek from The Doors. During Oliver Stone's 'The Doors' movie, Billy Idol's character memorably tells Ray to "Fuck Off Ray". So obviously Fannah christened the hapless bespectacled record shop dude 'Fuck Off Ray', a name we adopted with glee. I can remember his look of utter mystification, complete bafflement: "Who are these people, why are they telling me to fuck off and my name's not even Ray?"

I had been to their night the week before and it had been packed, so was disappointed to find when I arrived that it was empty except for me and my poor long-suffering mates who I'd convinced to come along. It was empty because Fuck Off Ray and his hapless crew had cancelled the event, pulled all the promotion but neglected to tell the club or me. I played my allotted warm-up, no punters arrived, no DJ came to relieve me. The bar staff yawned and cleaned the shelves. My mates drank bottled lager and the spotlights clicked through their motions. I carried on playing, wondering whether to just pack it in, then one of the DJs/shop staff turned up, handed me an envelope with an embarrassed grin then scooted off to tell security the night's cancelled before scuttling away. The house lights came on, I switched off the mixer and packed up my tunes. We drove home and I spent my wages, an envelope containing a single, lonely £10 note, at the McDonalds drive-through on the Old Kent Road.

The Amphib started his own night, the brilliantly named Diurnation and I played there a few times. "It means people of the night, Harold," he said, bristling slightly at my reaction to the name. "Then why not call it People of the Night, or Night People or anything that sounds less like both diarrhoea and urination?" I asked, to no avail. The Amphib always followed his own particular path, oblivious to fashion, trends or other people's opinions on things like calling house nights Diurnation. My memory of that particular night was playing my house music to a clued up South East London clientele, one of whom approached the booth to ask me if I was going to play any dance music tonight.

Looking back at all those warm-up gigs, they were all characterised by the same naive hope, that someone would hear me, someone influential, and that they'd come up to me and offer me some kind of DJing job. As though early Saturday evening in a pub in Brockley is where you find most of the decent club promoters from the UK, all of whom are talent scouting. This belief was born from the over-exuberance of many dancers and clubbers who would come and congratulate you after your set and offer you DJing work that they didn't really have to offer. At least one person would always say they're connected to someone or somewhere and they'd love to get you in. I used to find this aspect of the job utterly thrilling, as every new opportunity was a chance to DJ in front of a new audience and a step closer to what I had now decided really should be my goal: of earning a living from DJing.

Television and films have given us a generally misguided picture of how any path to success unfolds. Fiction concertinas events, squashing lengthy time frames into mere seconds. It cuts out huge swathes of real-life incidents – failures, disappointments, hold-ups – and edits out much of the waiting and procrastination in order to move the narrative on. It was rare that someone would say "Mate, we've got to have you come and play" and then next week you'd be playing the opening slot. Lots of people were just really high, wanted to tell you how much they were enjoying it and got a bit carried away. Others possibly thought they were making a sound business decision but come Monday morning changed their minds. The path to new gigs rarely comes from a promoter coming up to you mid-gig and saying "Hey, I just heard your set and I've been looking for someone who DJs like you, we should get you to play at our parties for a huge fee". Although weirdly, that's the secret fantasy of every DJ of the fourth tier and below.

I came away from many early gigs with a clutch of work offers that mostly came to nothing. At all those early gigs, I secretly, quietly, barely consciously, hoped that this might be the night where I got heard, noticed, picked up, transferred to the big time. As though that was how it happened. It only took a couple of years for me to realise that job offers made at four in the morning from people on drugs should be taken with a pinch of salt.

Every gig taught me something, even if it was something as simple as the fact that Dan Hartman's 'Instant Replay' only works on a dance floor for about a minute, minute and a half, tops.[5] I had an interesting mix, from an imaginary psychologists' point of view, of quiet self-confidence tempered by raging self-doubt and the constant threat of the black cloud of gloom descending. I thought I was a good DJ but also worried about gigs. Will they like my tunes? Wait, aren't all my records rubbish and I'm just a great big idiot? And then I would ascend to brief heights of elation when a gig went really well and it turned out that I wasn't a great big idiot after all. I mixed at home obsessively. It seems like a strange thing to spend so much time on, now that the beatmatching element of DJing is no longer a required DJ skill. It was partly that mixing tunes together is fun, but it was also because I loved the music so much, that it wasn't enough to just buy it, listen to it and play it. I wanted to smell it and eat it and in lieu of being able to actually physically consume music, constantly mixing it together at least allowed you to immerse yourself fully in it. And of course, as a DJ, you could listen to two tunes at the same time: double music!

5 Perhaps it gives everything away too soon, there's not a great deal of difference between the verse and the chorus and once you've heard them once, there doesn't seem to be much point in going through it again. And then when Dan starts his post-second-chorus scatting, someone usually comes up to the booth and asks you to stop playing Leo Sayer.

It's not especially relevant to the book, but I feel that for the sake of balance, Dan Hartman's other big club record 'Relight My Fire' featuring Loleatta Holloway, a tune so massive that there isn't a font big enough to do it justice, should really get a mention as we played it around this time too and it's a stone-cold classic. The full-length version of 'Relight My Fire' was called 'Vertigo/Relight My Fire' and came with three minutes of string-soaked cosmic disco instrumental goodness before finally kicking off into another six minutes of epic disco heaven. Featuring proto-house pianos, storming orchestration and the performance of a lifetime from vocalist Loleatta Holloway, you get a grand total of nine minutes and forty six seconds, every single moment of which was, in contrast to 'Instant Re-play', utterly playable.

Normal people bought their music from Woolworths or Our Price, or some other now-defunct high street retailer. Not us. We had specialist shops just for us, run by DJs, full of nothing but 12" vinyl, slip-mats and mixtapes. They existed in every London satellite suburb, and there was a huge clump of them in Soho. I would exhaust myself searching for records, heading out to the suburbs once I'd covered every central London record shop at least twice in one day.

White-labels were promotional records, so-called because their labels were usually completely blank. They came out in restricted numbers to a restricted audience, to promote the record before general release. Access to decent promos was another clear indicator of which DJ tier you were on. Some DJs got sent white-labels in the post, with a feedback form, asking them when they played it, how it went, would they play it again and asking for marks out of ten. There was a period in my life when this was my dream, to be sent promos.

As a low tier DJ, white-label promos were difficult to come by, although occasionally a friendly record store assistant that you'd spent years grooming might slip you a precious white-label which you'd treasure as though it were a rare gem. A promo might not be available to everyone else for weeks, or even months, so DJs loved them. It might even end up not released at all, in which case you've got yourself a rare DJ-secret-weapon.

A white-label had way more cachet than a normal release, it signified that you were a genuine part of the DJ community. Promos are now usually delivered digitally and it's not difficult to get on lots of promo lists. In fact, it's an irony not lost on the older DJ community that the only time you hear DJs talking about promos now is when they return from holiday and then announce via social media that they've got hundreds of promos to plough through.

If you headed into central London on a Saturday afternoon record shopping trip – Black Market, Reckless, Choci's Chewns, Fat Cat, Zoom, Flying Records – you'd likely bump into other DJs you half-know, also doing their shopping for that night, looking for something new, maybe picking up their bag of tunes that the shop had been keeping back for them. I used to watch with genuine envy when someone could just swan into Black Market Records in Soho and be handed a bag of pristine new releases, imports, promos, white-labels and rarities that had been saved for them. Along with being sent promos, having a record shop assistant keep a bag of new tunes behind the counter for you was the dream we all aspired to.

Eventually, I would achieve bag-held-behind-the-counter-for-me level, but only at Cruisin' Records in Welling, not in any of the Soho shops. This was a clear reflection of my place in the DJ hierarchy. A bag of tunes held back for you at Cruisin' records Welling? Then you've reached tier five of the DJ pyramid, maybe even tier four if there are some white-labels in there. If you get a bag kept back for you at Black Market, you're more likely located in at least tier three or higher.

We all had our preferred record shops. My favourite of the out of town shops was the aforementioned Cruisin', Welling's finest, mainly because the atmosphere was the most fun. Run by Ralph Smith, Friday evenings you'd get a bunch of house DJs all hanging around waiting for the van to turn up with the latest releases, snapping up the new vinyl like the eager little DJ crocodiles we were. Record shops on Friday evenings were vibrant, fun, full of chat and laughter with just a little edge of professional jealousy if someone else scored the last copy of something brilliant. Gathered around the counter, giving the thumbs up or down to a new tune, "I'll take a copy of that too", "Had this on promo last month". It was like membership of a private faction, full of its own codes, DJ jargon, and in-jokes.

Listening in-shop means you had to imagine yourself in the centre of your own dance floor in a few hours, at peak time during your set. What is this tune going to sound like then? Yes or no, in or out, you work your way through until you are left with a pile of about three times more records than you can afford. Listen to them all again. Lose another third of them. Spend more money than you meant to. Go home happy. The train ride home across the Thames as the sun was setting on an early Saturday evening, with a couple of bags of fresh vinyl for tonight's gig, will always remain one of the absolute favourite journeys of my life.

Fannah meanwhile had decided university life wasn't for him and had been sniffing around a converted live venue in Woolwich, which was being redeveloped into some kind of nightclub. He somehow talked them into interviewing me for a resident DJ role before they opened, and I got the job. I think my interview involved us talking about my mixtape that I'd brought with me and me telling them their promotional flyer made their venue look like a leisure centre. They agreed to pay me a flat fee every Saturday night and a record allowance. Yes, that's right, they paid me a certain amount of money each week specifically to spend on records. On top of my wages. I couldn't quite believe my luck, whilst also simultaneously feeling that this was the logical next step and that maybe, this was a sign that I could actually 'be' a 'professional' DJ.

So I began my Saturday night residency at Woolwich's Eauzone club. They had a brilliant sound system in there, with a superb toothless sound engineer in attendance all night. I can't recall exactly what I played on that first night, but luckily Fannah somehow kept his cassette collection from those days, so I have a DJ mix of mine from 1994. It's very fast. We used to play our music substantially pitched up to match the energy of the times and to suit our own need for speed. Featuring UK house from labels like Soma, Junior Boys Own, Stress, Sun-Up, Global Grooves, some US house dubs from Strictly Rhythm, Emotive and Nervous, some techno, some Italian piano house, lots of music I have no recollection of ever buying, a few vinyl wobbles in the mix and bags of enthusiasm. If you caught me DJing in '94 you'd be treated to a few long transitions à la DJ Sasha, some key-matched mixes which I remember being particularly pleased with, and way more cheesy vocal samples than I remember playing.

The Eauzone DJ booth was initially embedded way up in the wall in the corner, pleasingly away from the dance floor and the DJ could look down on the entire room, but people wouldn't immediately know you were up there. It was a perfect set up. I loved it up there. The whole beginning-of-the-night ritual was sheer joy. Get a few drinks in, chat to the bar staff, most of whom were my mates anyway, wonder where Fannah was, head up to the booth, sort the records out, set the monitor levels, angle the little lamp just so. Move your drinks to the other side of the decks, shift the record box around a bit, get a few tunes out, where's the ashtray, what are the levels like, how's that system sounding. Put a record on then go and walk around the empty club, frowning slightly at the sound system, listening for any obvious problems, even though there was a full-time sound engineer in attendance; it was all a part of the ritual. I loved it.

There were pillars and a low ceiling along one side of the main room and stages at either end. The club's initial marketing featured an aqua theme and there was definitely a dolphin in their original logo. Most of the interior was blue and the bits that weren't were gold, with huge swathes of the walls covered in found objects: toys, key-rings, trinkets, costume jewellery, all set into the plaster and sprayed blue or gold. It was about to become the seat of the next stage in my DJ career, my first club residency.

In a nice bit of rave synchronicity, my friends and I had done some of our most serious raving of the last few months at a warehouse venue in Plumstead, which was run by the same team now running the Eauzone. The boss was Alistair Barnum. He had managed the lead singer of a 70s pop band after they broke up and then had a brief pop career of his own in Japan before settling into a lifetime of hustling around the edges of the industry. He always had a plan, was always one for the long game and always had an eye for a bargain and a deal. Overflowing with bonhomie and brilliantly told anecdotes, he was the nearest thing to a raconteur we had ever known. Edgy too though. There was something else lurking underneath those twinkling eyes; there was always an ulterior motive, a plan, a strategy; always.

Barnum used to wear a medallion on his lapel. Later on, when we pieced together the debris of those years, we discovered that he had told each of us an entirely different plausible story regarding the medal, its provenance, and what it meant to him. I think maybe he was testing out how far he might be able to mislead us, or how gullible we really were. Or perhaps he was just bored and enjoyed fucking with us. He was an expert manipulator, enticing people to do his bidding based on vague, rarely fulfilled promises.

Barnum was much smaller in real life than he appeared, but you'd never know unless you met him when he wasn't wearing his cowboy boots which had big lifts in them. He came out into the street in his socks to greet me once when I went to visit his home studio and I briefly got vertigo. He was recording a piece of music that he wanted to tie-in with the World Cup of that year, and he wanted it to be a contemporary club record, so had asked me to drop by to provide a few pointers, based on the fact that I was playing the very latest club tunes at his club. For everyone else that year, USA 94 was about the fact that neither England, Northern Ireland, Scotland or Wales had qualified, but for Barnum it was all about an angle for a hit. I tried to be diplomatic about the leaden 80s style cliché-laden pop romp he was cooking up and attempted to get him to let me 'have a go' on his impressive synth collection. He demurred.

He and his team had done a superb job of converting an ex-live venue into a rave den. During the refurbishing, Barnum had sneaked in at night to move the guidelines carefully set up by the builders during the day to make his floor a couple of inches higher; he always wanted to be a couple of inches higher. The venue was split into the main club and a bar area; there was a decent-sized indoor balcony, offices, and space for a recording studio upstairs.

For the first Saturday night, I had spent my record allowance and duly handed in the receipts before taking to the decks. Four hours later we closed early, entirely empty. The Eauzone had huge overheads. Lighting rig, sound system, sound engineer, my records.

The licence stipulated that there had to be ten door staff working for the club to open, and Barnum had elected to be independent of any brewery, so the stock prices were sky high too, not to mention they were paying me and a Friday night resident as well. Meanwhile, they'd done virtually no promotion, merely expecting to repeat their Plumstead warehouse success where they had opened a club and hundreds of eager ravers had simply turned up. This was different; times had already moved on.

A few weeks in and the club was in deep financial trouble. Barnum had quickly realised that Fannah could be a useful asset, especially if he bought his paying student audience with him and so set him up as 'Bar Manager' with questionable wages and even more questionable working conditions. Thus entrenched, we got a date for our first BYO at the Eauzone, whilst I took over DJing at the struggling Friday nights.

We planned, flyered, worried, discussed the order the DJs would play in as though anyone would care, and we bought records. On the night of our first Eauzone Blow Your Own, Fannah and I arrived early to soundcheck, dress the club and to worry some more. We sat and had a couple of drinks alone in the bar, quietly anxious, smoking cigarettes, tapping ash, waiting to the sound of the air con and the hum of the fridges. We both went upstairs to the office and looked out to see a fucking great queue. We got 600 through the door, and they drank the bar dry, one in one out all night.

Late into the night of our first Blow Your Own party at his club, Barnum and I took a moment together on the balcony, looking down at the dance floor. Every available surface, floor, stage, podiums, speakers, bits of the club that definitely weren't for dancing on, had someone dancing on it. Wolfie had just dropped a massive great piano break which was virtually drowned out by the whoops and cheers of most of our mates and some other very happy young people. Barnum turned to me with a big grin and said "It's like you've hired a rent-a-crowd and their only instruction was 'act like you're having the very best party of your fuckin' life.'"

For a few months, DJing was my only source of income – I was actually a real, working DJ. Once Fannah was in at the Eauzone, he took over the Saturday night promotions and started getting other decent parties in, many of which I got to play warm-up at as resident, a lovely little golden period for me when I got to DJ with established, grown-up DJs.

Following the success of Blow Your Own, my Eauzone residency and the various gigs I was getting around London, not to mention university gigs, this was when I really started to work and to learn. You realise just how much of DJing is rapport and communication. You learn that practising in your bedroom is a great foundation and that honing your technical skills is important, but you also quickly realise that there is nothing that can really prepare you for somehow helming the emotional flow of a room for a few hours.

And you realised that DJing is much more than peak-time Saturday night; it's those drizzly Tuesday night slots in Ilford that really are the makings of you.

BIG TUNES AT BLOW YOUR OWN AT THE EAUZONE

Firefly featuring Ursula Rucker – Supernatural (Original St. Louis Mix)
Mood II Swing featuring Carol Sylvan – Closer (Closer Dub)
Underground Sound of Lisbon – So Get Up
Deep Dish Presents Prana – The Dream
Solitaire Gee – Slumberland (Rhythm Invention Mix), The Teaser
Twangling – Twangling (Three Fingers In A Box)
The Shaker – Just Lick It
Taiko – Echo Drop
The African Dream – All The Same Family

Bump – House Stomping
Kristine W – Feel What You Want
Red Eye – Cut It
Punchunella – San Trancisco
G.O.D. – Limited 1
Cover Ups – Vol 1 and 2
Danny Taurus – Lies EP
Ramone "LL" Ropiak – Ropey Trax Volume 1
DJ Duke – Unreleased Dubs Vol 1 and 2.
Fire Island – There But For The Grace Of God
X-Press 2 featuring Lo-Pro – Rock Da House, Hip Housin'
Sure Is Pure – Out To Lunch EP
Movin Melodies Production – The Ethics EP
Alcatraz – Giv Me Luv
Nush – You Girls
Subliminal Cuts – Le Voie Le Soleil
Heller 'N' Farley Project – From The Dat Vol. 1
Shades Of Love – Body To Body (Keep In Touch) (The Junior Vasquez Remixes)
Blast feat. V.D.C. – Crayzy Man
Sweetest Day Of May – Joe T Vannelli – Greed Mixes
Grooveyard – Watch Me Now
Xen Mantra – Golden Delicious (Dandy Lion & Burdock Remix)
Lex Loofah - Jacked, Freaky Deaky
Lisa Marie Experience – Do That To Me (Mix 3)
Delicious Inc. – Delicious Poem

8

THAT'S THE WAY LOVE IS

Time has slowed down. I am mid-gig, Greenwich University student union upstairs bar, early 90s. I'm staring intently at two copies of the same record, one on each deck. I have been mixing them together. One of them is playing, deliberately, a single bar behind the other, so when I switch from one to the other, I can repeat the last four beats. It's a method that vinyl DJs used to use to perform a rudimentary live remix.

You play your copy of, for example, 'To The Beat Of The Drum' by La Luna which has a vocal sample that goes "To The Beat Of The Drum Bang, To The Beat Of The Drum Bang Bang". Then you play the second copy in time but exactly one bar behind the first. Then you can slam the crossfader back and forth between the two and rearrange the vocal, so, for example, you can make them say "To The Beat Of The Drum, To The Beat Of The Drum, To The Beat Of The Drum, To The Beat Of The Drum". Push the second tune forward by half a bar and you can make them say "To The Beat To The Beat To The Beat To The Beat". Or indeed "Bang Bang. Bang Bang".

This may sound like a bizarre practice and admittedly written down, it looks fairly ridiculous. However, in the early 90s, when you were DJing to a room full of bug-eyed party loons, most of whom were familiar with the tunes you were playing, pulling off a little trick like that used to make them totally lose it. It all seems so innocent now, almost a little naive, now that a DJ can get the stems or multi-tracks for a tune and remix it live with ease with no risk of the mix falling out of time. But attempting tricks like this live with vinyl was another matter. If you lost concentration, you could forget which was which and leave the wrong one playing, causing the entire room to suddenly lose their groove. And as we've already established, causing the room to lose their groove is a bad thing for DJs to do.

This is exactly what has happened to me: I am now lost, switching between the two songs one bar apart, trying to orientate myself and remember which track is which. However, the decision is taken out of my hands by a raver I vaguely know called Steaming Joe, who has bounded over to the decks for a sweaty handshake, misjudged the distance he needed to travel, his size, his momentum and indeed my wish for physical expressions of affection whilst mid-mix, and has careened into the table, sending the decks, mixer, drinks and ashtray flying. I'm left standing with my headphones still on, in front of a collapsed table and a surprisingly unbroken pair of Technics 1200s.

Steaming gets up and attempts to disentangle himself from various cables. He's given himself a bloody nose and, from somewhere in the mêlée he's gained a large black mark right down the middle of his face. He looks a bit like a painted warrior of rave who's travelled by horseback through the night to deliver some urgent missive from the acid house chieftains. "Sorry everyone", Steaming announces, while trying to pull a musty wrap of billy whizz out of his jeans pocket. "It's alright though, I've got plenty of go-powder", before falling over again and this time definitely breaking the arm of one of the 1200s.

Out comes the back-up deck, a greasy Citronic belt-drive, rickety but workable and the party continued, albeit with no more two-copies vinyl trickery. Mixing two copies together was a clear sign that my DJ confidence was growing. As it did, deciding what to play slowly took over from thinking about mixing as my main concern. In day-to-day life, rapport with someone either happened, or it didn't and there were some people that perhaps you'd never really 'click' with. And it seemed like this was true with DJing too. The trick was not to become fixated with the one or two people standing at the sides scowling, the ones that you just couldn't seem to connect with and instead play to everyone else. The entire room will rarely be going for it all night. More often there's an ebb and flow to it all, and there might be a couple of people who just aren't that into it, others who absolutely love it and all the shades in between. You just have to work with what you get.

A DJ friend of mine once got himself a gig at legendary New York club Twilo after many years of grafting at the DJ coal face. Twilo was something of a DJ holy grail gig, somewhere for the true believers, the house soldiers. He was playing his tunes and a girl came up to the booth: "What kind of music do you call this?" she politely asked. He smiled a wry smile and said "Deep house", to which she responded, "Right, because I call it shit". Later someone asked for a Mariah Carey song before spilling their over-large cocktail on his records.

I had a techno-obsessed DJ friend who used to run his hand along his record sleeves, waiting for some kind of quantum-level energy-based inspiration to stop him at the exact perfect record for this precise moment in time. He claimed that every piece of vinyl he'd ever played had picked up some non-specific 'vibrations' and could on some level make themselves known to him at the perfect time to drop them in the mix.

Not me, I used to flick through a few tunes, straining my eyes looking out into the dark, trying to imagine what would work perfectly next. I'd regularly select a tune, pitch it up and begin to mix it in before changing my mind, whipping it off and frantically grabbing something else to mix in instead. Decisions, decisions, decisions. It's an odd thing; for 'choosing' to be such a central part of the job of DJing, but DJing really is just about collecting, then choosing.

Lots of the house music from this period featured instrumentation, layers of samples and plenty of chords and melodies. There were lots of songs too, with verses and choruses. This high level of musical content meant that putting a smooth blend together sometimes presented the DJ with (albeit very low level in the greater scheme of things) problems, as mixing together songs that aren't in complimentary musical keys often sounds awful. Here you would have to decide to let selection trump the mix. It might be a little lumpy getting there, but it was always better to scruffily mix in a great track than to perfectly mix in the wrong track. Always; still is.

As soon as a DJ starts to prioritise their selections based on how well they can perform the transition, rather than on the inherent musical qualities that make a particular record the right one for a particular moment, they've lost. Fear of performing a less than perfect transition is a threat to the DJ's ego. If you're looking for the definition of a good DJ, it's a DJ who can take that hit to their pride, the hit of performing a far from perfect transition for the sake of playing the right tune at the right time.

This topic is a chance for all DJs to point out that it's the music that's the most important thing and they'd rather hear a set of good music mixed badly than bad music mixed well. They're right of course, but also, there really is no excuse, particularly if you're getting paid, particularly if you're using digital DJ gear, to not make a brilliant job of the technical side of things as well as the all-important choosing part.

With house and techno music, the mix is an important part of DJing, not as important as the music itself, but it's more than just a tool or process to transition from one piece of music to another. It's an art form, or at least it's a craft. Done well, mixing can really create anticipation and excitement. I'm not referring to the turntable scratch-antics of hip hop turntablists, their thing is an entirely different craft, far closer to musicianship, requiring the kind of commitment to Repetitive Strain Injury and Carpal Tunnel syndrome that most house DJs simply lack. The suite of tools available to the house/techno/disco DJ is subtler than scratching and cutting. It's about utilising the mixer in tandem with the minimal and repetitive nature of the music to re-edit and rearrange it for maximum dance floor tension, and eventually, for maximum impact.

Sometimes though, you just get your selection wrong. You pick a tune that you think will work, you carefully mix it in, but when it drops it's way weaker than you remembered, or it changes the mood too suddenly, or not suddenly enough. For a DJ it's not great news, especially if they're playing in a club with more than one room and it makes everyone leave. Sometimes it only takes one bum selection and the mood can switch and the trickle out the door turns into a flood.

I did a decent floor clearance at the Eauzone once. I was going on at midnight, maybe 1 am, things had been brewing nicely, a good pace had been reached so I decided that I'd entirely break the mood, drop the tempo by perhaps 10 BPM and play (the sophisticated and intriguing but not really suited for this particular peak moment if I'm honest) 'Light of Jesus' by Fila Brazillia.

This record is not only quite slow compared to the galloping house and techno we generally favoured at the time, but it also has a very long and beatless intro. So that gave us all plenty of time to stand around while the energy steadily left the room like air seeping from a puncture. Ah, I thought to myself, that's not gone down well, I've made a mistake with that. My stomach contracted, and I suddenly felt very self-conscious. Some people wandered off to the bar. Other people stayed and looked at me. There was nowhere to hide. This intro really was way longer than I remembered. Prickles of embarrassment. More people wandered away. I started frantically rewinding the previous tune to its beginning to cue it up so I could drop its initial 32 bars of drums under this never-ending intro. But it didn't matter; the classy mid-tempo Fila Brazillia beat kicked in and perhaps another quarter of the room left the dance floor.

DJ moments like these are a bit like when comedians die on stage. Doesn't feel great at the time, but how you deal with it can be the making of you. Generally, if you clear the floor, you probably need to try doing something different to what it was that cleared the floor. DJ folklore tells of pioneering DJ heroes like Nicky Siano or Larry Levan who would play a record, clear a floor, then play it again eight times in a row, digging in and using the sheer force of their personality and their confidence in their taste and abilities, to insist that their audience come with them, and love this new record as much as they did. These are great and inspirational tales, and the very best DJs have genuine faith and belief in what they do, but it hardly needs mentioning that I am not Larry Levan or Nicky Siano, and sometimes, you just have to acknowledge that you got it wrong, and then fix it.

Having substantially dropped the tempo, I now had the option of speeding things up again and every DJ knows that most basic, elementary trick of programming: people respond to the music getting a bit faster. What you need is a beatless breakdown to do a sneaky transition to a faster tune and then when it kicks off again at a higher tempo it gives the room a massive lift. I stepped down from panic mode and selected an appropriate tune, did a lazy fade from one to the other and within a few tunes, my dancers were all back on the floor. Dancers and clubbers, they're always quick to judge, but just as quick to forgive.

I realised that there was a little truth at the heart of the whole episode. I had just really wanted to play that record: it sounds superb on a big system, I'd tried it out earlier before the punters had arrived. I knew it was too slow, but you DJs out there, you know how it is with your new tunes, you always want to play your new tunes... I should have put on something to match and increase the splendid churning mood created by the last guy (I think it was Panno), but instead, I'd made it about me and what I wanted, rather than the club night. And as soon as you do that as a DJ, you're doomed.

Playing at the Eauzone got me working with the kind of DJs who were playing most weekends and running their own parties. Whilst I understand that a club residency with a record allowance isn't going to fall into everyone's lap, if at all possible I would recommend supporting other good DJs as a great way to learn the craft. I learnt a lot.

Some DJs approach the whole thing so differently to me; some of them are genuinely rough with the equipment and their records, taking a frankly cavalier approach to looking after their vinyl, smashing the crossfader around, throwing tunes and sleeves about the booth, mixing in and out for entire records, never leaving the EQ alone, working it. But I also noticed that these same DJs would sometimes just let a good tune play if they felt that was the right thing to do. I learnt that sometimes you've got to work the tunes and really let the punters hear the mix, and other times, you should be playing music good enough that it needs no embellishment from the DJ.

It was at the Eauzone that I learnt the true power of the B-sides of US vocal house records. Having favoured euphoric Italian and UK progressive house as the base of my DJ sets, I began to develop a more subtle approach via my growing love for the dub mixes and instrumentals of Strictly Rhythm, Emotive, Hi-Bias, Sex Mania, 8 Ball, King Street et al. Someone once told me that the difference in voltages in the electricity supplies of the UK and the US contributed something to the variation in sound between UK and US house records. Whatever the explanation, there was something in those American records, some bit of sonic magic nestling in the gaps between the heavily swung hi-hats, claps and kicks that dance floors just couldn't seem to resist.

My friends tended to have a healthy attitude towards my DJing success. Crofty was a small, unassuming presence in day to day life, who at night would light up like an incandescent firework, and was a constant party-companion through the years. His mood was mercurial, his loyalty and commitment to whatever half-assed entirely impractical, implausible or clearly untrue opinion he'd just this second thought up as strong and stubborn as his dedication to hedonism and to his beloved Tottenham Hotspur. For such a small man, his capacity for substances was surprising, his appetite for the party impressive. He used to stand in front of the booth willing me to drop a mix and at the merest hint of platter wobble he would joyfully clasp his nose with two fingers and waft the air with his other hand, as though to dispel a foul odour. "Phwoar what a stinker" he'd gleefully roar. Fannah would inevitably join in: "Call yourself a DJ? You couldn't mix cement".

Crofty & Fannah had known each other since they were kids. Over the years, Fannah – large, strong, aggressive – had pushed

Crofty – small, unassuming, mild-mannered – through a window, caused the pair of them to be barred from several establishments in Brighton, strangled him into unconsciousness 'in fun' and generally acted like a loveable, needy bully. Despite all this and I'm guessing here, but also at least partly because of all this too, they were the very tightest of friends. They had their own at times impenetrable secret coded language, communicating largely through film quotes and they rarely used anyone's real name.

Although there were still nights when it was virtually empty, things at the club seemed to be improving. Fannah had started booking decent underground parties who brought their own crowds and I got to DJ in the bar at many of them. One night I played after a well respected and very good DJ. I was very pleased to be DJing 'with' him and felt to some extent that I had 'arrived' and was, if not part of DJ royalty, at least DJing quite near DJ royalty. So after the briefest of handover pleasantries, I pitched and cued up my first record and then perfectly mixed out of his last record. I then intended to take the needle off it and hand him his tune.

What I actually did was take the needle off my record, the one that was playing. This makes an awful, scratching noise, obviously amplified through the top of the range sound system at full peak-time pelt. A few people screamed; most people covered their ears instinctively. For a split second there was just the 'tst-tst' in my headphones of the other record still going and the general hum of a nightclub: the fans, the power amp, the clink of bottled beers from the bar. This moment of silence can't have been more than a second, yet it seemed to take as long to pass as the rise, decline and fall of the Roman empire.

No one really noticed exactly what I'd done, but they were all pretty certain it was my fault, so there was some desultory cheering and quite a bit of 'Sort it out for fuck' sake', all of which was perfectly reasonable. I went red and my mouth went completely dry, both of which were really helpful tactics for dealing with stress, nice work body, thanks. I quickly flipped the crossfade, put my tune back on and then frowned ostentatiously at some imaginary off-stage sound engineer who'd just made a pretty big imaginary fuck up.

I played my first 'back-to-back' session with another DJ in the Eauzone bar. Back to back simply means that you both take turns to play records, one each. It's fun, exhilarating and also slightly nerve-wracking. You never know what the other DJ is going to play, so your usual style of DJing, where you might think a couple of tunes ahead and have a few 'definitely-will-play's lined up for later, all goes out the window. Instead, it's a real test of certain DJ skills: your ability to listen, hear, watch and respond, and the process can really stretch you as a DJ. It makes you play better and try harder, and there's nothing like the thrill of live mixing out of a tune you've never heard before.

Back-to-back DJing requires you to be in the moment, neither planning nor reflecting. It pulls a DJ out of their comfort zone and out of any lazy habits they may have got into. I was as guilty as anyone; I had mental notes about groups of three or four tunes that I'd played together previously that all really complimented each other. Sometimes I'd use these as building blocks to construct my sets around. Or sometimes when I played a tune, I would automatically reach for another certain track to play next, because they just worked so well together. Playing back to back pulls all that away from the DJ and leaves them with just their music collection and their judgement. It removes the crutches of knowledge and planning and requires the DJ to simply feel, observe and react. Back-to-back sets are the off-road driving of DJing.

On this occasion, my DJ partner was reading the crowd perfectly, tune after tune, and had just put on another corker. I'm flipping through my record box looking for the next selection and there it is, the perfect track to mix with this one. I know in my DJ heart that this tune I'm choosing will complement the last one perfectly but also take the dance floor a step up. I pitch it up, cue it, ride the crossfade and mix it in. And I'm thinking, this sounds brilliant, it fits together with the last track perfectly, I'm on fire tonight. And then as I complete the mix and hand him back his record, I realise that the reason it sounds so perfect and fits together so well with the other tune is that the record I've chosen is, in fact, the exact same record that was already playing.

Another error that I used to make, I estimate perhaps one gig in four, is the 'Why-aren't-my-headphones-working?' scenario. You go into the DJ booth; there's some other DJ on before you, you shake hands, "Nice set" you say. "About five minutes I think," they shout back because they've spent two hours in the mix, have the monitor on full whack and can't hear a thing. So you hang around a bit while they play their last tune, you get your tunes out, get your headphones out and put them around your neck, trip over their cable so stick the plug into your trouser pocket.

He finishes, you take over, you're feeling a little bit of adrenalin, you fumble around a bit for your first tune, put your headphones on, cue up the track, you can see on the mixer that it's playing, but you can't hear anything in your headphones. You try to ask the previous DJ – who's waiting to leave and join his mates ignoring you on the smoking terrace – for help but he's no use. His tune is about to finish and you still can't hear anything in your headphones. Your throat goes dry as you wonder how you're going to play the entire gig with broken headphones until at the last second you realise that the headphone cable is still in your pocket and not plugged into the mixer. This triggers a simultaneous double emotion-blast of relief and embarrassment. You plug your headphones in and hope that no one noticed. Honestly, one in four gigs.

There were always a few practicalities to consider when taking over from another DJ. You may have to negotiate your way through that difficult moment when they appear to be putting on another tune when they're already over time. Or that slightly annoying moment when they hand over to you and their last track has ten seconds left to play.

When you take over you need to decide what to do with the tune they've left you with. Essentially, how you mix out of it will demonstrate your opinion of the tune and if it's not working, it's just got to go, even if cutting it short bruises your fellow DJ's ego. Some DJs like to make a grand entrance when they begin their set, dropping a piece of music with a two-minute beatless orchestral intro to announce that they have ARRIVED, and now the music will COMMENCE. Sometimes this is exactly what a dance floor needs, a complete reset. Sometimes though, it's just the DJ showing off. I generally went for the smooth transition if at all possible, just keep the vibe going, but like all DJing decisions, this one depends on what you think your dance floor truly desires at that particular moment.

There's one clear, single unwritten rule of booth etiquette though: when you plug your headphones in, that's the signal that you're on and they're off, from that moment on, you're driving. Their record is still playing and they'll be waiting for you to mix out of it so that they can go and have that piss they suddenly realise they really need, so you'll often find yourself mixing with the previous DJ and their mates breathing down your neck. And if you want to know what it feels like when they all leave to take their drugs somewhere else simply take a drive in a car full of monkeys then let them out.

Then of course at some point, unless you're finishing the night, you'll need to hand over to the next DJ. This used to be a remarkably straightforward affair: you put on your last record and unplug your headphones, they plug theirs in, put a new record on, mix it in and then give you back your record. Pat on the shoulder, shaky hand, nice one, great set and we're done. This still happens but also, sometimes DJs turn up with a bunch of controllers, a drum box or two and a Mac that they need to plumb in around you while you carry on playing, and they might need to knock through that dividing wall and install a Wi-Fi router before starting their set.

If you're the last DJ you get to finish the night. The people on the dance floor in the last couple of hours are likely to stay till the end, or they'd have left by now so you might be able to get away with all sorts of left-field selections. But then again, a thinning dance floor can be a fragile thing and you can't be too cavalier. You'll need to leave them on a high and finish with a really good record. Sometimes you choose something crowd-pleasing, something people know, sometimes it's a current big tune, but more often a classic, drawn from the ever-growing collection of classic dance music. The last tune should be a song to tie up the evening, create a musical moment, an audio goodbye. Some DJs go for an out-and-out banger, and that was always my preferred option, but many prefer to pick something utterly obtuse but somehow appropriate; all you have to do is make the perfect selection to end everyone's perfect night perfectly. No pressure.

And then the actual moment when the music finishes and the lights come up, the hum of air-con or the click of the lighting rig becomes audible, and suddenly everyone's 7 am rave face is harshly lit. The artifice is torn down so quickly, it's like being shaken awake from a dream you didn't want to end.

But the British love a pantomime, so soon the 'one more' routine was instigated. You get to the end of the night, security comes over and gives you the nod, you fade out the track, they put the house lights on, suddenly everyone catches sight of each other in the light and it's like we're all in Michael Jackson's 'Thriller' video. And then the rave-zombies all start shouting for one more. If they make enough noise, and there hasn't been too much trouble that night, security might allow you one or two more records. Someone drops the lights, you play a killer tune and everyone goes bonkers again for a bonus few minutes.

DJs then have to get their shit together, power down the amp and mixer, try and gather their belongings whilst shaking hands with happy punters who are looking hopefully for an after-party. From helming a magical underworld of debauched sonic adventures and pleasures of the flesh, DJs suddenly have to deal with the very prosaic issues of getting paid, finding a cab and not forgetting that their headphones are still plugged into the mixer, a fact all too often not recalled until the following day.

After the DJ's ears and their music, headphones are the single most important DJ tool. They used to come with a jack connection (bear with me), a chunky plug that connected them to the mixer so you could hear what you were doing. Then headphone manufacturers decided that we all actually needed a mini-jack connection – a tiny plug that could fit into a laptop or phone but would be too small to fit into a DJ mixer – with an added removable adapter which would enable headphones to be plugged into a mixer. These headphone adapters are some of the most precious items in DJing. Many's the DJ over the years who forgot their adapter and arrived at the mixer ready to drop their first killer tune, only to find they can't plug their headphones in. I'm the kind of person who has spare headphone adapters in my record bag, a back-up in my pocket, with a couple in each shoe just to be on the safe side and so have been able to act as a DJ hero for other DJs a couple of times.

Fannah and I spent evenings playing records and plotting our next moves. We would audition potential new tunes for the job of being the last track of the night, taking our role as party-makers deadly seriously. He had a vision for BYO that involved worldwide success, an accompanying record label, then a studio, eventually our own club, all the records we could eat – we just had to navigate the choppy waters of South East London's clubland first. And define our sound, come up with a visual image for our marketing, do some ads for pirate radio, get some posters printed up, employ a flyer team, court the music press, get our DJs on promo lists... whilst keeping on the right side of whatever criminal gang ran the venue we were working at – and somehow we could turn our little night into what we knew it could be.

That was the plan and Fannah and I hustled, learning on the way, with mixed results. Aside from many great Eauzone parties, he also once got me booked for some awful posh girl's awful party in a massive house in Pimlico. We carted the decks across London on the understanding there would be a sound system at the house but there wasn't, so I ended up trying to play through their shitty hi-fi while they all complained in posh voices about how it wasn't loud enough and that the DJ didn't have Whigfield's 'Saturday Night'.

Then Fannah got bored-drunk and started 'comedy' rugby tackling the poshos who had no idea how on earth to handle this previously charming but now also slightly frightening, sweating beast, until he tackled the smallest bloke there who promptly jumped up and punched Fannah in the face. Who predictably punched him back. And then weirdly, they asked us to leave. The short period of time that it took to unhook my mixer from their shit hi-fi and pack up my decks was probably only a couple of minutes, but it seemed to stretch out into an oppressive, awkward eternity, soundtracked by Fannah inviting the "wealthy tartlets and cushion-soft page-boys" to rugby tackle him back, to make up for "the misunderstanding".

Generally though, the early 90s were a great time to DJ. Dance music culture had gone overground and sometimes it seemed that everyone I knew was somehow involved in nightclubs, record shops, DJing or promotion. Everyone listened to DJ mixes and soon it seemed that anyone in the pub could tell if a DJ was making a mistake in their syncing of two tunes and could spot a 'trainwreck' mix coming a mile off. A generation became adept at hearing and appreciating the intricacies of DJ mixes and in turn critiquing any DJs who couldn't perform the role properly.

The amount of self-criticism that I would put myself through if I made an iffy selection or a wobbly mix was way out of proportion to the actual mistake. Whilst striving for perfection might get you good results, it's good to do that striving in the knowledge that you'll never actually achieve that perfection, and from time to time you'll make mistakes. And hey, it's ok to make a tiny DJing mistake occasionally. Young-me didn't really get this and I used to beat myself up if I thought a gig had gone badly. By badly, I merely mean the whole room wasn't going for it the entire time, or if I'd executed an imperfect transition.

Growing up through acid house had given me a slightly false expectation of what DJing could be like and my view of success and what was a good or bad night was skewed. In rickety middle-age, I now see that those first few years of acid house and rave were unique and that the particularly intense atmosphere of those times was a result of many colliding factors. New drugs, new music, new ways to consume them; a particular government, a particular existing underground scene, new technology and the synergy between all the various elements. The extreme levels of euphoria of the acid house and early rave scene proved more difficult for DJs to replicate as the years went on.

There are many elements required for a DJ gig to be classified as a great gig, and sometimes all the ancillary stuff, the location, the hotel, the hosts, can influence how a gig feels. In some ways, it's impossible to name the best gig I ever played, it depends what you mean by best. The most fun? The best music? The best sound system, crowd or some other factor? However, out of all of them, I can pick out one single booking, where everything aligned perfectly, which I've nominated as The Favourite Gig Of My Career™ (TFGOMC). It took place a few miles from my flat in London, in an unremarkable venue, and was entirely unexpected. I suppose on some level I'm still hoping that it will somehow be beaten, but as the months turn into years and into decades it seems extremely unlikely. I've played gigs where I got paid more, gigs with larger crowds, in better venues, on better sound systems. I've played with more of my mates present, or where crazier things happened, gigs that steadily moved from hedonism to debauchery and beyond, parties that went on for days. When parties go on for days, things can really start to happen, and you really get the measure of people too. This was none of those things but still has a particular place in my DJ heart.

It took place over 25 years ago, was finished by around 3:35 am and was on a student union campus, not even a real nightclub. Trip hop[6] had arrived by this time, meaning I had a broad range of BPMs

6 Trip hop was essentially hip hop without rapping and with added extra production weirdness. It was a great genre with a crap name and terrible reputation, somewhat justified by an unfortunately low-hit-rate-to-the-number-of-releases ratio. But its central conceit of sidestepping MCs and rappers and putting the beats, scratches and sam-ples centre stage, concentrating instead on the mood, the texture, the surface sheen of the stolen audio and the delicious crustiness of those sampled drumbeats still yielded some pretty tasty results in my opinion.

to play with, from deathly slow tripped out beats through mid-tempo Balearica to house, techno, breaks, and jungle, from around 80 bpm to around 140. Although I didn't know that it was going to be TFGOMC, I knew I was getting seven hours to play with, and a captive audience of off-it, up-for-it studes and their mates.

I knew that I couldn't work out exactly what I was going to play across seven hours, that would be crazy, but I did concoct a simple plan. I started with some tempo-less ambient drifty type stuff. Then, over the course of the evening, I slowly increased the tempo, from very slow at the beginning to very fast by the end. It was a simple, straight forward, dumb/obvious approach and, as you have probably worked out simply because of the name of TFGOMC, it was a technique that turned out to be extraordinarily effective. Having no other DJs to consider, think of or accommodate in any way clearly appealed to what I now realise is quite a controlling aspect of my character and I couldn't wait to get on it.

The venue was called The Bunker and was, perhaps unsurprisingly, underground. I had two record boxes and a record bag. I was going to have to play plenty of B-sides and track fours over my seven hours. As I slowly upped the tempo, shifting each record a notch or two on the pitch control, I could feel the tension growing in the room, like a fire that just needed a little stoking, before it crackled into life. There was some decent pillage in there that night. By about ten, we all knew something special was happening. The room locked in. I looked to see if any of my mates or my girlfriend had turned up, but no one I knew came. I think maybe there was an international football match on, or maybe they just didn't fancy another crap night out in south London.

Tweak the pitch slider, turn up the bass, mix in a tune with a little more drive than the last, increase the tension, refuse to give in to it, no big tunes yet, save the big guns, instead seduce an entire room, until they let their guard down. By 11 I felt a sublime apprehension through my body. If they were going off to what I was playing now, what were they going to do when I started dropping peak-time tracks? And so the night drove on, everything simply accelerating: time, temperature, anticipation, tempo, intensity.

And it happened; the dream gig, where every single selection is the right one, for those people at that moment, and somehow every single tune just raises the fever that little bit further. There was disbelief on some peoples faces, as we all together took it a notch higher, and higher. I started getting butterflies. The illuminated people dancing on the packed floor in front of the decks, on the tables and chairs around the edge, the bar staff dancing on the bar, every single space was occupied by bodies moving to the beat, all generating this incredible amount of energy and heat.

And that final, no-holds-barred last hour, we all shouted ourselves hoarse, the steam rising from us and gathering on the ceiling before falling down as club rain. Our damp clothes clung to our skin, hands were clammy; my fingertips wrinkled from the moisture. The roar when our favourite tunes dropped, every single body in the place feeling the exact same emotion at the same moment in time. And for the entire night, not one record jumped or skipped. Every selection landed perfectly, every transition went smoothly. There was no build-up of fluff on the needle, the sound system was big, bad and heavy. No one asked for requests, people gave me cigarettes, drinks, substances, sweaty handshakes, huge grins and damp hugs. The party went off.

Perhaps for big-time DJs, this kind of thing happens every weekend. Maybe they spend their entire summer season in Ibiza utterly killing it every night, playing special seven-hour sets and making the magic happen in an almost casual fashion, night in, night out. For DJs like me, it was a rarity. I had played a lot of slow warm-ups and a lot of quiet room twos, and a few peak times too, but a whole evening like this wasn't the norm, it was exceptional, memorable.

I don't remember leaving or getting home that evening, but presumably, I did both those things. My brother's lovely daughter attended Greenwich University a generation later. I told her that I played my favourite gig there and she said that she and her mates used to have a few drinks in their halls before heading down there of an evening.

No one cares about that gig except me, it means nothing to anyone except me. There were no promoters or club owners there who witnessed my DJ skillz who then realised that they had to book me. I've generally felt OK about my career, such as it was, with all its ups and downs, but it always felt odd that no one I know witnessed that night and I've never spoken to anyone who was there. It only exists in my memory.

HAROLD'S EARLY/MID-90S US HOUSE FAVOURITES

PM Dawn – A Watcher's Point of View (Todd Terry Remix)
Lou2 – Freaky – (Alternative Mix)
House 2 House – Harambee
Mateo and Matos Present Relapse – Feel Funky
Danny Tenaglia – Bottom Heavy
Nate Williams – Light Speed (Roy's Red Dog Mix)
George Morel – Let's Groove
Cynthia M – Love Storm
Simone – Hey Fellas
Pleasure Dome – 8 Minutes Of Techfunk, 12 Minutes Of Dreams
Roy Davis Jr. – Heart Attack
Tribal Liberation – The Motherland EP
DJ Duke – Lost In The Grooves, Turn Up The Rhythms, Back To The Bass
Ralphi Rosario 's Energy Factor – A Sexual Factor E.P.
Junior Vasquez – X
Eric Kupper – The K Scope Project
Masters At Work Present Nu Yorican Soul – The Nervous Track
Mood II Swing – Move Me (Alternative Mix), One Your Knees

9

SWEET HARMONY

"Play it nooooooooooow. Play it now or I'll jump in the fucking sea I swear". This is Charlotte. It's Charlotte's 22nd birthday and she wants me to play 'Show Me Love' by Robin S. We are not at sea. I don't have 'Show Me Love' with me, I stopped bringing it to gigs a few years back. This has made Charlotte furious but also resourceful and she starts singing the signature keyboard riff to help jog my memory despite me telling her I know the tune but simply don't have it with me: "Boo boodle boo boo, boodle boo boo, boodle boo boo, boo boo... for fuck's sake, you must have it you... you fucking... DJ, you're a fucking DJ. Wait. Oh. Broooagggh. Agh. Oh. Oh fuck". Charlotte has been sick down the outside of my DJ booth.

A DJ's experience of boat parties is related precisely to their position in the DJ pyramid. For those near the top, a boat party might mean gently cruising the Adriatic coast, DJing on a pair of solid gold decks to lots of beautiful people in expensive sunglasses. When I hear boat party, I think of a fat, greasy barge, moored near Embankment tube station in London, split level, each with its own unique variant on the damp-smell template. Not one of the floors were even, many of the doorways were lethally low and there was just enough, very slight, movement of the boat to induce nausea in a few punters.

I played a few parties there, mostly for a smart-shoes and sun-tan crowd, who desperately wanted to be moored off Ibiza, and did their very best to act as though this were the case. Sipping cocktails as the sun went down over an oily Thames, their pristine shirts, skirts and hair-dos gently ruffled by the evening breeze. But then everyone just got riotously pissed, banged up all their pub-coke and descended into Dionysian dishevelment.

As a DJ you are often something of an outsider, watching the carnage unfold. Other times it seems like a good idea to at least try to approach the level of the punters. At the boat parties, I tried both methods, neither was overly successful. There's just no preparation for a night in the company of the British when they're on a mission to get utterly arse-holed, there's no single strategy that you can count on. The British getting fucked up at the weekend is all laughs up until about 10 pm, after which anything can happen.

I had experimented with various alcohol and drug combinations while DJing over the years and discovered through the course of my research that not all combos were conducive to playing a decent set. I was once kicked off the decks because I was tripping and had forgotten I was DJing and instead had become fixated on getting the kick drum in sync with my heartbeat. Acid will heighten your senses but it's not especially useful if you need to work out why the left channel has gone dead when you've only got 30 seconds to sort it out before the current tune ends.

Alcohol was good, although not too much, just a couple of loosen-ers before you go on, a few when you're playing, no beer or you'll be pissing all night and you've got to be behind the decks for the next few hours so it's shorts and shots. I learnt this one the hard way; the toilets in some clubs were miles from the booth, and navigating your way through a peak-time crowd, pushing your way to the front of the toilet queue and getting back to the decks before the tune finished was often a challenge and indeed occasionally impossible. On one occasion I was playing a long set, had drunk too much, was given an additional hour to play so put on a tune, tramped off to the loo, and it was only mid-piss that I realised that it was actually pretty quiet out there and oh no, the tune's finished and I'm here having a piss and I'm not in the booth putting the next tune on. Pausing only to agree with the toilet crew that the DJ had obviously fucked up, I then had to-run, Groucho Marx style, low to the ground for camouflage and to minimise panic, pop up in the booth with another tune and bang it back on.

Cocaine, again, like alcohol, can be great for gigging, but only in very small doses. A little cheeky line here or there, perk you up a little, give you a little false bravado for a bit, it's not the worst thing a DJ can do. But there's always a line with cocaine (ho ho), one that is depressingly easy to cross. Take too much suddenly, it's not good, it's bad. Coke engenders an over-confidence, in both your abilities and your music, and in fact an over-confidence in everything. This is not especially conducive to DJing and generally tiresome for those who have to deal with you at the time. And then you have to cope with the crippling shame the following week when you realise how terribly you acted.

Smoking a zoot out the back of the club before you go on always seems like a great idea, but if you then find yourself on the decks too high to properly function, suddenly it's no fun at all. If you've never over-indulged with cannabis, then you won't know that when it stops being fun you get what is commonly called The Fear, a drug-induced paranoia that sees danger lurking around every corner, and menace in every social interaction. Is everyone looking at me? Why are they all looking at me? Am I looking at me? Did I say that out loud? Say what out loud? Wait... Does everyone here think my records are shit? Oh no, all my records are shit, I've been found out and I've forgotten how to work the mixer etc.

The Fear can manifest on acid too, only the sensation is ten times worse. Fannah and Crofty once convinced themselves on an LSD-flavoured walk home that they were about to be the victims of what Fannah later described as a "high-level organised mugging". Their response to the threat was to simply lie on the pavement, place their wallets on their chests and fearfully chant "We mean you no harm".

I used to get pretty nervous before gigs. If a DJ tells you that they don't get nervous before a gig, they're either lying or they've not understood the gravity of the situation. Some DJs feel it in their gut, others in their chest, some go quiet, some can't stop talking, some will need to shit. Me, I always needed to piss just before I was due to go on. These pre-match nerves, aside from the fact that you were at a party where there were usually loads of drugs were a big factor in DJ drug use; and some alcohol, weed, coke etc. to "calm you down" before a set is extremely common, as common as you would imagine. It's a wonder that more of us didn't end up with serious drug problems.

Ecstasy wasn't particularly conducive to DJing either. I know some DJs who thought it was, but you only had to listen to them DJ on E to know that it wasn't. That whole in-a-bubble-of-fluffy-loveliness isn't quite the mindset needed to helm a club for a few hours. All that falsely-created empathy was great, but a DJ needs to be able to take control of a room, whereas someone on E just wants to find out where you're from and tell you how amazing your skin looks.

Amphetamine was great for concentration and for playing long sets but tended to make the DJ frown, get a taut jaw, hollow cheeks, grey eyes, and generally look a little bit like a cliché scary drug user. Then the week after you'd taken it you'd cry if you momentarily lost a sock or if your cat looked at you funny.

DJing on ketamine? Someone once gave me what I thought was a pretty stingy line of coke just before I DJed, but it wasn't a stingy line of coke, it was a perfectly respectable line of ketamine. I remember coming up early into my set, sweating profusely, breathing hard, trying to ride it out. Time went weird, I didn't know how long records had been playing. My motor control was severely affected, then I got tunnel vision. I stood unmoving, listening intently, trying to understand the audio information that was coming in through my headphones, but all my senses were altered, time-dilated. I began to think about what I was thinking about, and then temporarily became absorbed and assimilated by space-time itself, which made the mixer really hard to use.

DJing isn't like piloting a plane – if you crash a mix no one dies. It's more like driving a boat dragging one of those inflatable bananas that you can ride in the sea when you're on your Mediterranean summer holiday. It's easy to get carried away and then you look up and see that you've left them all behind you in the ocean, bobbing in your metaphorical wake.

DJing is a job that takes place in a party atmosphere but it's still a job. People give you a wage in return for turning up and entertaining a room of paying punters. I quickly found that low-level dabbling before the set was the best approach, but I played many gigs with just a couple of drinks and loads of fags. The aim was to get a taste of where the crowd is at whilst remaining compos mentis enough to be able to spot if there was fluff on the needle or to keep a stumbling punter from knocking over the decks. Inevitably, this was a tightrope most DJs walked to a certain degree. Some had stronger constitutions and could seemingly deliver peerless sets whilst utterly spangled, others simply couldn't.

I once saw a DJ fall asleep standing up at the decks. I once saw a DJ take so much coke that he actually instigated the "don't you know who I am" conversation with security *on his way out*. I once saw a DJ so drunk he curled up and went to sleep in the booth mid-set. I once saw a DJ leave the booth, join the dance floor and when the tune ended, a punter took over because the DJ had forgotten he was playing. I once saw a DJ pour vodka into his eyes to 'perk himself up a little'. I once saw a DJ try to take a handful of pills by heating them through tin foil to smoke, as though they were heroin. I once saw a DJ in one of the UK's finest nightclubs take off most of his clothes, roll around on the floor and attempt to drink poppers, before simply smearing the bottle's contents over his near-naked body.

We all suffered some effects of the party lifestyle, it's just that we accepted it as part of the whole package. If Saturday night was going to be this good, then inevitably there would be some kind of low during the week, and we all became experts in spotting the signs of a midweek crash and specialists in how best to get through it. In some ways DJing is a tough job, to do well at least. You have to be part entertainer, part technician, part curator, part presenter, part sound engineer, part group-psychologist. Being an expert in human behaviour and different forms of communication helps too. You have to be able to unleash a riot of sound, whip up a crowd into a group-frenzy, but somehow still maintain control of the volume levels and prevent it all going into the red: it's an odd mix of shaman and geek, requiring a unique skill set to do well.

As DJs became more and more visible in clubs, dealing with and indeed speaking to your audience became more and more a part of the job. Some of the things that people have done to me when I'm right in the middle of mixing two 12"s together include:

- Talked to me about their relationship
- Sung me a song
- Attempted to interview me for DJ Mag or Mixmag, I forget which
- Attempted to take my phone number, contact details, current biography and itinerary for the coming months
- Praised my DJing/tune selection
- Criticised my DJing/tune selection
- Talked in depth about their DJing experiences and how they in some way relate to this evening
- Asked me to look after their coats/bags
- Asked me to look after their suitcase
- Asked where the toilet/bar/exit is
- Asked where the DJ is ("I'm the DJ" "Right. Do you know where the cloakrooms are?")
- Asked what time the next DJ is on/what time am I finishing
- Given me records

- Presented me with a pineapple (not as often as records, just the once actually).
- Asked to use the mic to MC over my tunes
- Demonstrated their MCing skills in my ear
- Tried to push me over (a member of the public, a promoter who'd booked me, and on more than one occasion, Fannah)
- Jumped on my back (Fannah)
- Done that thing where they sneak up behind you and nudge the back of your knee with their knee so you lose your balance (Fannah and Panno)
- Tried to kick me off the decks
- Tried to steal my record box
- Stolen my coat
- Thrown glitter on the decks
- Sprayed me with perfume
- Flyered the DJ booth (in what, if you think about it, might be one of the most pointless exercises ever committed by any sentient being)
- Offered me drugs
- Tried to sell me drugs
- Tried to buy drugs from me
- Tried to get in the booth to take drugs
- Showed me their drugs on their tongue as they took them
- Spilled their drink on the mixer/the coat pile/the floor/the decks/my tunes/themselves/other people/me
- Asked to charge their phone
- Asked to play a song off their phone
- Showed me their song request on their phone
- Taken a photo of my face, two millimetres from my eyes, with a flash, whilst screaming "Let's fucking 'ave it".
- Asked me "What have you got then mate" before looking through my record box uninvited
- Knocked the needle off the record that's playing

- Walked into the decks table, made the record skip, spilt their drinks, dropped a cigarette on the platter, didn't even notice
- Cut the bass on the mixer
- Attempted a cheeky rewind
- Switched the mixer off
- Switched a deck off
- Tripped and pulled the mixer off the table while falling, leaving it hanging off connected only by various cables, still functioning perfectly well
- Fallen on the decks
- Put my headphones on and pretended to DJ whilst I was deep in my record bag

All part of the job.

I shared mid-90s line-ups with DJs like Mr C, Jazzy M, C.J. Mackintosh, Dave Dorrell, David Holmes, Nick Warren, Billy Nasty, Trevor Fung, LuvDup, Matt Jam Lamont, all of which for me was a big deal. When you're an up-and-coming DJ, the list of who you've played 'alongside' is important. 'Alongside' can mean many things in clubland though. It can mean that you follow them at peak time, or that you warm-up room three hours before they arrive and your paths never actually cross. Getting your name on a decent flyer was another important step in the rise to DJ credibility and success, another rite of passage.

I still have a few of the flyers, my name sitting alongside a list of other unimaginatively named low-tier-ers: Mick Pierce, Andrew Delaney, Kieron 'DJ' Douglas. All of us are hopefuls, desiring that somehow our name would do that thing when it becomes more than just a name, and becomes synonymous with the glamour and excitement of clubbing, that our name might be lifted to the heights of a Carl Craig or a John Digweed.

We carried on putting on BYOs at the Eauzone as well as our occasional forays into wider clubland, but there was a definite tension growing between the DJs in the BYO crew. I was still searching out euphoric tracks and funky US dubs, whilst the rest of the crew were discovering the newly birthed tech house sound.

The euphoric piano break, born from Italian house was a production trope that had been gloriously fresh just a few short years ago but had begun to feel over-used. Despite the best efforts of some prog-house producers to keep knocking out piano tunes, the genre had become not exactly sordid, but some clubbers and DJs became a little embarrassed at the innocence and joy of the preceding years. It was almost as though they resented being played a tune that was so obviously signposting to them when to put their hands in the air, that they no longer appreciated being so brazenly manipulated. And as commercial piano-house or 'handbag' house crossed over into the UK charts, the antidote was brewing in London: tech house was evolving on the dance floors of the Heart & Soul, Release, The Drop and Wiggle parties and at The End nightclub. It was a more raw yet sophisticated sound than what we had previously played at BYO, taking the acid house ethos but framing it in a less euphoric, darker, more underground fashion. It was a sound that Panno and Hawkman wholeheartedly embraced and, of course, one that would go on to define the rest of my music career.

Meanwhile, things at the Eauzone began to sour. Despite the success of the weekend parties, the club was still struggling. Barnum first cut wages and then stopped paying them altogether, so I grudgingly left as resident, doing occasional guest spots and DJing in the bar during the week for £20. Fannah stayed for a while longer on the basis of promises that were clearly never going to be kept. Compromises were made regarding club security, so the venue generally became more hazardous and at times had quite a threatening atmosphere. We felt the whole thing getting away from us. Barnum wasn't around so much anymore. Fannah was often left at the helm, a kid out of his depth, attempting to placate creditors, local gangs, security, DJs and promoters, and address the low-level criminality which was now flourishing.

Also, the club had inevitably come to the attention of Electric Ed (his nickname apparently derived from an unsavoury incident with a car battery and a debtor) who ran a nightclub a couple of miles away. He sent a henchman to the Eauzone one evening who informed Fannah that although he deserved a cheeky slap for opening a club so near to theirs, Eddie instead was merely going to insist Fannah buy four crates of Red Bull (which was relatively new to the UK at the time) off him each week to keep him sweet. No one ever bought it and the cellar slowly filled up with boxes of unwanted caffeine drinks.

The Eauzone was open during the day as a bar and became something of a hang out for low-level criminals. Lots of the remaining staff were wandering around utterly zonked on the sedative Mogadon. Sometimes it was hard to know who was working security and who was just hanging around waiting for a 'delivery'. The chain of command began to fail, there was no leadership, the bosses were never available. No one wanted to answer the phone anymore. It felt like there were no adults around.

It seemed as though everyone from the local estates came to the club to sort out their differences, and there were occasional running battles between gangs. One night the decks were stolen, brazenly walked out by a pair of local wide boys. An amp and a couple of monitors went the next night. Another evening the back doors were stormed and a brief intense local turf war took place under the main stage. Discipline was breaking down. The mood darkened.

Crofty was helping out behind the bar and managed to fall into the cellar and knock himself out, seeing in the New Year in casualty whilst frightening the bejaysus out of us. Fannah was threatened frequently as part of his day job, mostly with pretend guns, but occasionally with real ones. Some of the punters shat on the floor of the toilets and then stuck cigarette butts and toilet soaps in it, leaving behind bizarre shit sculptures.

The day-glo paint job and house-family bonhomie couldn't hide the tension and menace that hung over the Eauzone. Local businesses claimed that heroin use was rife at the club. They were wrong, it wasn't heroin, it was cocaine, amphetamine, ecstasy, sedatives, barbiturates and steroids. The club had debts and then under pressure from the local community concerned about drug use, lost their entertainment and alcohol licence following a police surveillance campaign.

At the time we were pretty bitter about it. Fannah had put his heart and soul into the Eauzone and ended up working for little or no wages. All of us, in our youthful naiveté, had done occasional gratis stints behind the bar and we had all invested a lot in the venture, in different ways. Our bitterness was in direct proportion to how much faith we'd put in Barnum's various half-promises, insinuations and manipulations, but all of us felt that the club could have been so good, but for a long line of bad management decisions. The Eauzone is just a brief footnote in London's clubbing history, but at the time, along with the Ministry of Sound, it was one of only two venues south of the river with a 7 am licence. It was kitted out with a killer sound system, a heavy-duty lighting rig, looked great inside and was a multipurpose space with huge potential. And yet...

Our last Blow Your Own at the Eauzone was a strange affair. Not as well attended as others, but still with a respectable amount of bodies on the floor, the music now meandering from one end of the house spectrum to the other with no real focus. I was on early, and I remember at maybe around 2 am Maurice, the toothless sound engineer told me that whoever was on the decks should be "Fucking well fucking kicked the fuck off, this is fucking shit". Fannah dutifully booted our guest Guy of Gisborne off the decks after he'd dropped a couple of mixes, and spent the rest of the evening being berated by G of G's girlfriend. The night limped on.

Now, if this had happened to me in recent years, perhaps we'd have pulled the old 'fuse has blown' trick. It's a fantastic piece of DJ pantomime, something of a last resort, but every DJ should get to do it at least once in their career. You cut the music out entirely and pretend the sound system's gone down. You have a tune cued up and ready to go, one that goes straight in with a massively banging intro, no build-up. You hold your nerve for at least a minute, checking connections, looking genuinely worried, acting out the role of a DJ desperately trying to get the equipment working again until people start to feel uncomfortable/begin baying. Hold your nerve. You have a brief pre-discussed pantomime with the sound man, then all of a sudden, you drop the massive tune and everyone goes completely bananas. It's a complete reset, a reboot, and it allows you to supply a space for everyone on the dance floor to reset their mood too.

But I wasn't that DJ yet. Instead, I watched as everyone carried on playing records that weren't really working and our precious club night haplessly shuffled to an ignominious end. My memory assures me that it was raining when I left the venue by myself at half seven Sunday morning and there were no minicabs.

We did another BYO party back at the university, but the original cellar bar had closed and anyway, we really weren't gelling as a DJ unit anymore, and the atmosphere was dismal. Our precious party simply faded away, essentially because we weren't really sure what we wanted to play anymore. Quite how we managed to go from a strong, well attended night to something that just wandered off and died is hard to work out.

Panno and I having a punch-up definitely hadn't helped. I had broken my knuckle on his head, and was eventually wrestled off him by Fannah, who would later joyously tell the tale of how he was having a poo at the time when our flatmate Arty came running up the stairs to get him: "Harold and Panno are having a fight!" The most ridiculous thing about it was that it came about because months earlier I'd asked him when he was getting off the decks at one of our parties after he'd over-run by like, five minutes. Just that. We really did take it, and ourselves, terribly seriously.

My insistence on big anthems was perhaps starting to grate on the other DJs who had been getting into much more underground music. Ironically, were we to jump forward just a couple of years in this tale, the underground tech house scene would be where I released hundreds of original tracks and remixes and jumped up a couple of tiers in the DJ hierarchy, to, briefly, the level of 'hotels and flights paid for, a decent amount of sheets for a couple of hours DJing'. However, first we had to ruin Blow Your Own, and then I had to drift about for a couple of years, trying to scrape gigs while wondering if this DJing lark was really going to work out.

I continued DJing at the university but it was less fun now that everyone I'd known had left and I was just a jobbing 'dance' DJ. The wild abandon of the early 90s was fading fast, clubbing was changing, it's always changing, and for students, it seemed that the commercial sounds of 'handbag house' were what was wanted. With its associated smart shirts and glam dresses, it seemed to me to be a slow return to the discos of the mid-80s.

I don't remember my last university DJ gig; much like Blow Your Own, they just seemed to slowly fizzle out. My only real regret about the Eauzone was my failure to capitalise on it, to turn it into anything bigger. I'm not sure what I thought I should have done different but I very much felt that I had had a residency, paid, decent regular gigs and lots of opportunities, yet a couple of years down the line, I hadn't progressed with my DJ career at all.

Sometimes I think I just wasn't the right kind of person to be a successful DJ. I wasn't fun enough in real life, I was too serious, unapproachable, not that easy to get on with. I often felt separate from others, happy to be the DJ at the party because when I DJed everything was brilliant. But the other stuff, the peripheral socialising and networking that is essential to DJing success, that came much less easily to me. I've often felt that this weakness was probably at the heart of any failure to make more of opportunities that came in the next few years. I was an obsessive nerd when it came to music and could helm a party, and that used to be all that was required of a DJ. But I wasn't a rollicking party animal or centre-of-attention raconteur, all of which seemed to be more and more expected of a DJ.

In the late 80s and early 90s, you just had to find good tunes, and hustle for gigs. When I first went to a nightclub, pre-acid house, the DJ was often one step up from a children's entertainer, playing bad music to a bunch of smart-shirts in a club with a no trainers policy. But the late 80s saw the DJ slowly step out of the shadows and begin the journey to centre stage, from nerdy technician to dance floor hero, as large numbers of people started to have extraordinary nights helmed by local spinners, many of whom would go on to form the initial DJ top tier. Acid house turned the DJ into part-shaman/part-cultural curator/part vibes-facilitator.

It was perhaps inevitable that some DJs would start to receive the kind of fan worship that had previously been reserved for pop stars. We watched it slowly unfold over several years, as 'our thing' gradually became co-opted by mainstream culture before becoming mainstream itself. Soon DJs were being put on pedestals, literally. At the Eauzone, the booth had started being tucked away, high above the dance floor. By the end of our time there it had been moved to the centre of the main stage and wasn't a booth anymore, it was a podium. It was a perfect illustration of the power of the market to enact cultural change, to subtly warp the emphasis from community-generated events to individualism. The booth became a table on a plinth right at the front and centre of the main stage, as though the DJ were a rock performer or singer. Pushed to the centre, DJs were then expected to 'perform'.

This is often contrasted with early raves where, as the cliché goes 'the dancers were the stars'. Some clichés are simply a by-pass to critical thinking, a handy, meaningless phrase to fill a space in a conversation. Some clichés though, they exist because they contain at least a kernel of truth. In fact, I'd take the whole idea a step further and say that not only are the dancers the stars but any DJ who truly believes that it was them and not their audience who 'made' the night, has fundamentally misunderstood what DJing is about. Without a willing audience, a DJ is just a lonely nerd playing by themselves.

Thinking back to those bacchanals at Telepathy, Labyrinth, parties in abandoned industrial spaces and in clearings in forests, it really was us out on the dance floor or indeed forest floor that made the party what it was, and you mostly didn't really know or care where the DJ was as long as they played good music. Our dancing, our bonhomie, our clothes, the way we interacted, how we responded, this was what made a good night into an unforgettable night; it was us.

If you put a DJ on a stage expecting them to perform then they may well feel they have to do something. Hence the growth in DJ 'moves', the litany of contemporary DJ pantomimes from the 'Jesus' and the 'heart-hands' to the 'ow-these-knobs-are-hot', or the ever-dependable fist-pump. All because everyone is looking at DJs who ironically have less to do than ever before because now the technology can do most of the tricky technical parts of DJing for you.

Some DJs began to pretend that they were performing filter sweeps on records live, moving sliders and knobs that weren't actually doing anything, just to give the punters a show. I could never bring myself to pretend I was doing something I wasn't, but I understood why they did it – stood in broad daylight with several thousand people all waiting for them to do something. If you treat a DJ like a rock star, putting them on a stage as though they were a performer, then merely wearing headphones, gently frowning whilst cueing up the next tune and smoothly transitioning simply won't cut it.

I had a few gigs where I definitely felt the pressure of the audiences' gaze upon me, gigs where perhaps they were used to a more animated DJ. Sometimes I would dance about a bit more, or adjust the EQ knob with more of a flourish than was strictly necessary but just couldn't bear any further levels of fakery. It was always half-hearted. You can't fake a performance; you either dive in and give it your all, or you decide – as I generally did – that I was there to present music for a party, not to perform. I usually made an unspoken deal with my crowd: I'll play the very best music for them and in return, they'll dance and have a great night – and none of us will have to prance around like a prick or pretend to be doing something we're not.

But the faceless anonymity of the DJ and accompanying punter participation that acid house celebrated just didn't fit in with how the entire entertainment industry infrastructure is set up. It's not commercially viable in its raw authentic form, doesn't have mass appeal, it's too extreme, too underground, but that just meant that commerce and capital worked hard to water it down: throughout the 90s house music, clubs and DJs became big business.

There's been a constant push and pull as mainstream culture appropriates bits of dance music/DJ culture, driving the underground into new forms and new 'stuff' that the mainstream can't yet stomach. The growth in the pantomime of DJing is one of the results of this ebb and flow and has spilled over into the public perception of what a DJ is: an exuberant disco-monkey, ruler of the after-party, crazy monarch of the week-long debauch. This idea of what a DJ should be is somewhat at odds with the reality of my personality.

As my wife rightly points out, if I have a superpower, it is the ability to immediately locate and then perfectly define the melancholy in any given situation or event. This isn't necessarily what people want or expect to get when they book a DJ for a party. I was a music obsessive, someone who could pick out the right tune for the right moment, and mix it perfectly, that's what I did well. But all the ancillary stuff, the performance, the air punches, the post-gig networking and so on, not so much. For my entire career I've wondered if I had just been a bit more fun, would I have been more successful? The answer is – cheer up Harold, stop dwelling on the inevitability that the answer is probably yes.

10

IS THERE ANYBODY OUT THERE?

The Eauzone was empty and boarded up, but depressingly, Wolfie and I both got office jobs at a publishing company across the town square from it in Woolwich. Worse still, I did alright at my new career and was steadily promoted until I found myself working as a marketing manager for several electronics industry journals such as Microwave Engineering and Electronics Times. I didn't like it. I don't suppose many people there did. The boredom was partly mitigated by the fact I could afford to buy more records and trainers now that I had a proper job, but only partly.

I DJed at peoples birthday parties, playing Stevie Wonder, Chic and JBs records. There was another lost raver in the marketing team I worked in, Johnno, who was also pretending to be normal. He and I put on a couple of nights in an extremely shiny South West London bar. They were poorly promoted, ill-attended, sad little affairs, soundtracked by the very finest US house and garage, expertly mixed, echoing off the mirrors and chrome of the empty room. Johnno was a true house obsessive; he would play you a record, tell you why it was great, then stare at you intently, waiting for the part that made it great to happen so that he could nod in affirmation, yep, that was still the bit that made it great.

I put on a night called Terminal 2 in a venue in Shoreditch with a friend who had an enviable music collection and no DJing experience (DJ Barely, great name). The flyers we produced were a thing of beauty with the images and name all fitting together tastefully and with a logo and matching font. I say 'we', but it was produced by DJ Barely's graphic designer at the magazine he worked at. I wonder how many promoters and DJs' graphic designer mates have been conned/bribed/begged to knock up a decent flyer for unsuccessful club nights? That would make a nice coffee table book, 'Great Lost Flyers of 90s Unsuccessful Club Nights'.

We distributed the flyers studiously around the bars and pubs of south London and put an ad in Time Out magazine. We had some lovely posters printed up, and carefully navigated the treacherous waters of south London club poster sites. As previously mentioned, poster territory is serious business in nightclub land. The thing about dedicated poster spots is that they're always full, so inevitably you have to put your poster over someone else's poster, which can be taken as a direct attack. Even if the event you're postering over has already happened. I've witnessed a feared club owner bright-red and spitting with rage, riling his troops up for a minor war all because someone postered over one of 'his' spots with ads for their rival night. Good old traditional south London clubland with its quirky little traditions.

Drawing on our knowledge from various gigs and promotions we'd been involved in over the years, we established where we could put up our posters without fear of having our door over-run on opening night in revenge. It turned out that these were all places that no one could ever see in their normal day to day life. And also places that the police will arrest you if they catch you trying to put posters up.

We had previously discussed at length exactly which genres we should mention on the flyer and they included, eventually, 'Basement Funk' (don't know), 'Fried Noodling / 80s Analogue' (again, not sure) and 'Proto-Disco' (I know, I'm awful). We naively imagined that the late 90s were still a time where you could merely promise to play good music and people would turn up. People didn't turn up, not really. It was ok, but we barely (ho ho) half-filled it, and despite our great tunes we weren't asked back. It had taken me a few attempts but I'd finally realised that simply booking a nice little venue and promising to play really good music wasn't actually promoting, even if the flyers are divine.

DJ gigs in bars are a very different affair to a gig in a club. DJs of tier three and above don't have to play bars if they don't want to, they'll just be getting club, rave or festival gigs. If top tier DJs play a bar gig, it will be on a beach in Croatia with a crowd of attractive, up for it people all on decent drugs. Back in reality, obviously each gig brings its own challenges, but the bar gig ranks pretty low in the DJ gig hierarchy. Lower if there's no entrance fee, lower still if you're playing on a tinny, plastic and bakelite PA and the bar manager keeps telling you to turn it down. Which they will, it's in their job description or something.

If you're DJing in a bar, there are no carefully supplied DJ journeys, not really. You're supplying sonic wallpaper. You might get some folk to dance for a bit, you might not. People might tap their foot absently when the conversation briefly falters but clearly, people haven't gathered in a bar to lose themselves under the strobe to the sound of the bass bins. They've come for a few drinks and a laugh with their mates. The bar manager will tell you to turn it down a bit mate.

The smoking ban in the UK, whilst obviously a triumph for public health has made it harder for DJs to hold a room together too. If people in the bar keep going out for a smoke it means that DJs have to keep going out onto the smoking terrace to air punch or do a nifty heart hands before going back inside to mix the next tune, which is really annoying.

Bar sound systems are often poor, and the more you increase the volume, the worse it will sound, reflecting back at you off all the mirrors and cold flat surfaces. Again, "Yeah brilliant mate, really good, can you turn it down a fraction, cheers." Punters will come up and chat with you, not even asking for requests, just if they're a bit bored on their way back from the loo. And unlike a club gig, as you're not under the same pressure conditions you would be were you headlining a club, you can chat with them too. Double-edged sword that. Still, I'd rather have someone complain about the music than completely ignore it. It's tough for a DJ to make selections based on responding to the mood and whims of a room when all the room is doing is shouting over your music.

For a bar gig, you might be booked for the entire evening and long DJ sets generally bring their own challenges, not least of which is eventually needing a piss. If you had a mate with you, you could nominate a 'piss-mixer' to mix in the next tune if you don't get back in time. It's either this or put on a Fela Kuti track. Both Wolfie and Fannah did the occasional 'piss-mix' for me over the years, something that would give Fannah the terrible fear until he'd successfully executed a passable two-bar fade of two records I'd selected and pitched-up for him, at which point obviously he would suddenly become king of the DJs.

When BYO had finally keeled over and died, Fannah had moved to Brighton. I had stayed in London and eventually moved offices to London's Docklands. I wore a shirt and tie, attended meetings where I had to discuss our market profile, our latest campaign and other terrible, terrible things. I went to conferences and pretended that I didn't hate every moment. I took people's business cards that I would later roach as if proving to myself that I was still actually underground, I was still acid house. I wasn't, I was a marketing manager. My immediate boss was working towards becoming a functioning alcoholic, and got edgy every day at 12:55 pm, in case anyone put a call through to him which might delay his rush to the pub for as many pints of Stella as you can drink in a lunchtime. I had two suits, a grey one and a black one, both were shit. The only thing that made the whole thing bearable was the money.

I couldn't take my real, actual job seriously, because it seemed so ridiculous and so utterly divorced from anything I valued or held dear. I still just wanted to work in dance music, nothing else. Despite going through this DJing dry patch where I only played out occasionally, I still very much thought of myself as a DJ who also happened to be a marketing manager. I still bought too many records, still mixed them together at home, still went to listen to other DJs, went to clubs, bought the magazines, argued on the emerging online newsletters and forums about what the definition of tech house might be. Everything else – real life, proper job – though it took up most of my week, it was all just a collection of weird, stressful tasks that I had to complete daily to earn money.

Throughout 'Harold Heath: The Marketing Years', Fannah had decided that it was his mission to bring tech house to the UK's south coast and had been steadily putting on some of the best parties of the late 90s in Brighton – and he got me down to play at some of them.

House music split off and subdivided into many interesting directions in the 90s. I chose tech house because I loved it, but I loved lots of other music in the 90s too: drum & bass, downtempo/trip-hop, funk and, of course, other types of house and techno. There were many different musical paths I could have taken. Indeed, Fannah and I fully embraced the downtempo vibes of the output of Mo Wax and Ninja Tune and spent many hours one summer trying to perfect our turntablism-moves. But there was also the fact that tech house was physically near to me: we lived in South East London where the first Release parties took place. The Heart & Soul parties that Panno and Hawkman were raving about were just over the river in Stratford, Swag records was a few stops on the train away in Croydon; my future path in dance music was in part due to simple chance, timing, and proximity.

Those few precious gigs with Fannah in Brighton really made a big difference to me in the lean, late 90s. I worked in such a straight environment, pointlessly slogging away at a thankless task to generate capital for shareholders, in an industry so dull it had been declared by the UN as a site of national disinterest. Dressed the same as everyone else, a clichéd interchangeable cog in the machine, hating every minute and beginning to understand the heavy lunchtime drinking. But Fannah provided me with regular hits of visceral underground culture and hedonism to remind me what being alive was. Just getting back into that world, away from wearing a stupid suit and tie and discussing our marketing strategy for the Coventry conference was a relief.

Like so many DJs before and since, the next logical step was learning how to produce my own music, a task I happily devoted the late 90s to. All my productions were influenced by the tech house scene and the tunes I heard on the dance floor at Fannah's Brighton club nights. This was one of those brief almost mythical dance music golden ages, when a genre was young, fun and uncomplicated. Tech house was a party-friendly scene full of producers doing interesting things, labels being bold, and people putting on parties that had all the hallmarks of acid house. Long, lost weekends jacking on the dance floor, then floating my way through another after-party, all the crew in attendance, chatting rubbish for hours, sharing endless spliffs and lukewarm cans of lager with strangers.

One evening we played at the Pressure Point in Brighton and Fannah had booked a big US guest DJ, big in a famous way but also in the big way too. The DJ booth was only accessible by a ladder that led up through a tiny hatch and bless him he got stuck. The sight of his big arse half out of his trousers, wedged into the hatch, his chubby legs wiggling with slight panic, stuck with me. It doesn't matter how famous or successful you are, you're never too famous to get your fat bum stuck in a weirdly small DJ booth entrance.

A few years previously, we used to go out and rave all night, eventually roll back in utterly exhausted sometime the next day, and cocoon up together around someone's gaff. In Brighton the club nights often ended at 3 am, which was no time to go home, so the after-party became very important, and Brighton was extremely good at after-parties, with the infamous post-rave afters Club Magnus, Brighton's secret after-hours unlicensed residential nightclub, often stretching on for days. Fannah used to lord it up in the kitchen, alternatively entertaining and low-level torturing guest DJs with equal aplomb. He once held an impromptu kangaroo court to 'try' an interloper who had taken advantage of Magnus's good nature and moved into a tiny shack he'd built under Mags' stairs to live there rent free. Fannah and crew quickly reached a verdict and carried out the sentence of eviction there and then.

It was at a late 90s afters round Fannah's house, that fabric DJ and all-round tech house legend Terry Francis brought along a Roland MC303 'Groovebox'. This was a silver box covered in knobs and buttons, about the size of a small chunky laptop, that could produce beats and basslines and you could use to make rudimentary tracks. I was instantly attracted to its flickering lights, many buttons and the fact that you could bosh out a tune on it in no time.

Having been DJing since the late 80s and only gigging sporadically at the time, I was going through a stage of never completing mixtapes, endlessly experimenting with a four-track cassette recorder, adding sound effects and trying to mix more than two records together at a time. I was bored, idly wondering about how I'd like to get the drums from one track and mix them with the vocal from another, but put a different sound effect on it. And whilst being a great DJ doesn't necessarily mean you'll be a great producer, there is some crossover between the roles, and I'd arrived there, right at the crossover point, where I wanted to take the process of DJing and re-arranging pieces of music further.

Sometime in the mid-90s, I'd made some rudimentary tracks round Slim Jim's house. In fact, I had even made a tune 'for' my then-girlfriend for her birthday. Yes, I actually did that, I spent a bunch of evenings around Jim's house where he lived with his mum and dad, telling him what I wanted him to do on Logic, then gave a cassette of the recording to my poor girlfriend as though that were a decent present. I think I got her something else too, an actual present rather than just a fuzzy recording of some conga loops and an acid bassline. I hope I did.

Making tunes with Jimbo meant working on his computer, but as at the time I worked in a stupid office on a stupid computer all day doing my stupid job, the very last thing I wanted to do when

I got home was work on a computer. But Terry's Groovebox represented something different to me. It was like a cross between a musical instrument and a sequencer which meant you could press play, and then add and remove sounds as it played, composing in the moment while the music played, turning controls rhythmically in time to the beat. This seemed very different to me to drawing notes in on a computer. Besides, every time Slim and I returned to a project, his computer made all the drums and synths playback with piano notes which we would then have to laboriously reset, which this machine never seemed to do.

I never bought a Roland MC303 in the end (it had MIDI limitations if you want to know why) but I did set about amassing recording equipment. This was a very happy time for me as I had a purpose again, and over the following months, I built a ramshackle home recording studio. There were a few decent second-hand shops in south London where you could pick up old guitar pedals, out of date drum machines, and once a super weird brown and orange Eastern European synth that had only one good sound and was prone to sending strange MIDI signals as though it were trying to communicate.

I bought filter clones, handmade synths, lots of cables, made long effects chains of guitar pedals, sampled the sound of a lorry going over a bump outside my house and generally luxuriated in the creative process and the equally exciting fun of acquiring machines, with lights, dials and buttons. My main rule was no computer, so my set up was built around a mixer, a pair of Yamaha hardware sequencers, a couple of groove boxes, a sampler, some sound modules and a rack of compressors and effects.

I tried to learn the secret hidden knowledge of mastering my tracks, endlessly comparing my productions on different sound systems, thinking it was done until I tried it out in the car where it would suddenly sound weedy and weak. If you can get your production to sound good in your studio, standing outside your studio, in your headphones and in the car, then you might just have a good mix. I got an audio splitter and collected old stereo speakers, so I could switch my mixes between my studio monitors and the kind of speakers that my music might be heard on, striving to achieve that perfect sonic balance, the tune that sounds killer everywhere. I played an early track to Crofty who screwed his face up in disgust informing me that I had accidentally invented 'soft techno'.

So many hours, days, weeks, months and years, energy and effort, just spent with my machines. I genuinely loved house music and the process of creating it. I used to run home from work like a kid running home from school, just so that I could get into my studio and maximise my music time. I used all my work holidays in my studio. I sometimes would wake with an idea and it would excite me so much I would have to get up and go and work on it, wrapped in my duvet at 4 am on a Tuesday night. I would switch on the gear and begin a piece of music or a beat and forget to eat or to go to the toilet, and just get lost, slipping into a dream-like timeless state which only the base physical demands of my body could eventually pull me out of. If I'd had a nutrient-rich drip and a catheter hooked up, I could have spent days, weeks at it.

I once took my newest drum machine on a holiday with my then-girlfriend, the same one who was the lucky recipient of my first production, so that I could programme beats in between socialising and being normal. Sorry Leanne, I really was rather over keen on the whole production thing wasn't I.

My obsessive nature and inability to leave things unfinished were a major factor in my finishing productions. I was also aided by the fact that my mixer, the desk with all the sliders where all the different sounds are mixed together, was analogue. This meant that all the settings like volume and EQ levels were changed by hand with every new song that I made. So I couldn't leave something unfinished, go and work on another song and come back to it as I would lose all the mixer settings. Therefore, I had to finish each piece of work before I could move onto the next – so I became good at finishing projects.

I had soon produced a couple of albums worth of material, most of which I then abandoned, as each week I learnt a new technique that made my previous production sound hopelessly amateur. How I laughed at last week's effort, why, I hadn't even side-chained the bassline compression, what a fool! I gave out my early efforts to DJs and label bosses. It wasn't hard, Fannah was booking lots of them to come and play in Brighton. They were all at the after-parties I was at. Feedback was positive. I felt I had momentum. Fannah announced that he was going to manage me. I readily agreed.

Fannah and I made lists of record labels that we thought should sign my music, and lists of DJs who we thought should play it. He approached promoters for me, hustling for DJ gigs. We considered possible artist names. He utilised every DJ and producer contact he'd made as a promoter, speedily absorbing info, gossip, improvising when needed, finding out about contracts, technical riders, blagging it when all else failed, relying on his good nature and charm to see things through. Fannah loved to plot and plan, his boundless enthusiasm infecting anyone he spoke to. He was the classic industry mover and shaker, appearing confident but sometimes not entirely sure of what he was doing, carrying on regardless because things seemed to be going well. He should have had that on his business cards – Fannah DuPont: Will Carry On Regardless For 15%.

The summer of 2001 was an eventful time for me as my first 12" release coincided with two other big life moments. I met my future wife and was made redundant from my stupid marketing job. I'd met Annie briefly at Slim Jim's birthday booze-up at our local Lewisham battle cruiser the Frown and Wanker. I fell head over heels in love with her in perhaps three minutes. I had never been so sure about any matter of the heart, I was certain, just plain certain within a couple of minutes that if I could just spend some time with her, we could be together forever.

Unfortunately, we were both involved with other people. I quickly and quietly ended my current relationship the following week and then when Annie sent a group email asking if any mates knew of a temporary job going, I convinced my half-cut boss we needed an assistant and offered her a role helping me with some upcoming conferences. She took the job and over the course of a summer of electronics exhibition marketing, brandies and Silk Cuts, a summer I'll never forget, she fell in love with me too.

My redundancy was, perhaps surprisingly, nothing to do with this grand scheme and was instead the result of the company changing hands and me arriving back at work on Monday morning after a week away to find a new job description on my desk. I was lucky. I hated the job and my suspicions that a company couldn't just make you do a different job to the one you were contracted to do were confirmed by my union and they instead gave me a decent redundancy package. I happily took it and spent it on updating my studio.

At the start of the twenty-first century, starting a career making records seemed like a reasonable endeavour, when in fact, from a business point of view it was a laughably bad idea. When I first started making tunes, colleagues and mates were getting £1000 advances and shifting thousands of copies of their vinyl releases and this was the low end of the vinyl industry: the next tier up were getting larger advances and selling way more copies. In just a few years the arse would well and truly fall out of the vinyl market.

In fact, with exquisite timing, my vinyl-releasing career perfectly spanned the period from when vinyl sales were still, just, a viable option for a label, through the period when labels and distributors were closing every week, to a time when sales income for an artist like me fell to just a few pounds as vinyl became an economically unsustainable model.

Didn't know all this at the time, wouldn't have cared anyway: Fannah and I were on a mission and nothing would stop us.

HAROLD'S TOP CLASSIC 90S TECH HOUSE

Calisto – Get House
Ravi Mcarthur & Tom Gillieron – Another Crap Night Out In Eltham
Floppy Sounds – Ultrasong (Studio B Remix)
Presence – Sense of Danger
The Mingers – Emancipation
Soggy Plop - Hairy Scary
Silverlining – Precision Spanner
Animus Amor – And On
Pure Science – Brighter Dayz (Californian Sunshine Mix)
Housey Doingz – Ride EP
Makesome Breaksome – The Vision
The Usual Suspects – Nightstalkin'
Blunted Dummies – House For All (Eddie Richards Mix)
Mood II Swing – Do It Your Way
Janice Robinson – Children (Joe T Vannelli Tribal Dub)
Circulation – Scarlet (Mix B)
DJ Sneak – You Can't Hide From Your Bud
Hot Lizard – 165... Drop EP, 'The Theme' (Love from San Francisco Mix)
Swag – Drum Hydraulics EP
Outa The Blue – The No Boundary's EP
Blaze – Lovelee Dae (20:20 Vision Main Mix)
The Ron Honey Experience - Nitedrive
Klarky Cat – Gumbo
The Timewriter – Letters From The Jester

11

RHYTHM IS A MYSTERY

The Escape Club, Brighton, late summer 2001, about half-past midnight. Fannah has just handed the very first record produced by myself in my home studio to a DJ and it's about to be played for the first time in a nightclub. In the process of writing this book, Fannah confirmed in a series of emails to me that he definitely remembers it was well-respected DJ Jane Fitz. Or DJ Lottie. Or Alison Marks, he's not sure, it was a long time ago Harold.

There's an air of disbelief to the whole thing, but he's definitely given it to her. Wonder when she's going to play it? It might be next week. Fuck, she's cueing it up. The Escape in Brighton was a small venue and it was midweek. The club wasn't packed but there were quite a few of us on the dance floor. She mixed in my track. I wondered if she was annoyed to have someone like Fannah essentially insist that she play it, if we'd broken her DJ flow. He could be somewhat pushy which generally worked in my favour in such matters. I was strangely distracted. Around me, people were dancing. Not losing-it-dancing, but not wandering off the dance floor in disgust either, they were definitely dancing. And something was coming out of the sound system that I recognised, but it didn't really sound like my tune. Any working DJ will tell you, tunes can sound entirely different over a club system to how they sound at home or on headphones. Such was the case here.

My strange, lumpy, amateur production was full of lower mid-range that I could now hear were muddying up the production, along with about ten other things that I immediately hated too. Why was that synth noise so loud? And what was it doing there anyway? What had I been thinking? And that hi-hat pattern is literally stupid, it might be the stupidest hi-hat pattern that was ever programmed.

No one else thought any of these things. No one else thought anything much really, a couple of people whooped at the drop which was nice. And Fannah did lots of drunken roaring, as was his way. Still, just to be on the safe side, I decided that I was an awful producer and that this, my best work to date, which had been signed to a respectable techno label as part of a five-track deal, was actually really poor and I was just an imposter. In effect, I'd just publicly found myself out, so I decided it was probably for the best if I just retired to join a monastery and spend my days self-flagellating in lifelong remorse and recrimination at my abject failure. Fannah suggested that I might be over-thinking it and that I should get the drinks in.

I had signed my first ever record deal with Stickman Records in July 2001, the same month that a talented programmer called Bram Cohen presented his latest software to the world at the yearly 'Defcon' hacker conference in Las Vegas. It was the BitTorrent protocol, a piece of technology that would ease the global move from paid to free music. File-sharing sites where you could download music for free already existed in 2001, but the process could be lengthy, depending on how many other people around the world were attempting to access the same file. Torrenting vastly expedited the process by inverting it. When lots of people were trying to file-share the same song, download times increased. With torrents, the reverse was true and the more people simultaneously downloading a file, the quicker the process. Free music for everyone, hurrah!

The Mp3 had been invented in the mid-90s and it facilitated a new age of digital audio slipperiness, where music could be moved around the internet easily and speedily. This quickly enabled free access to all music that had ever been recorded, along with software, books, films and TV programmes too and changed forever the nature of how we think about and consume music. The digital model has directed the development of new products and services and succeeded in turning most music consumers into renters rather than owners. And for dance music DJs and producers, as digital took over the record industry in the early 2000s, lots of things changed:

- Earnings from releases dropped substantially as the profits from a download, and then a stream were substantially smaller than from a physical copy.
- Lots of recording studios, vinyl distributors and record shops closed as they became redundant and home software replaced them.
- DJing became way easier as it automated some of the tricky technical stuff.
- Production and distribution of dance music became way easier too via studio software like Logic or Reason, ably assisted by the fact that you can move digital files around for free and that a digital record label has virtually zero setup costs.

That's quite the collection of effects for one industry to absorb in the space of a few years, and it was pretty chaotic for a while. Still is in many ways. People in business talk about one door opening as another one closes, but for a few years the music industry was like an endless Matrix-esque corridor full of doors slamming shut whilst countless other new doors were simultaneously being blown open.

There were unexpected side-effects too. As record producers and artists earned less and less from their releases, they started to look to DJ gigs to make up the shortfall, leading to a glut of DJs, ably assisted by DJ technology that made the whole job a lot easier.

With freely available digital music came technology enabling DJs to play digital files. Early DJ CD players were all-in-one machines with a front panel packed with rubbery buttons and they were all required by law to have a time delay between pressing any of the buttons and the machine actually carrying out any of its functions, rendering them near-impossible to mix with. I once agreed to DJ at a party but on arrival found a set of prehistoric CD decks, all rubbery buttons and confusing interface, of which only one deck actually worked, while the other one just seemed to angrily eat your CDs. We had to use a minidisc player for the other 'deck' and put them both through a small studio mixer with no pre-cue listening or crossfade. No one cared though, they just danced to the music and laughed and cheered at the lumpy clashing transitions.

DJ gigs like this where the equipment simply won't allow you to do any mixes at all are rare, even rarer now that you can DJ a perfect set off your phone and Bluetooth it directly into the brain ports of your virtual friends, but they do happen occasionally. It's liberating, if a little nerve-wracking, to be able to abandon any DJing techniques at all and merely play tunes, clumsily, one after another, with the gaps, silences and overlaps that a DJ would usually avoid, generating a very different kind of excitement in the room. It's DJing stripped bare, down to its very essentials: simply selecting good music.

Then Pioneer CDJs began appearing in DJ booths. For a while, no one knew where to put them, but then someone figured out that you could make stands and have them above the record players. Then over the course of a few years, the lids were put on the Technics vinyl decks and they became big shelves for CD wallets.

However, the arrival of digital DJing has been far from smooth. Dance music and DJs have a strange relationship with technology. On the one hand, we are all committed futurists, with our abstract sounds, our cutting edge genre mutations and our ridiculous sci-fi themed artist names. On the other hand, dance music is oddly conservative, obsessed with its past, constantly looking back to and sentimentalising golden 'old skool' eras.

Even me and the BYO crew had indulged in some club-nostalgia a few years back. Somewhat bizarrely, having been clubbing for only a few years, in the mid-90s we decided to put on a 'Back to the Old

Skool' rave. This was the same mid-90s when contemporary house music was brilliant and the scene was really strong all over. There was fantastic dance music being released in loads of different genres, some superb DJs coming through, DJs had started to travel internationally a few years back so now access to decent contemporary DJ sets was far less limited than it used to be. So obviously we picked this moment to do an old-skool party.

We had met a well-known hardcore rave DJ, let's call him DJ Bassman to avoid any recriminations, and he was going to be the centrepiece of the event. All of which was looking like it would be a jolly good beano, until a couple of weeks prior to the event he turned up at our flat unannounced at two in the morning with the biggest bag of drugs I had ever seen. He then proceeded to chop out a line straight out of a comedy sketch. It must have contained at least ten grammes. Then he chopped out another and then did them both, one for each nostril. Looking back, I've always assumed that it couldn't have been decent cocaine, it must have been substantially cut, because surely, if it was decent cocaine, nosing up 20 grammes of it in a few seconds would kill you.

So when writing this book I went online to try to research how much cocaine you can take in one go before it might stop your heart. The prognosis depends on many different factors including but not limited to body size, tolerance, amount previously consumed etc. but in laymen's terms, if you put what looks like 20 grammes up your nose in one sitting, you're probably asking for trouble. Anyway, moments later this all became moot as in mid-conversation, sitting in our kitchen, a smooth and steady stream of blood comes gushing from his nose, presumably containing most of the drugs too. Bass stands up, puts his head back and holding the bridge of his nose says "I'm going out for a Cornetto, you lot want anything?" Great exit, never saw him again.

To me in sunny south-east London, deep into the underground house scene and spending my days sampling old records, when I first heard of digital file-sharing and Napster in the late 90s it seemed like another world. It was something to do with American college nerds, technology, and possibly math rock music, whatever that was. Culturally, it just seemed like it was a different world to underground house. I was completely blinkered by my love of the club scene and DJing and ran headlong into a market that was in the middle of a digital revolution. Pretty soon there would be no barriers to entry to becoming a DJ or a producer, and that market would be flooded with near-identical home-made house music, the vast majority of which was available free to those who chose not to pay.

Back at the start of the 21st century, I had figured all I needed to do was release one 12" a month, turn in as many remixes per year as possible, and get a couple of decent gigs a month, together with maybe some less decent ones, and I'd be able to call it a living. It would be a small living, a bachelor living certainly, but a living nonetheless, and a living that I could then develop into something bigger. I knew some people who were essentially doing the same thing. Some supplemented their careers with studio engineering, mastering, or promoting parties. It wouldn't be a grown-up, pay-the-mortgage, put-the-kids-through-school living, but that could come later.

In the meantime, I figured I had a direction and I would be able to build up my professional music career, rising through the ranks, selling more records, getting better gigs. My ultimate goal was to have my own professional studio where I remixed the stars and produced my own genre-defining music, which I could then play at my exclusive club residencies. I hadn't mapped out the stages to achieve this, but things seemed to be going well, so I kept my head down and churned out tunes which Fannah duly punted out to labels.

Considering the tidal wave of change that was about to wash over the industry, our scheming seems naive and quaint now. But scheme we did. We were young and didn't really care about anything much but parties and tunes. We weren't really paying attention to technological developments with the potential to revolutionise the entire industry, we were busy. Fannah got me DJ gigs and got my tunes signed. The plan was working, but we were like a pair of happy, hapless traders who'd just successfully opened a corner shop in the ancient Roman city of Pompeii in AD 79.

I had been sent a few promo copies of my first 12" several weeks before release, which I had to go and pick up from the post office. I opened the parcel in the street, pulling out a pristine 12" with my own music from my little studio on it. There was all that stuff about achieving goals, reaching the next stage in your career, recognition, credibility etc. but for me, having my record pressed on to vinyl fulfilled a deeper need, that inexplicable urge that I'd always felt, that drove me to DJ and later to produce.

Listening to music wasn't enough. DJing wasn't enough and neither was pretending to be Nile Rodgers on my battered Fender copy. I always wanted more from music, perhaps more than it could deliver, but getting a tune pressed on vinyl somehow brought me closer to whatever it was I was searching for. It was a little bit like I had given birth to a musical baby, which I understand does sound really weird. But if you really love music very much, then you get certain urges, and when the time is right, you'll make sweet love with the music, and then a few months later, the tunes-stork delivers a 12" of your productions.

Credited to Malachi and put out on well-respected Canadian techno label Stickman, 'Where's The Soap' was the strangely-titled A-side,[7] with the superior 'Scuba' relegated to the B-side. Stickman

7 There's a tiny strain of comedy in UK tech house, a welcome relief from the po-faced seriousness. Wiggle DJ/producer Nathan Coles released records under the name 'Soggy Plop', Ravi McArthur & Tom Gillieron released a tune called 'Another Crap Night Out In Eltham' and production duo Big Hair put out an album called 'Imagine Being Chased By A One Man Band'. No doubt influenced by this, I chose to give my first ever release the hilarious come-dy title of 'Where's The Soap' in reference to a Dave Allen joke. (Two nuns in a bath, one says "Where's the soap?", the other says "It does doesn't it"). I obviously didn't know that the one track with the stupid name would be the first thing I ever released. The other tunes that Stickman signed off me were called things like 'Scuba' and 'Sang-froid', not genius

had signed five of my tracks that they released across two 12"s. For a new artist, this was a pretty good start to a recording career. Despite having been a part-time DJ since the late 80s, I still hadn't come up with a suitably cool DJ name so Fannah suggested I call myself Malachi, after a character from the 1984 horror film 'Children of the Corn'. There is now a much more successful artist recording as Malachi. Many years after my first release I had a job writing promotional copy for a music management agency and had to write a promotional email listing all the achievements of this way more successful-than-me Malachi.

And then, of course, one night, you get to play YOUR OWN RECORD. Is this OK you think to yourself? Is this a singular act of enormous narcissism? It's not, it's not a singular act of enormous narcissism, it's a great idea. I'm PLAYING MY OWN RECORD, as a DJ being paid to play records!

Listening to those releases now, nearly 20 years after I made them, they sound bizarrely fast. We were younger, fitter, leaner then, and the tunes sped along to match our energy. Those first two EPs feature five lumpy, galloping productions, overflowing with ideas and enthusiasm, and low on technique and polish. I was trying to emulate the productions of producers like Charles Webster, Asad Rizvi, Bushwacka, names that are, within underground house circles, by-words for quality. Their records are clearly a product of the dark arts, simultaneously detailed and precise while also somehow being tough and raw.

I didn't really achieve my goal of musically emulating my production faves, and instead produced my own oddball lolloping take on the tech house template. There are records and remixes that I made later in my career that I was proud of, as well as several that I

---

titles by any measure but an improvement on a spelling pun. Really, I would have rather my first EP had a super cool name, like 'Space Robot Battle War Lasers' or or 'Cybermatic Love Machine 5000 XL' but it didn't. It was called 'Where's The Soap'.

would be content to never hear again, but my earliest work simply sounds odd. I remember where some of the sounds came from (I had just bought a Tri-Wave Pico Generator, a hand-built synth which sonically resembled what I imagined a pebble might sound like if you were so mean it you made it cry), but the finished productions sound strangely unfamiliar, as though they came from someone else. Still, Stickman thought enough of them to sign a handful and put them out.

I gazed at my records, the ones encoded with my music, marvelling at the newness and the real, actual-ness of them, turning them over in my hands, finally getting one of them out of the sleeve and smelling the new vinyl. I was 30 and had been buying tunes since I was a little kid. Now I had made one. Two, if you counted the B-side. It's a proper rite of passage, receiving a card through the letterbox that you're pretty sure is going to be your first-ever release, heading off to the post office and picking it up, bringing it home, looking at it, playing it for the first time, in blinking disbelief.

My first ten releases were spread across a bunch of record labels, most of them decent, a couple not so much, and most if not all came from Fannah's efforts. We felt that we had momentum, all it had taken were those two Stickman releases at the beginning of the century, now I had credibility and could get my stuff heard by other labels and be taken seriously. I still have some emails between Fannah and me from that time, and his enthusiasm and drive for my success was relentless: "You're the king mate... onwards and upwards... a long road is ahead but we can do it man, two contracts signed in January already, let's keep it up...!"

Looking back through our emails from then I was surprised just how busy Fannah was promoting me, and just how much interest there was in my tunes. I was also amazed at all the deals we didn't quite clinch, with artists and labels who went on to operate in DJ tiers way higher than I ever reached, any one of which could have changed how things worked out, both for my recording career and

Fannah's management career. The music business is so full of ifs and buts, it's amazing there's room for anything else.

I didn't realise at the time that I was witnessing the end of an era in audio production. The digital revolution which would pretty much end vinyl as a format would define the nature of my career from now on. It had of course already substantially impacted on it, not least by facilitating my ability to sample other artists and record my own music at home. My first releases sold a few thousand copies on vinyl, my later releases just a few years later would sell a few hundred downloads, my more recent releases might get ten or 20 paid downloads and a few plays on Spotify. Over the years some music on streaming platforms might get included in playlists and streamed many times, but at my level, this doesn't really add up to much at all and certainly isn't comparable to physical sales.

Now you could argue that this is because my music has become steadily worse over the years or that I have become steadily less popular and both these may well be true, but also clearly, generally people are buying less music than they used to and profits for artists are smaller per unit, even over the lifetime of a stream.

There seems to be a general feeling across much of the music industry that streaming has 'won' and that this is just how things are now. I'm not so sure. Streaming income is far smaller than the income from physical mediums and this is inevitably going to affect how musicians work. It may be that "musician" becomes a job only available to those who are already financially stable. It may be that the ubiquity of streaming platforms like Spotify changes how and why people make music.

I feel as though we still need to work out exactly how much we value music and understand that unlimited access to everything all the time maybe shouldn't be the only goal of music platforms. The idea of us all simply acquiescing to one giant music supplier to whom we'll pay a monthly fee in order to rent what we used to own hardly feels like progress. You can't uninvent streaming, or for that matter bit-torrenting, file-sharing or taping songs off the radio, but when huge sums are being generated in the music industry while the majority of the actual creators are struggling to make a living, this feels unsustainable – it feels to me like it's far from over.

However, in the early 2000s, this was all in the future and my initial tracks were released only on vinyl, cut by an engineer onto an actual, tangible physical medium. I didn't go to the studio to see my first record being cut, as it happened in Canada, but I went to the cut of some of my other early tunes. You get the tube out from London to somewhere Godforsaken in Zone 6 that you've never been before. Take a cab to an industrial estate, wander through a variety of receptions and corridors until you arrive in a windowless, weirdly-shaped room packed with all sorts of esoteric, baffling, top-end whizz-bang audio equipment, all connected to a cutting machine. It's a device that's about to do some actual, real live magic, right in front of your eyes.

You bring them your DAT tape, they put it through their machines to make it loud and shiny. They do an A/B test, ask you what you think and you can't quite believe your ears, they've made your tune sing. Then, and here's the alchemy: through the lathe they somehow get the music onto the master lacquer, which is used to produce a 'stamper', which will then stamp the grooves into hot vinyl, producing records. Utter magic. If this happened now, I would Instagram/Twitter/Facebook/show-off and un-humble-brag the fuck out of it. Then, I just drank it all in, had a chat with the nice engineer man and went home.

Around 300 million years before then, the sun rose one morning on a young earth, its rays warming the shallow waters of the late Palaeozoic oceans. The seas were bustling with prehistoric little creatures and microscopic plants and animals, all going about their prehistoric marine business, storing up energy derived from a star 93 million miles away. Living, dying and sinking to the sea bed, over millions of years, layer after layer of organic matter falling to the bottom. It all gets compressed under the sediment, the colossal pressure and passage of time somehow producing planetary transmogrification, transmuting the organic matter into oil.

And then millennia later, someone pumps the oil out of the rock from a couple of miles under the sea. It's transported through pipelines, taken across oceans by tankers and then we perform another trick. This time, by industrial and chemical processes the oil is broken down into ethylene, butadiene, propylene and other by-products. The ethylene is combined with chlorine, polymerised, and then converted into a plastic polymer called polyvinyl chloride: vinyl. It arrives at the pressing plant a few weeks before me and my DAT tape. And there, via a process that I still can't quite comprehend, the prehistoric matter created hundreds of millions of years ago becomes host to a tune I knocked up in my home studio on my sampler. If that isn't a miracle then I don't know what is.

12

LET THE MUSIC USE YOU

A recording studio, Deptford, 2002. I'm part of an oddly mixed demographic which includes a smattering of amateur UK garage MCs, a burnt-out tie-dye roadie and the percussionist from an 80s ska band. Belting out Spandau Ballet's 'Gold' into a mic is an acne-scarred bloke with a rectangular shaped head, plastered with jet black, dandruff-flecked, over-gelled hair. Such is his volume that we can hear him perfectly well through the walls of the soundproofed vocal booth. He decides to change songs, generating a general collective tutting and sucking of teeth from the room, several of whom are super keen to get on the mic and prove their MCing skills.

The vocalist is called Lee, he runs the karaoke in his local pub in Eltham and fancies himself as a singer. He's short, fat, always moist, indiscreet (he showed me a topless picture of his girlfriend on his phone within a minute of meeting me; he was married), with a deep, gravelly voice. And Lee wants to be a singer. But deep and gravelly isn't enough. You need at least in-tune as well. Deep, gravelly and in-tune, that could work, but without that crucial third element, the whole thing falls apart.

The Labour government of the time provided courses to get people like me back into paid employment, or at least off the jobless lists for a few weeks. I jumped at the chance to do a state-funded music technology and sound engineering course. Most of the other pupils were either long-term unemployed or kids who had only been out of school for a year or two. In this particular lesson we were learning, bizarrely, how to record to analogue tape, using a huge 32 track desk and a massive tape machine, a skill that was about to be made largely redundant by the widespread availability of home recording software.

Lee switched to the classic soul show-stopper 'The Dark End Of The Street'. It's a song which is precious to many soul fans, as the most famous version was recorded by the fiercely talented but fragile James Carr, the lyrics imbued with extra layers of meaning and emotion from Carr's tragic tale of mental illness and hospitalisations. Carr's performance is exemplary. However, Lee had never heard of James Carr, he only knows the song from the film 'The Commitments'. I tried not to be snobby about this but didn't succeed because I was exceptionally snobby about it.

Lee belted out 'The Dark End Of The Street', sweating, huffing and puffing, going red in the face, sometimes hitting the melody, sometimes missing it. He came out of the booth looking pleased with himself and said, with no trace of irony, that when he sings it at the pub he does karaoke at, no one ever claps and he can't understand why. His words hung heavy in the air. No one said anything. A couple of people stared at their shoes, a couple of others stifled a giggle. "It's because you can't sing in tune," I said. Not sure why, I'm not usually the type to dish out harsh truths, but I'm pretty sure it was a Tuesday after a working weekend when, as any DJ will tell you, the mechanics of the brain are severely compromised, patience is tissue-thin and emotions are raw. Lee went out for a smoke saying he wasn't crying, he just had something in his eye. I felt awful; he didn't have anything in his eyes, except the tears of a shit pub singer, and those are some of the saddest tears on earth.

About a mile away was another recording studio, the legendary (for me, my mates and the burgeoning global tech house family) Strangeweather studios in Greenwich. Around this time, Fannah sent some of my music to a label called Surreal, a label we were both really into. Iron Mike ran Surreal. It was hardly an appropriate name for a mild-mannered bespectacled bank employee from the Kent suburbs. He wanted to sign one of my breaks tracks and I went round his house in Sidcup one night to play him a load of my other demos, intending to put together a two or three-track EP. The problem was he didn't like any of the other tracks, so he decided to get a remix done by someone from Strangeweather to complete the EP. This was something I was exceptionally pleased about and was how I ended up there one evening.

I bought my sampling drum machine in with me and hooked it up to their massive mixing desk. They had a Mac, racks of outboard and two walls of vintage synths and drum machines. Strangeweather was a dream-come-true studio for me, an analogue knob fest, the air dusty with cocaine and loaded with ego. Several big personalities, each as big as their mixing desk, worked there, churning out a series of early tech house corkers under a variety of pseudonyms.

I'd programmed a handful of drum loops, using several classic Roland drum sounds and was playing them back into the Strangeweather sampler. Producer and recording artist Pig Bwoy was manning the equipment, and he asked me to "Run that 909 again" and I didn't really know what he meant. Now any house producer will tell you that Roland's TR808 and TR909 are the two best, and most distinctive sounding drum machines in the world. And any house producer should be able to distinguish between the boom of an 808 kick drum and the thwack of a 909 kick, and the electro click of the 808 snare compared to the toppy smash of the snare on a 909. But, complete greenhorn that I was at the time I had no clue at all that I had created a drum loop using 909 sounds, I had just programmed sounds that I liked.

We finished transferring the samples. "I've done a dub mix as well, do you want those parts too...?" "Nah, we're good" frowned Pig Bwoy, already lining the stems up on the Mac.

My Surreal track ended up being one of the deals that didn't work out and was never released. Years later I interviewed Mike for an article about his label and he said he thought the parts got used on some other remix on the label, but he couldn't remember which one. I've never managed to spot them in any of the Surreal releases. I expect one of the scholars on the Oxford University degree dedicated to early 2000s UK house will establish the fate of my drum loops at some point in the future.

Getting signed to Matthew 'Bushwacka' B's Oblong label in 2002 marked a significant development in my production career, and helped me in my journey up the DJ pyramid. He was one of my favourite producers at the time and getting my work out on his label was another stamp of credibility for me. Oblong was home to many great records, including Bushwacka's 'The Healer', a sublime slice of house music, all shimmering chords and bitter-sweet tension, and now my odd clunky productions were there too. My tunes weren't original, I had literally learned my craft by listening to good records and copying them, some of Bushwacka's records in fact. But I was still using esoteric sound modules, lots of sampling with almost all my outboard space taken up with compressors rather than effects. All of which contributed to a fresh, almost naive approach to the house music template which seemed to be popular with record labels and DJs.

'Time To Slide' was released on Oblong in November 2002. You can pick up a vinyl copy of it online for less than a quid now. I still really like it. It reminds me of going to Wiggle parties and Fannah's club nights in Brighton and of trying to remember every musical idea from every record to use later in my productions; fun times. But most of all, it reminds me of people coming up to me on dance floors and yelling 'Time To Sl-i-i-i-de – To The Dance floor". I don't like all of my recorded output, but this one is cool.

So by day I would produce underground house music, record mixtapes and work occasional awful temp jobs. Two evenings a week I'd head off to Locos, and once, maybe twice a month, I'd play a 'proper' DJ gig.

Like many other seismic cultural changes, I don't remember when the internet happened in my life. But by the time I was releasing music, house music networks were changing and developing quickly. Instant messaging meant you could easily chat and strike deals with labels in other countries, or continents, forging a lovely little connected house music family. One evening I had so many message windows open that I mistakenly agreed to do a remix swap with someone who shared a first name with someone else that I actually wanted to work with.

Another great use of the internet for dance music generally and DJs, in particular, was to notice that things had changed, which brings us neatly to a brief sub-section of the book that I'm calling:

Things That Are Different To How They Used To Be That Old DJs Notice Are Different Now:

- All DJs used to really want to get promos, now DJs moan about getting too many.
- We all used to dance facing each other, didn't know where the DJ is, now everyone dances facing the DJ.
- DJs in the olden days didn't have Instagram or Twitter or cameras or film or anything did they.
- Nowadays kids at the disco are all on their phones, aren't they?
- And the DJ can't leave the equipment alone.
- And showing off, they're always acting like Johnny Big Trousers, we never used to do that.
- Music/clubs/venues/DJs/drugs/and other things aren't as good as they used to be.
- The music's changed and I'm not sure I like it.

As previously mentioned, DJ and dance music culture is a curious mix of the progressive and the conservative.

Paradoxically, despite the growth of the internet and all its attendant messaging technology, during the early 2000s I used to phone people in the industry and receive phone calls regularly from labels I was working with. In 2003, we'd chat about tunes, about gigs, remixes, pressings, covers, club nights, and exchange any gossip. I'm aware that this next part makes me sound like an old man angrily shouting into an uncaring void, but this just doesn't happen now. People tend to email, text or message, apart from a couple of times a year at music industry conferences where we arrange meetings with people that work around the corner back home.

I've had long working relationships with label managers/owners who I've never actually spoken to outside of email, or even seen. Their labels have started small, risen and eventually folded and throughout we never met, and I wouldn't recognise them if I saw them in the street.

I used to like chatting to the people who ran record labels, all types of human behaviour was represented in their numbers. One or two were weirdly boring which I always found simultaneously surprising and disappointing. The music industry isn't supposed to have dull people in it, their place is in the straight world, the world that we're all trying to escape from. Yet within the bohemian idyll I imagined dance music to be, there were plenty of label owners that were straight down the linc business people. Others were stoned immaculate, trusting in the energy of the earth, or ley-lines or that mythical acid house energy to guide their promotional strategies. And some were famously unreliable.

There's one well-known European house label whose reputation for paying artists is so bad that if you announce online that you've signed a deal with them, you'll receive a flood of 'You'll not be getting paid for that mate" messages. I recorded a couple of EPs for them and they never paid me, and instead endlessly recycled the nine tracks I 'sold' to them on compilation albums, repackaging their back catalogue again and again, never ceasing, just pressing on with Borg-like intensity in their relentless drive to exploit others' compositions for their own gain. If nothing else, I admired their work ethic.

They once pretended they couldn't speak English when I called them up, after having answered the phone and taken my initial enquiry in perfect English. True story: I once called another label owner up, chasing up an advance, and he told me that he had intended to pay me earlier that day, but when he had gone to the bank to do the transfer he couldn't find the door to get in. No lie.

The music business has always been shady as fuck, from Don Arden robbing the Small Faces or Jimmy Page pretending he wrote old blues songs, to new releases being bootlegged and DJs miming their sets. Payola, pre-sales to achieve high initial chart positions, dodgy clauses hidden deep in contracts and misplaced royalties, all that and much more has been the history of the music business. House music was full of illegal bootlegs, stolen tunes, uncredited producers, illegitimate samples, cash-hungry promoters ripping off DJs, punters getting mugged by over-priced drinks at raves, but still, taking all this into account, there was still some kind of financial equilibrium.

There was, at some vaguely unspecified but definitely pre-digital period, a balance of DJs, the low numbers dictated by the relatively high financial and time/effort access requirements. To be pro you needed to buy some decks, a mixer, an amp, speakers and some recording equipment. Then you would have to continually buy new, expensive music. Then you have to nail the practical skills of DJing, which required practice and perseverance: acquiring the skills was a twin investment, time and money, the two big ones. So this filtered out many casual wannabes from ever actually trying to become DJs. There were ups and downs, winners and losers; you got knocked for your DJ wages sometimes but there was still the chance to carve out a living as a DJ.

It might be, like mine, barely scraping by, constantly substituting the low income with dead-end or temporary jobs. Or like some of my peers, a half-decent one, but there was a living to be made from all aspects of the music business. Capital was generated and exchanged; there was real, actual work going on, generally carried out by people who had some kind of clue what they were doing, and many of them were specialists in their field. Services were rendered, invoices were raised, fees were collected. There were experts eeking out a wage at all points of the process, from programmers and mastering engineers to record sleeve designers, distributors, records shops, all the way through the chain.

Digital changed everything.

Previously, all the dirty dealing had taken place within the music industry itself, behind the scenes: artists and DJs got ripped off by managers, who got shafted by labels, label execs were taken for a ride by managers, a circle of mutual abuse. But this was something different, suddenly, the 'fans', those who professed to love the music, seemed content to steal music.

Once music could be converted into digital zeros and ones and be instantly swapped between hard drives around the world without cost, then everything changed and the equilibrium that had existed before simply disappeared. And aside from the erosion of music's value, digital technology lowered access to production, music distribution and DJing too, so that pretty much anyone could 'do' any of those previously skilled tasks. Change began to unfold exponentially and unstoppably.

There was a period in the early 2000s when vinyl distributors just kept going bust, owing labels thousands of pounds. You'd open your email and receive another note saying a label who owed you a few hundred quid couldn't pay you because their distributor had folded owing them money from their last five releases. Sales kept dropping, pre-orders were down, profits were way down, the business model buckled and then broke.

We saw all this and continued to make music. I had a high production rate, dedicatedly turning out what I thought were ever-better tunes, signing more record deals, ticking off personal goals: my first US record deal, my first four-track EP, my first remix. Deals got worse. Advances fell. There was a period where you had to ask for an advance whereas previously it would have been offered. And then advances were off the table entirely and profit splits became the norm. Sales plummeted and still we continued to create music. The industry, broken, ruined, slowly started to wonder what it was going to do about the free music culture. DJs still bought music, but not many other people did.

The older generation was appalled as a new generation wholeheartedly embraced free music. We couldn't believe what was happening to the industry. All rules were being broken, all bets were off, we were in freefall. But me and almost all my mates in dance music, we still continued to make music. A couple of wiser souls saw the writing on the wall and just left, seeing that the business model was dead. But most of us continued to create house music whilst our sales continued to drop.

Music fans had been sending a very clear signal to the music industry for a few years that they wanted music in digital form. The larger music industry stuck its collective head in the sand, bizarrely sued a few low-level pirates and fiddled while a generation learned to love free music. Now, music fans were going to stick it to the man, show these big corporations who was boss, and they were going to do it by paying for monthly broadband, paying for Mp3 players, laptops, iPods, iTunes, for phones and 18 month contracts; they were going to set up direct debits to a number of large corporations to enable them to not pay one penny to the artists, singers and bands whose music they professed to love.

And something else odd was happening too: the idea of somehow restoring value in music, something that had become completely free, resurfaced in the fetishisation of 'things', rare vinyl first editions, obscure remix double packs, elevating the format above the actual music, surface over content. I loved vinyl as much as the next DJ, but despite its many charms, I loved it because of the music it contained. People in the industry began a long, boring decade of arguing about which music format might be superior, an argument that you can still easily reignite online if you're not careful.

As the structures of the traditional music industry crumbled around me, I continued to spend my time DJing underground house parties and producing underground house music, the profits of which couldn't possibly sustain me financially in the long term. This is the point in the book when I'd like to say why, to offer some insight into how the continual diminishing returns didn't diminish my ardour for making music. Looking back, I'm still not really sure why though. It seems trite to say, but at the heart of it, I just really loved it. And it's hard to let something you love go.

I hadn't begun making records to get more DJ bookings, but it happened anyway. I got booked via someone I'd never met introducing me to someone I didn't know on AOL's instant Messenger (that was, briefly, how things worked), to DJ a weird gig in Mayfair with, I'm fairly certain, DJ Rob Mello playing too. It was weird in that it may have been London's tiniest basement bar and the cupboard-esque dimensions only just about fitted the DJs and our mates. Quite what would have happened if anyone else had shown up I don't know – luckily, literally no one came.

Promoters began to approach record labels I was on to offer me DJ gigs, including my first invitation to play in Bulgaria: "Club name is Black Box in Sofia – capital city of Bulgaria with capacity 700 person" went the email. Sounded good to me. And in contrast to my gig in Mayfair a few weeks previously, around 700 people did actually come.

I still believed that there was a place waiting for me, nearer the top of the DJ/producer hierarchy, and that if I worked hard I could get to a level where I was selling more tunes, getting the kind of DJ gigs that would constitute an actual living, perhaps get my music licensed for TV and films, maybe produce and remix bigger artists. I eventually did get a couple of my pieces of music used on TV, and it was a nice little earner, but providing the promotional campaign backing music for Channel 4's exciting new US soap 'Brothers & Sisters', whilst an achievement of sorts, does not a sync career make.

Another reason to continue producing was that my ego really loved reading all the positive DJ feedback from my releases and the magazine reviews. DJs used to say nice things about my tunes a couple of times a month. Imagine that: you open up your email, and there are forty-odd compliments from your peers in the industry. Granted, half of them are variations of "Nice track, will play", but plenty of them will tell me I'm great. What's not to like about that? My ego loved it. I loved being Harold Heath. If I just read the DJ feedback to my tunes and the record reviews in magazines, if I stayed in a tiny warped tech house bubble, I was successful.

However, I was raised Catholic, and there was no lasting contentment for a sinner like me, not with a watchful deity I didn't believe in noting and judging my every move. I was lapsed which means that I don't believe in God, yet simultaneously felt the effects of his non-existent gaze, a relic from my childhood upbringing. So I would contentedly read some feedback on my latest release, enjoy the brief dopamine feast this afforded me before the inevitable process of guilt and self-denial began.

Instead of wallowing in the cardinal sin of pride, I opted for either envy or lust. I constantly compared myself to more successful DJs and producers, criticised my own music for not being as good as that of my heroes, for selling less, wanted to be playing better gigs and to record for better labels. I possessed a latent guilt, that I shouldn't have been there at all, that I wasn't a genuine producer or artist. I always worried I was about to be found out, that if not God, then definitely someone else, someone real, would twig that I wasn't actually an authentic producer, but some kind of bluffer, a faker. I was just cruising through, making it up as I went along until someone had the wherewithal to point out that I was nothing more than an interloper.

Another reason I was continuing to produce even though the music industry was burning all around me was that I was getting much better DJ gigs as a direct result of my 12" releases. I was a 'name', a name that hardly anyone knew, and one whose tiny spark of fame would soon go out, but a name none the less. I had released a bunch of tunes on decent labels, had a bit of radio play, had played some decent gigs here and there, my name was on a few 12"s and I had done lots of remixes. I got good reviews in the music mags.

The only people who might have recognised me would be DJs, promoters, labels who signed my stuff, people who worked in record shops and maybe a few clubbers. And this already small demographic would be drawn from the tiny pool that was the international tech house community rather than the larger dance music industry. But my continued success led to bigger and better DJ gigs.

The fees improved. Someone once paid me £800, two nights in a hotel and my flights to play records for two hours. This seemed very good to me in 2005. As the money got better so did the time slots. And I finally managed to get myself to the DJ level of 'gets sent 12" promos' at exactly the point when everyone realised that they couldn't afford to send out 12" vinyl promos anymore, and began emailing out a bunch of Mp3s every fortnight instead.

A pilfered vocal sample and the bassline from a Layo and Bushwacka cut (under their The Usual Suspects pseudonym) called 'Nightstalkin' from the golden years of tech house in 1998 was the inspiration for my next big release 'Long Relationships'. 'Nightstalkin' is an underrated masterpiece of funky tech menace and really should be much better known. For 'Long Relationships' I tried to replicate the b-line, knowing full well that I wouldn't be able to, but in the process of attempting the theft would steal some of their notes, mood and their groove, and that would be enough. I was right. As is always the way, if I'd known that it was going to be one of the most popular things I ever produced, I definitely would have spent more time on it, but it came together super quickly.

Looking back this was a creative lesson that it might have been helpful for me to learn sooner rather than later in my career. Most of the best stuff came speedily and unselfconsciously and years later, I've realised that it's the same with writing words. The times when I spent ages tweaking at a riff or idea trying to get it to be good were often wasted compared to those brief moments of inspiration. I mixed 'Long Relationships' down super quickly too and it was snapped up by the first label we sent it to.

They were Urban Torque. The first time I ever spoke to Jason (great hair and big ideas) and Leigh (no hair and an excellent dry wit) in person I thought Jason was on cocaine because he just wouldn't stop having ideas and telling them to us. He wasn't, and it turned out he never ever took drugs; he was just always having ideas and telling them to us. His business partner Leigh was in contrast more laconic; together they made a superb team. They loved 'Long Relationships' and it turned out, loved lots of other tunes I made too. I don't remember how I first found them, it was probably Fannah who made the initial approach, but it was the start of a long relationship (haha) with a most excellent record label.

'Long Relationships' also brought my music to a wider audience, including one of my DJ heroes Colin Dale, a serious player and much-respected originator, who signed me to his DJ agency. I used to tape his radio show off Kiss FM. There comes a stage in this game, when people who were previously distant, special, who you idealised, suddenly become just people you work with, people you know. I once walked into a club where Colin was DJing and he saw me and put on 'Long Relationships', kindly providing me with a very cool memory. Colin's agency once got me a cracking gig in East London and before and after my set I took drugs with a live performer that I interviewed ten years later about his being straight and off drugs for several years. I had completely forgotten that we'd met and banged up some lines together and when I introduced myself he had to remind me "Funnily enough we've met before actually..."

'Long Relationships' was my first release that got widespread, as opposed to just tech house, DJ support. So many firsts in this game. First mixtape, first signing, first warm-up gig, first review in DJ Mag, first headline gig, first overseas gig, first festival gig, there's always something else to reach for, each as exciting and at the same time as strangely everyday as the last. 'Long Relationships', with its credible big DJ support and BBC Radio 1 airplay was a springboard up onto the next tier. DJs who I'd previously been fans of were suddenly contacting me to tell me they loved my music.

Eventually, you find yourself on the same bill as one of your heroes. At which point it usually turns out that they're a disappointingly normal person. The best you can hope for when you meet your heroes is that they're not a complete nightmare.

One day, one of your releases gets signed to a label that you used to buy and you have to somehow match this new version of yourself with the concept of being someone who records on Oblong, a label whose every release you've previously loved. Now I'm on Oblong. I'm one of them. It's like slowly getting entry into ever more hallowed areas of a private club, only to find it full of people just like you, rather than the creative geniuses, tortured artists, mavericks, renegades and raconteurs you were hoping for.

Sooner or later you get the remix parts from the studio of a producer whose work you've admired for years, which raises the twin spectres of self-doubt and imposter syndrome. Generally, I did well on the bigger remix challenges. I was really pleased with my re-rub of Terry Lee Brown Jnr., someone whose records I had been buying since the mid-90s. (German producer Terry Lee Brown Jnr. isn't the only person called Terry I've remixed fact fans, there are two others, Terry Vernixx and Terry Grant).

My remix of Shur-I-Kan's 'Kissing' is a particular favourite of mine, it's brilliant, but only because every single part he supplied me with was amazing. Even his handclaps were superior. The bassline was so perfectly balanced, so even, it seemed to possess actual weight, and the percussion was precision-tooled rhythm perfection.

I somehow wangled a stab at remixing Asad's 'Slippery Heights'. Now, 'Slippery Heights' isn't a well-known house record which is an injustice, for it is extraordinarily good. Impeccably produced, with exquisite vocals and a killer hook, it's a perfect blend of glitter ball sheen and deep, thundering house. I got the parts and used some chord inversions I was particularly fond of and produced a weak, muddy, quiet remix of a brilliant record. Worse, I put the sublime vocals of Mel Dymond way too low in the mix. And the very worst thing about it is the chords I use are lush, the idea I had for it was good, it was just very poorly executed.

When people go on chat shows and talk about their long lives in showbiz, they always say they had no regrets. Me, I've got loads and near the top of the list is doing a sub-par remix of a classic tune. Should've got help mixing it, should've taken more time, should've made it the classic remix it could have been. Didn't though. Don't even know why. It was up on Beatport but for some reason it's been listed incorrectly and when you click on my remix you erroneously get some other clattering technoid workout by some other artist, a fact I was faintly relieved to discover.

Asad also remixed 'Long Relationships' and unsurprisingly turned in a great re-rub that came with a wholly original breakdown. Paul Woolford also produced a superb bouncy futuristic remix too; both artists whose work I've continued to buy over the years, and they both introduced me to the experience of wondering if their remix is better than my original.

Pete Tong played 'Long Relationships' on his Essential Selection radio show and Annie, Jimbo and I gathered around the radio to listen. When you finally hear your own composition on BBC Radio 1, the radio station that was on in your house every day when growing up, that was on in warehouses and garages and factories all over the UK and that everyone listened to when we were kids – these first moments are often odd rather than full of joy. There's a healthy portion of disbelief and confusion, a cognitive dissonance as your mind adjusts to the new reality: it really is your song coming out of the radio. Then there's a flush of success and pure ego pleasure, accompanied by mad silent dances of glee.

Pete Tong says "And that was Harold Heath" and then, here's the weird bit. He doesn't pause, before taking a deep breath and saying, "Harold's been plugging away at the industry since starting out as a DJ in the late 80s, but has only been producing for a few years. He's had a string of releases on some of the best labels in underground house and with this track is definitely stepping it up a few gears, with DJ support from some of the biggest names in the biz... Harold, mate, we're all rooting for you." Pete Tong didn't say that. He said "And that was Harold Heath" and then introduced the next record.

He didn't even say "And that was Harold Heath. We continue." You realise, in those moments of jubilation and success, that the music industry doesn't actually revolve around you, it hasn't been waiting for you to show up and it won't miss you when you're gone. And one day, you'll definitely be gone.

This is the kind of realisation and general outlook on life which makes me such fun at parties. Anyway, Pete Tong played it and Annie and I danced around our tiny grey back room in Lewisham. Slim Jim, showed his enthusiasm in the only way he knew, which was to adopt a different-from-usual facial expression, and move parts of his body if Annie or I looked at him.

So Annie and I danced and whooped and celebrated the no doubt soon-to-arrive riches and fame that a play on Pete Tong's show would inevitably bring, and Slim moved some of his body parts in ways he thought might be appropriate for the moment. I recorded it on cassette, and somewhere I've also got a recording of another appearance on Radio 1 where I had to take part in a quiz. I had to guess a fruit or count a cloud or something, I forget. There was definitely banter involved, although if I'm honest, I don't think it was top.

SOME CHOICE HOUSE I PLAYED IN THE MID 2000S

Plej – Lay Of The Land
Lawnchair Generals – Stop Frontin', The Truth
Charles Spencer - Board Meeting
YSE – Bounce Back
Solaris Heights – Rivers
Explicit Theory – Touch Your Body
Mazi – Interplay
Kerri Chandler – Bar A Thym
Trevor Loveys – The Bounce
Asad Rizvi – A Hora

Asad Rizvi featuring Mel Dymond – Slippery Heights
Ian Pooley – 900 Degrees
John Dahlbäck Feat. Erika Gellermark – Nothing Is For Real (Warren Clarke Remix)
Shur-i-kan vs. Milton Jackson – I Want It (Milton Jackson Remix)
François DuBois – Blood
Tom Gillieron – 4 Get Me
Hipp-E featuring feat. Lamont Moerhaus – Dance Wit Me (Dub)
Greenskeepers – Polo Club (D's Book Learnin' Dub)
Terry Lee Brown Jr. – Bar Snack

13

TAKE ME AWAY

MIAMI WMC 2005

A hot summer night. Not a drab, British, drain-scented hot summer night with KFC debris bathed in street-light orange. A Miami hot summer night. Neon adventure, ultraviolet glow, hot rods, palm trees, there's a tattooed muscle-man dude with a fucking great snake walking down the street at 2 am like that's a normal thing to do, that kind of a summer night. Rushing, a film of sweat even under the air-con, cotton clothes close to the skin. There's more sky here than in the UK. They say everything's bigger and better in the US. Certainly, the quantity of bacon they gave me at Denny's earlier in the day was bigger than you get in the UK and instantly endeared me to America.

Miami Winter Music Conference, the annual international dance music get-together, until Amsterdam Dance Event rather stole its thunder in recent years. A week of conference sessions, networking opportunities and parties. The one event that everyone in the industry has at some point suggested "It's not as good as it used to be", with that weird dance music emphasis on constantly regenerating nostalgia. I bought a conference ticket, never went to one conference session. Picked up my conference bag from a swanky hotel, and wandered around a languidly dull pool 'networking event' for a bit and then never went back.

Me and a small crew of other producer/DJs piled into a taxi, leaving one party to go to another, after getting a call from Jason and

Leigh. I had just accidentally consumed seven too many hash pipes with another DJ and sat in stunned stoned silence as everyone in the cab (in my memory there are eight or nine people in there, and they're all walking around, there can't have been more than four of us and obviously on reflection I realise that we were all seated) pretends to be American with awful American accents for the entire journey. Love a cab journey in a foreign city at night though; there's nothing like it. I'm the kind of person who's genuinely intrigued by the difference in street furniture around the world. You go to some places and the street signs, the traffic lights, even the manhole covers are different from home. Imagine that.

We are on our way to a BBC Radio 1 mansion party. Yes, it was described as a 'mansion party'; essentially it's a house party but in a mansion. I'm sure that Pete Tong will be there, he's a BBC Radio 1 DJ, and he'll probably recognise me from that time he played my tune on his show a couple of years ago. Or get introduced to me. Or ask to be introduced to me more likely, and he'll be all like "Mate, I played your track on my show that one time, did you hear it?" and I'll be all like "Oh yeah I think I remember that, nice one Pete, appreciate it". The party is accessed through respectful conversations with massive, sweet-smelling and immaculately preened security staff outside the sweet-smelling and immaculately preened security wall with barbed wire and machine-gun posts. I'm really high. There probably weren't machine-gun posts.

There's a lot of neon and coloured sparkling lights, water features and tasteful sculptures. It's one of those ultra-modern rich people's houses where you're not sure if you're indoors or outdoors, where you think you're walking into a room but find yourself in a mini garden with a curved slab of marble on a plinth symbolising freedom. With a water feature. The floors are also made of marble I think, although I'm no expert in mansion floor design. The words start to rotate in my brain "marble floor maybe marble floor maybe". It has a comforting rhythm to it; snap out of it, Harold. Those floor tiles, so smooth and shiny. I'm distracted at the thought of how cool they would be pressed against my hot face. Cool, flat tiles, smooth, calming. Marble floor maybe marble floor maybe. I'm not going to lie on them though, even if it seems like a very good idea. Instead, we're led past more things on plinths made of black and gold; then through a sumptuous, I don't know what the name of this room is, a sumptuous debauch-chamber?

We go through some kind of half door/half artwork; crisp gravel under feet, then soft grass, we're outside where the temperature, even after midnight, is shocking after the air-con of the house. The heat is heavy, slowing everyone down, it's everywhere, not just in the air, but the surfaces, the walls you lean against, the bar when you rest your arm on it, everything's high temperature, ice cubes melt in moments, matter gently buzzes with heat.

I get introduced to a man who's wearing an LED t-shirt. His thing is he plays along with DJ sets on his harmonica. I'm totally taken by the flashing blue lights of his t-shirt, which perhaps he mistakenly thinks is interest, so he gets his harmonica out and starts 'jamming' with whatever record was on, steadfastly holding my gaze as he puffs through his precision blues riffs.

He was, technically, very good indeed. He could play loads of notes really fast up and down his mouth organ. Sounded awful though. "It's in the wrong key" he explained. I don't know if he meant the song or the harmonica. "I play with..." and he dropped a well-known DJ's name, "...we've done loads of gigs together, he bumps the tunes, I bring my mic along – I've got a special mic connection for my piece" – by piece he meant harmonica, I don't know why he called it his piece – "We jam sometimes for hours on end". "Why?" was my stoned but very genuine response.

I never heard what he said back to me, I'd already moved on to other matters in my mind. Perhaps he quietly left the party, choosing to walk home rather than get a cab, reflecting on what he was doing with his life, and that central question – why? Perhaps it was a pivotal moment for him and he woke the next day with a clear head, put all this mouth organ piece nonsense behind him and got into marketing LED t-shirts, but I never heard because Jason from UT wanted to introduce me to famous DJ #58 and famous DJ #64, members of DJ tier two.

He made the introductions and they briefly acknowledged me, then, expert social instigator that he was, Jason just faded back into the party as though he'd never been there. Meanwhile, famous DJ #58 turned back to his conversation with famous DJ #64 and the pair of them studiously ignored me, making a point of not meeting my eye or responding to anything I said, but carrying on speaking as though I wasn't there, as if they'd agreed previously to make a point of ignoring anyone introduced to them. Brilliant. I said something suitably witty like "Great, see you later then" and wandered off back inside, where Sasha, my DJ hero from 15 years ago, was playing a set of bleepy electronica.

In 1991, at the absolute height of the rave honeymoon period, we'd gone to Cambridge Corn Exchange for an Eclipse rave purely to hear him play. He played that Whitney Houston a capella 'I Wanna Dance With Somebody' sped up to +8 over an Italian piano track, which he used to do a fair bit at the time. We all thought this was very good fun, and then later he dropped Moby's 'Go', the first time I had ever heard it, its impact on a couple of thousand loved up dancers almost profound. That tune, oddity that it is, with no bassline, a piano solo made up of a single chord, and a massive steal from a TV theme, is another example of dance music's ability to take a few disparate elements and re-mould them into a wonderfully epic new thing.

In Miami, as if in tribute to those days, a single breakbeat came rattling out of the smoke as Sasha ever-so-briefly dropped a snippet of 'Bombscare' from Two Bad Mice, a classic rave track from 1992. Just a glimpse in the night of a time long past and then it was gone, as quickly as it had appeared.

Dust, smoke, hot vapour, neon sound and wandering, shimmering conversations. Cocktails that looked like you could wash and condition your hair with them; confusing the natives: many Americans struggled with my accent at the best of times, but a conversation with 4 am-slurred-drunk-but-also-still-totally-wired me was, I imagine, something of a challenge. At one point I met famous DJ #70, and, intending to compliment him on his latest release that I had been playing, I attempted to introduce myself. It was later reported back to me that my earnest opener was "I'm from which part are you from England?", a bold conversational gambit no doubt, a sentence that with its multi-layered levels of meaning and possible intent still baffles me to this day.

Famous DJ #29, who at the time was riding the crest of an extremely successful DJ and production career was comfortably settled into what I presume was a prohibitively expensive white sofa, looking extremely happy. By this point in the evening utterly off his rodders, making little sense, with a bottle of champers in one hand while a pair of beautiful women shovelled drugs into him and several stately peacocks balanced precariously on or near him. Again, looking back, not entirely sure about the peacocks, but the overriding theme was opulence. I don't think I've ever seen anyone, before or since, look so utterly content with their lot in life as Famous DJ #29. It was like a film director had told his prop team to assemble the parts for 'extraordinarily happy and debauched DJ scene: take one'. Famous DJ #29 had been releasing loads of highly successful records and was DJing everywhere and I remarked to one of the more approachable peacocks that I'd been DJing for probably as long as he had, and he seemed to have done a much better job of making a success of it than I had.

Someone from our party, not me I'm pleased to report, had semi-passed out on a sculpture with their hands in their pants so we were politely asked to leave: ("Your friend" a calmly angry Spanish accent said to me, "he goes too far"), so we headed off into the night ending up at a slightly creepy strangers' house. A sprawling warren finished with dark oak panelling throughout, with a tasteful ivy-framed patio and small pool, where we did laughing gas and schnapps with creepy old vest-and-sandals guy as the sun rose.

My first and only WMC. Staying up for a couple of days, sleeping it off, then a huge meal at Denny's and off for another couple of days, play some records, exchange records. Lost my voice and my headphones somewhere, people gave me other records, constantly amazed and jollied at the welcome I get everywhere by DJs who play my music. Hanging out with people I've been chatting online with for years and as is the way with these things, people who work a few miles away from me in London. Clubs, bars, hotel rooms, terraces, roof parties, after-parties.

Nightclubs in Miami are cooler inside than the temperature on the streets. Ultraviolet garish bars, huge carpeted clubs, with seemingly infinite back rooms and layers of VIP areas and backstage access. Calling the headliner who's on the decks to get him to convince security to push us through the throng to the VIP, then through the VIP into the back room and just when you think you've been let into the inner sanctum you notice a dark corner roped off from the rest of the room.

You realise that it's probably like a Russian doll in nightclub-form; at the back of each secret VIP party there's another, and another, each more exclusive than the last until you get to the final, tiny room. It's so exclusive you can only get in if you're dead, and if you sneak a peek through the gap in the door, you'll catch a glance of some lost souls who never left their final after-party, each waiting in the shadows for their turn to tell the others how successful things have been going for them lately, whilst doing endless lines of dusty grey ghost cocaine.

By the end of the week, I was painfully aware that I'd soon be back at Locos, no doubt drinking bottles of Becks and moping. I briefly went into denial, the combination of lack of sleep, substances and alcohol twisting rationality. Maybe Annie and I could just like, move out here – right? I got on well with the guys at the three gigs I had here (three!), what's to stop me using those contacts to build up a DJ career here in Miami? I bet vest guy's connected right? Later that day, I made my way back to the airport and inevitably, therefore, back to Locos.

I have no recollection of the flight home, I was flat out the entire time. When I eventually woke at Gatwick, I had been dead to the world for so long that the volume of the crack my neck made when I first stirred woke up the couple snoozing next to me.

Back at Locos the Monday after my Miami trip, drinking heavily, the contrast between my present situation and the previous few days was stark. In Miami I'd been someone, man, I'd been like Jimmy in 'Quadrophenia', when he was down in Brighton over the Bank Holiday when it all 'meant something'. And now I was back in the Locos basement, heavy with jet lag and come-down, making a far from triumphant return. I tried to mix some commercial dance tunes together, something like Modjo's 'Lady' or Armand Van Helden's 'You Don't Know Me', in an ill-fated attempt to bring some of that Miami magic back with me. To no avail, of course, someone simply suggested I played 50 Cent's 'In Da Club'. Again. Which was ironic because I had just got back from a week in da club and we weren't in da club now, we were in Los Locos, where students go to get pissed and where dreams go to die.

Annie and I moved from London to Brighton. The day we moved out, we awoke to find ourselves inside a police cordon due to a stabbing on our road. I drove up and down from Brighton to Covent Garden twice a week to DJ at Locos, getting back around five or six each morning. I got a part-time job at Sussex University in 2005, a year of contrasts in the context of this tale. On the one hand, I had many successes in my career and looking back, apart from the continuing drop in sales, things were going pretty good for me. I was prolific, Urban Torque were going to release my album, my music was getting decent press reviews, my tunes were getting DJ respect and plenty of club plays. I was getting a few nice bookings with decent conditions and pay; things were generally looking up.

However, although generally things may have been looking up, specifically the traditional music industry was looking down at an abyss of terminal decline. It had reached the point where decisions needed to be made about turning off the life support and letting it die. CD sales had consistently fallen for years; revenue from downloads was still way lower than expected and hadn't filled the gap left by the drop in physical sales. The big four record companies continued to lay off staff and shut down divisions of their corporations, then they became the big three as Sony and BMG merged.

My trip to the Miami Conference had featured plenty of talk about the impact of digital, despite some parts of the industry remaining committed to vinyl as though it were a matter of family loyalty. Everyone: labels, DJs, producers, were all talking about formats. Was vinyl dead, were we somehow betraying our culture if we switched to CDs? What could we do about sales? They had been steadily falling for a few years now and the issue was unavoidable. Everyone I spoke to had a different opinion on what should be done and what was the best course of action for the industry. We were united in our disunity. Meanwhile, the actual real music industry, the big corporations, had already been planning and scheming how to monetise the new digital territory; organising, negotiating and manoeuvring while we swapped vinyl promos and wondered about the future.

It was at WMC 2005 that I first heard a DJ say records were now just adverts for your DJing. This initially seemed heretical; all my life I'd treasured records, now I was making them and a DJ was telling me they would never earn us any money again and should be treated as nothing more than a sonic billboard to hawk your DJing services. This was one of the perhaps inevitable results of the continuing general process of devaluing music resulting from file-sharing and then torrenting. Music was slowly morphing into a mere advertisement for other services. What a cultural fall from grace, from holy sacrament, communion-creator, sanctuary, muse, aphrodisiac and precious art form, down to nothing more than an advert.

Digital formats largely took over from vinyl, which obviously substantially affected a culture that was based around vinyl. It costs a fair bit to press up and release a record, including printing the labels and the covers, getting it mastered and cut, and the cost of physically moving them around, each link in the chain, from pressing plant to record shop via distributer all need to be paid.

Digital distribution via Mp3s cut almost all these costs, thus reducing the financial investment needed to release music. The cost had previously acted as a gatekeeper, and although there had always been plenty of bad music pressed onto vinyl, digital really threw those quality-control gates wide open. Accessible and affordable music-making technology and the ability to distribute music digitally at little or no cost led to everybody deciding they'd better start their own digital label to punt out as many tracks as they could to make up for the short-fall between physical and digital profits. Over the course of a few years a new, barely functioning underground house music industry of low cost, low profit and high product-turnover emerged.

It was into this cheery world, and with exquisite timing given the general collapse of the industry and the specific collapse of CD sales that I was about to release my first album, on CD, the classic 'Hole Funk' by Harold Heath. It was a dream come true. I finally had a chance to make an album, just like Gil Scott Heron or Carl Craig or Trevor Horn. It didn't quite turn out like any of those artists. I was pleased with most of it, though.

I wanted it to be dense, rich, full of interesting diversions, beguiling musical distractions and to have enough in it to withstand repeated listens. The whole project was guided by some of the most familiar tropes in dance music album production. Here goes: I wanted it to be different from my 12" releases which were specifically made to be played by DJs, in the club environment. In 2005, the concept of the album as a whole still existed and I wanted to make something that took in broader influences beyond house music. I wanted it to withstand home listening, rather than be simply a collection of club tunes. I had been making non-house music at home for years but had never released it. Now was a chance to make an album as a cohesive whole; a collection of different moods and tempos. It seemed important at the time. My desires regarding this album were remarkably similar to the 50% of dance music producers who try to stretch out a little on their albums. The other 50% simply produce a collection of club bangerz in their particular style. My attempts to be different were as clichéd as everyone else's.

I agonised over the length of the breaks between each track (on the CD they're all different, deliberately so), the label and I gave much thought to the overall composition and sequence of songs. The final track finishes with a rich chord played on a rising pad that then drops out as the last cymbal crash is pitched down and fades out, sounding exactly like the broken mirror of life falling into the eternal black hole of fate.

Listening back to it, I'm pleased with most of 'Hole Funk'. It has some cool moments. Lots of nice funky sampling, chunky beats and an interesting, wide sound palette. I played some guitar and Slimbo Jimbo's rickety old bass guitar on some of the tracks. I thought some of it was a bit soundtrack-esque, and I really liked how the downtempo non-house tracks had turned out. Its success was its mix of naiveté and confidence.

It was far from perfect. We should have done some album edits, cut down some of the longer tracks to maybe half that length, removed the long DJ mix-ins and mix outs that some of the tracks featured, and a couple of the tracks are weak compared to the others, but overall, I can say I like it. Pete Tong mentioned it on his radio show. DJ Mag gave it four and a half out of five. I write for DJ Mag now and I'm hoping that one day they'll reinstate my missing half a point and award me the five out of five that we all know I actually deserved.

The whole thing was made on a couple of semi-pro groove boxes with a load of archaic outboard, with no computer at any point, until I had to utilise Slim's Logic skills to get the vocals recorded. There's a nice deep house vocal track towards the end of side two, 'Feel The Love' featuring a lovely hippie from Brighton called Katie. This was one of my first attempts at recording vocals. I had bought a new mic and preamp, a mic stand, cables, and I'd constructed a vocal booth, from covering an old wardrobe with blankets and quilts. She insisted on recording her vocals whilst sitting cross-legged on the floor, barefoot, holding the microphone close up to her mouth.

If you've not recorded vocals before, it's one of the biggest challenges in studio engineering. We all hear voices so often, we're so familiar with them that if you fuck with them at all, it quickly sounds wrong. Additionally, mics are highly sensitive and can easily pick up the low-end vibrations of a truck outside the house, or distort at the 'pop' of the 'p's and 'b's of the English language. Therefore you're not meant to hold mics when recording because they'll pick up any movement you make and ruin the recording and you're meant to keep a certain distance from the mic otherwise it will distort. I'd learnt about recording vocals at college but doing it for real was way harder. You had to interact with a human, one who may insist on sitting cross-legged on the floor, holding the mic tightly to her lips and swaying, eyes tightly clamped shut in order to summon her muse.

Over the next few years, I recorded lots of singers that I used on my tunes using variations on my wardrobe booth prototype. Working with singers teaches you a lot about dealing with people. Singers really have to lay themselves bare when they perform, and depending on their attitude and how you deal with them, it can be a fraught or smooth affair.

I once recorded a couple of UK garage tracks and used a local singer who, bless her, for some reason dropped into a 'swing your partner by the hand' square dance cadence early on in the session and then just couldn't stop. Each take was great for the first two lines, but then at the third, she went into do-si-do mode. Despite lots of encouragement, fag breaks, a cup of tea and a biscuit, she couldn't remove the square dance voodoo once it had appeared. We had to abandon the recording and she glumly do-si-doed her way out of my wardrobe.

Then there was the enigma that was Bruce Zulu, rapper and vocalist, who unknowingly provided me with another great little clubbing first, my first in-club sing-a-long. Bruce wrote and performed the vocals for 'Be My Friend' which was on my album and released as a single with remixes the following year. We recorded his vocals in Jimbo's home studio in Catford, under a single bare electric light bulb, with Jim 'engineering'. 'Be My Friend' was a stab at hip house and has a chorus, a plaintive four-note refrain which unsurprisingly goes 'You Can Be My Friend'.

One night I played it at the Pressure Point club in Brighton where there were a few of the London tech house crew in attendance, and a couple of Wiggle regulars sang along to my song. This might be one of my favourite moments of my career. It wasn't a big thing, just some party people together under the strobe, singing my song back to me. I'd had a drink and sung along too at the top of my voice. You can do that when you're DJing in a club, no one can hear anything except the tunes, so you can proper belt it out.

I got to put some acknowledgements on the CD sleeve. This was also one of the best bits of my career; acknowledgements on the sleeve of my album. I'd read sleeve notes on the backs of records, on that awkward fold-out thing that came with cassettes and CDs, now it was my turn. I thought long and hard about what would be appropriate. And also cool. And also street. And would also suggest that I hadn't spent a long time thinking about it, but also showed that I cared. And that was also still cool. Ironic really, I can't imagine that over the years since many people have pored over the acknowledgements and thanks on my debut CD.

Anyway, I thank Leigh and Jason and the vocalists, Katie and Bruce, because I was brought up properly. I send 'big' love to Annie;

then you thank family don't you, so I go on to thank my Mum and Dad, I think because I was ridiculously proud and thought an actual physical album would confer some credibility on my music career, whilst perhaps showing that I wasn't wasting my time with it. Weirder still, I also thank my brother and sister who really hadn't contributed much to my tech house career to date. I stopped short of thanking God, thank God, and instead moved onto Fannah and his family, mis-spelling his eldest son's name (classy, apologies Isaac), before sending my regards out to various members of the international house music family.

Urban Torque thanked both Annie and me which was a nice touch. They knew she was integral to my success. She supported me through the whole album process, when I was struggling with muffled vocal recordings, or worrying about track listings in a way that suggested these issues were really important. In fact, if I review every single endeavour I've ever undertaken since we met, Annie has always had my back. She doesn't get much of a mention in this tale as her dance music world peaked in the intensity of early 90s rave and the polished conga loops of tech house didn't really appeal to her, and that's not really fair because there wouldn't really have been a career had it not been for her.

From 2001 when we first met, Annie had been a constant enthusiastic, positive presence in my career, encouraging me, pushing me on to actually network rather than just talk about networking and generally being the best wife a DJ could ever want. Essentially, you should read this book with the knowledge that everything that happens after 2001 has a clever, funny, beautiful woman in the background, quietly organising, supporting, looking out for and looking after me.

A Springsteen-obsessed university colleague very kindly bought a copy of my album and then, baffled by this electronic noise with no proper lyrics and struggling for something to say about it, described it as 'pleasantly hypnotic'. I played it to my Mum and my sister. My sister was momentarily vaguely amused and my Mum, whilst proud and genuinely pleased for me, asked me to turn it off after a couple of songs bless her.

We had an album launch party for 'Hole Funk'. For some reason, it was in a club in Leicester. I played some music and another DJ played off CDs, and I remember thinking how terribly cosmopolitan it must be to be able to go to a gig with just a few CDs and a bag with some clean pants in it rather than lugging two stupidly heavy record boxes. I played a nice little set and was having fun; someone from Mixmag or DJ Mag, I forget which, had turned up with his girlfriend to interview me. He looked bored to tears and approached me mid-mix to ask me some questions. I said "One sec mate", slid the crossfader across, lowered the volume on the outgoing track and took off my headphones. But he had already left. I briefly caught his girlfriend's eye looking back over her shoulder at me with an unreadable expression on her face as they slipped out.

To help promote the album Urban Torque enlisted a photographer and arranged a 'shoot'. I wasn't sure of the etiquette, so I brought along a case with several different hats and coats, reasoning that if I changed hats and coats throughout the day, then I would cunningly fool future magazine readers into believing that I'd had more than one photoshoot. We also took some photos of me dressed in a vintage RAF pilot uniform which I had hired for the day, to lean into the old-man-ness of the name 'Harold' and to attempt to break away from the terrible monotony of cool DJ photos.

We headed off down the beach, I changed hats and jackets a couple of times and then got out my drum machine and headphones. Sat on Brighton beach, my headphones plugged into my trusty Roland TR606 drum machine, I tried to look convincingly like the kind of person who often pops down to Brighton beach to sit and programme his 606 whilst staring moodily off into the middle distance. Props. I brought props to my first photoshoot.

The idea being if you have a pair of headphones in your photo, then people can see that you're a DJ, likewise, if you've got a drum machine in shot, then you're a producer. I'm secretly a little proud of my naiveté. I also brought along my previously mentioned Tri-Wave Pico Generator, a photogenic square silver box covered in silver knobs that looked like it could double up as an unreliable time machine. I held it up sagely, and the photographer got his minion to shift the light reflector so it was right in my eyes and I had to squint. The photos came out pretty good, and I used them for years, still do, even though now I'm bald and then I had hair, or perhaps because I'm now bald and then I had hair.

At least with the RAF uniform shots, I looked a little different from the other clichéd DJ and producer promo photos, which tend to be in front of a graffiti-covered wall, looking moodily off to the left whilst wearing your best trainers. Again, I think that my experience with a press shoot was probably quite familiar to many low-level DJs, so much so that I believe the majority of us generally followed this particular arc with regard to promotional photos:

- No photo, just a snazzy online avatar.
- First few releases, their mate with a camera takes a couple of usable shots of them standing in front of some graffiti, (wearing their best trainers), looking off-camera, not smiling.
- Get interviewed by a magazine who take some decent shots in front of modern buildings.
- Use three shots from this session for the rest of your career. Uncredited.

'Hole Funk' got good press reviews and great DJ feedback. Lots of my DJ heroes played tracks off it and charted it. One evening a few weeks after its release, Leigh and I were at The End nightclub in London. The DJ put on a tune, and Leigh, ever the alert A&R, starts nodding along. What's this he says, it's really good. I listen, it is good. It sounds familiar. Yeah, it's pretty cool, I say. I think I've got it on 12" maybe... We are facing each other when the truth hits us simultaneously: we're listening to my record, on his label.

HAROLD HEATH SUMMER 2007 MIX CD: 'BEAUTY & THE BEATS'

Terry Lee Brown Jnr. – Chatterbox
Logan – Flash (Charles Webster Remix)
Roland Van Den Toorn – Yoghurette (Replika's Tasty Dub)
YSE – Bounceback
Shur I Kan – Future
Afrodrops – Nice Cream
Fred Everything And JT Donaldson – Theme
Fred Everything And JT Donaldson – Listen
Bryan Jones – Let It Go
DJ Disciple – Deep Underground
Coles And Coker – Sweat Bomb
Santiago And Bushido – What's Your Name
Chris Harris And Dominic Martin – Dig It
Peter Black – Cream (Asad's Silverlining Re-rub)
Gui Borrato – It's Majik (Terry Lee Brown Jnr. Remix)
Funk D'Void Featuring Jay Leblone – Lovin (Hipp-E Mix)
Nikola Gala And Scope – Hoping For You (Scope's East Life Remix)
Julian Sanza – Everything
Joshua Collins - Lilo (Harold Heath Remix)
Sam Ball – Past, Present And Future

14

PLASTIC DREAMS

2006 and a digital revolution had swept through the international music industry, up-ending all the old rules and certainties. Profits for artists, producers and labels had drastically shrunk and music was available free if you didn't want to pay for it. DJs had proliferated exponentially like germs on a particularly fetid and fecund petri-dish. As part of my fast-paced business-focused response to the demands of an ever-changing global marketplace, I joined MySpace in January of that year.

Jason in one of his advisory diatribes had strongly recommended I get on MySpace to promote my music now that my album was out. I needed an online presence apparently. I didn't think much of it at first; you had to choose colour schemes and photos, then upload some music and supply updates. You could customise it, but it was a template so you could do what you wanted within the narrow confines of what was provided for you, no more no less. A step in the reduction of scope and possibilities of the internet. You could also 'rank' your top friends, which was weird.

Within a couple of years, everyone was moving over from MySpace to the even more regimented Facebook, where you didn't even have the false sense of control garnered from being able to change the background colour to 'personalise' it. Instead, they controlled every aspect of it apart from your profile pic, And it turned out that they owned everything you put on there and quietly made note of your every keystroke. But again, everyone said it would be useful for my career; then they said it was essential so on I went, in April 2009. I began posting my DJ mixes and links to my ever-growing appearances on poorly thought out hastily thrown together compilation albums. Over the years tracks of mine appeared on albums describing themselves as tech house, techno house, deep house, nu-disco, disco-house, chill house, tropical house, yacht house, beach house, pool house, gym house – yeah I don't know what the last few are either.

I began to get a better response to my DJ mixes via Facebook than on my website and I let the domain renewal lapse. Nobody was interested in my tiny corner of the internet, with my DJ mixes, links to press about my album or reviews of my tracks. No one cared. I don't blame them, there were way more interesting things to read online. So we all wandered trustingly into the loving embrace of Facebook, leaving our outmoded personal websites to simply wither away into the virtual ether.

I played more gigs in Bulgaria and the Czech Republic in the mid and late 2000s and they were some of the very best of my career. The clubbers there really, really, loved tech house. United in their passion for a scene that had grown substantially since the mid-90s, they were proper dedicated house stalwarts, each and every one of them. The type of crowd who cheer when you mix in a clipped hi-hat.

To briefly be a minor, mid-tier DJ star in Eastern Europe in the mid/late 2000s wasn't exactly what I had always dreamt of, but it was pretty cool. I loved those gigs. I felt completely self-contained; sure of what I had to do and happy to do it. I was just there to work and whatever other hedonism or adventures I encountered or partook of would be down to fate. I felt that a booking that included a decent wage, flight and hotel meant that they trusted me to play whatever I thought was best, so I did, and it worked. I felt confident in what I was doing: I just got on with the job I loved.

They whisk you off from the airport in a cab that has a completely unplaceable but not entirely unpleasant scent, and before you know it you're climbing seven flights of stairs to a radio station to give an interview. They ask you for interests outside house music and you intend to say something about enjoying quality science fiction films and novels but are fried from the flight and hungry, so you just end up telling them plaintively that you "really like spaceships" instead.

If you've got time it's off for a meal in a local restaurant where you get introduced to lots of people and drink many toasts of whatever local spirit is preferred. Most people might not be speaking English. Long, hot parties, steaming club nights, raves on boats or in disused swimming pools, longer after-parties, half empty-rooms with the sun already streaming through the windows, but no one's stopping. The long-termers don't mind the space or the light, they've travelled through the night together and come out the other side. Scene devotees, hardcore clubbers, they're like puppies, you have to wear them out, and they'll need a long after-party before they're finally ready to give it up. Some of them, you know they'd never leave if you just carried on.

Sometimes these kinds of sparse daytime sessions can be the finest to DJ at. A sense of glorious unity is born from spending a whole night together, like dance floor soldiers who've served a long campaign and are now bound for life. That sublime tension and release that the very best house music delivers works its inevitable magic again, with the mid-morning sun streaming in and illuminating everyone's smiling faces and tired shuffling feet.

Once a promoter's mate picked me up in his tiny red sports car, the type where you're so low down you can't see in other car's windows when you pass them, and we passed every fucking car in Bulgaria that night on account of him driving at four hundred miles an hour. Fat-headed, flight-jacketed, completely silent after the initial introductions, foot to the floor, wordlessly speeding in a torrential thunderstorm with visibility down to 30 feet, languidly resting a single finger oh so casually on the very edge of the steering wheel.

A promoter once booked me and then got so pissed he tried to kick me off the decks after my first record so he could have a go. He tried a couple more times before being bundled away by a kindly pair of punters.

If you get straight on the decks straight from a cab journey, the shock can be visceral. A period of acclimatisation is ideal but not always possible. Sometimes you simply have to push through the dance floor and take over. And it's already rammed in there, so hot, humid too and the air is so thick, and you realise that you're already coated in a thin film of sweat and you're beginning to self-baste. Dropping straight into the extreme environment of the modern nightclub, the shock can make you want to piss, or shit, give you a dry-mouth or shaking hands, depending on your body's preferred reaction to pre-show adrenalin.

It's so loud you can feel various parts of the frequency spectrum in different parts of your body, the bass comes up through the floor and rattles your gut. The top end is piercing, making you flinch, the volume is all-encompassing. All you want is a smoke and a drink, but no time now, this is what you came here for, pick that first tune. The first tune of your set: what a delicious decision.

On and off, this moment had been in the back of my mind for the last few days, and the closer this moment came, the more I thought about it. What will I play first, what will work – and of course you never know until you're there in the thick of it, in this most bizarre extreme work environment. One in which, were the job conditions described to you, you might have second thoughts about working in:

Wanted
Experienced mood manipulator, crowd controller, group psychologist, children's entertainer, shaman, musical devotee, genre expert and tech nerd. You will be responsible for the entertainment of several hundred paying customers, most of whom will be in some way inebriated.

Hours
Variable, always late, some jobs might be two hours, some might be two days.

Working Conditions
The job will involve extremely loud noise pollution for its entire duration. You'll be working in a hazardous environment with high temperatures, high humidity, and high levels of smoke. There will be constant visual stimulation from bright lights and strobe effects. You may need to travel through a time zone or two to get to work.

Wages
Variable.

Perks
May include, and generally be limited to, free drink and drugs and a vague hard-to-define sense of satisfaction if and when the party goes off.

In the mid/late 2000s I could command a few hundred quid with accommodation and some kind of transport for a UK gig, and a few hundred more with travel and accommodation for a gig in Europe. Sometimes I lucked out and got more; sometimes I was happy to take less. Never played for free, except for friends birthdays. Playing for free just makes it harder for anyone else to get a decent wage. That's why unions were invented. Shame we've never had a DJ union to campaign against Free-Js. Playing for free is the sure sign that someone is playing at being a DJ. Never play for free; you're worth more than that. And if you're not then you really shouldn't be out DJing. DJs should be experts, specialists, the kind of people worth paying.

I played a bunch of my own releases at a night in Manchester, to UK house heads who knew my stuff, loads of them singing along. In 2008 I had finally played at Wiggle in London, a personal goal. I had been entranced by the Wiggle DJs for years; Eddie Richards was a genuine DJ legend, he'd been DJing in London long before acid house broke and Terry Francis and Nathan Coles were both brilliant on the decks. The Wiggle crowd were easily the most discerning crowd I'd ever DJed to. Fanatics all of them, some of them had been raving at Wiggle since the mid-90s.

You knew you'd get a quality night of DJing at Wiggle. Legend told that in the vinyl days, DJs would be kicked off if they dropped two mixes in a row. I was nervous, still playing mostly vinyl, the decks right at the front of the dance floor on a slight stage, the lights bright and hot, my hands a little shaky. Proper butterflies, needed a piss as soon as I got on the decks even though I'd just had one. I can't remember a single tune I played. It was something of a DJ highlight for me to play there and I only have very happy memories of the night with lots of my friends on the packed dance floor.

Fannah, having given me the most amazing start to my career, had gone and had a pair of splendid children and wasn't really available to hold my hand anymore. My agency DJ gigs were great but few and far between. Instead, I, with no manager or anyone who knew anything about anything, managed my own bookings.

You go out there never really knowing what you're going to get. Your plane ticket is paid for so you know they're good for that, but what the rest of the weekend might be like is always at least partly a mystery. You might end up not putting your hand in your pocket the entire weekend, treated as some kind of VIP, getting drinks and meals and treats bought for you, as though you were something special, and not just a bloke from London who makes tunes with a sampler.

There is one sure test of someone's character: if you want to know what a person is really like, then see how they act when they get treated like a low-level superstar DJ. When they get driven from an airport to a hotel, then taken to a bar for drinks, given some drugs, driven to a club, bought more drinks, introduced to loads of people as the star of the evening and then put in a booth to play some music. How do they then treat people? It's difficult, in practical terms, to actually apply this test. But if you can arrange it, you can learn a lot about someone when they're put in that situation.

I heard of DJs who turned up and always demanded prostitutes be arranged. Or who insisted that certain drugs had to be supplied before they'd play the gig. Some DJs had drugs as part of their rider. I heard of a DJ who insisted on a microwave in his hotel room so he could dry out his ketamine and another who employed a personal drug mule for international gigs. Others had reputations for always getting too messed up or for being rude to punters. Our tech house family was so close, if someone did something out of order at a gig, by next week people in several other countries would know about it. European promoters became a source of stories and gossip, some good, some bad, about the various exploits of UK tech house DJs.

There was one DJ who was always described as 'larger than life', who for a year or so, seemed to have always just played last week in the club I was playing in. I was never able to live up to his wild Keith-Moon-of-tech-house antics, and used to wonder if they preferred to book him because he was more fun. They probably did.

You might get paid before you go on, with a whisper and a clutch of notes pressed into your palm, or an envelope slipped across the decks whilst you go into the mix. You might end up in the alley behind the club watching the promoter quietly slip away in a cab having not paid you. You might get a third of your fee and end up winning the argument and getting another third. You might take pity on a promoter whose night was ill-attended and come to a deal. Or you might not.

This isn't always a world of contracts. At least it wasn't at the level I worked at. We had written agreements sometimes via emails, and hotels were usually pre-confirmed. And if I worked with an agency then I'd get a contract and maybe even an un-needed technical rider (a pair of decks and mixer please), but otherwise, the scene often survived on word of mouth, your word was your bond, and an online handshake sealed the deal. You go out to gigs blind, not knowing anyone, trusting that your accommodation and payment are going to happen and nine times out of ten they do. Unsurprisingly, most people who put on parties simply for the love of putting on parties are the kind of people who'll pay you if they can.

Most times you get looked after very well, but I've experienced all shades of the accommodation spectrum from a plush hotel with crisp, clean sheets, thick carpets and quality room service, to stark rooms filled with old mattresses and ice on the inside of the windows. Five star gaffs with too many swimming pools and unfinished hotels with live wires sticking out the walls, and doors that open straight out into the frosty night on the fifth floor. Windowless cold-war era vaults, basements repurposed as crash pads. Sometimes it's just someone's sofa during an after-party. Sometimes simply nothing, just a wide-eyed few hours hanging around an afters until you can get back to the airport.

I never much liked going back to the hotel. I was aware of the fragile and fleeting nature of my success and I felt that these particular adventures had a finite lifespan and intended to make the most of them. I didn't want to spend any of my precious DJing trips abroad alone in a hotel room. Anyway, a hotel room is way too quiet after DJing, after all that interaction, all those people and stimulation, it's too much of a contrast.

Besides which, a hotel room post-gig gives you the time, and the heavy silence, to reflect on the last few hours. Tonight I had a geezer, and it's only ever men who ask this, come up to the booth and ask me if I'm gonna play a bit harder mate. I say I will if he'll dance a bit better mate.

How do requesters arrive at their decision to approach a DJ? It might take them a few minutes because the dance floor is so rammed with people having a brilliant time. Pushing their way through, sorry mate, 'scuse me. Finally making it to the front, but the booth is up on a stage so they've got to climb up on stage and then go and stand next to me. I'm mid-mix, but I nod to him anyway. He starts talking but I'm not really listening as I'm already listening to three separate things at once (track one and track two in my headphones and the whole mix through the monitors) and you want me to lip read as well? Go on them mate, it's obviously pretty important if you've come all the way up here, and there it is: "Can you play a bit harder mate?"

Now more sure of myself, such suggestions from punters wouldn't play on my mind, but in my first well paid overseas bookings, I would inevitably focus post-gig, on the one minor, meaningless, low-level, barely-existent criticism, above the rest of the party-goers who were loving it, whooping and hollering to their heart's content. I'd be thinking about can-you-play-a-bit-harder guy.

Despite best intentions, inevitably sometimes you end up after DJing in a hotel room by yourself. TV seems puerile, pointless, and there's not going to be any sleep for hours. Could have a bath. Try and rest. I'd happily have stayed at the afters but it was winding up, everyone was going home. I could have drunk, chatted and vaguely danced for a few more hours yet. Even though my feet hurt and I've been up since Friday morning and I'm not even sure what day it is but I think I've got to fly home sometime later today and what's that buzzing?

Reflect on the gig. How did it go? Was it good? Did I do a good job? Should I have played a bit harder? More and more they're expecting to be entertained, looking in anticipation at the DJ, waiting for something brilliant to happen that they can see, observe, say they were there, without realising that the only brilliant thing that ever happened in these circumstances was when everyone got down. Seriously, what's that fucking noise?

Got to get a cab to the airport in a bit. Serge said he'd send someone to get me but I'm not convinced that will happen. The noise. It's the hum of the mini-fridge, next door's air-con, a shower two doors down, the huge boiler in the basement gently reverberating through the structure. It's coming from the building itself; it's the background drone of a medium-sized European hotel. It's in my ears too, late-night tinnitus squealing away its own little conversation, just waiting for me to listen and focus in on it. Hotel rooms after gigs produce quantum tinnitus: the more attention you pay, the bigger it gets.

Tonight's party had been so loud, so hot, so dark, my senses were severely compromised on arrival. Mid-set I had a couple of dodgy mixes, just a couple of barely noticeable wobbles really, nothing to worry about, but the horror of it all, public mistakes, the shame. I'm supposed to be a professional. But then at other points in the evening I was utterly killing it, hanging onto the faders on the mixer for dear life, looking out at the faces in the dark, riding the rhythms, in full control. A night of contrasts, ups and downs. A night like life.

Got to fly back home in a few hours. Drink some tepid concoction from the minibar, drop a valium and try to sleep. The post-gig state of non-sleep exhaustion. The thick carpet, duvet, long curtains and soft furnishings of the room soak up external sounds, allowing the normally hidden audio soundtrack of bodily functions to rise to the front of consciousness. A high pitched tone from your ears, the throb of blood in your veins, the roar of breath on a pillow. Occasional shivers. Taut jaw muscles and even your hair and fingernails feel weary. Don't know if you're too cold or too hot. Involuntary movements and twitches, aching stretches. The substances haven't left your body properly and although you're too tired to move and lack the resources to hold yourself up anymore, your body is too busy thoroughly sweating it all out to allow sleep to come yet.

The further in time I travel from our early experiences of house music, the harder it is to achieve the levels of sheer excitement and energy that characterised them. It couldn't last, not in that full-on intensity. So many things are different now, not least of which there is no novelty factor, nothing of what we are doing is new anymore and there are few surprises. Things change. Not every DJ gig can be as intense and euphoric as they were when we first started raving, but I still over-think the post-gig analysis.

Sweating it out. Eyes determinedly open. Ears ringing. The sound of my heartbeat, every flutter of my eyelids amplified, all senses still pharmacologically heightened, my nervous system in a state of divine fight or flight from the adrenalin of the gig. Simultaneously tired yet alert. Restless, stretching, fidgeting. Loud silence. Thinking about how the weekend's gone, baseless doubts suggest themselves. Should I have played different tunes, could I have done a better job, do I need to practice more, buy different music?

My thoughts rush in and out, half-formed, intense and imbued with strange associations and disassociations; things don't quite fit, they've stopped making complete sense. Shapes or shadows seem to move in the corner of my eye, but dissipate when I try to focus on them. Dislocated ideas clamour for attention with an underlying soundtrack of some awful piece of music I've not heard for years, Boney M, Haircut 100, or the music from the Shake 'n' Vac advert. My brain generally doesn't play me an entire song in these circumstances, it likes to loop a very small part of the song, say the pre-chorus, and it prefers a part I don't know the words to.

So not only am I tortured by, for example, the banal chords of Belouis Some's 'Sometimes' on a constant loop but also, I don't really know the words, so my mind inserts nonsense words instead, that another part of mind then attempts to decode. It's all quite wearing. My brain once chose to transpose the lyrics from the hymn 'Colours of Day' into the Oasis song 'Slide Away' that I barely know, for the entire duration of an MDMA comedown.

Sweating. Close my eyes again. The silence isn't deafening, but it is very, very loud. Muscles feel drawn, desiccated, my mouth dry, sore. In the left hemisphere, a headache wearily begins to assemble itself. Now that the alcohol is working its way out of my system I'm becoming more myself again, less Harold Heath the character. The uppers start to wear off, the false confidence and bonhomie falling away from me like aged plaster off a wall. They leave behind a mind now preoccupied with critically evaluating last night. How much did I betray my soul? I'm giving it a 6/10 on the shame-scale, which I can handle; it's been way higher in the past.

I can't relax, my mind running through every detail of the gig, every track selection, every mix, moments in disco-time that are already fading in other peoples' memories still occupy my thoughts. I think it went OK. Could have gone better. Could have gone worse. Maybe I should have played a bit harder. Maybe, perhaps, should have, could have... As dawn's grey light creeps through the gap in the curtains, my feet still tapping to a beat long since ended, I have no idea if any of what I'm thinking is true or false.

2005 BEATPORT CHART: 'HAROLD HEATH'S AUTUMN WINNERS'

Part of a DJs job is returning charts. You do a summary of the new music you're playing this week or month and then send it to retailers and post it online. If nothing else this is great as it means that years later, with a bit of luck the chart might still be online and you can work out exactly what you were playing in Autumn 2009. DJs submit charts primarily to support the artists whose music they play and to demonstrate to potential bookers the kind of DJ they are, but if we're being honest here, also to promote their own tunes too – hence the appearance of two of my tunes in this chart of mine from 2009.

Candy Dealers – Street Delight (Harold Heath's Re-rub)
Harold Heath – Lovebird EP
Dan Curtin – Other
Jake Island featuring Alec Sun Drae – Can You Feel It (Fred Everything Lazy Days Vocal Mix)
Jake Island featuring Alec Sun Drae – (Do It Like This – Shur I Kan Mix)
Scope featuring Sandra Lima – This Rhythm (Florian Kruse & Nils Nuernberg Remix)
Luca Doobie – Attica (Makam Remix)
Leon featuring Corrina Joseph – I Follow You (Detron's Springtime Leaves Remix and Dub)
Wonderland Avenue – Get Back (Topspin Mix)
Hussle - Shenoda

15

KEEP THE FIRE BURNING

With DJs now fully centre stage, acknowledged as bonafide stars, more and more people were aspiring to the role. DJing had become cool. Things like Ableton Live, Traktor and CDJs made it much easier to 'be' a DJ, in the same way that having Instagram on your phone made it easier to 'be' a photographer. So models, pop stars and celebrities all started 'having a go' at 'being' a DJ.

Meanwhile, anything I had ever produced was freely available on YouTube or SoundCloud if you wanted it. Alternatively, for a very reasonable fee you could join the world of illegal but unpoliced online music sites and have access to my entire back catalogue and indeed the back catalogue of pretty much any other dance music producer or artist you could think of. Obviously, the artists and producers never saw a penny. That was the convenient way to do it, take the waiting and organising out of stealing music, just get it all there for you, neatly packaged up for download. Of course, you could still torrent all the music you wanted, all for nothing – well, not quite nothing, you'd need to pay your internet service provider for a decent internet connection, and of course you'd need to pay for your computer or Mac. So someone was profiting off all this 'free' music, it just wasn't the people who actually made it.

As the decade went on it seemed that every week someone else I knew would start a record label, essentially because it was 'easy' and near-zero cost to do, and because you could, in theory, get more of the profits rather than split them with an external label. But this logic would only work if there were way fewer labels, whereas instead everyone set up tiny labels that sold tiny amounts of their music. It was indeed easy to set up a record label, but way more difficult to run it as an ongoing concern. People made more music. I was still getting asked for music by labels, but always now on a strictly 50/50 split, no one gave any advances any more. I couldn't blame them, sales were tiny. But still we carried on.

There simply wasn't enough DJ/producer careers to go round anymore. There were more DJs and producers every week, and fewer people buying music than ever before. Sometimes, reading the DJ promotional feedback on my releases, I idly wondered about how we were giving our music away to the one tiny slither of the population who might actually be inclined to pay for it. I was receiving the sales figures (sometimes, from some of the better-organised labels) and I could see the sales were tiny and becoming more so month by month. That could have been the dance music industry sales sector slogan throughout the 2000s: 'Becoming more tiny month by month'.

Ironically, as profits at the lower end of the music industry dwindled into virtual nothingness, my productions were picking up support from some of my favourite DJs, people I had admired for years. I had spent enough time working in my studio by this point, got to know my monitors pretty well, understood how to get the best from my limited collection of machines. I'd collected a few nice bits of studio gear over the years, nothing too exotic or exciting, just enough to churn out decent-sounding tracks. I'd completed some courses in sound engineering, spent a bit of time in better studios with better producers and this all contributed towards an if not golden period in my production career, then certainly a fairly shiny one.

I achieved goals, surpassed my earlier aspirations of what I could achieve as a producer, but there was no corresponding financial reward, just lots of kudos amongst my peers and some of my heroes.

Listening back to some of my later productions, I genuinely think there are some quality moments. It's just a shame that they were lost in a sea of other house music, none of which you needed to pay for anyway. I turned in a pair of remixes for UK house producer Ross Couch's label of an artist I liked, Spin Science. Chunky, well-produced, interesting drums, lots of nice musical touches and arrangement flourishes. I did a main mix and a stripped-down dub for both tracks, the low end sat beautifully, the percussion was fresh, and I was really pleased with how they all turned out. Sold fuck-all.

I had given up DJing at Locos. Going to bed at 6 or 7 am twice a week is cool, obviously, but have you tried a conventional sleep routine? My last gig there had been another classy night. A tiny girl snuck into the booth behind me, did some booth dancing, knocked over my Becks before leaving me with a truly foul lingering fart. Someone locked themselves in one of the toilet cubicles and then fell asleep, so the door had to be taken off at its hinges. And then another bloke ended up being taken away by an ambulance having fallen off a table while doing 'The Timewarp'. I wasn't playing 'The Timewarp' at the time. Standard.

My DJing adventures continued. I played a warm-up at The Egg in London and the following week played as a headliner at Jamm in Brixton. I met the resident from a legendary Northern club brand who talked about getting me up to play. A few days later I got a booking to DJ in Kuala Lumpur. One of the agencies I was registered with contacted me about a mini European tour. But most of this led to nothing much or nothing at all.

I made some tracks with a producer who had a beautifully specced studio space in South London. He'd engineered a couple of UK number ones, worked with some big names, a stand-up guy on the house scene. He signed a few tracks from me to release on his label. Listening to one of them, he said: "Yeah, it's great we'll definitely sign that." I was well pleased. "Yeah," he continued, "just have to remove all the pads and strings and chords first, obviously."

He and I played a few DJ gigs together and one evening a singer and microphone appeared during my set. Meanwhile, the producer is looking slightly sheepish, like he knew this was going to happen and hadn't quite got round to mentioning it. I wasn't sure what to make of this, was it going to be a brilliant moment of musical synergy? No, no it wasn't. One thing it turns out that I'm good at is communicating clear directions merely through my facial expressions, and I was able to cancel the sing-a-long-tech-house session merely by looking simultaneously angry, annoyed and agitated whenever he tried to melisma over my tunes.

One rainy Thursday evening sometime in the 2000s Fannah, Crofty and I went to dress a club in Reading (our mate ran a company designing and producing massive custom inflatables for clubs and we occasionally helped out). Darren Emerson was headlining the main room and breaks DJ Tayo was in the back room. Emerson was fine, but Tayo was superb, peerless, just so good, one of the finest DJ performances I'd ever heard: in the back room, on a Thursday evening. In Reading. This would have been a challenging gig for any DJ, but he absolutely smashed the place up. Yet here it was clear to see, the best DJs simply don't always 'make it'. Maybe our idea of what constitutes success is skewed. That evening Tayo took an unpromising situation and briefly wove some genuine musical magic, bringing a room together in unexpected abandon; he just tore it up. Surely that's the epitome of DJ success right there.

I was briefly made resident DJ of a Brighton party called Lovestick who put on some decent local bashes. Their flyers were subtle, tastefully shaped like a great big penis. I jumped at the chance of some local DJ gigs: there really is nothing like being able to wander home when you've had enough rather than have to navigate a national border or two before getting to your bed.

The promoters invited me to their minuscule central Brighton flat one evening and spent about an hour and three spliffs getting round to asking me to be 'exclusive' to them, meaning I wouldn't play for any other promoters in Brighton. I was getting literally zero other gigs in Brighton at the time and therefore this was a request that wouldn't affect me in any way, so obviously I objected on general principle instead.

It was exactly this kind of behaviour that held my career back. I should have been a networker, a player, the kind of guy who just said yes to stuff. But instead, I was a stickler for some kind of personal integrity that no one else cared about or even knew about, a standard of dignity that couldn't be wavered from. Something in me objected on a personal level to anyone making any kind of DJ related demands on me, even if those demands would affect me in literally no way at all.

However, my personal integrity wavered slightly when around this time I got a booking in Dubai. I was paid £1000 for two hours DJing, with a couple of days in a five-star hotel and flights thrown in which was obviously great, but it was quite an odd affair from start to finish. The UAE authorities enforce a strict moral code on their citizens, although Westerners could drink alcohol in the hotel bars. Perhaps I should have considered the lack of liberty for UAE citizens and the harsh reality of life for foreign workers in UAE before I took the gig. I like to think I would now. But I didn't; I took the gig.

Grooverider had done ten months inside a Dubai jail for having a bit of herb on him and everyone was edgy about the UAE customs. There were tales of people getting locked up because the police claimed to have found a roach stuck into the tread of their trainers. There was a rumour that they swabbed your headphones and you'd get a four-year stretch if they discovered any trace of drugs. We all remembered sharing headphones and doing lines with other sweaty fingered DJs and worried about getting through customs. Apparently, a very well known DJ had bottled playing at the venue the previous week for precisely this reason.

All these thoughts were in my mind as I strode purposefully through their palatial airport. When I got to customs a bored-looking man in a brilliant white robe vaguely shuffled through the stuff in my bag. "What is on these CDs?" he asked me. "Music," I answered. "Why do you need so many?" I wondered whether to tell him about how the art of DJing, whilst made up of many elements, was essentially about selection and juxtaposition, and therefore having a large collection to choose from was vital. But I didn't say that, I said something like "Oh I'm a DJ, it's my job, I'm playing a gig here in your lovely country."

He stopped idly rummaging in my bag and looked me in the eye at "lovely country", which had inexplicably come out sounding savagely sarcastic. He held my gaze just long enough for it to be uncomfortable, then hissed over his shoulder at his two colleagues. I inwardly cursed my ability to imbue words with erroneous sarcasm at inappropriate moments. They both came over and examined my bag through the X-ray screen, poring over the CDs, and speaking very quickly to each other.

My body decided that now would be a good time to try out its 'stereotypical suspicious person' moves; I could feel my pulse quicken and my mouth became dry. A small tremor of fear formed in my gut. I began to wonder if the way I was standing looked guilty or innocent. They all stopped talking and looked at me, the three of them blank-faced, empty-eyed. "Fuck," I thought. Then they burst out laughing and the bored dude said: "DJ! Have a pleasant stay in our lovely country."

Club 360 was located at the end of a curved spit so you felt that you were in a bar in the ocean. It was a circular venue with an open-air terrace. You had to get a golf cart to take you there from the hotel. The booth was out on the terrace under the stars with a lovely sound system. You're not allowed to have your drink with you in the DJ booth in Dubai. There's a little shelf just outside the booth, its only purpose to house the DJ's drink. There was a member of security whose sole job was to put his hand in front of me like a barrier and meet my eye with a slight tilt of the head every time I forgot and tried to bring my drink into the booth. The gig itself was brilliant fun, I remember veering off into a few old classics and personal favourites and it all going swimmingly.

The night before the gig I went out with the venue manager and his mates, and we went to a massive bar packed with suntanned English and Irish. Everyone was really hyped because Alan was about to perform what I was informed was going to be the highlight of the night, perhaps of my whole trip. Alan, a pinkened, weathered expat in his late 50s took to the mic and belted out Neil Diamond's 'Sweet Caroline' to the absolute delight of the utterly ratted audience who roared their approval. Odd place, Dubai. We went on to a nightclub which again, was a disconcerting experience. Entirely substance free, with a very famous UK DJ nearing the end of his career playing an absolutely awful 'I-could-not-care-less' set of re-edited 'classics'. We sat around getting bored-drunk, then I went back to my super luxury hotel and took advantage of room service to order Black Russians and club sandwiches. Everyone in the hotel called me Mr Harold, which I rather liked.

To add to the general air of weirdness, prior to the gig the promoter had been in a battle with the bar manager and both of them were offering to pay for my flights and pay my wages, each saying that the other was a con artist who was trying to rip the other off. A week of increasingly stressful emails and phone calls ensued, with each accusing the other of ripping them off, each assuring me that they were honest and true, the other guy was a borderline criminal, it was their job/reputation at stake here etc. All the while, the date was coming up quickly.

For a small time DJ, this was a big gig, and I found the whole thing baffling and perturbing in equal parts, not wanting to choose incorrectly and inadvertently lose someone their livelihood. The hotel emailed me asking me to finalise the booking with the bar manager so I eventually did so and the gig went ahead but neither promoter or bar manager turned up. It turned out that the actual promoter went on putting on his successful night for years there afterwards whilst the other dude, the one who booked me, went into, I think, building theme bars in Dubai. The whole thing left a sour taste in my mouth and I unsurprisingly wasn't booked to play at 360 again.

I was driven back to the airport, said subdued goodbyes to my host who apologised for missing the party, but he was so pissed he'd got sick and couldn't really remember much about it to be honest Harold, sorry mate. I flew back home with a growing sense of anti-climax, although, it has to be said, £1000 richer, so I could hardly complain.

Around 2010ish another avenue opened up. I was interviewed over the phone by a DJ for his radio show. Once the interview was over, we continued chatting and he began hinting at something, but I couldn't quite get what he wanted. "Would you be up for, you know, a bit of engineering, helping me out with some tunes?" he asked. I thought he meant helping him mix and master his productions. After a long and awkward conversation, it turned out that actually meant: would I record some music to specification and then sell it to him for him to put out under his own name? "I can't be doing with learning all that Cubase Logic stuff," he told me, "it's really hard, I've not got the time."

This is called ghostwriting – when you sell your composition for a flat fee and the buyer puts it out as their own. On the one hand, this is everything that is wrong with the music industry today, everything that has gone wrong with the precious scene that I've loved for so long. People who can't be bothered to even learn how to make a tune they just want to put a few out to see if they can get some DJ gigs out of it. Where's the shame? How can this be ok? On the other hand, he appeared to be offering £300 per track. I hadn't made £300 a track for a few years. By this time, I had a young son to support. I thought about it and then agreed to the deal.

I was straight with him from the start, I told him I thought it unlikely that he'd make back his investment in sales or streaming revenue, and that DJ gigs didn't automatically follow a few releases.

After about a year and a half, we agreed to drop the price to £150 as he was beginning to see or rather not see the fruit of our labours. It was good money for work I enjoyed and if at the same time I was a terrible hypocrite then so be it. Hypocrites have got to eat too. I had bags of underground kudos but kudos doesn't pay the rent. Try it, see what your landlord says.

In the second half of the 2000s, I put out some of my best productions and played some of my favourite gigs at London parties like Asad's Reverberations, Paul Soul and Christian Vargas's Sizzle parties in Brixton, lovely Liz Edwards' and Rochester's Kerfuffle party and DJ Jane Fitz let me play in the bar at her Peg party. Asad released an original of mine on his Reverberations label, featuring what is probably the best bassline I ever programmed. I did loads of tunes and remixes for UK house label Lost My Dog and worked with Miami's Dutchie Recordings, who by the end of the 2000s were pretty much alone in the entire music business in giving me an advance from time to time. Juan who ran Dutchie was never in it for the money anyway though, he just loved house music. Another middle-aged soldiering DJ, forever in love with the 4/4 beat.

Although rapidly growing, tech house was still a very intimate scene and if you played in London there would often be a bunch of other DJs and producers you knew in attendance. I played at the Secret Garden in South London, one of those rare bookings of mine that is free of self-doubt: this was definitely a great gig, I even have the emails from attendees to prove it.

A wide-eyed stranger approached me after I got off. "What time are you on?" he said, simultaneously rubbing his hands together and shuffling his feet. "Just finished. I was DJing for the last three hours. You were on the dance floor in front of the booth for the last 90 minutes. We shook hands several times." "Awesome," he replied, nodding his head vigorously. "Awesome. And what time are you on?"

I got booked to DJ at a festival in the Yorkshire Dales, which was described as a 'summer chill-out party with a boutique festival vibe' but which was more like someone had bought a load of broken tents, filled them with bits of sound systems and added a couple of battered burger vans into the mix. The flyer very clearly stated that there were several reasonably well-known DJs and artists playing on the main stage. Not many materialised, although I think I saw Mix-Master Morris in his silver tracksuit at one point. I still have the flyer and apparently, a pre-fame Calvin Harris was booked to play too, although I suppose it could be someone else with the same name. The 'main stage' was a filthy old rust-ridden flatbed truck with a phenomenally loud and lung-threateningly pungent generator so at least they'd delivered on that.

I wasn't going to be playing on the main stage in the evening as planned, I was now going to be playing in the afternoon in one of the 'satellite arenas'. Which turned out to be one of those large white marquees with windows that they use for catering weddings. I eyed up the rig in my 'arena', and began doing calculations in my head of exactly which part of the gaffer-taped and exposed-wires set-up was going to electrocute me first and in which direction I would likely be thrown.

The sound system had been set up uniquely, in that the main speakers had been placed facing the decks as monitors and the much smaller monitor speakers had been positioned as though they were the main system. How we laughed as we attempted to reposition them whilst negotiating the slippery boards that had been dotted about the muddy floor, in a kind of shit Crystal Maze DJ challenge.

So: bright daylight and no lighting rig, with a mixture of greasy boards or quagmire underfoot. Sound rig is a health and safety nightmare held together with tape and chewing gum, there's a tiny crowd of hippies sitting in a peace-circle drinking cider and smoking hash and a white girl doing a spiritual interpretive dance by herself. And I've not even started playing any music yet.

My couple of hours on the decks went very much as you would expect a poorly-attended DJ set in a windy wedding tent to go.

Slowly. Halfway through, the hippies became more wide-eyed and enthusiastic as their drugs kicked in. It could almost have been a beautiful moment in our crappy tent, but they spent ten minutes excitedly asking for psy-trance records I didn't have and then left en masse, dreads flailing in the late afternoon wind. I remember handing over to the next superstar guest DJ, whose facial expression I guess, must have been an exact mirror image of my own.

He began to mix his tune in, in an utterly pointless attempt at 'keeping the vibe going', when it was clear to all five of us in attendance that the vibe had never even visited this field, let alone our tent; we weren't even on the vibes' sat nav at this point. Then no doubt struck by the sheer futility of it all, he gave up and artlessly slammed the crossfader across to an entirely uncaring, near-empty, musty old wedding tent.

As the light faded things seemed to be descending. Hardly anyone who was billed to play was actually there and many were leaving already. Those that stayed were a hardcore of saucer-eyed, outsidey hedonists, already too spangled to leave and doomed to stay in the festival-that-never-was for the rest of the night. Soon all who were left had accepted their fate and there was a rapid decline into a full-on substance debauch from seemingly every punter, with an ever-increasing general gurn level.

There was a sense in the various tents that anyone was being let on the decks. There were growing rumours among the remaining artists and DJs that no one was getting paid. I had negotiated a small fee. The promoter was apparently still on site, but clearly he was making huge losses, had given up any sense of responsibility and the whole thing was plunging into chaos.

I heard that his mask was slipping, revealing the desperate chancer beneath, that he had lost it, gone native even. It wasn't quite like 'Apocalypse Now', that would be an exaggeration, but there was a definite sense of impending doom. People began to light wind-beaten fires while I searched for a promoter who didn't want to be found, who was dressed in jeans and trainers, in a dark field full of zombies and hippies also dressed in jeans and trainers.

In what was the single positive event of the day, I eventually found him, standing by himself quietly gazing across the vista unfolding before him. We had a fantastically restrained English conversation, with him insisting that there was no money and how he wouldn't be able to pay me anything and me calmly and rationally explaining how there must be some money and at least bung us a few sheets for petrol. I remember him and I looking out at the carnage that had been his festival dream. A light drizzle had started. Someone was playing very fast psychedelic trance, someone else had started beating a bongo drum, just perfectly out of time with the trance. With the forlorn sigh of a man who has given up, he silently handed me a few crumpled notes. For a second I considered giving him them back, or half back, then I pocketed the lot and left him to it.

I drove straight from this monstrosity of a booking down to London to play at a tiny festival that was beset by technical problems, overcrowding and bad, bad toilet smells. Stayed up the entire weekend, razzed the car, missed our mates' wedding, ruined my new Adidas Stan Smiths, lost my fucking headphones again, burned through way more sheets than I earned, spent the following week on a vicious comedown. The glamour of the DJing life.

You search for the music, haunting record shops and online stores, devouring charts and playlists. You buy the tunes, you spend hours putting together mixes, you post them online, you send out promos, you push and cajole and hustle.

You tell people that you're a DJ. You have to explain awkwardly at family gatherings what it is you do to blank-faced uncomprehending relatives. Young nephews and nieces will see you and mime holding headphones to one ear whilst rewinding a piece of vinyl without really knowing what they're doing. You get gigs in local pubs and clubs. You're playing in room three at 10 pm. You put on your own parties, you play wherever you can, along with countless other no-name DJs. You play at your mate's house parties, your sister's birthday, you agree to play awful warm-ups, your perfectly worked out set bouncing around a completely empty room.

You get booked for gigs that never happen. You travel to warehouses that are being busted as your cab pulls up. You play a squat party where someone spills their warm Red Stripe on your mixer and your mate's records get nicked. You learn how to ask promoters for your fee. And how to have a discussion about all the reasons why they don't have your fee.

You follow your favourite DJs, attend your favourite club nights. Listen to their mixes over and over again, CDs or tapes on repeat on Sunday comedowns. You play them in the car, obsessing over how the DJ manages their transitions and their tune selection, replaying your favourite sections, trying to explain to your partner why it's so good. You improve, you work hard, you get better. Your parties are going well, you're getting a decent local rep, you get offered some warm-ups. Festivals, bars, clubs. Keep on posting those mixes, keep on promoting your night and your tunes, chasing the DJ feedback, network network network.

You make a tacit agreement to sell your soul, just a very slight, low-level transaction, more of a temporary-soul-rental arrangement than full-on sale. You start to get offers, you're more than ready to handle it. Finally, some decent gigs. Gigs at nice venues, with quality gear and well kitted out DJ booths. With a nice hotel and flights all paid for. It's irresistible. And how, when you get offered all this, could you not try your very hardest to be the very best DJ you could be?

Every week, me and countless other travelling DJs went off to work in clubs, raves and festivals. We would get flown to our destination, be met at the airport by the promoter or the promoter's mate, put up for a night or two in a hotel, taken out for dinner and furnished with whatever hospitality was available. We would travel to far off cities where people thought we were special enough to pay to come to their country. This is the DJing I had dreamed of, where I could play exactly what I wanted, and where the club would be full of music fans, people who were really into what I did. And in return for the flight, hotel, wages, hospitality and low-level adulation, you go to work.

You stand in a DJ booth in a club or on a stage, delivering a set of upfront dance music to clued-up clubbers. You have a rack of decent equipment in front of you, a pair or even a bunch of Pioneer CDJs, Technics 1200s or 1210s vinyl decks and a mixer packed with effects. You've been doing this long enough that unfamiliar equipment doesn't throw up any surprises anymore. You're expected to know your way around the gear and to be able to cope if there are problems, to at least be able to perform some kind of basic technical troubleshooting. You should know not to redline and how to deal with an earth hum.

Your role is clear. You have to supply a killer soundtrack, the audio excitement for the night. There's no room for half-hearted performances or 'off' nights. There might be a couple of hundred or a couple of thousand paying clubbers here and certainly, if you were gigging in some parts of Eastern Europe in the early 2000s, you might well be getting paid more than some of the punters will earn in a month for a few hours work. Every track, every mix has to count.

You keep up to date with new music, with releases and remixes from your favourite artists and labels, as well as reviewing new producers' work too. DJs still playing vinyl visit the few remaining record shops, where the staff keep a bag of new releases behind the counter for them to go through. You become a regular at the Post Office, picking up vinyl. You wonder idly about where to put up the next inevitably needed shelf for the tide of records which is slowly encroaching on your room.

You endlessly trawl product in the online shops, shifting through the countless new releases. You get sent tens of email promos every day and you set aside a time every week to plough through the sound-a-like, throwaway fodder to find the gems, the unique, the quality and the ones that might get played for a few months.

You pass on going down the pub with your mates and spend your Saturdays hunting for records and your evenings mixing your new tunes together. You are secretly pleased when people cancel plans at the last moment so you can get on the decks and record a mix. You obsessively listen back to your mixtapes, play them to your mates, play them in the car. You do the best 90-minute mix you've ever done in your entire DJing career, at home in your bedroom and then realise that you forgot to press record.

You build up a collection of music, become an expert in your particular field. You learn about the music you play, where it comes from and who makes it. You learn individual tracks inside out, what happens in them and you have a database of hundreds of arrangements in your head. You know where the parts are that you can use to transition to another track, and which tunes are really difficult to mix.

You can accurately log BPMs by ear and identify your favourite artists by the sound of their snare or hand claps. You start to understand that almost intangible thing that makes a record capable of creating special moments on a dance floor. You understand the importance of context to your craft. Your technical ability grows, as does your experience and you become more confident. You are well able to deliver the goods, to turn up and rock a party, big or small, full or half-empty, in any city in the world. You arrive fuzzy from the flight with a bag full of brilliant music that you can barely wait to share. This is DJing.

I LOST A BUNCH OF MUSIC FROM THE LATE 2000S BUT DEFINITELY REMEMBER PLAYING THESE

Daniel Kyo – Droid EP
Nick Dare – Dub People (Burnski Open House Remix)
Fred Everything Thing & JT Donaldson – Here Come The Beats
Asad Rizvi featuring Lauren Kitara – Apathy
Shur I Kan – Gripper
Johnny Dangerous – Clear My Mind (Aki Bergman Remix)
Mood II Swing Presents Lem Featuring Tara J – Reach 4 U (Mood II Swing Dub)
Matthew Bandy – Derty Werk (Asad Rizvi's Reverb Rerub)
Jimpster – Dangly Panther
Stimming – Kleine Nachtmusik
Terry Lee Brown Jnr. – Softpack
Ross Couch – Way Of The Samurai EP
DJ Disciple – Deep Underground
YSE - Bounceback
Fernando Fuentes aka Cue- Feels Good
Fred Everything featuring Lisa Shaw – Here I Am (Shur I Kan Remix)
Milton Jackson – Randoms
Inland Knights – Back Chat
Coles And Coker – Sweat Bomb
Yankee Zulu – Bullfrog

16

ENERGY FLASH

Brighton, 2011, about half-past midnight. We're at Riki Tik's, a long thin dark town-centre venue that goes way further back than you'd expect from its tiny facade. I'm on the decks. This is the launch party for my second album 'Family Affair' on UK label Lost My Dog (LMD). I am positively humming with bonhomie and well being, if ever so slightly unsteady on my feet.

I focus my vision squarely on the lights flashing in front of me on the mixer and decks. Such pretty colours, the reds, greens, blues and oranges, all so friendly and beguiling... Need to do something though: mix the next tune in. From somewhere, my semi-automatic suite of DJ skills have been ticking over in the background whilst I have been entranced with the lights and I seem to have already selected the next song. Get in the mix. I reflect as I slowly bring up the volume of the new track whilst simultaneously gradually reducing the bass on the other, the fresh layers of percussion causing the dance floor to whoop with delight, that I really love DJing.

There's a photo of me at this gig, I'm wearing a white t-shirt with a big question mark on it; by 2011 90% of famous DJs in the world dressed resolutely in black T-shirts. There was something about the black t-shirt as a fashion choice, it was the ultimate play-it-safe option. It's dull, conservative and fitted in perfectly with the larger world of dance music's then trajectory.

Something called EDM was happening, something that became as ubiquitous and as numbingly dull as the black T-shirts all DJs wore. To be frank, EDM baffled us. Electronic Dance Music. Doesn't even make sense. Aren't all the other electronic dance music genres Electronic Dance Music? A cultural signifier of the greater cultural stupidity that was unfurling. A weird bastardisation of club culture rising up like a dumb, grinning, gurning black-T-shirted Colossus, bestriding clubs, festivals and then stadiums. "Make some motherfucking noise," it exhorted us. "When's the drop?" it memed.

Just a few years previously DJs often played records whilst collecting glasses and wiping tables at venues. Whilst me and my mates had been scuttling around basements, room twos and raves at weekends, the larger world of DJing had lost touch with reality. DJs were on altars, being worshipped by thousands of people, as though they were rock stars. And then some of them were actually rock stars as famous people began to get DJ bookings simply based on their celebrity rather than any DJing ability.

EDM rose in tandem with the growing ubiquity of social media, and so the excesses were amplified and distilled, as were our reactions to it. EDM's attempt to rebrand the DJ as a dance music rock star was a part of US entertainment corporations attempts to get hold of some of these dance music dollars they'd heard so much about. Repackaging the whole thing in a structure that already exists, that they understood, DJs were marketed like rock stars, raves were rebranded as festivals and became hives of high production values and corporate sponsorship.

We railed against the music, awful bosh electronic noise, filled with endless drops, breaks and rises, stapled onto 16 bars of pristinely produced sub-nursery rhyme level synth riffs before another breakdown. EDM seemed to be entirely composed of surface sheen and it was relentless, there was no let-up in its continual sense assault. EDM music seemed to exist in a state of constant panic that if it let the dial drop below ten for even a moment then its attention-weak audience would lose interest.

With EDM came the growth in pre-programmed DJ sets, where the DJ selects all the music beforehand, then records it mixed together and 'mimes' DJing – this actually happened. People actually did that. You had to have stuff pre-recorded so that it synced correctly with the pyrotechnics, which again, just shows how utterly backwards and wrong the whole thing was. If a DJ ever had any value at all beyond owning lots of great music, it was in their ability to respond to their audience. This was the literal opposite.

What's notable of course is that the whole 'PLUR' ('Peace, Love, Unity & Respect') movement which sprung up among the young EDM raver community was remarkably similar to the vaguely idealistic, tolerant hedonism of the original acid house crew. It's almost as though there's some kind of instinctive urge to get together, to share, to participate and create, and it crops up at even the most commercialised, unexpected moments.

However, that's where the similarities pretty much ended and anyway, in our old age, we seemed to be slightly less accepting than we had been 20 or 30 years ago, mainly because we couldn't see past just how embarrassing their DJs were. Real, actual DJs cringed whenever a grinning black T-shirted EDMer appeared on TV and pretended to tweak a control on the mixer. If nothing else, it gave us something to collectively rail against whilst refining our online profiles.

Riki Tiks in Brighton was a long, long way from stadium EDM. This Lost My Dog album launch was the week following my Dubai date. I'm DJing with someone else's headphones, as I left my headphones plugged into the mixer in the United Arab Emirates (AGAIN). A girl is leaning into the booth, asking me about something called a Flo-Rida. She spells it out for me: "F-L-O-R-I-D-A – it's like Florida, but it's two words, you must have it." Predictably, I don't.

LMD released some of my best stuff, and I did some of my favourite remixes for them too. I was genuinely sad when they folded in

2015. After a good ten years in the biz, their shutting down was a clear signifier for me. In 2015 I found myself in the slightly odd position of working for LMD and writing copy for their tenth anniversary/retirement release which included tracks and remixes from me.

I felt strangely sentimental about LMD's retirement. When I'd first started working with them, I still felt like my career was on the up. I was about to sign my first album, I'd been to Miami, getting good feedback, good offers and so on. But now a decade had passed and I'd barely scraped a living from DJing and production and had taken dead-end jobs to concentrate on trying to 'make it'. I'd released a lot of music and remixes, played some decent gigs, got better at doing what I did, and I was nowhere nearer my vague ill-defined goal to 'make a living from DJing and production' than I was ten years ago. Meanwhile, in the years since my first release in 2001, the music industry had undergone such change that it seemed no one in my circle of DJs, producers and labels really had a handle on it at all yet.

I'd worked with LMD for years, for most of the time they'd been around. They were some of the most stand-up guys in the industry, paid what they said they would when they said they would, had their shit wired tight, stuck to the thing they were good at, put out a couple of classics. I still play their release 'Bounceback' by YSE, a timeless slice of UK deep house. Seek it out if you're a DJ, it's a very good tune, I think I even played it at the launch party.

Running an underground house record label was becoming a luxury few could afford. There was little point in A&Ring, mastering, producing artwork, promo-ing to DJs then promoting through the label's socials if you only sell a few copies or pick up a few pennies from streaming, it's unsustainable. Many labels realised that despite success and industry recognition, kudos wasn't enough, the endeavour was financially unsustainable unless they were prepared to do it purely 'for the love' and so they simply stopped.

My LMD album wasn't really a full artist album, it was a collection of my best singles and remixes that I'd done for the label over the years, together with a few new tracks. I was proud of it though, it's a decent record of my music. Another little achievement for me, something to file away in the win column, to be secretly pleased with, quietly proud of. I still appeared to be doing well at the time, the music press still reviewed my stuff, not as much as they used to, but the album got nice little write-ups here and there.

My tiny critical success was, of course, dwarfed, fairied, pixied even, by the EDM behemoths. DJs had become deities on plinths to be cheered, affection for the person who bought a bag of tunes to the party had become twisted into hero worship. It was reflected in the content and character of electronic EDM music, which became more bombastic and simplistic, even as production values constantly increased, making this empty vessel more fizzy, shiny, and massive than ever before. Smashing you in the face, screaming in your ear when you should put your arms in the air, when you should cheer and when you should dance.

Rave by numbers, not even by numbers, rave by three simple steps, just three single states with no deviations: the breakdown state where you all cheer like it's space-armageddon, the drop state when the kick and bass come back in and briefly re-energise the crowd, then the rest of it, when everyone stands around either vaguely swaying or on their phones.

It's easy to rail against EDM, and forget that countless kids actually really loved PLUR and the synced pyrotechnic EDM shows. For some of them, it was a route into more underground scenes, the kind of scenes that could pass my music-snob-test. But it's easy to rail against it because it was a cultural bed-shitting of epic proportions. Having invented house, techno and hip hop, the US seemingly decided to take a massive turd on their beautiful, life-changing, epoch-defining cultural creations and create EDM. Parts of Europe really ran with it too, don't think we didn't notice, Sweden and Holland.

Take a few simple elements of dance music, exaggerate them, distil them, to the exclusion of any subtlety, charm, sophistication or complexity. Bleach it white, straighten it out so it floats free of its Black and gay roots and replace the soul and the funk with bombast, surface sheen, glitter, shine and faux epic-ness. And above everything else, centralise the break, the build-up and the drop. The music stops, then ever-so-slowly it builds inexorably back up to a peak, a climax, frantically trying to generate tension where there is none – how can there be tension when you all know exactly what is going to happen next?

As though the yawning creative gap at the heart of this music could somehow be filled with a huge, coldly-calculated two-minute breakdown in the middle. The drop and build technique had been stretched out, exaggerated, centralised, became a standard EDM practice, perfect to document with Instagram, with ever more hysterical synth risers, ever crazier increasing intense hyper builds, until it eventually, inevitably became a sad worn-out trope, empty of all power and meaning, all in the space of a few years.

In the early 70s, pioneering DJs like Francis Grasso and Kool DJ Herc were discovering the power of breaks – that part in the record where the music drops out leaving only the beat which instantly, inexplicably always makes dancers dance harder – and using them to create a whole new sonic world. Now in 2011 that power was being weaponised into a technique of audio crowd-manipulation, to stave off the inevitable boredom that resulted from watching a plastic DJ on a huge festival stage.

Meanwhile, I continued to create music, do remixes, hustle for gigs and work a few days at the university each week because, well, because that's what I did. I tried to branch out. I attempted to make music for commercials and TV. I joined some agencies and composed a load of library music that no one ever used. I gave a few DJ lessons and considered other options.

I had a substantial back catalogue, including several vocal tracks that would lend themselves to a live band approach. Why don't I just put together a band of talented musicians to play my stuff and get work playing festivals. Easy! Everyone says that all the money that musicians no longer make from sales, they can make from gigs. Everyone actually used to say that. So that was my next plan, and so began the sorry tale of Double HQ. Double HQ was the name given to my second band, my first being the short-lived but probably better art college band Purple Kevin twenty-five odd years previously.

But Double HQ was a commercial plan, not an artistic endeavour and this approach wasn't really where my heart was at so, therefore, looking back, it's easy to see that it was doomed to fail from the start. The plan was I would recruit musicians. All they had to do is learn the simple chords and arrangements for a few of my tracks. I'll play most of it from my computer, they play bass, drums and sing alongside my electronic trickery. I'll stand behind my laptop, perhaps wearing a leather jacket, pretending to play the keys, triggering sound FX and doing filter sweeps. We will be The Harold Heath Quartet, for there are four of us, so-called because Harold Heath is an old-sounding name and I had an idea for a photo session where we were going to be all dressed up in 1920s gear, photographed in sepia accompanied by a pair of gramophones and some archaic recording equipment. Each member was going to perform in a variation on Edwardian dress. I shortened the name to Double HQ for no reason other than I thought the words sounded cool together.

I would arrange a gig where we would perform our songs, we'd film it and use the footage together with my extensive back catalogue to market ourselves to the festival circuit, where we would be sure to command serious fees. We would fill the gig with our mates so that it looked like we were popular. I thought of myself as a Machiavellian house music puppet master, carefully pulling the strings in the background, using my young band of eager talent and the tiny amount of industry kudos I had at my disposal into convincing the larger festival circuit into booking a low-level house producer as a live act. I bought a leather jacket to wear on stage: I had a plan.

I recruited musicians from the local music college in Brighton. An eager drummer, who was well kitted out with equipment including a practice booth in his home, and who could do lots of cool fills, but who didn't seem able to actually learn the songs. We practised for months and months and he was never able to work out a way to know where he was in the song. Instead, I ended up the night before the gig, recording lengthy commentaries for him to listen to on headphones during the performance, with a metronome and me speaking instructions: "...there is a break in four bars, four, three, two,...", "...the chorus is approaching in eight bars..." like some kind of musical sat nav.

We planned to go abroad, to Europe and the US as soon as possible, although he had neglected to mention his recent spell in prison for drug offences, which might have hindered our plans for US domination.

The bass player was an old man in a young man's body, with memorably broad legs and he was generally unhappy about something. The first singer was nice but then got throat nodules, so we got a second singer who was also nice and also super-focused on success, a quality I greatly admired.

We hired rehearsal rooms in Brighton and endlessly ran through three-minute edits of a handful of my vocal tracks. The drummer still could never work out where we were in the song. The singer did ok. The bass player wanted to do a bass solo in some of the songs. We practised, thought about what we should wear on stage. I had a leather jacket, so I was golden. They played along to my synths, samples and programmed loops, I fiddled a bit with the keyboard doing the occasional tweak of the resonance knob. We practised and practised but weirdly, never really got any better. Making a band sound good was an entirely new area to me, one I'm afraid to say I didn't excel at.

We booked the seaside Concorde venue in Brighton for our promo gig. I wondered how the drummer was going to play if he didn't know where he was in the song. I wondered if it was really a good idea to give the broad-legged bass player a solo in one of the songs. I wondered if the singer's head down, legs akimbo, single finger pointing to the sky pose that happened at the end of every song was really the kind of thing I wanted.

The night of the gig came round. We got all of our mates down. Sound-checked on the main Concorde system. Set up the cameras. Set up a feed from the mixing desk. I checked and doubled checked all connections, I gaffer taped things, took off my leather jacket cos I was getting hot. Did a second soundcheck. Checked the recording levels, checked the cameras again, checkity-check. People arrived. We sat out back and smoked and thought about the gig. I checked some more stuff.

Someone, can't remember who I got to do it, announced us and we bounded on stage like eager puppies, to play the easiest gig and in fact the only gig we'd ever play. We ran through the set, made a few mistakes but got through it. It was fun. I had put my leather jacket on again, like a rock star, and I jumped around behind a keyboard like all the best dance music artists have done throughout the history of dance music. The band mostly held it together, although the bass player had elected to use an effects pedal he'd never used before for some reason and this seemed to spook the drummer who stopped playing and gesticulated at his headphones meaningfully mid-song at a couple of points. My friends were kind and cheered anyway.

The recording was poor quality. The singer was capable, finger-pointing pose or not, but she'd not had a great night. The monitoring wasn't as good as it could be and she was really unhappy with how she sounded. Didn't blame her, the recording wasn't kind. I edited it to the best of my ability, got it down to a nice little length showcasing our best moments. I then spent a few weeks punting Double HQ. I remember having a nice chat with someone running a classy little festival up north, the kind that I could see us playing at. He opened up the video link I'd sent him while we were on the phone and watched it while we chatted. He said that he'd liked some of my Harold Heath releases over the years and that I seemed nice. He also said that we weren't very good and the video wasn't very good and that we were unlikely to get any work from it. He was right, it wasn't and we didn't.

Double HQ later met in a pub to have a final argument about the money we were never going to earn before we went our separate ways. I couldn't get through to the singer so had to leave a final voice mail telling her I was finishing the band, which felt like a shit way to end things, as well as faintly ridiculous, at my age, to be ending a band via voicemail but she either didn't or couldn't answer her phone.

I had built a website and recorded us, trying to incorporate bits of their playing into remixes and dub mixes of Double HQ material. I'd spent a few hours each week in hot smelly rehearsal rooms, as had they, trying to get them to just play along with my stuff, but there was clearly something wrong in my leadership style, it hadn't worked: some essential thing that I couldn't even define, let alone develop or work on or buy or supply was missing.

I was exhausted by the whole thing. During rehearsals, I'd taken to sitting on a stool. Sometimes I would go out for a moment just to sit and rest somewhere comfortable, pretending I was going to the toilet. I was disheartened by the affair and in particular, my inability to control other humans and bend them exactly to my will, which it turns out isn't as easy as it sounds.

Perhaps playing music, wearing a leather jacket and having a singer who could point really well just wasn't enough of a show. Stadium EDM had redefined how dance music was presented, introducing pyrotechnics, glitter cannons and face-melting light shows. All synced up perfectly in time with the pre-programmed music, just in case anyone hadn't worked out where the breaks and builds were, it was spelt out for them in hyper-neon blindingly illuminated metaphorical letters, ten thousand feet high, on fire, in space: here's the drop, here's the build. And here's the heart-hands.

EDM was the logical result of one of the many skirmishes between commerce and art that have constantly used dance music as their battleground. If there were a metaphorical noose, it would begin to tighten at this point in our story, if there were shackles, they would begin to rust solid; tightening, restraining, containing and limiting DJ culture. EDM and its surrounding whizz-bang world represented a reduction of potential, the limiting of possibilities.

New lines were drawn about what was expected from DJs and what wasn't. The injection of finance into dance music that drove EDM redefined dance music into a shallow, surface-only copy of what it could be, tricking a generation into thinking that standing at an event and filming a DJ was a cool thing to do. The primary DJ skills – selection, empathy and communication – were simply erased in the rave new world of EDM. And in their place, EDM offered bombast, songs programmed to soundtrack Instagram moments and all the glitter, smoke and 'show' elements you could handle.

But of course, this didn't happen in isolation, culture isn't simply foisted upon us, we react and interact with it, reject it or accept it, we're all involved in a constant cultural conversation, a to-and-fro. EDM didn't prevent artists, DJs and producers from continuing to release stunning electronic music and generally pushing forward into the future with the authentic ethos of acid house. It's not like quality dance music culture was simply killed by EDM.

However, it was still bewildering to see EDM unfold internationally and the idea of the DJ become so removed from what we thought it was. Even if in the greater scheme of things EDM eventually grew so far away from actual clubland as to be an irrelevance, it left a scar. It left a mark on the culture, on the expectations of what audiences thought a DJ was and should do, and how they thought an audience should act as well.

Dance music's collective revulsion at EDM was simply a sign of just how life-affecting acid house and it's ensuing cultural changes had been, and how much it still meant to all of us. We felt as though there was some kind of spiritual battle to be won, that we had to defend everything DJing stood for. It turns out that we didn't win the battle or the war, but that the enemy, having trained a generation to expect a DJ to 'perform' and rinsed our scene for filthy lucre, simply sat back and continued to let the money flow in.

Maybe there's never an end to this war; maybe we should think of it as an ongoing campaign to maintain authenticity, a fight that may never end but one that's worth fighting anyway.

I was DJing in Brighton regularly around this time as well as picking up a smattering of European gigs. I had been befriended by a local promoter, DJ and producer Will Sumsuch. Sumsuch was a bit younger than me, way keener, terribly enthusiastic, and most of all, he still really 'meant it'. He adopted me to come and help him conquer Brighton's nightlife, which seemed like a great idea.

Sumsuch still felt that there was a future in running record labels, putting on club nights, creating remix packages, and most of all, at the heart of every creative decision he made, that quality would win out, no matter what. From the outset, our approach to the whole endeavour was entirely different from each other and his dedication and belief began to bring my own growing ambiguity more clearly into focus.

We'd bonded over the various industry war wounds we'd picked up over the years and used to joyously recount tales of the worst rip-offs we'd experienced, who was an utter nightmare when she was behind the mic in the studio and who didn't actually make their own records.

We were DJing each week at Riki Tiks in Brighton, so we made one Saturday night my album launch party. I invited all my Brighton crew and they all turned up, as well a few faces from the tech house scene. I was on form, DJing-wise and had a great gig. Went outside to steal a cigarette off someone having given up smoking when my son Jake was born but still desirous of a few post-gig puffs when drunk. Got lost in a chat-hole for a bit, and by the time I had returned most people had left. I was exhausted and felt unwell, so limped away from my own, virtually empty launch party before the end, a move I was not particularly proud of.

Next day, I thanked everyone who came down last night as was customary on Facebook. What it really meant was "Hey everyone, I'm launching an album and I want you to buy it so here's my album launch party, aren't I great". Someone replied to say that they'd turned up late and I'd already left, and thus the whole fragile artifice of 'Thanks everyone who came down last night' simply fell apart.

But Sumsuch still believed. He was very keen to continue our night, to brand it and give it a concept, come up with a name that tied it all together, all things that I was less concerned with. I was concerned with how we might get people to come to it. He was too but thought that a concept and cool name combo would be the way to do it. I thought he was wrong but had no answer to the promoter's eternal question: how to get people to come to your night?

Truthfully, the real answer is to be young and have lots of mates, as hopefully a bunch of them will turn up and they'll bring their mates too. That's how we did it 20 years previously, and it worked brilliantly well. And at this level, away from actual nightclubs, this is how many legendary club nights began, a bunch of mates and their mates getting together for some nocturnal subversion in the backroom of a pub or bar.

Here was the challenge for the middle-aged DJ. Firstly, I no longer have large amounts of casual friends that I hang out with at the student union bar and nearby pubs instead of going to lectures. Secondly, the much smaller-than-20-years-ago group of friends that I do have, are likely to go out clubbing two or three times a year as a special occasion as they have jobs and families and are in their forties. Therefore, the business model that previously worked so well simply doesn't exist for the middle-aged DJ. Also, Harold Heath isn't really a draw; he might draw maybe ten people out in Brighton, on a good night. But that's not enough is it, even in a tiny place like Riki Tiks.

Sumsuch didn't care about any of this, he just believed. The promotional material he wrote spoke of a "music-led genuine alternative" for Brighton, as though ensuring that the music was really good in a

UK city-centre venue would guarantee people would come to your event. It wasn't 1991 anymore. I admired Sumsuch's belief and commitment but was too jaded to share it.

My concerns were borne out by the low numbers who came to our house night, no matter how much beautiful music we were playing. These were very different DJ gigs to when you're paid to be the headliner. We had a fragile deal with the bar manager, fragile in that it was based purely on numbers. Get enough bodies in and you can play your tunes, if numbers drop there's plenty of other DJs who reckon they can fill it on a Saturday night. In these kinds of situations, the bar manager really doesn't care what you play, and probably again, isn't really fussed as to how exclusive the music you play may be. He just wants to sell beer and spirits, so all he needs from the DJs is that they bring their mates, or do enough promo to attract enough bodies. That's all. There's no other element to the relationship. And this is of course very different to being booked to play a specific niche of music for a particular club night.

We struggled to keep the room filled most evenings. We all called in favours with mates, acquaintances and Brighton faces, encouraging them to come and help us build something. There was no door charge; people stopped in on their way somewhere else. Sometimes we'd create a vibe and get a tissue-thin hold on the dance floor, but it was such a small venue that it only took a few people to leave or go and have a fag for it to look empty. and eventually, they'd all drift off. We got a few low key guests in, ran a few ads, made some flyers, put some posters up, made promotional mixes and promoted the nights on social media.

This is the slog of promoting in a medium-sized town. I was lucky to have Sumsuch and local DJ hero Danny Fantana as partners, this kind of stuff was a lot more fun when shared. Playing to a single, pissed-up couple who aren't so much dancing as holding each other up as they stagger around the dance floor is way more bearable when you've got a mate in the booth with you.

Standing behind the decks, considering my next completely irrelevant tune selection, I think back to better gigs, when the collective warmth of the crowd created so much heat that condensation fell from the ceiling like disco rain, and when every tune just killed it. Then look around the room again, the beats echoing off the walls and floor back at me.

Three pissed blokes have joined the dance floor. They laugh as they do 'funny' dancing. I sigh, wonder what the fuck to put on next. Four girls join the funny men and do normal dancing which instantly makes the men cease their comedy moves. Three new people have appeared at the edge of the dance floor, nodding in low key appreciation, not quite ready to commit, but open-minded. A group of, I'm guessing from the look of them, comic shop workers arrive, dispatch a couple of lower status nerds to the bar and the rest hit the dance floor. A small handful of people have returned from smoking, a couple of other people wander breezily into the growing throng. Fantana and I look at each other in disbelief as another shit night in Brighton briefly becomes more fun.

I pick a tune, something big, something to reward a room of people who don't really care if we play them deep house, tech house, progressive house or whatever really, they just want to have a dance with their mates. I've got a few re-edits of disco tunes with me that I can weave in with a couple of disco filter cut-ups, with maybe one or two 'classics' thrown in, and I can trick them into dancing to some proper underground deep house without them even realising it. Before you know it I've got another tasty little set of tunes coalescing in my head, and with a bit of luck, I'll keep these fuckers here till closing time.

And here goes DJing again, the contrary craft that it is, just when you're pissed off with aching legs, tired ears and two drunk bored punters on your dance floor, suddenly there's a little spark of audio excitement and human communion, and you can whip it up into a private sonic firestorm, just you and a handful of people who fancy losing it in the dark for the next couple of hours.

17

LAST RHYTHM

"Are you sure you're alright to play?"

"Of coursh imma right t'play. Fucksake like. Imtoallyfine."

DJ Name Removed is alright to play. We've booked him for one of our Brighton parties. He's turned up in a T-shirt with his own name emblazoned on it – red flag right away – and then proceeded to get utterly pissed. Then about an hour ago his bird-like wingman Glenn gave him some drugs "to perk him up like" but whatever he's taken has made his speech even more slurred and his movements even slower. He's now lumbering around the club like an oiled disco sloth, seemingly unaware of what's going on around him. He's got a feather boa from somewhere and his shoelaces are undone. Later he'll lose one shoe entirely. At one point he seemed to be having a low-key chat with his reflection.

"OK, well if you're sure you're alright, then you're up: get on the decks."

"I'm fucken brilliant like. Toa'ly ruckin ready. To'aly."

He doggedly heads off in the direction of the bar. I steer him back in the opposite direction to the DJ booth and place his headphones in his pudgy, clammy hands. He looks at them like a dog that's been asked to do a crossword but then seems to snap out of it, successfully plugging them into the mixer. He looks like he's going to make it, so I foolishly slope off to the bar where before I've ordered my drink the music stops and the jeering starts. With a heavy sigh I wonder will I find him asleep?

Unconscious? But no, I find him in the booth, fully awake and fast heading into the angry/surly stage of his intoxication, having turned off the music to argue with the woman who wanted her feather boa back.

DJ Name Removed eventually capitulated and returned her boa before commencing on a truly awful set where he played the same tune twice on two separate occasions, fudged most of his mixes, plunged the room into silence once and generally did absolutely every fucking thing fucking wrong. We kicked him off early and I honestly don't think he even noticed. On the following Monday he posted 'big shout going out to the Brighton massive who came down for my gig on Saturday' on his Facebook, as though he had experienced an entirely different evening from the rest of us.

We had met him and booked him via Facebook. Social media seemed to offer an answer to the challenges of promoting house nights and indeed of the difficulties of marketing your music too; you could easily contact any DJ or producer you wanted and there was an audience you could, in theory, sell to if you knew how to 'engage' them, thus sustaining your career. Although the exact details of how you translated engagement into a living remained hazy.

I was a late adopter of the mobile phone, and likewise social media, but I succumbed eventually. Unwillingly at first, until I noticed how good those little likes and shares felt, then I bought into the whole thing. If this was how you had to promote your 'brand' to get more DJ gigs then so be it. I announced online when I was playing, shared links to my latest remix and posted mixes. It showed that I was still a working DJ, credible, and worthy of booking.

And so was born the contemporary tropes of DJ social media content, a modern tragedy in itself, as those not particularly blessed with charm, charisma or wit attempted to appear charming, charismatic and witty online. DJs began posting their chart placings, as though anyone except their mums cared: "Blessed to be at #27 on the Beatport Melodic Underground Deep Tech House Chart!" At some point, a DJ decided to announce that they had 'big things coming', whilst neglecting to inform their 'fans' what that thing might be and other DJs seemed to think this was a great marketing and promotion tool too. Indeed, many DJs began to use the term 'fan' to describe someone whose sum contact with them had often amounted to nothing more than clicking 'like'.

People began to refer to the corner of their bedroom that contained a rickety desk, pair of monitors and a laptop as their 'studio', and then simply as 'the lab'. If a lonely intern had, in the course of their weekend downloading several hundred promos, left the world's emptiest compliment – "downloading for Richie Hawtin" – on a release, it was magically re-spun in the press release into "Big support from heavy hitters including Richie Hawtin".

Most of all, every Sunday there was a stream of "Thanks to everyone who came down last night" posts from DJs who had warmed up from eight till nine at their local wine bar. This became the new normal: DJs and producers presenting an image of themselves as successful, working, sustaining a career in the music industry. I did it too, even as it gradually became less and less true. I chose to promote it as true anyway.

Most of my wages now came from my job at the university in Brighton. Sales of my music earned tiny amounts of money. Gigs were the only reliable source of music industry income and there were lots more DJs than ever before and therefore way fewer gigs to go round. DJs tended not to post about their actual jobs in the councils' regeneration team or as sales manager for their town's second-biggest tile retail outlet; they posted about parties, remixes and releases.

Instagram arrived in 2010, a photo site in which to promote our audio culture. A perfect match for a dance music industry turned upside down. DJs and producers like me all began to slowly create a vast online hall of smoke and mirrors where we led parallel lives within our virtual, functioning underground house music industry. In fact, most of us were scrabbling around, working several jobs, watching music sales steadily fall month on month, playing fewer gigs. And still, after all the extraordinarily clear writing on the wall, we were still plugging away, making tunes, doing mixtapes and hustling for gigs, because… because… I found it hard to answer why anymore.

I still loved DJing and production with a passion that wasn't matched by anything else in my life. Being born without the sport gene, I didn't have a football team to follow, I didn't like any sport really, or cars, or motorbikes or walking holidays. I hadn't started running marathons or learning about craft beers or doing any of the things other men seemed to like. I didn't care too much for anything really, except my wife, my boy and my music.

Meanwhile, my beloved tech house had undergone a metamorphosis. It had begun as an underground movement based on eclecticism which placed a high value on the musical knowledge and selection skills of the DJ. By the time I started to release music in 2001, it was no longer a scene created from DJ selections; now producers made records that were specifically tech house. Over the next decade and a half, the genre slowly but surely grew in stature, gaining confidence, eventually expanding to fill every space in clubland that it could.

Like every genre, as the tech house sound became more popular, it was inevitably compromised, simplified and then codified. Certain stylistic quirks like the highly polished percussion, that Chicago 'bmm-tsst-bmm-tsst' rhythm and breakdowns featuring white noise were emphasised and then exaggerated whilst other more nuanced features were dropped. The sound became more accessible and less idiosyncratic. It stopped surprising or beguiling and instead simply delivered the very specific goods.

Tech house had evolved into the genre of choice for DJs who worked in 'big rooms'. People talked about 'big room' tech house, and they meant really simple, obvious tracks that worked on a huge, mixed demographic, the type of tune that might work in a massive nightclub in Ibiza. The definition of what tech house actually was, and could be, shrunk, its boundaries tightened, a prodigious irony bearing in mind the free programming choices of the pioneering DJs that created the whole genre in the first place. By 2016 there were articles in the dance music press entitled 'Why Tech House Just Needs To Fuck Off'.

But there was still plenty of support for the UK tech house scene across Europe and in the early 2010s. I was still getting infrequent but decent overseas gigs. They tended to be organised by a certain breed of promoter, the kind of person who puts on a party because if they don't, there won't be a party. They create magic where there was none, purely out of expediency and force of personality. Often these promoters were deceptively easy-going and laid back, but with an underlying rock-solid unswerving dedication to making the party happen. The DJs get all the props, most of the glory and a nice pay-cheque; the promoters though, who put up the money, take all the risks and make it happen for everyone else, they're as essential to the whole endeavour as any record spinner.

I was flown to Athens to play a couple of times by Lee and Adreas, a gentle pair of house-loving souls who were trying out club promotion. The night of the first gig Lee was robbed on the street, her bag snatched by a motorcyclist. Then we discovered at the last minute that the venue was flooded and we had to move the party. We had a superb night, I DJed for hours on end, really digging in. Annie had come along for the ride and got so pissed on European spirit measures that she lost her shoes and we had to carry her home.

Last minute cancellations tend to happen more at the lower end of the DJ market. I was once booked to play a party but when we arrived the police had already shut it down, citing licence infringements, council regulations, incorrect building usage, smiling on a Saturday, the whole lot. There were lots of folk milling around in confusion outside, all casting long shadows on the hot tarmac from the lights of the police vehicles; but Andre who was promoting ("We make party, ya?!") decided we could relocate to his mate's city centre bar.

So we got what seemed like a long succession of cabs and lifts-from-friends to a dark, cosy city centre bar with a tasty little sound system. Andre got into a heated conversation with someone then beckoned me over and introduced me to the DJ who played here every Saturday night who wasn't at all impressed with the idea of me taking over. I could see his point, but a bunch of folk from the original venue had made it here, and I felt obliged to deliver seeing as I was being paid to be here. DJ man grudgingly said I could do an hour or so.

He was clearly pissed off though and did something to the amp behind me as I'm mixing in my first tune; maybe he turned off some of the speakers or turned the master down, I'm not sure, but it's suddenly hard to hear what I'm playing over the chat of the punters and before I've barely registered what's happened, he's in the wind. A group of punters came up to the decks to complain to me at length about both the volume and the style of my music. There's some low level jostling – nothing heavy, just young bucks flexing their muscles – but things were getting away from me a little. Andre was nowhere to be seen so I figured if I could just get the music volume back up, maybe everyone would chill.

Instead, a fight breaks out, security comes over and start throwing out anyone in the decks area, and they gently but firmly remove me from the building sans headphones as well. Just for once, I thought, I'd like to be kicked onto the decks.

Andre the promoter has already been chucked out too and is beside himself, assuming that with my connections and level of fame I'll have him blackballed from tech house for ever more bless him, as if I'd blame him and as if anyone would care what I said about anything. But that's the nature of being the guest DJ, there's always this sense that if I'm here, if they've paid for me, that I must therefore be famous, influential. Whereas in fact I'm not, and it would take a lot more than a few tech house gigs a year for me to have any sway or influence, anywhere.

Anyway, we both have a sense that we've had enough of this bullshit for one evening. A determination descended upon us both; it was a hot night, we were still young – well he was – and we were fully charged, ready to go. Andre starts swearing quietly, then more loudly. "Motherfucking shit! Bastard sons of whores!" and, one he got off me: "Cunting fuck!"

And then with the confidence of someone who really wanted to put on a party and has had quite a lot of drugs, Andre put his hands on my shoulders and looked deep into my eyes. He stared deep into my soul, his jaw unable to keep still, a fine layer of perspiration on his forehead. "Harold – we will go to the one place they'll never expect us to go – we're going back – we make party, ya?!" He'd hit upon the idea of going back to the original venue – which was closed by the police for being unsafe and inappropriate and indiscreet and all those things just two hours ago. We're going back because the party has to continue, has to happen.

The thing is, Andre's planning on driving us, and fired up as I am, I'm still aware enough to wonder if he's really able to drive. "Are you sure you're good to drive Andre?" I ask as he buckles himself into the passenger seat. He assures me he is but wants me to direct him out as he's in a tight spot. "I don't think you're OK to drive Andre, you're in the passenger seat." He got out of the car, walked around and got in the driver's side. "I'm fine to drive Harold, let's go." "No you're not, give me the keys". He had a hint of mania in his wide, wide eyes: "We're going back Harold – we're going back!" He puts the car into reverse, looks over his shoulder and hits the accelerator at which point both he and I very quickly find out he's actually in first gear as he drives straight into the car parked in front.

We didn't make it back. But best of all, Andre blagged us back into the bar, the resident DJ was nowhere to be found so I just got back on the decks, with the volume now mysteriously back at full pelt and we did indeed make party, ya?

Back in reality, the music industry no longer made sense: the kids paid a monthly fee to huge corporations so they could steal music from their favourite artists. DJs had become awful faux-rock stars, thousands of people stood in rows looking at them instead of dancing together to their music. In the face of a reality where the old certainties had fallen away, producers and DJs like me retreated online and constructed a virtual fiction instead, an online successful dance music world, one that was reassuring in its simplicity. And once we created it, we started to believe it. We neglected what was actually happening offline and instead began to live online, where we were still seen as successful, and we internalised any online approval as success, even if it was the approval from strangers in a constructed reality. We created a simplified, cartoon sketch of ourselves and we looked out through its eyes, seeing a simplified, cartoon sketch of the world.

Those ten years when social media really consolidated its hold over us, between say 2005 and 2015, although feel free to have your own arbitrary decade distinctions if you wish, for those ten years, we closed our eyes. Many of our banks were corrupt, major corporations avoided tax, everyone's personal information was stolen, but no one was prosecuted. We retreated to the warm glow of the internet even as it started to reduce us.

Social media didn't save my career although it did help me get some more gigs, remixes and releases, including my one and only gig in France, not at a club but in an Airbnb basement. Journeying home through the Monday morning rush hour to catch the Eurostar via the Paris metro system, carrying a heavy record box and a bag, I was sweating profusely, puffing my way through an alien, albeit stylishly dressed Parisian underground, attempting to decipher the unfamiliar metro map on no sleep; I became evermore confused.

One particular concourse was absolutely packed. I intended to politely push my way through the enormous crowd saying, as you would in England, "Excuse me, thank you, excuse me, thank you". Now my grasp of the French language is pretty loose, but I know how to say "Pardon moi, merci". However, in my fried state, I didn't say this once. What I actually said to every French commuter as I moistly pushed past them was, for some reason "Bonjour, bonjour, au revoir, au revoir". So imagine if you will, a similar situation in London, perhaps Charing Cross station at Monday 8 am. There's a sweating, confused French DJ, laden down with his luggage which he keeps dropping, pushing his way through the crowd of commuters and in a thick French accent, he keeps saying "Hello, hello, goodbye, goodbye, Oh, hello, hello, goodbye goodbye..."

This might be the period in my musical career of which I'm most proud, the tunes I released worked on the dance floor and I was happy with lots of them, proud of some of them. I would get great DJ feedback from DJs I idolised but they didn't sell well, and a music career as an underground house producer and DJ was becoming an ever less likely venture, particularly at my lowly level.

I was dismayed to hear from colleagues around the world that I wasn't alone in this; it was disheartening to realise that there really was no comeback. Income from downloads or streams took over and physical releases became rarer and rarer. The potential income for the artist was substantially less and we all felt it. For a few years, I had been able to ask for £300 advance for a remix. This fell to £200, £150, £100, then people stopped offering advances and offered 50/50 profit splits.

I had almost always provided two remixes – a main mix and a dub mix – to justify my standard fee of three hundred pounds. It was easy as I inevitably piled too many ideas into the main mix and could just cut out a few of them at the end to create a dub. But as the income continued falling I quietly stopped providing people with an unasked for dub.

I could see that a certain number of gigs a year would constitute a living, but every week more DJs arrived, eager to get on the decks, to fill in if anyone took a night off. Every week, more and more of them, everywhere, self-professed vinyl-junkies, sudden obsessive converts to the DJing cause, fresh-faced, newly arrived, ready to rock the party. And plenty of them seemed happy to break the golden rule: they'd play for free. The fact that people would now offer to DJ for no money just showed how twisted peoples' idea of what DJing was had become.

DJ gigs for me, when they came, came via social media, DJ agencies and word of mouth. I still bought lots of music; although aware that I could get it for free I paid for it, downloaded it, burnt it to

CD, drew a spiral or an eye or an otter or a spaceship on the CD so I could identify it, and took fat CD wallets out to gigs with me.

A few years later in 2017, Snake Eyes booked me to play at a gig in London before DJ Bill Brewster, a very well-respected DJ of whom I was something of a fan. I got there and took over from the young DJ who was on before me, who did a cartoon double-take at my battered old CD wallets then catching himself said "CDs, like, I totally respect that", as though I was some old relic from the past, a curio from DJ days gone by.

I had made a very slow move from vinyl to digital DJing. Civilians won't understand, you weren't there man, but us DJs, we lived through the format wars and we bore the scars. You had to learn a whole new set of justifications for your particular chosen format, and there was an entirely new suite of digital DJing mistakes to make. I did a great one on a live radio show, accidentally pressing the play/stop button on the tune that was playing without realising. Doing this makes the tune replay a split second loop over and over like it has got stuck. I stared in mute incomprehension at the CDJ and its many controls, listening to a single momentary sliver of audio looping, wondering what I'd done and what I could do to fix it before the radio host rushed over and hit play again.

Digital DJing was also the facilitator of the pre-mixed DJ set, which enabled your average plastic DJ to mime their way through a gig. The realisation that this was starting to happen, in retrospect, feels like a turning point for DJing, although perhaps it was just another step in an unavoidable trajectory.

I never got to DJ in Ibiza, Chicago or Berlin, either miming or for realsies; no one ever asked and I didn't really know how to make myself more successful than I already was. It was Eastern Europe and the UK tech house scene that tended to book me. Proper underground audiences, proper sound systems, serious business, always the same, always different. The same shock as the heat and volume hit you when you first enter, that initial disorientation from the lack of light and the sheer volume, coupled with a tightening in the stomach. Then the acclimatisation and settling in to play your beloved tunes, your collection you've painstakingly curated, the one thing that you've been really good at, collecting tunes, finding the very best music.

Then you get to play them to the faithful, and for a few hours get completely out of yourself. It was such a fun thing to do, such an exciting world to be involved in. It wasn't really glamorous. The floors were sticky, the people really high or drunk or both, the venues often down-at-heel, the wages sometimes better than others, and occasionally club owners or promoters did decidedly uncool things. But it did have a certain charm of its own, a unique attraction. It was illicit, sometimes debauched; hot, hilarious, extreme, it was everything that being young and running around in a disco was all about. Essentially I just wanted to be at Gary's Disco in the youth club in Bury St Edmunds for the rest of my life.

The thrill of being up when everyone else, idiots that they were, were wasting their lives asleep. Only we in our exclusive clique, our undercover private gang, only we knew of these secret rites, clandestine celebrations: our thing. Where the music would be overpowering, and where we could dance for so long that there was no way we could go to work the next day. We opposed the dominant ideology of the ruling classes without even knowing it. We were anti-work, dedicated hedonists, and because we realised the importance of our hedonism, we worked at it. It meant a lot to us. It did that thing that academics and social scientists say, it gave us meaning. It meant something.

Night people, night places, there's just something inherently intoxicating about the nocturnal world. Arriving in the dark when everyone else around is safely tucked up in bed asleep. But not us. We descend into the basement, where it's too hot, too loud, and where the night people are having another party.

I make my way to the decks, put my tunes down, look around, think about what I'm going to play next and feel that familiar mix of nerves and excitement. There really is nothing like it.

18

CAN YOU PARTY?

I had just turned five years old in July 1976 when Tavares spent eleven weeks on the UK chart with 'Heaven Must Be Missing An Angel', peaking at #4. I have no recollection of ever hearing it on the radio or seeing Tavares on the TV but I do remember singing it all through the long hot summer. I had realised that when I hummed it to myself it made me feel good, providing a brief power boost meaning I could run faster – running is very important when you're five – as though the 4/4 drum beat and the soaring disco strings imparted to me a minor set of superpowers.

When you're a little kid, the peak of excitement in your day is often something like when you get on your bike and ride it really fast, or you go up to the top of the road to run down as fast as you can. I used to 'rev' my pushbike, by spinning the pedals a couple of times before I set off. I had a long-standing deal with fate. If I successfully spun the pedals fast twice in a row, then I would definitely be able to ride faster. Likewise, by simply forming my hands into blades when running, I could run way faster than the unthinking masses who were my peers, still foolishly clenching their hands into little fists whenever they ran. And with Tavares, I had discovered that playing a soundtrack in your mind also had a similar effect: you simply play a good song in your head and you can fly.

I also realised that you could wear a song out and that the power of a song was finite: you could hear it too much and get tired of it and it would lose its hold over you. I distinctly remember hyping myself up in the changing rooms before swimming by singing Tavares and then cautioning myself not to overdo it, in case it became stale and lost its power. I held it back, in my memory, like a rare treat to be savoured, instinctively understanding that the thrill of a fresh, exciting new piece of music might not last and therefore had to be deployed carefully. For as long as I can remember, I have been holding back the biggest tunes for later in the DJ set in my head.

DJing and I were clearly well suited; we had got along just fine for years. But as with any relationship, eventually we hit some hard times. By the time LMD closed in 2015, a few years after my second album was released, my world had shrunk. Now I was in my early 40s, a house producer whose records sold tiny amounts, whose DJ gigs had steadily dwindled. Worse than all that though, I'd developed something that was eventually diagnosed as Chronic Fatigue Syndrome.

It took me so insidiously that I'd barely noticed it creep up on me. I ignored the onset for years. I began to feel more tired. I drank coffee to wake up and ate fast food to save time. I drove to gigs, stayed up late, then drove home. I woke up too early in the mornings and instantly set about making more tunes. My legs began to ache at the end of the day.

I had started DJing for Snake Eyes again God bless him, he was running a lovely bar in East London and gave me Saturday nights for a few months. It was a bar gig, but a bar with a decent sound and a big space for dancing. I played what I wanted, lots of funk and soul, disco, house and all sorts, in many ways the ideal gig. With lots of time to play with, I would revisit my music collection each week, resurrecting things I'd not played for years. It can be occasionally disconcerting, to pull out an old record, experience that same familiar musty smell and a small note of recognition at the cover you've not looked at for 12 years; then to play it and for the sound to trigger memories long forgotten.

I first heard Cloud One 'Disco Juice', the strangely time-signatured underground disco classic at a party in maybe 1989 and then never heard it again till DJ Nick The Record kindly included it on a compilation in the 90s.[8] I dropped the needle on the vinyl and from the very first second I was immediately transported back in time to an aircraft hanger somewhere in East Anglia a decade earlier. A huge rush of lost memories burst up into my consciousness in parallel with a powerful yearning for something wonderful but long gone.

At Snake's latest venue I'd replaced a DJ and saxophonist double act, and most evenings someone would ask when the sax player was going to come on. I would play tunes for six or seven hours. One early morning travelling back to Brighton, my vision went fuzzy. I had vertigo and the room was spinning, even though I wasn't in a room. More pressingly, I had the worst pain I'd ever experienced in my life, concentrated into a cold, hard sphere, slightly less than a centimetre in diameter, above my left eyebrow. Some homeless people and a couple of police paused their conversation to impassively watch as I was violently sick in the street. I picked up my record bags and carried on into Victoria Station to wait for the first train. I was sick all the way home. Unfortunately, there was no toilet on the train, so I threw up in a number of different bins.

The next day I felt better, so thought it best to ignore it and carry on as before. It happened again a few weeks later. It started to happen more often, perhaps once a month I would have an aggressively violent migraine and a night of alternately shivering and sweating nausea. My legs ached after standing up and DJing for hours on end. I began taking more hot baths to soothe them. Then they began to ache whenever I stood up. I went for massages, looked into vitamins and supplements. Then they started to ache all the time. I went to the doctor who suggested I was tired.

8 It has one extra beat in it, which means, music nerds, that if you try to clap along with the snare, eventually you'll find yourself one beat out.

DJ gigs, when they happened at all, were more difficult. I put it down to old age. One day I was running for a train and I fell over. I was always in a hurry, always trying to fit as much in a day as possible, forever working out schedules where I could wring maximum value out of every available second. I looked back at the perfectly smooth concourse, baffled by the lack of anything that could have tripped me up. My legs had simply given way because they were so tired. Someone helped me onto the train. I had fallen heavily, ripped my jeans and my knee was bleeding embarrassingly copiously. It was another warning sign that I studiously ignored. I was too busy, man, really didn't have time to pay any attention to the many, in hindsight, very clear signs that a problem was developing.

I began a gradual process of slowing down. I could do slightly less every day. I could last for slightly less time each day. Tasks began to grow in size as my ability to do them diminished. It began to take me longer to get places. I had been a fast walker all my life but over a couple of years I slowed down to a tiny-paced old man shuffle. It took ages to walk up the hill to my house. One day I had to stop and rest halfway, watching people zoom past me. Then I stopped walking up the hill at all and got the bus. The idea of just quickly going anywhere, just to pick up some milk or go to the post office began to fade and everywhere slowly moved further away from me.

My world got slower, quieter, parts shut down, temporarily unavailable, then things slipped into a period of stasis. My legs ached constantly. I was tired and irritable. Annie and I began planning, even for simple trips, to account for my inability to carry out normal tasks at a normal pace. We argued because I was bad-tempered, because I was tired and my legs hurt. I was constantly angry at myself for not being able to fit as many things in a day that I wanted to. I felt scuttled, stymied, thwarted, frustrated. One day Annie suggested that I might be ill.

I went to a doctor who took samples and tested them and then referred me to the hospital, who also took samples and tested them too. The tests eliminated the big scary illnesses and left me with the non-diagnosis of Chronic Fatigue Syndrome. A cover-all term that they give to anyone who complains of tiredness, fatigue, aches, headaches etc. and who can't be diagnosed with anything else. In one way, it's a great diagnosis as it means you've not got anything life-threatening. The flip side is that there's no scientific agreement on the causes, symptoms, treatment or cure of CFS.

They signed me up for a CFS support group. My legs hurt. The support group was on the other side of town and was a huge effort to get to. Quiet, broken, ill people gathered together in a sterile, dimly lit community centre to share how tired they were. I walked places very slowly, head bowed, hood up, taking tiny little steps. CFS, or sometimes they called it ME: Miserable Exhaustion, ho ho.

If it sounds like the first half of the second decade of the 21st century was dark for me, then that's really not the case. These were years full of love and light. Annie and I had a beautiful young son who was terribly good fun, and which also meant that I got to play Lego and watch cartoons a lot, something I thought was just wonderful. I looked on with disbelief as every day I fell in love with him more; he truly was the bringer of joy.

I was married to a most excellent wife, we lived by the seaside, I got to make music for at least some of the week, and I was occasionally flown to play music for lovely people. I was a very lucky man. However, they were also years that I remember as grey, foggy and slow, with small horizons, low expectations, and of constantly aching. Frustration mixed with embarrassment at my failing abilities. Unsure of whether I should tell people about it, I retreated and quietly fumed.

Everything was murky, dim, low temperature. I could never seem to get warm enough. I felt like I was made out of that muddy grey-brown Plasticine you get when all the colours have been mixed up. If I lent against anything, it felt as though it would leave a mark in my flesh, that my body could no longer spring back into shape, but would yield to all outside influences. I despaired at my inability to do tasks and worried that my wife would become tired of my tiredness, tired of me. She never did, not for one second, through the very worst of it.

The cold winter skies that could be overcast for weeks felt somehow heavy, clay-like; the low temperature slowed me down, as though it took the very last of my scarce energies by osmosis. Everything felt weightier, duller, like walking through deep, freezing mud. I sought out quiet, low stimulation, low stress. Beige inertia. I wanted a comfortable seat, warmth, muted light. My aspirations shrunk. The occasional gig offers required careful consideration. Annie and I would plan with close attention the journey, working out how I could travel back, how soon I could rest, weighing up the wages with the price I would pay the following week. DJing tired me out. My legs ached.

Strategies to cope and to enable me to continue to function were enacted. I kept a yoga matt and a cushion under a stairwell at the university where I worked part-time and would sneak off for a nap once or twice a day. I continued to produce music and it provided a safe harbour, somewhere where I still felt like myself. But I was not really able to get out and promote it.

I tried to learn how to pace myself. It turned out that for my entire life I had been fabulously impatient without ever really being aware of it. I had rushed through my days with the unconscious assumption that most people were just weirdly slow and it would be great if they could just step aside cos I'm coming through, got things to do. I was that person behind you in the queue, tutting if you delayed for a millisecond. I was in a hurry, all the time, every day and every night.

I had packed as much into every moment as I could. I was obsessed with time, with making every moment count, not allowing myself to rest or recuperate. Consequently, I was often late, or stressed or in a hurry, as I was unrealistic about what I could actually fit in, in a single day. It gradually became clear to me that in fact, everyone else in the world wasn't slow and stupid: I had just always been in a hurry.

I was still getting occasional European DJ bookings and for a while was unable to accept the gulf between what I wanted to achieve and what I was actually physically capable of. So I accepted gigs that I perhaps wasn't really fit for and my brilliant wife would send me off with migraine pills, protein bars and a carefully worked out route to a city in another country, precision planned to minimise physical impact.

As ever, the gigs themselves, those precious moments when you deliver the beloved goods to the faithful, were fun-filled, over-stimulated adventures; house music all night long was our mantra, for life. Those few hours when you're playing your tunes, you really do forget about your own frail, physicality, but the corresponding post-gig fall-out became worse, perhaps as a pay-off for the few hours of adrenaline-fuelled freedom from pain and fatigue.

There was also the associated after-party shenanigans, with the constant expectation that a visiting DJ would be a party-animal, raconteur and all-round good-vibe merchant. I wanted to be those things but by this point what I wanted more post-gig was a hot bath and to somehow relieve the continual aches. Instead, here goes another sun-lit session of drugged up people stumbling around to my music in happy abandon, seemingly indestructible house music acolytes who would contentedly keep going for as long as I would. It was what I had always wanted: for people to want to dance to the music I was playing. It was a shame that it was beginning to hurt so much.

I would watch them sometimes from behind the decks, all those wonderful disco people, still dancing, still laughing, secretly envious of their staying power and stamina – such stamina! I wanted that, but my staying power had left. Instead, stubbornness held me up through those overlong weekends.

I was floating around the edges of a very big DJ sea, lacking the energy to swim any further, barely staying afloat. There seemed to be more DJs every day, as though they were being churned out by a factory production line, and none of us older DJs seemed to be retiring. This was the context in which my illness and my reserved, reticent personality collided, at a point in my career when networking and the general socialising post-gig were becoming ever more important.

Slowly all these elements coalesced into the slow-tail off of my DJ career. I felt a sneaking suspicion after some gigs that my giving up and going to bed before the requisite 48-hour sesh had reached its end somehow reflected badly on me. DJs were meant to be unstoppable groove machines with huge personalities, always up for a party, always ready to go, a welcoming receptacle for alcohol and substances, just wind them up and watch them go.

Promoters or resident DJs would, more often than not, offer drugs. I would, more often than not, take at least some of the drugs. Ever wary of my own rules on the subject, of the need to stay sober enough to steer the ship but stimulated enough to see it safely to harbour the next day, walking the line between necessity and indulgence, drug use became purely functional as my health worsened. The quality of substances varied wildly across Europe. I wouldn't really like to know what obscure adulterants I've consumed over the course of my DJing career. But it was always to the same end; to enable me to continue to be DJ Harold Heath, for just a few more hours.

A basement club, Sofia, Bulgaria, the walls painted matt black, exposed pipework along the ceilings. Who-knows-when o'clock. Everybody's temperature is rising. The smoke machine appears not to have an off switch. Grinding my teeth, bitter taste at the back of my throat. I'm playing my first tune, peak time, apprehensive and excited. An air of anticipation, those early set nerves, settling into my groove. It's so familiar now, yet I never tire of it, the thrill of playing my house music over a hefty system to bacchanalian warriors of the deep.

A moment later and I'm gently chewing on the insides of my cheek. Relax my face, take a deep breath. Slight tingles down my arms into my fingertips. Love this monitor setup, sounds solid up here. I'm not in a booth, I'm on a stage, but there are enough monitors and sound system equipment stacked around me for it to feel suitably cubby-like. Stop chewing your cheek. It's a four-hour stretch. Plenty of time for DJ indulgence, to play five US garage dubs in a row, each one sparser than the last, cutting between the beats at high speed until the room is locked into nothing more than a kick drum and a hi-hat. House music all night long.

Although the recall of entire nights can be disjointed, I often remember the moments when I played particular tunes, and this night was the first time I played Asad's monumental vocal tune 'Slippery Heights' – his original, not my weak remix – to a full club. It felt like we were all levitating. These are the past moments I treasure the most, just a clear, unsentimental memory: a room full of joy and beautiful music.

My headphones are damp with sweat, there's a line of half-empty bottles and glasses piling up in front of the decks. There's a club full of paying punters in front of me and with a few musical nudges, we can temporarily halt reality and embark on a journey of fantasy, joy and profane worship, providing I get my shit together. Grind, flex, relax. I focus in on the job, listening intently to the tune in the headphones, lining up the beats then getting in the mix, forgetting about everything except the sound and the mixer in front of me.

Transitioning between the two tunes, creating a new, fleeting musical moment, holding onto the two volume sliders and smiling out into the darkness, all concerns in my head and outside this room simply recede into the night. It doesn't matter anymore, nothing matters, except the next record, and then the next record. When I was DJing in the nightclubs and wine bars of mid-90s South London, all that mattered was the next record. When Gary's Disco was at its height in the late 70s, all that mattered was the next record. The next record was all that ever mattered.

After a long weekend, then come the hugs, long goodbyes, stretched out farewell conversations, a last drink, a toast, an exit that takes 45 minutes. I take a cab to the airport, alone again, low-level radio in a language I don't understand, the smooth motion of the car calming, soothing. The unfamiliar streets contribute to a sense of sleepless unreality. Images shift, seeming to change as they move out of sight, the edges of my vision are fuzzy. I need to rest, but have to get through customs and onto the plane first; numb to the procedures and questions, head down, following whoever is in front of me until I'm finally in my seat next to the window. The engine on the wing appears worryingly rickety. The flight attendant is about 14-years-old, has three haircuts and once the main door is shut, gives the handle a little tug, like he's checking a car door he's just locked.

A nauseous, claustrophobic flight, the airport journey, stairs, corridors, suitcases on wheels, standing in slow moving queues, struggling home via trains, buses and cabs. Singly focused on the bed waiting for me at the end of the trip, in Brighton on the south coast of the UK, which we flew over on the way back and I could see clearly from the plane in the dawn light. Heading back down from London, over the Thames again, realising it's somehow Monday morning rush hour and I'm surrounded by clean, pressed commuters, all of whom can smell me. The odour of nightclubs; the smoke machine, stale cigarettes, alcohol-on-the-turn, rogue perfume, nocturnal debris. Eau du Debauchery.

Back home, it's silent, my wife at work, my son at school. Everything looks, feels and smells familiar. No more surprises here, back to normality. It seems extraordinarily quiet. There are letters on the doormat; someone left the milk out this morning. Day to day life ticks over whether my weekends are spent playing records to 500 people in a club, or building Lego spaceships with Jake.

Later that year Colin Dale's DJ agency got me a tasty booking in Prague, but my flight details changed at the last moment, meaning I would need to be at Gatwick for 4 am. I briefly ummed and ahhed, concerned that I would just be too tired. I worriedly called Colin to back out of the gig but he calmly talked me down and it all went ahead. I got to the flight just fine, had a great gig, and the following day got gently drunk in a cosy bar while the snow fell softly outside. However, it had become clear that I was in the wrong job. DJs really need to be OK with long hours, early flights, late nights and so on.

You can't really be a DJ if you can't take late nights.

19

BREAK OF DAWN

Late summer 2001, East London. I'm behind the decks in another backroom of another pub, which we've hired for Frostie's birthday. Another slightly iffy sound system, another slight surfeit of eager DJs and another audience of friends, friends-of-friends, acquaintances and who-are-theys. But this time, there's something different and in hindsight, this DJ gig took on great significance. In fact, it might be the most important DJ gig I ever played.

A punter comes up to the decks. In DJ world, this is the classic opener to around half of all DJ anecdotes; it's like 'A priest, a rabbi and a minister walk into a bar'. A short man with thinning curls, rosy cheeks, big glasses and an even skim of perspiration comes up to the decks to shout at me that I'm essentially playing his record collection. That's what he bellows, two inches from my face, his eyes bloodshot, his breath ripe. "Mate, you're essentially playing my record collection."

"Awesome!" I shout back and give him a brief thumbs-up, which seems to satisfy him. There were a few potential smart-arse responses that had queued up in my mind but I've got other things to deal with. I'm on edge. My future wife is on the dance floor in front of me with her then-partner. We have spoken only once, that fateful time at Jimbo's birthday drink-up, when I instantly fell in love with her, and this is the first time I've seen her since then. I feel like a teenager. A couple of hours ago getting ready, I changed my shirt way too many times before finally deciding on this awful shirt that only a complete idiot would ever wear. Play it cool Harold.

Summer 2001 was just before I asked Annie to come and work for me in Docklands, just before I signed my first records to Stickman, a long and eventful summer. Dave Glasses comes back up to the decks and goes into further detail regarding his theory that, judging by the music I've been playing this evening, he and I have similar record collections.

I'm trying to be polite to DG, but I have no room in my head for his continued development of the 'we've got similar records' theme, as I'm trying to think of what tune selection I could make that could simultaneously keep this fragile little dance floor going, whilst stopping my future-wife-but-then-virtual-stranger Annie and her now-ex-then-actual-boyfriend from dancing together. I choose 'God Made Me Funky' by Headhunters, an epic extended 70s funk jam which develops into some far-out jazztastic atonal soloing. I think it worked. I like to think of it as the most important selection of my life; a few years later Annie and I were married, at what was easily the best wedding I've ever been to.

I didn't trust anyone else to make a good enough job of wedding DJ, so I meticulously programmed, mixed and pre-recorded the music for the entire day, from the pre-kick-off hanging-around section, to the song we sang during the ceremony and then through the rest of the reception and party into the night. Brilliantly, a local promoter – Magnus, remember Club Magnus earlier in the book? – turned up for a drink or two and flyered my wedding reception for an event THAT NIGHT, as though my extended family of Irish aunties would be interested in a techno bash on the seafront.

I love that people still tell me my wedding had the best music of any wedding, (although I bet they say that to all the DJs they know who get married). DJing and music had been there at every juncture of my life, a constant presence. And I kept returning to it, beyond when that was a sensible decision. I loved this DJ life, even as it inexorably slipped away from me.

Being ill definitely affected my DJing more than my production career. If your legs are really tired and aching, you can still produce a tune at home from a chair, even if you feel awful and luckily I still felt able to create. And although I do seem to be locked in an eternal love/hate relationship with my own productions, there's plenty of Harold Heath tunes from the 'Sick & Tired Years' that I still like. However the income from releasing music fell with every release; DJ gigs, which you were offered because you continued to release cool music, was where the money was at. I was producing music that enough people thought was cool enough to offer me DJ gigs but was becoming too unwell to play them.

I was still hungry, I've always been hungry, but now I was like a hungry man in a dark, unfamiliar kitchen: I had to move very slowly and carefully. I was increasingly unable to sustain the constant promotion, mixtapes, promo feedback, gig announcements, 'Thanks for coming down last night' statuses, chart returns, and all the peripheral administrative stuff that a working DJ needs to stay on top of. In my compromised state, the stress surrounding DJ bookings, the travel, the missed sleep, the exhaustion, all began to outweigh the benefits.

I didn't want to stand up for long enough to play a decent gig anymore, ridiculous as it sounds, not unless I was airlifted to and from the club. After-parties had become physically torturous, the aches in my legs constantly gnawing away at my attention and sucking out the last of my tiny energy reserves. When I got tired my cognitive abilities were severely compromised too, decisions became difficult, my emotions were muted, damped down, or they would race to the other extreme and rational responses to situations sometimes seemed out of reach.

But another big factor in the slow wind-down of my DJ career was that Harold Heath had peaked. My musical moment in the sun, when my releases were regularly reviewed in Mixmag or DJ Mag had ended. My tunes still got good feedback from DJs but generated little in the way of meaningful sales or streams. Fresh, new, more interesting artists had appeared.

Established producers who had been my peers had either overtaken me or dropped out. I had plateaued. And if you're in the music industry, you have to keep going up, you can't simply plateau. If you're not always going up, then the fact of your peers going up beside you makes you look as though you're going down, even if you're actually just stationary. In dance music, you only get to be a new artist for a while; now I was an established artist with a dwindling fanbase, who couldn't get out and earn from DJing. This was a far from an ideal situation to find oneself in.

I went through weeks where every time I sat down in my studio I came away pleased, then other periods where I worried that I had run out of ideas. Some of the EPs I released were great; some weren't. I got to remix some of my favourite artists during this period and was generally pleased with the results but there were more prosaic matters to consider. If I wasn't getting DJ gigs from making music, and my income from sales of my music was constantly shrinking, how could I justify carrying on spending so much time on a pursuit that generated such little income, when I had a young son and a hard-working wife? I couldn't.

It was hardly a perfect storm of events that ended my DJ career, more a moderate light wind, a temperate north easterly breeze made up of my failing health and falling income from production, in a music industry that had way too many DJs and no use for another medium-to-good house DJ/producer.

Eventually, my health issues meant I had to slow down. I tried eating better. I took vitamin supplements, ensured my meals were balanced, increased my intake of green leafy vegetables, drank more water, ate less processed food. I got a new bed, made sure my bedroom was dark, banned digital devices from bedtime, made an effort to get a proper night's sleep.

I began exercising regularly, ever so gently, so slowly at first. I decided to get strong again. I did a push-up. The next day I did two, the following day three. Then I stalled for a week. Eventually, and it took months and months, I could do 50 push-ups. The recovery was as slow and insidious as the onset. And I never really recovered, not back to my previous levels of activity, but that's the point really, my previous levels of activity were unsustainable, that's why I became ill.

The improved diet, better sleep, graduated exercise, vitamins, careful resting, managing my energy levels – as I write it down, I'd forgotten how tedious it all was – it eventually started to have positive effects. I feel that my world has slowly re-grown again, and the idea of heading across town no longer fills me with dread. I have had to continually reappraise my ideas of how far things in Brighton are from each other and am pleasantly surprised at my ability to walk to places that previously seemed impossible for me to ever get to on foot.

Even so, my illness, whatever it was, there's still a shadow of it hovering around in the background, a faint hum just at the edge of consciousness. An awareness of my vulnerability and of the vast difference between then and now, between being young and indestructible and the inevitable limits of age. Each Halloween, Annie and I look back to when I was unable to do twenty minutes of trick or treating with her and the boy before heading home to rest my aches and pains, and we can see the progress I've made.

But it took a few years and pretty much neatly tied up the end of my DJing career. Making a comeback was never really going to be an option. It's hard enough to maintain regular gigs when you're at the top of your game, but when you're a few years out, recovering from CFS, and you were hardly a major star anyway, you have to be realistic. Also, I'm aware of the sad truth that the DJ lifestyle was clearly a factor in my becoming ill, and to go chasing after a chance to become ill again would be foolish in the extreme.

My returning health meant I was better able to work at jobs that actually paid money, retraining first as a music technology teacher and then taking up as a music writer. Being in a position to write for the magazines I pored over as a teenager and to interview people whose music I loved was a middle-aged surprise that I wasn't expecting and have absolutely loved. Aside from a stint on a Brighton pirate radio station and the very occasional friends party, for me, DJing in public simply retreated into the background.

I still listen fanatically to new music and to old music, still put together playlists, create DJ mixes at home, and listen to tunes in terms of where they might work in a DJ set. I still think about DJing a lot, sometimes with misty-eyed nostalgia, but sometimes with the view of someone who did it for years wondering what the fuck happened. I forget that most people didn't spend hours, days and weeks of their lives in record shops looking for tunes or spend their weekends in clubs and raves. This isn't most people's lives, it was ours, it was DJs.

I think back to all those hours spent looking for tunes, and how for years shopping for music and DJing meant everything to me. It's odd really, consuming as a hobby, turning the produce of major corporations into firstly the tools of your trade and then later into memory-receptacles.

If your record collection is old enough, a flick through it can take you back to when your concerns were much smaller and less serious than today. Like many in middle age, I worry about the environment, politics, the future for my child, the bills, will my hair ever come back. I think about my own health and mortality; I hope my teeth make it. I reflect on friends with failing marriages, with health issues. But if you'd like to visit a place where none of that existed, then simply listen to your 30-year-old music collection, it can trigger the most vivid of memories of what it was like to be free of such worries, to never had even considered such things. Music can momentarily make you feel carefree again.

That's why you have to make sure your kids have access to good music, so that when they're old and the world weighs heavy on their minds, they can simply listen to a song from their childhood and allow it to work its transporting magic. When I was young music meant a lot to me. It generated feelings that I couldn't express then and I struggle to fully articulate now. It still does. But I loved music so much that I really thought that other people should hear it too, really hear it, the way I did. I still do. This was why I first began DJing.

But over the years, motivations around why I was a DJ subtly changed. The sense of love and sharing always remained, but I would be lying if I said that my motivations remained as pure, innocent and naive as this throughout the rest of my DJing career. If only life were that simple, that you never changed, or grew, or reassessed anything but clearly, as the years went on, the reasons for DJing subtly developed and changed.

I really liked being good at something. I was always really good at something, whether it was possessing the best backspin in Bury St. Edmunds (still talking about it, 35 years on), or DJing. I never thought of myself as a competitive person but looking back over my life I clearly was very competitive indeed, just mostly with myself rather than with anyone else. Whatever I did I devoted myself to completely which was probably also a factor in getting ill.

There was also an element of ego to DJing. It was irresistible, the urge to briefly bathe in the adoration which was actually directed at the piece of music you'd just played. It was the music that was causing the emotional paroxysms across the room, but occasionally, you'd allow yourself the dirty luxury of momentarily sharing in the glory, because it was you and you alone, who picked that one perfect piece of music for that perfect time, and so you secretly, guiltily, suck up a bit of that energy for yourself, knowing full well it's not really yours. You didn't make the record, you just pressed play.

Gradually over the years my naive DJ evangelicalism has not so much faded, as been tempered by experience and maturity. How terribly dull. I don't know that I could survive in my middle age if I still took DJing as seriously as I used to. Also, my wife would probably have left me, for any number of reasons were I still the same over-focused, blinkered, driven DJ of my twenties.

Comparisons to others used to blind me to the reality of my low-level success. Now that I look back, I'm more at peace with my career. I didn't guest at the world's best clubs, and maybe you never heard of anyone I remixed, but there are many measures of success. Weigh up the luck I had, weigh up the joy to sadness ratio of my time in the music industry and on balance, I'm content.

As previously shared at the start of the book, I played a brilliant parents and kids rave in 2017. Looking out into the daytime crowd, all face-paint, hot excitement and day-glo noise, it wasn't actually that dissimilar to some nightclubs I've played at. Fun though it was, it was hard for the gig to not take on a weightier dimension in my mind. Just hearing all those songs again and seeing the age of some of the parents gave me a stomach-lurching overview on how many years had passed; inevitably I thought back through my career of DJ gigs.

I had my moment, lived my dream and was lucky to get a chance to DJ to clubs full of people who'd paid to come and hear me. Lucky lucky lucky. I failed to get as far as I wanted, but I'm not sure that I would ever be satisfied, whatever level I made it to. Even if I'd ended up as a DJ headliner at The End, Cream, Space and that new venue on the Moon, as well as resident of my own private members club on a secret paradise island, whilst remixing Miles Davis or Marvin Gaye's back catalogue in my spare time, I would still probably be unhappy and dissatisfied, no doubt planning on how I could remix Jesus, play a gig in Atlantis or some other unattainable goal. Success really does depend on how you define it.

Through it all, my deep love of this music that has soundtracked my life has never changed, my ardour never dimmed, the flames have never dipped, even for a moment, even in the deepest depths of ill health, even as the industry changed and ran out of money, never leaving me. It's a part of my very physicality, there's still a fervent wish to listen hard to extract that emotional hit from music, and then find someone else and make them feel the same.

And even playing 25-year-old records, in a tent, in the day time, to slightly ragged parents and their way over-excited children, eyes still meet when a tune drops and that unspoken thing, that shared experience, that sheer joy – it's still there. Someone just caught my eye and quietly mouthed 'Hardcore!' like we used to shout when we were in the depths of a rave and we would cheer and roar as we rode the wave of shared emotion and music-glee. This time it was a middle-aged man, paunch barely held in by his Superdry cardigan, with one child on his shoulders and another balloon-clutching toddler holding his hand. In many ways, this gig is brilliant.

My dance music career descended so slowly it was imperceptible, like when your kid grows up in front of you and you can't see it day to day but every now again you are shocked by how old they look or how grown up they sound. My boy is here today in the marquee, eleven-years-old, as ever quietly into the music in his way, but more interested in the free sweets and chance of lemonade. I remember being so young that the possibility of lemonade was a substantial contributing factor in how good a day you were going to have.

DJing and music have given my life shape and direction, filled my head with potential, hopes and dreams, targets to strive for, made me endlessly happy, given me such satisfaction. So many lost happy hours spent making music and DJing, totally immersed, Lost In Music. And even now that it's over, if I ever got the call, I've still got my headphones, I'm ready. I'll always be ready, I'll never stop being a DJ. Although I will definitely need a very strong coffee first.

Success is relative; it depends on who you compare yourself to. There were plenty of other wannabe DJs who never reached tier five like me, who wallowed in tiers seven or eight for their entire careers, probably countless more who never even left their bedrooms. But I salute them all, and the culture that we all helped create, because I know that even just dropping tunes in your house with your mates, being excited about music and falling in love with it all, that in itself is a success.

16-year-old me, listening to my soul records, gazing out of the window of my red and white Habitat 80s bedroom as another summer evening passed me by, young me would be bursting with excitement if he had even the slightest clue at what lay ahead.

I was about to enter a world that would define who I was. I was about to have some of the best times of my life, attend some of the wildest parties ever organised and it would all be soundtracked by some of the most revolutionary music humans had ever produced. This was a life-changing culture. All those records, every single drop of dopamine that my brain produced when I bought another 12", all those gigs, the terrible warm-ups, and those unforgettable nights of pure adrenaline and sublime anticipation when it all came together. Young me would find it hard to believe what lay ahead, the sheer joy of it all. I like to think that young me would have been happy with how it all turned out.

SPECIAL THANKS TO EVERYONE WHO BOUGHT THE BOOK ON PRE-SALE

Mark Allister, Dean Anderson, Marie Anderson, Sharon Andrews, George Ankrett, Sally Armstrong, Magnus Asberg, James Atkinson, Richard Austin, Rehana Awan, Lee Berry, Rebecca Bailey, Dave Bain, Rares Balauta, Ryan Bassett, Martin Barraclough, Chris Berry, Neil Bopperson, Dale Bracewell, Melanie Brett, Ben Bristow, James Burt, Adam Carter, Shaun Chapman, Paul Church, Rich Clarke, Mark Collings, Nick Cooke, Thomas Coulling, Ben Davis, James Decarte, Tom Dent, David Dick, Helen Dickinson, Constantin Dimov, Josh Doherty, Alexander Drewniak, Lee Drummond, Andrew Dunn, David Dunne, Stephen Ellis, Paul Field, Tim Forrester, Mike Foy, Chris Frost, Chris Garlinghouse, Rob Gear, Jost Gerischer, Michael Goggins, Giles Goudge, Rob Gray, Thomas Greenan, Adam Guda, Neal Gustafson, Lee Guthrie, Catherine Hamilton, Aidan Hanratty, Robert Hardy, Craig Harrop, Jonathan Hart, Jon Harvey-Lindon, Timothy Hazell, Andrew Higgs, Ben Hindle, Claire Hines, James Holloway, Guy Hornsby, Phil Howe, Sean Johnson, Chris Howell-Jones, Russell Hunt, Ergin Hussein, Anba Maria Jamieson, Michelle Johnson, Shane Johnston, Richard Jones, Dom Kane, Si Kemp, Kevin Knox, Steffen Korthals, Paul Layden, Andrew Lloyd, Tom Lown, Erik Lyngvær, David Maclean, Marcus Madgwick, Ann Majic, Doony Marrero, Alex Martin, Andrew Martin, Hayley Martin, Gordon May, Marni McArthur, Alister McDermott, Marlon McKetty, Alain Miguelez, Fazakas Miklos, Gary Milne, Andy Moore,

Alex Moran, Donal Moran, Leigh Morgan, Wayne Morgan, Robin Munro, Joe Naylor, Jamie Odell, Tim O'Malley, Stuart Parkins, Michael Parsons, Dave Paton, Joel Pearson, Carlos Perez, Samuel Plisskin, Helen Portas, Stefan Prescott, Ali Purbrick, James Radford, Rayees Rashid, Alex Rose, Matt Rowley, Hannah Saunders, Thomas Saunders, Wayne Saunders, Matt Sayers, Diane Scott, Jeff Scroggin, Dave Simpson, Zoe Spicer, Tom Steel, Tony Stevenson, Ian Straker, Leigh Strydom, Daniel Torres, Japhy Turner, Jodi Turner, Maria Turner, Stephen Turner, Yvonne Turner, James Twyford, Keane Ullathorne, Maurits Verwoerd, Ornette Waite, Andy Ward, Daniel Watts, Tamsin Watts, John Weissinger, Simon Westfield, James Williams, Tiggy Whitham, Sarah & Paul Whittaker, Dan Willett, Adrian Winter, Alex Woodhall, Mark Woon, Brendan Wrixon, Robin Wylie, Charlie and Lou.

ALSO ON VELOCITY PRESS

JOIN THE FUTURE: BLEEP TECHNO & THE BIRTH OF BRITISH BASS MUSIC

MATT ANNISS

Since the dawn of the 1990s, British dance music has been in thrall to the seductive power of weighty sub-bass. It is a key ingredient in a string of British-pioneered genres, including hardcore, jungle, drum & bass, dubstep, UK garage and grime. *Join the Future* traces the roots, origins, development and legacy of the sound that started it all: the first distinctively British form of electronic dance music, bleep techno.

Based on five years of research and hundreds of interviews, *Join the Future* is a radical alternative history of the rise of British dance music during the late 80s and early 90s.

STATE OF BASS: THE ORIGINS OF JUNGLE/DRUM & BASS

MARTIN JAMES

As UK government legislation, standardised music and bad drugs forced the euphoria of the rave into the darkness, a new underground movement emerged – jungle/drum & bass. Drawing on interviews with some of the key figures in the early years, *State of Bass* explores the scene's social, cultural and musical roots via the sonic shifts that charted the journey from deep underground to global phenomenon.

Originally published in 1997, *State of Bass: The Origins of Jungle/Drum & Bass* extends the original text to include the award of the Mercury Prize to Reprazent and brings new perspectives to the story of the UK's most crucial subterranean scene.

FLYER & COVER ART

JUNIOR TOMLIN

Showcasing the mastermind behind some of the most iconic rave flyers and record covers of the late eighties and early nineties, *Flyer & Cover Art* is a comprehensive insight into Junior Tomlin's incredible back catalogue.

30 years since he designed his first flyer this book documents his work across 160 pages, with commentary and draft sketches provided by Junior himself. The book is 25cm square, printed on premium 130gsm full colour paper. It is the first time his work has been documented and presented in such a comprehensive, cohesive fashion.

BEDROOM BEATS & B-SIDES: INSTRUMENTAL HIP HOP & ELECTRONIC MUSIC AT THE TURN OF THE CENTURY

LAURENT FINTONI

Bedroom Beats & B-sides is the first comprehensive history of the instrumental hip-hop and electronic scenes and a truly global look at a thirty-year period of modern music culture based on a decade of research and travel across Europe, North America, and Japan.

Combining social, cultural, and musical history with extensive research and over 100 interviews, the book tells the B-side stories of hip-hop and electronic music from the 1990s to the 2010s and explores the evolution of modern beat culture from local scenes to a global community via the diverse groups of fringe idealists who made it happen and the external forces that shaped their efforts.

SYNTHESIZER EVOLUTION: FROM ANALOGUE TO DIGITAL (AND BACK)

OLI FREKE

From acid house to prog rock, there is no form of modern popular music that hasn't been propelled forwards by the synthesizer. As a result they have long been objects of fascination, desire and reverence for keyboard players, music producers and fans of electronic music alike. Whether looking at an imposing modular system or posing with a DX7 on Top of the Pops, the synth has also always had an undeniable physical presence.

This book celebrates their impact on music and culture by providing a comprehensive and meticulously researched directory of every major synthesizer, drum machine and sampler made between 1963 and 1995. Each instrument is illustrated by hand, and shown alongside its vital statistics and some fascinatingly quirky facts.

WHO SAY RELOAD: THE STORIES BEHIND THE CLASSIC DRUM & BASS RECORDS OF THE 90S

PAUL TERZULLI & EDDIE OTCHERE

Who Say Reload is a knockout oral history of the records that defined jungle/drum & bass straight from the original sources. The likes of Goldie, DJ Hype, Roni Size, Andy C, 4 Hero and many more talk about the influences, environment, equipment, samples, beats and surprises that went into making each classic record.

This is the story of music forged from raw breakbeats and basslines that soundtracked a culture of all-night raves, specialist record shops and pirate radio stations. It's the story of young producers embracing and re-appropriating new technology, trying to best their peers and create something that would have hundreds of people screaming for a rewind on Saturday night.

TRIP CITY

TREVOR MILLER

In the summer of 1989, when *Trip City* was first released with a soundtrack by A Guy Called Gerald, there had been no other British novel like it. This was the down and dirty side of London nightclubs, dance music and the kind of hallucinogenic drug sub-culture that hadn't really been explored since Tom Wolfe's The Electric Kool-Aid Acid Test. Maybe this is why Trip City is still known as "the acid house novel" and an underground literary landmark.

But for 2021, *Trip City* is back in this all-new incendiary incarnation – including a new introduction by author Trevor Miller, a foreword by Carl Loben (*DJ Magazine* editor) and a vinyl reissue of the A Guy Called Gerald soundtrack.

DAFT PUNK'S DISCOVERY: THE FUTURE UNFURLED

BEN CARDEW

Daft Punk's *Discovery* is a record that looked into the future and liked what it saw; an album that predicted the electronic music explosion, YouTube and the end of privacy, while dragging soft rock back into vogue. *Discovery* was not only one of the best albums of the 2000s, it was one of the most prophetic – the kind of record that makes you wonder: *how did they know?*

This book is a homage to a fascinating, troubled beast of an album that casts a huge shadow over the 21st century, as *Discovery* reaches its 20th anniversary.